# PRESIDENTS' DAY

## SETH MARGOLIS

**DIVERSIONBOOKS**

Also by Seth Margolis

*False Faces*
*Vanishing Act*
*Losing Isaiah*
*Perfect Angel*
*Disillusions*
*Closing Costs*
*The Semper Sonnet*

Diversion Books
A Division of Diversion Publishing Corp.
443 Park Avenue South, Suite 1008
New York, New York 10016
www.DiversionBooks.com

For more information, email info@diversionbooks.com

First Diversion Books edition February 2017.
Print ISBN: 978-1-68230-697-0
eBook ISBN: 978-1-68230-696-3

For Carole

# PART I

TUESDAY, NOVEMBER 2

# CHAPTER 1

Harry Lightstone climbed Mason Street toward the top of Nob Hill. Perhaps he should have availed himself of the car and driver the organization had placed at his disposal. He'd visited San Francisco dozens of times, but somehow he never quite remembered just how steep the hills were. Whose idea had it been to build a city on the back of a giant camel? And who had booked him at the Fairmont when the convention, where he'd delivered the keynote address, had been at the Saint Francis, a thousand feet closer to sea level? He exercised five days a week—free weights with a trainer and at least a half hour of cardio—and still he was sucking air, never mind that he was climbing at a snail's pace. Even at fifty-six, shouldn't all that exercise count for something? He was the same weight he had been the day he graduated Princeton. Press profiles often described his face as "craggy" (his enemies called it vulpine). He tended to look best in black-and-white photos, which was just as well, since his face was in one newspaper or another almost every day of the week. Black and white brought out the shadows cast by his jutting cheekbones, the just-short-of-rakish overhang of his lush gray hair, the meditative thrust of his lower lip. "Yon Lightstone Has a Lean and Hungry Look," one columnist had headlined a recent screed in which his ambition had been attacked. Got it wrong, as usual. He was undeniably lean, but hunger, in the metaphorical sense at least, had never been a defining trait, which was almost remarkable, given how far he'd come. He hadn't been born with ambition. He'd married it, quite unintentionally. Lean he might be, but Marcella was the hungry one.

7

Half a block ahead, a woman turned onto Mason from Sutter Street and began to climb. She had on very high heels, but even without them she'd be five ten, perhaps even five eleven. He sped up, thrusting his arms like pistons to help propel him up the near-vertical slope. How did she manage to move so quickly perched atop those shoes? Excellent proportions for a woman that size. Perfect, in fact. He wanted a closer look at a woman who wore three-inch heels despite her height. Goddamn hill, he'd collapse of a heart attack before he got a frontal view.

He was a few feet away from her when she fell forward, onto her knees. Unable to stop himself in time, despite the incline, Harry bumped into her and buckled to the sidewalk next to her.

"Damn these shoes," she said. "And damn these hills."

Even on her knees she was a magnificent presence, sharp features highlighted by a deft application of makeup, the lush dark hair billowing from her scalp adding a precious half inch to her stature.

"Let me help you up," Harry said as he struggled to his feet. He extended a hand and, after a moment's hesitation, she took it. Despite her initial uncertainty, it seemed to him that she let him do all the work in hoisting her off the pavement. He felt the full weight of her in his right biceps, and as she slowly rose to her full elevation, like a corn stalk shooting up in fast motion, he felt that familiar and bafflingly erotic combination of potency and weakness. He had raised her up. He was dwarfed by her.

"Thanks. I might have stayed on the sidewalk all night if you hadn't come along." Her voice was throaty, almost gruff, with an insinuating lilt. She brushed off her knees, and when she stood erect he was again struck by the size of her, at least two inches taller than he was, aided by those heels, of course. She had the legs of an athlete, sturdy rather than sleek—a serious tennis player, perhaps.

"I'm...Herbert." Harry angled to the left of her so that she was on the uphill side, adding an additional two inches to her height advantage.

"Danielle," she said, extending a long arm. They shook

hands. "Are you heading up?" She indicated the top of Nob Hill, three steep blocks ahead of them. When he nodded they began their ascent.

"Are you from here?" he asked.

"I'm staying at the Mark Hopkins. You?"

"The Fairmont. What brings you to San Francisco, Danielle?" He felt unable to rise above cliché in the presence of such a woman, though shortness of breath wasn't aiding articulation.

"Business. You?"

"Business," he said.

"What kind of business?" Molded by her lustrous voice, the question sounded fraught with implication. He said the first thing he could think of.

"Consulting."

"Huh. Me too."

They looked at each other, sideways glances that acknowledged the mutual lie, and he knew that an early night in bed with the day's newspapers and briefing books was not to be. At the top of Mason Street she stopped and turned to him.

"I could use a drink," she said, not at all out of breath.

"There's a bar on the top floor of the Mark Hopkins," he said. There was also one at the Fairmont, but he couldn't possibly bring a woman back to his hotel, even a "consultant."

"Excellent." They turned right onto California Street. He had to take extra-long steps to keep pace with her. He fell behind her once they entered the Mark Hopkins, the better to avoid being recognized. He sensed all eyes were on Danielle, anyway.

In the elevator she pressed the tenth-floor button.

"The bar...is on the...roof," he said, still short of breath.

"The minibar is in my room."

He didn't have an immediate reply as he considered a number of possible reasons for her apparent haste to hop in bed, none of them having to do with his craggy good looks. Harry Lightstone was nothing if not a realist.

"You're not a..."

She gave a coy smile. "Do I look like a hooker?" She placed her hands on her hips.

He gave her a quick scan, taking in all six feet of her. He was no judge of fashion, though his wife spent a small fortune on clothes and accessories. A large fortune, actually. But Danielle seemed dressed conservatively, if anything. Did hookers wear cream silk blouses and navy skirts? Well, if she wasn't a hooker…

"Do you know who I am?"

"Should I?"

He felt his dick stiffen at his good fortune. He'd been more or less true to Marcella for twenty-two years, the first fifteen or so because he'd been generally satisfied—or perhaps too busy to stray, the last seven because he'd been too afraid of getting caught, which had everything to do with his public life. More or less, because there was that one time with the tennis pro from his club in Pittsburgh, a tower of a woman with deltoids like hard cantaloupes. But he'd stopped short of doing anything technically adulterous. It was all about technicalities in his business nowadays. And he'd come close with a woman he'd met in a chatroom, crossing the line he'd prudently erected between his online life and what he thought of as reality. They'd met for a proper cup of coffee and she wasn't nearly as statuesque as she'd led him to believe—a major disappointment, in fact, but a relief, too, as he hadn't been tempted to proceed beyond caffeine.

Danielle unlocked her room and crossed it in two magnificent strides. After snapping the curtains shut, she turned back to him and he nearly swooned at the prospect of what was coming.

"So, um, about that drink," he offered. "Vodka?"

She opened the minibar and removed two small bottles of vodka, which she poured into one glass and handed to him.

"Nothing for you?"

She stepped so close to him that her breasts grazed his suit jacket. She reached around and pulled his head toward her, crouching slightly to maneuver her lips onto his. She smelled of lilac and musk.

"I've always…I've always had this thing…" Damn, still out of breath. "For really…I mean, you're so…tall." He put the glass down.

"Some men are intimidated by my size," she said as she unbuttoned her blouse. "You're not intimidated, are you, Herbert?"

Harry shook his head, but in fact his heart was threatening to push through his chest, and fear, the sense of being helpless in her presence, was certainly a part of it. He ran his hands along her broad shoulders, then down her long arms. He crouched to his knees and let his hands drift down her skirt, along her calves to her feet, which he noted, approvingly, were large—at least a man's size eleven. He registered the cream blouse hitting the floor.

"I can't do this," he said with as much conviction as he could summon, pulling away from her.

"I think you can." She picked up the glass and held it to his lips. "You're not the least bit intimidated by a woman like me, are you, Herbert? You're more of a man than that."

"I've never done this before." Technically. "You see, I'm—"

"I see that you're here, on business. Like me. No one needs to know. No one needs to care…"

"If only you weren't so…" But words failed him, as they almost never did, and vodka had weakened whatever sense of caution was left. It wasn't about her, anyway. It was about him, about that dizzy sense of feeling at once small and vulnerable and completely protected. Powerless, for a change, but safe.

"I like a man who knows what he wants, Herbert, a man like you."

"Perhaps if I could just see…"

Slowly, he lifted her skirt, sliding his hands along her bare thighs, relishing the astonishing…scale of her. Danielle was correct on one point at least. He was a man who knew what he wanted.

• • •

In Manhattan, Julian Mellow answered the phone before the first ring had ended. Not his usual cell phone; this one had been procured for him for this call alone. The bedside clock read one thirty, which meant he had been asleep for about an hour, if you could call it sleep. He often wondered if he ever fell into a true slumber. Some mornings he woke up (if you could call it waking up) and spent the first moments of full consciousness trying to determine if he'd actually slept. Dreams and conscious thoughts had a way of merging seamlessly at night. It had been two years since he'd had a truly satisfying night of sleep. Two years, two months, and three days.

"Yes," he said softly into the phone. On the other side of the bed, Caroline rolled onto her side, away from him, and yanked the covers over her shoulders. His wife had no trouble sleeping.

"It's Danielle. The...person you—"

"I know who you are."

"I forget, what's your name?"

"I never told you. How did it go?"

"Perfectly. Check your email. I just sent the file."

"You had no problem getting his attention?"

"He's a height freak. I know the type. Looked up at me with these huge, adoring eyes, like I was his mother."

"I'll check my email. Goodnight, Danielle."

"What about my money?"

"The second payment will be delivered to you tomorrow morning."

Julian hung up and got out of bed. He walked to his bathroom (Caroline's was on the Fifth Avenue side of the master bedroom, and had a view). He glanced at his reflection before moving to the toilet. *Had* he been asleep when the phone rang? His blue eyes looked alert, his skin taut. Even his hair, unusually thick and dark for a man of fifty-one, looked tousled rather than unkempt. No one had ever called him handsome, but as a younger man he'd had no trouble attracting women. He was no longer much interested in attracting women but they came at him still, though he was enough of a realist to know that it was his position on the *Forbes* list of the four hundred wealthiest Americans (somewhere near the top, he guessed, never bothering to check anymore) and not his good looks or charm that drew them.

He entered his study, turned on his computer, and logged on to the account he'd established to receive a single email, which, as Danielle had promised, was waiting for him. BigDanniXXX@gmail.com. Two clicks on the email's attachment launched a video player, which he maximized.

The first image was of the back of a woman's head. She was standing slightly to the left of the camera and appeared to be alone. But he soon became aware of a low murmuring and then saw the top of a man's head, thick gray hair just clearing the bottom edge of the frame. She must have activated the camera while he was exploring her lower regions. Smart. A few moments later the man stood up, but his face was obscured from the camera by her head and billowing hair. "Move over," Julian whispered at the monitor. What if she'd gotten the wrong man? "Show me the face!" There was some muffled talk, mostly from him, letting her know he never did this sort of thing, suggesting without any conviction that they stop even as his hands moved greedily along her body, and then Danielle began moving to her right, easing her companion with her so that they were both in the exact center of the screen. Then she slowly sank to her knees, and as she disappeared from the monitor she revealed her companion's face in close-up.

A very, very famous face. Harry Lightstone, senior senator from Pennsylvania, chairman of the Senate Foreign Relations Committee. A publicity whore, apparently, since he'd accepted a less than glamorous speaking engagement on Election Day. True, it was an off-year, twelve long months before the presidential election, but the media would be focused on local races thought to have bellwether qualities, leaving little chance of Lightstone's address making the evening news. He was a conservative Republican with ties to the party's extreme right wing, and, most relevant for Julian's purposes, a long-married father of two who had the strangest, most unlikely obsession with very tall women.

"I'm pulling down your zipper," he heard Danielle say, a bit louder than was probably called for. "Unbuckling your belt. Oh, someone's happy to see me."

The blow-by-blow narration was unnecessary and risky,

though apparently the senator hadn't caught on. His expression and the guttural moans emanating from the mouth that had delivered countless speeches from the floor of the Senate told the story clearly enough. Still, getting a blowjob from a giantess would probably not be enough for what Julian had in mind. Men had survived worse. He rolled his mouse over the fast-forward button and moved the clip ahead. Danielle stood up and began to undress the senator. He reached around her and removed her bra, releasing two large, perfect breasts, which she pressed into him at about shoulder level. Even at fast-forward speed, even knowing that the protagonist was perhaps the fifth most powerful man in the country, the movie was a sordid bore. And still no money shot, nothing he could really put to work for him.

The clip fast-forwarded along, the actors' movements jerky, like panicked mice. Finally, they made it to the bed, Danielle practically pushing him onto his back, revealing the senator to be in decent shape and modestly endowed. Danielle jumped onto the bed and stood over him, legs astride his body. She still had on her skirt but was otherwise naked. With her back to the camera she began to unfasten her skirt but stopped and said something inaudible to the senator, who shimmied down the bed so that his feet dangled over the end. She went to the head of the bed and turned to face the camera, positioning herself just behind the senator's head. In full view of the camera she unfastened her skirt and let it fall to her ankles, revealing to the senator and to Julian—and to no one else, if the senator behaved as expected—an impressively large, semihard penis.

WEDNESDAY, NOVEMBER 3

# CHAPTER 2

At the breakfast table Wednesday morning, Julian was on the phone (his usual phone) when Caroline entered. She had on a floor-length silk robe and heeled slippers—the look of a 1940s movie goddess. Caroline was an aristocratic beauty, with a long, disdainful nose; pale blue, skeptical eyes; and full, disapproving lips. That she was the daughter of a mailman from Natick, Massachusetts, with a younger sister who, blessed with the same genetic raw material, had become a popular performer at a local strip bar, only added to her appeal, for Julian was drawn to people who, like himself, were the products of their own stubborn imaginations.

"I can't talk right now," he said quickly into the phone when he saw Caroline. "The plane leaves in one hour. There will be a passenger boarding in San Francisco. Say nothing to him. You'll return to New York on a commercial flight. I'll call you once you're in the air."

"Who was that?" Caroline asked after he'd hung up.

"An employee."

She poured coffee from the pot that Inez, their housekeeper, had earlier placed on the sideboard of the small breakfast room, which separated the kitchen from the formal dining room. "Since when do you ferry your employees on the jet?"

"It's early," he said with a sigh, and picked up the *New York Times*. The governor of New Mexico had announced the previous day that he was a candidate for the Republican presidential nomination, a late entrant. That swelled the field to four, with the first primary three long months away.

"It's about Matthew."

He stopped reading but couldn't look at her. They'd grown distant in recent years. She was a psychologist with a thriving private practice, had been since before they met. She used her maiden name—Stepinack—and few if any of her patients had the slightest idea that she was married to one of the world's wealthiest men. She'd never cut back on her hours even as he'd grown increasingly successful. Each morning she walked several blocks east from their building on Fifth Avenue to a sunless, ground-floor office off the lobby of a far less glamorous building on Second Avenue. Neither of them talked much about their work, though both were consumed by it. And yet she could still read him like an old, familiar book.

"What does sending a jet to San Francisco have to do with—"

"It's in your voice," she said, "the way you sounded when you were starting out, putting those first deals together, as if everything depended on getting it right. You haven't sounded like that in twenty years."

"I have six deals in the works. This afternoon I have a board meeting—I can't honestly remember which company—and then I'm giving a speech to a group of business students at Columbia. And tomorrow is more of the same. Do you really think it's about Matthew?"

"I know it is," she said quietly.

The name lingered in the air between them; they both needed a few seconds to accommodate themselves to the new presence.

"It's always about him," Julian said quietly.

"He was my son, too."

Their eyes met, but just briefly. If anything, she'd been the more devastated by his murder two years ago, at least initially. After a week he'd gone back to his routine, but it had taken Caroline nearly a year to reenter her life. Her patients were referred to colleagues; she'd found it impossible to focus on the anxieties and disappointments of other people. When she did resume her life, she did so completely, with her habitual enthusiasm and energy. Not Julian. He went through the motions of being Julian Mellow. Perhaps if they'd had other children he would have been pulled back to life by the demands of parenthood. But they'd not been able to conceive after Matthew was born, and though he didn't believe in fate or omens or, for that matter, religion of any sort, he'd always held an unexamined faith that having just one child, a son, was his destiny. He'd been an only child too.

"I know you're convinced that I don't think about him as much as you do," Caroline said.

"Not true."

"You're convinced you feel his loss more deeply than I do."

"He was our son."

"I had to make a decision, the hardest of my life. I could spend the rest of my life grieving, or I could move on. Grieving was by far the more tempting choice—you do realize that, Julian. Grieving would have been much easier. But I decided to move on. You haven't."

"Do you have any idea what I've accomplished in the past two years? More than seventeen billion dollars in deals." Such industriousness struck him as monstrous, in light of what had happened to Matthew. Every deal felt like a betrayal, a movement away, leaving Matthew behind. But then again, so did the sunrise each morning, each tick of the clock by his bedside.

"Deals," she said, practically spitting the word. "You haven't moved on, not a single inch."

"I don't know how," he said, his voice barely more than a whisper. Sometimes he felt that if he'd spent more time with Matthew, been a more engaged father, less caught up in deal-making, his son's death wouldn't sting quite so hard, and so persistently. He had little to hang on to, few actual memories. The pain was about what might have been, not what was.

"I've learned to think of grief as a *thing*, a kind of object, something hard inside of me, something alien." She placed a fist over her chest. "A year after Matthew died I put that object on a shelf, a high shelf. I never got rid of it, never threw it away, I just put it to the side. It's always there, and sometimes…" She shook her head. "Sometimes I can't help but notice it, and it almost shocks me, the way it did back then. Those are bad moments, bad days. But I just couldn't carry it around with me, I had to put it somewhere."

"I can't do that."

"You mean you *won't* do that. Because you're too focused on revenge."

*What did she know?* He'd been scrupulous about keeping his plans from her, as much for her own protection as anything else. She'd asked about the second phone. He'd told her it had to do with a top-secret deal. For all his success, Caroline was the more ruthlessly practical. She *moved on.* He never really could. When she'd gotten

17

pregnant, shortly after they met, when he was penniless and she was just twenty-one, she'd insisted on having the baby, despite his reservations. *We'll figure it out,* she'd said. And they had. He stood up.

"I have to get to the office."

"It won't help, whatever it is you're planning," she called after him as he headed for the front door.

Perhaps she was right. It was too soon to tell. If it went well, then he'd know whether he'd done the right thing, whether he could finally move on. And if it went badly, he'd be destroyed, and she'd go down with him.

# CHAPTER 3

Three thousand feet over the Sierra Nevadas, Billy Sandifer gazed out the window of the Gulfstream G650. The jagged landscape was brutal, even raw, yet every hundred miles or so there'd be a single house, or a cluster of houses, and he'd wonder what was going on down there, who lived there, how they got there, whether they were happy to be that isolated. Sometimes his own life seemed equally inscrutable. What was he doing in Julian Mellow's private jet, on a mission that violated every principle he held, or had once held, or pretended to hold? He was living someone else's life, someone he hardly knew. His own self, his past—his soul—seemed as remote as one of the distant peaks glimpsed out the window, visible for one moment, then quickly left behind.

He lifted one of the plane's several phones and dialed the Newman Center back in New Jersey. He heard a recorded message. He'd forgotten how early it still was.

"I'd like to make an appointment to see my daughter," he said after the beep. "Rebecca Sandifer. I'll call back later."

The mountains ended abruptly, replaced by a flat green landscape of squared-off farms that seemed scarcely more hospitable. The flight attendant crossed the cabin and leaned over from the waist.

"We'll be on the ground in five minutes. Would you like anything else?" He'd almost forgotten someone else was on the plane. Like Becca, he sometimes lost awareness of other people.

"No, thank you."

She was quite beautiful, he realized—why hadn't he noticed before? And why didn't this matter? He was forty-two years old, unmarried. These things should matter.

"Buckle up, then. I'll see you in San Francisco."

# CHAPTER 4

In New York, Zach Springer heard the phone ring from somewhere in a dream that involved visiting his childhood home in suburban New Jersey, only instead of the familiar floor plan he found himself staggering through a maze of brightly lit corridors, doors opening into still more corridors. Disturbing, like all of his dreams, and yet he felt a powerful reluctance to wake up that had nothing to do with fatigue—he'd been asleep for eight hours, and he needed no more than six, as a rule. He opened a door, and then another, the ringing growing louder, but there was no phone in sight. He ran down a long hall, as white as a hospital corridor. The ringing grew louder and louder but still he found no phone.

And then he was in his bed, sitting up, groping through the piles of books and magazines on his nightstand, searching for his phone.

"Hello," he said.

"I woke you up."

*Damn.* He should have cleared his throat before answering. Sarah didn't sound disapproving so much as disappointed, which was worse.

"I was up late," he said.

"You were asleep an hour before me."

"And then I woke up."

He heard her sigh. "I need to get back to class. I just wanted to remind you to call that guy my principal knows, with the construction business." He heard a child's voice, one of Sarah's third-graders. "Miss Pearlman, can I stop now?" And then Sarah again, in a gentler voice, talking away from the phone. "If you don't finish the picture I won't be able to hang it up in our show…great, I'll be right back. Anyway," she said in a huskier, more clipped tone, "it's much harder to reach him in the afternoon."

Sometimes he felt less responsible than one of her charges at PS 87, the elementary school a few blocks from the apartment they shared on the Upper West Side. He hadn't had a paying job in three years, and had to be prodded into calling contacts for job leads.

"I'll call him now," he said.

"Have a cup of coffee first. You sound like…poo poo. I need to get back to the zoo."

"I love you."

"I know," she said, and clicked off.

He got out of bed pondering whether a woman of profound intelligence and inexhaustible kindness could stop loving someone simply because he was chronically unemployed, perhaps unemployable. Or did love take a back seat to practical considerations for even the most romantic of women once they reached their thirties?

They'd met when he was a ridiculously well-paid analyst at Mellow Partners, set up by friends. She was beautiful and intelligent and Jewish. He was not-bad-looking and successful and Jewish. So they both expected to hate each other but ended up moving in together six months after their first date. The marriage-and-children conversations started almost immediately. Then it all fell apart for him and they stopped discussing much of anything. She'd stuck around, but he wondered how much longer she would. Her teacher's salary barely covered the rent on their one-bedroom apartment, and his stash from the go-go years with Mellow Partners had dwindled to almost nothing. Sometimes he thought it was a race between which would run out first: his money or Sarah.

Guinevere, their old English sheepdog, met him in the kitchen. She'd been with Sarah when they'd met and still regarded him, from behind a shaggy fringe of white and gray bangs, with suspicion, rarely looking at him directly and approaching him only when summoned by a clap of his hands. Sarah, he knew, had already walked Guinnie, and her food and water bowls were still half full. From a box of Fig Newtons above the sink he removed two cookies and fed them to Guinevere, as he did every weekday morning. Their little secret.

He downed a cup of instant coffee, put on his biking gear, then picked up the scrap of paper with the job contact's name and number. He knew exactly what he should do. *Should* was always the easy part: call the contact, pour on the charm, ace the interview, get the job, marry Sarah, produce children, live happily ever after. Instead, he put the contact name back on the dresser. He pulled on a logo-covered bike shirt, pulled up a pair of padded-crotch Lycra shorts, squeezed into his Italian-made biking shoes, snapped on his helmet, maneuvered his $4,800 Orbea Orca racing bike (one of his last purchases as a rising star at Mellow Partners) into the small elevator, and headed downstairs.

In the building's lobby he ran into a neighbor, Jessica Winter, one of those ubiquitous Upper West Siders who, though far too young to be respectably retired (she looked about thirty-five), seemed never to work and yet appeared to have no trouble maintaining a comfortable lifestyle. It seemed unlikely that she survived on the ten dollars they paid her now and then to walk Guinevere.

"Where are you off to today, Zach?" To his dismay, she put down the grocery bags she was carrying, preparing for a full-blown conversation.

"Nyack."

"Wow. I'm so impressed. That's got to be, what, fifty miles each way? And at this time of year." Her eyes traveled up and down his spandexed frame. At thirty-five, he was in the best shape of his life; three years of unemployment had its benefits, chief among them the ability to take long trips by bike once or twice a week.

The body-clinging bike outfit actually made him look even more buff than he was, and the crotch padding in the shorts tended to act as a codpiece, a fact he deeply regretted as Jessica regarded him with undisguised interest.

"Not quite that long."

"Still…"

She was undeniably attractive, and for a moment he played out a scenario in which he followed her upstairs to her apartment and hammered the final nail into his own coffin. There would be something profoundly satisfying about casting off his last remaining relic of decency, accelerating the slow, inevitable decline by plunging right to the bottom.

"The bike does most of the work," he said with a modest shrug and a grin. He even patted the seat. That grin had launched a thousand one-night stands, or so it had seemed. There was a time when he dispensed it like a drug. It was a big, toothy grin that sent one side of his mouth north, the other south, forcing his eyes into a squint that somehow accentuated their blueness; inevitably, it was only after he smiled that women would comment on their color. He'd studied his smile quite assiduously in the old days when his star was rising and before he'd met Sarah. Apart from luring any number of women, it had played no small role in successfully closing many a deal at Mellow Partners.

"We should have lunch some time," Jessica said. "Since we're both around during the day. We could take Guinevere to the park."

"That would be nice." He brushed against her as he squeezed the bike through the door and hoped like hell that he'd never run into her in the lobby again.

•  •  •

He was five miles from Nyack, a small city on the Hudson River about twenty miles from the George Washington Bridge, when his phone rang. He debated answering it. He was on pace to make it to Nyack in under two hours, not his best time but faster than usual.

Some mornings he just seemed to fly along Route 9W; the uphills seemed gentler those mornings, the downhills longer and more numerous, his legs pumping in an unstoppable rhythm. He knew the route so well he was rarely tempted to look up from the pavement. Scenery was irrelevant. The journey was irrelevant. It was all about arriving. Biking, for him, was a very un-Zen-like endeavor.

He retrieved the phone from one of the pockets sewn onto the back of his shirt. The digital display revealed a familiar number.

"What's up?" he said, maintaining his pace.

"It's Charlie."

"I know." Even without caller ID, the flat, unflappable pilot voice gave him away.

"I'm on the ground at Signature, the private airport in—"

"In San Francisco, I know." He once knew every private airport in the country.

"Just dropped off your friend."

"He's not my friend. Was Julian Mellow on board?"

"Nope, guy flew solo. Apart from a flight attendant and two pilots."

Zach felt a sudden heaviness in his legs. He wouldn't make Nyack in under two hours. "I don't suppose he mentioned why he was going to San Francisco."

"He doesn't say much. This must be the fifth time I've flown him—"

"Third."

"Yeah, whatever. Always alone, never with Mr. Mellow. Never could get much out of him other than that he likes his coffee black. Never even told us his name."

"Okay, thanks for checking in."

"There's something else."

Zach steeled himself for the inevitable request for more money. Charlie was paid by the phone call, fifty bucks for each report of the comings and goings of Julian Mellow's G650. The information had so far been completely unhelpful. *Mr. Mellow is attending a board meeting in Detroit. Mr. Mellow and his wife are visiting friends in Palm Beach. Mrs. Mellow is attending a shrink conference in Chicago.* If Sarah ever learned that he was frittering away money on such nonsense, he'd be out on the street.

"We've already been through this; I don't have more money to—"

"I have a different passenger on the way back to New York. I'm in the head now, using my cell phone."

Zach pictured him in the bathroom, whispering into the phone lest his copilot spot him for the traitor that he was.

"Not Mr. X?"

"This guy's as far from anonymous as you can get and still be homo sapien."

"Who is it?"

"I don't follow politics and even I recognized him."

"Come on, Charlie."

"Harry Lightstone."

"Harry Lightstone is on your plane?" Zach had to focus hard to keep from veering into traffic.

"He was waiting on the tarmac when we pulled over to the terminal. Practically sprinted to the plane when we lowered the stairs."

"Alone?"

"Yep, and get this. He asked for a vodka with his bagel. Straight up."

"Are you dropping him off in DC?"

"Nope, NYC. Oh, one of the attendants is banging on the door, probably thinks I've got the runs. I got to go."

"What time are you landing?"

"Six hours and forty-five minutes, but—"

Zach clicked off, pocketed the phone, and turned his bike around.

• • •

# CHAPTER 5

Billy Sandifer stepped out of the Gulfstream and almost tumbled down the stairs when he spotted Harry Lightstone charging across the tarmac. Senator Lightstone hitching a ride on Mellow's jet? Wasn't that sort of thing illegal, or at least frowned upon? Well, the senator had a lot on his mind, after what happened last night. It was Billy who had found the girl on the internet, paying her half up front, then phoning to let her know where the senator would be.

The fuel truck was already hitched up to the jet. Quick turnaround. He'd already been informed he'd be flying commercial back to New York. He passed the senator about fifty yards from the stairs.

"'Morning, Senator Lightstone."

The simple greeting seemed to upset Lightstone, who broke pace for a moment, glanced nervously at him, and then continued his sprint to the jet. Billy had met many politicians in his day, back when he was a volunteer operative for a string of left-wing candidates. He knew the automatic response of career politicians to unsolicited greetings: first, the instant scan to determine if it was someone he knew, or should know; then, if it was nobody, the cordial brushoff—"Nice to see ya," or "Same to you, fella." Lightstone had executed the familiarity scan with practiced efficiency, but he'd failed at superficial pleasantness, which a politician of his experience and tenure would never do unless something were seriously bothering him. Well, finding yourself a tongue's length from a cock when you'd been expecting something very different had to be a mind blower, and learning, as he no doubt had earlier that morning, that your encounter had been immortalized on video might put even a polished pro like Lightstone off his game.

Billy had the car service drop him off on Market Street near the Civic Center. He paid the fare in cash and headed off on foot for the Castro. The day was warm and sunny, and as he walked he found himself enjoying the passing show, the more so as he neared the Castro and the show became increasingly flamboyant. He didn't give a thought to the task before him. He was good at that, focusing on the moment, to the exclusion of all else. He'd first recognized this talent shortly after Becca was diagnosed. He'd learned that he could effectively forget all about his daughter. It had scared him, at first, this ability to compartmentalize, as the self-helpers called it. But he soon saw it for what it was: a survival mechanism. Julie had no such talent, perhaps mothers never did; Becca's diagnosis had eaten away at her mother, slowly but inexorably, until her only recourse was to flee, leaving Billy to make the tough decisions. But perhaps his strength was really only that ability to forget things when he had to, things like principles and ethics and consequences both legal and moral. It frightened him, sometimes, what he was capable of, but then he'd put that fear aside, in its own sealed-off compartment, next to the one that held his grief and guilt over Becca, and move on to the next task.

It was a weekday morning and the Castro was quiet. Not that you'd mistake the neighborhood for anywhere else in the world. Billy walked briskly along Market Street and turned right onto Castro. Many of the neighborhood's bars and stores were still closed, but numerous coffee shops, most of them doing a brisk business, lent a sense of idle relaxation to the neighborhood. The beautifully restored Victorian homes lining the side streets looked especially handsome in the crisp morning light, defiantly proud of their excessive ornamentation, much like the neighborhood itself and many of its inhabitants.

Danielle lived on Church Street, which ran perpendicular to Castro. He didn't need a map, having been there two weeks earlier when he'd engaged her services. Finding the senator's fatal flaw had taken some doing. In Boston, while the senator was attending a dinner, Billy had used a pick set to get into his hotel room, where he opened the senator's laptop and inserted a USB drive, with which he rebooted the device and reset the administrative login password. Less than three minutes and he was in. So much for government cybersecurity.

He'd clicked on the little arrow to the right of the address bar and a pull-down window appeared, listing all the sites the senator had visited in recent days. Very helpful. In addition to the expected places—wsj.com, CNN.com, and several sites devoted to Lightstone himself—there were visits to such sites as Amazons.com (not to be confused with the online store) and toweringfemales.com. Billy followed the links to these and a half dozen similar sites, all devoted to the obsessive worship of tall women. Very, very tall women.

He walked up a short path to the front door of Danielle's house, a dilapidated Victorian painted yellow and maroon that had been carved up into small flats. He rang her bell several times before being buzzed in, then climbed a slanting wooden staircase to the third floor.

Danielle had on a floor-length blue silk robe with a fluffy feather collar, the kind of getup Mae West might have worn if Mae West had been six two and less demure. "You woke me up."

"I could come back," he said.

"Yeah, right." She pressed her lean body against the door frame to let him pass. The apartment was as he remembered it: one room, one window, a total disaster. Clothes tossed everywhere, piles of magazines and books forming low, makeshift tables, several of them supporting empty takeout containers. A scrawny gray cat on the windowsill looked up at him with huge, embarrassed eyes.

"I don't know why you couldn't just send the money," Danielle said. She sat on the king-size bed that dominated the room and served as its only seating area other than two black folding chairs next to a small dining table covered with dirty plates. She patted the bed. "Come, sit."

He'd rather saw off a limb with a dull kitchen knife.

"I have a plane to catch."

Danielle slowly crossed her thighs. "You know, you're very good-looking. You keep yourself in shape, I can see that. I'm guessing you're thirty, maybe thirty-five? A lot of guys go to seed long before that, but not you. And you've got all your hair. You ever think about hooking up with a girl like me?"

While she talked, Billy steeled himself for the task at hand—not the ultimate task, just the part that involved sitting next to her, touching. By the time he joined her on the bed he felt almost fine with what was happening, just short of relaxed. Because he wasn't there any longer, not on the bed, not in the room, not even in San Francisco. Only his hands and arms were there, and they knew what they had to do. Billy Sandifer was gone.

Danielle ran a hand along his right arm. "Wow, you really are in shape...I forget, what's your name?"

"Dan."

After a beat she broke into a deep, throaty laugh. "Dan and Danielle. I like that." As she began to unbutton his shirt, he took off his belt. "It's kind of bright in here," he said. "Could you lower the shade?"

He watched Danielle make her way through the piles of junk to the window, where she jerked down the shade, forcing the cat off the sill. There was an efficient athleticism to Danielle's long stride, to the way she yanked down the shade in one smooth movement. He would have to be careful.

"Perhaps we should do a little business first? You know, I almost had a coronary, making sure I intercepted your guy halfway up Nob Hill."

He handed her the rubber-banded wad of twenties.

"And another two hundred for this morning's amusement."

"I thought I was getting lucky."

"You are, Danny-boy. But a girl's gotta make a living."

He took out his wallet and handed her two hundred-dollar bills, which she placed in the drawer of a bedside table, along with the thousand. She mounted the bed in one effortless motion, straddling him. From beneath, she looked colossal, an Egyptian deity carved in sandstone. Her robe fell open, revealing a perfectly formed woman on top, a generously endowed man on bottom. He patted the bed. She looked surprised.

"Most of my gentleman callers prefer me on top."

"This one wants you on your back."

Danielle let the robe drop to the bed, then lowered herself onto her back. He felt nothing, saw nothing—because he wasn't there—as he climbed on top of her.

"It's nice to bottom for a change, especially this early in the day. Usually I work so hard." She sighed and closed her eyes, pursing her lips. He reached for his belt, quickly slid it under her head, then tightened it around her throat. Her eyes blinked opened as he maneuvered his knees on top of her upper arms, pinning her.

"Honey, this isn't my thing at—"

Her last words, an expression of sexual preference. Her legs flailed, her body bucked under him like a wrestler trying to push out of a pin. Billy wondered if there was a twelve o'clock flight out of SFO. As she squirmed he calculated his arrival time in New York, remembering to add three hours. Her head whipsawed back and forth. He'd try for a Newark flight, which would put him that much nearer to Becca's residence. He'd rent a car and charge it to Julian Mellow, who never seemed to care what he spent. Her head movement slowed, then stopped, and a second later her jaw went slack and her eyes relaxed to something like a horrified stare. He squeezed a few moments longer, for good measure. He'd call the airline from the cab and book the first flight to Newark Liberty. He released the belt and checked his watch. With luck he'd be with Becca before closing time.

Billy retrieved the $1,200 from the bedside table, put on his belt, and did a quick scan of the room to make sure he hadn't left anything behind. The cat jumped onto the bed, from which Danielle's giant legs dangled a good ten inches.

Out front, he walked briskly down Church Street, relieved that no one had seen him leave Danielle's building. The neighborhood was quiet, but as he approached Market he passed a man of about forty-five who did a double take. He picked up his pace. A moment later he thought he heard his name but he kept walking, concentrating on not breaking stride. He was probably imagining it. The man hadn't looked familiar to him, and no one recognized him anymore, the once-famous radical who'd aged two decades during eight years in jail. He didn't recognize himself.

He waited until he was safely out of the Castro before flagging a passing cab.

# CHAPTER 6

Zach Springer clocked record time back to the West Side, showered quickly, and changed into his post-Wall Street uniform—a Paul Stuart oxford shirt, left over from his Mellow Partners days and showing its age around the collar and elbows, along with jeans and running shoes. His three-year-old BMW, another relic from Wall Street, was parked a few blocks away. It had aged badly since he'd taken to parking it on the street; practically every time he saw it a new ding or dent had appeared, but he always felt a twinge of relief that at least it was still where he'd left it.

He made it to Teterboro Airport in an unusually quick thirty-five minutes. Way back when, he'd passed through Teterboro many times as he crisscrossed the country on Julian's Gulfstream, meeting with executives of companies they were considering buying. He parked and headed into Meridian Terminal, the one used by Julian. He recognized the friendly attendant who acted as a kind of concierge for the private jet set.

"Hey, Katrina."

"Long time no see." She gave his wrinkled shirt and jeans a quick once-over.

"Has Mr. Mellow's jet landed yet?" he asked casually. That sort of information was not given freely.

She hesitated a moment before shaking her head. "Any minute. Are you getting on?"

"Meeting someone." He waved at her and walked through the double glass doors to the tarmac. Off to the left a Delta jet ascended into the overcast sky, then circled lazily to the north. Could be the Newark to Boston flight. When the Gulfstream was otherwise engaged, he'd flown that route often for due diligence at one of the tech companies out on Route 128. Invariably he'd come back with negative reports that emphasized the company's lack of earnings or even prospects for earnings, the inexperience of its management teams, the perilously low barriers to entry that made it vulnerable to competitors. Julian had grumbled and scowled in frustration as he read the reports, and sometimes he'd call Zach into his office and berate him in a voice that could be heard in every corner of the sixtieth floor of 14 West 57th Street. But he'd never sunk a penny into any of the tech companies he'd sent Zach to investigate, most of which had later either gone out of business or teetered on life support. Zach had never received a word of thanks for saving his boss what might have amounted to a billion or more dollars, and then he'd been forced to resign in disgrace. His only mementos from those days were a rapidly dwindling bank account, a drawer of Paul Stuart Egyptian cotton shirts, a closet of useless Brioni suits, the BMW, and a court decree barring him from the securities industry for life.

The crescendoing din of an approaching jet pulled him back to the present, and a few moments later the Gulfstream was on the runway. It was not the jet he remembered but a gleaming new model. Mellow liked to upgrade every few years. The jet taxied closer to the terminal building and a moment later the stairs were lowered and Harry Lightstone appeared in the doorway. At the same time, a figure to his right darted across the tarmac. Miguel DeLeon, Mellow's driver. Zach stepped into the shaded area under an overhang. DeLeon took the senator's carry-on bag and led him back to the terminal. Zach entered the building before them, walked quickly through it, and exited near the parking lot. He was in his car with the engine running a half minute before Mellow's black Mercedes S600, DeLeon at the wheel, Lightstone alone in the back, pulled away from the curb.

Zach followed the car over the George Washington Bridge, down the West Side Highway, and onto West 59th Street. The Mercedes turned right on Fifth Avenue, then right again onto West 57th Street, where it stopped in front of number 14, a glass tower on whose sixtieth floor Julian Mellow pulled a good number of the strings that controlled corporate America. Zach doubled-parked several yards back. A moment later, Julian Mellow exited the building and got into the back seat of the Mercedes. The tinted windows obscured all three men from the outside.

• • •

"The car just turned onto 57th Street, Mr. Mellow."

Stacy Young, Julian Mellow's longtime assistant, stood in the doorway of his office, separated from his desk by an antique Laver Kirman that had, until ten years ago, covered the floor of the drawing room in the Villa Buonconvento outside Rome. Julian had bought the rug at auction at Sotheby's. Caroline, who had little interest in interior design, had outsourced the decoration of the apartment and the house in Southampton to a small platoon of architects, decorators, and art consultants. But the office was Julian's preserve. Against a panoramic view of Central Park, the large, sparely furnished room projected an understated refinement that Caroline's decorators would have disapproved of, assuming they ever bothered to drop by his office, the source of the vast river of money that financed their unstinting creative efforts. His desk was a Josef Hoffmann dining table, a starkly geometric piece that, in the six years he'd owned it, continued to buoy his spirits each morning. Along one wall was a sleek walnut credenza, also by Hoffmann. Above it hung a portrait of a woman by Egon Schiele, her garish face distended in an expression of what Julian thought of, approvingly, as amused horror.

"I'll meet the car in front," he told Stacy, who left him to relay the information to Miguel DeLeon, his driver.

He straightened the stack of papers he'd been reading, squaring their edges, and placed them next to a small pile of prospectuses, adjusting the position until both stacks were perfectly aligned. He crossed the office to an open door that led to a long, dimly lit, windowless room. Before closing the self-locking door, he glanced slowly around, as if checking up on a room of sleeping children. These were not children, however, but eleven pictures: two portraits of unknown men by Hans Holbein the Younger; an Albrecht Dürer woodcut; a Madonna and child by Hans Memling; two preparatory sketches of Habsburg royalty by Velázquez; a portrait of a young man by Jan van Eyck; two small preparatory drawings by Raphael for his great Betrothal of the Virgin; and the jewel of his collection, *Woman at a Spinet* by Vermeer, a painting believed to have been lost in an eighteenth-century fire at Hampshire Castle in Hertfordshire. Julian had purchased all of the pictures, including the Vermeer, from a network of private dealers renowned as much for their discretion as their taste. His name appeared nowhere on any bill of sale, and the pictures had been seen by no one other than himself since their purchase.

One of the richest ironies of his life was that the more wealth he acquired, the more privacy he lost. All friendships seemed suspect when viewed through the prism of vast wealth. Sometimes it felt like a giant, disfiguring boil on his face; no one could help focusing on it, no matter how resolutely they attempted to look away. But the subjects of the paintings in his private gallery wanted nothing from him other than to be remembered.

He closed the door, which could be opened only with the permission of a retinal scanning device mounted at eye level to the right of the door.

The black Mercedes pulled up to the curb just as he left the building. He was momentarily tempted to keep the senator waiting, because he could. But he had little tolerance for game playing, least of all from himself. Lightstone practically assaulted him when he joined him in the back seat of the car.

"What the hell are you doing? How dare you even think that—"

"Shut up," Julian said.

The senator groaned as if he'd been gut-punched. Julian watched as the senator registered what was happening, a sudden and complete transfer of power. From the leather pocket on the back of the front passenger seat Julian took out a set of headphones and handed them to Miguel, who put them on. Twenty years of high-profile buyouts had taught Julian that no one was to be trusted and no place, not his office or home or car, was secure, not with the sums of money he dealt in. Meetings in the back of his car were something of a Julian Mellow trademark, remarked upon in articles about him. Headphones for his driver were also mentioned, often as evidence of his paranoia.

"What the hell are you up to?" Lightstone said. His voice sounded thin, as if he couldn't quite get enough air. "How the hell—"

Julian checked his watch. "I have a conference call in fifteen minutes."

Lightstone observed him with slack-jawed horror. "Do you have any idea who I am?"

"Senior senator from Pennsylvania. Chairman of the Foreign Relations Committee. Of course I know who you are, as did Danielle last night."

He'd called the senator at four o'clock a.m. Pacific Standard Time, waking him. Julian had been characteristically succinct, ignoring Lightstone's groggy interruptions. *It's Julian Mellow. I have video of you from last night. You should understand that I'm not referring to your address to the Society of American Manufacturers at the Saint Francis. My plane will bring you back to New York. It departs at 10:00 a.m. Pacific time, Signature Airport, a private terminal near San Francisco International. If you're not on the plane I will share the video with the media.*

"You could go to jail for a long time for what you did."

"I think we both know that won't happen." Julian glanced

out the tinted windows at the crowds of tourists thronging the sidewalks on Fifth Avenue. He felt a million miles away from them. "Now, here's what's going to happen. Next week you're going to announce your candidacy for the Republican nomination for president."

"But I haven't decided yet. And it's a bit late to—"

"I've decided."

The senator's mouth fell open but no sound emerged.

"Everyone knows that you've been on the fence for months. You've even put together an exploratory committee. No one will be the least bit surprised when you throw your hat in. The filing deadline for New Hampshire is next week. No signatures required, though you'll need to put an organization together for later primaries, some of which do require signatures."

"Why?" was all Lightstone could manage.

"I need a friend in the White House."

"You can get the current occupant on the phone anytime you want."

"I speak to Paul Nessin regularly."

"Is this about taxes?"

"I can afford to pay taxes."

"Then why?"

The Mercedes turned up Sixth Avenue, passing several skyscrapers that Julian had purchased during the last real estate slump. He'd packaged them into a real estate investment trust and sold shares to the public in an IPO two years ago, netting enough to purchase a dozen Vermeers for his gallery, if only there were any to be had. Lightstone had never met a tax cut he didn't like, but the truth was, Julian had no problem with higher taxes, as long as they were directed at those who could afford to pay them. The antipathy of the super-rich to taxes never failed to amaze him. Those who could most easily afford to pay them were, in Julian's experience, the most vehement about the need to lower them, sending wave after wave of beholden politicians to Washington to make sure their views were appreciated when tax bills came to a vote. In his heart he didn't really care about tax policy one way or another, but it was certainly no dealbreaker as far as his support of Lightstone went.

"Are you even a Republican?"

"My affiliation is irrelevant." The government was a lumbering, inefficient, antiquated bureaucracy. But he knew the private sector—and human nature—too well to have any illusions about what *less* government could do.

"I've already come out in favor of another tax cut and against reinstatement of the estate tax."

"Don't you mean the 'death tax'?" Republicans were geniuses at branding. Few people thought of themselves as having, or inheriting, an estate. But everyone was going to die. "I don't concern myself with events after my death."

"Then why? Why put me through this?" His voice had taken on a whiny plaintiveness that was very unbecoming in the fifth or sixth most powerful man in the free world. "I'm chair of the Foreign Relations Committee. What possible interest could *that* have to you? Is there something about foreign policy that you're after?"

A shiver of vulnerability made its way down Julian's back. "Of course not," he said quickly. "All you need to do is announce your candidacy next week."

"You have no specific agenda?" He sounded almost hopeful.

"Nothing you need to know about right now."

A shadow of fear crossed the senator's face. "I can't believe this is happening."

"For God's sake, Harry. You pander to the money boys every day. Last week you agreed to support the energy bill only because it included a huge subsidy for a new shopping center outside of Pittsburgh. How much did the developer contribute to your reelection campaign last year?"

"But this…using video, entrapping me with…how did you know about…how did you pick…*her*?"

The Mercedes stopped in front of 14 West 57th Street.

"You'll find there's little that escapes my attention," he said as he tapped Miguel's shoulder. The driver took off the headphones.

"Take the senator to LaGuardia. The *shuttle* terminal." He extended a hand and was mildly disappointed when the senator shook it. Weak men were more dangerous than strong ones, he'd always found. If you could control them, so could someone else. The senator's wife, for example, was thought to call the shots on most matters of importance.

"I wish I knew what this was about," the senator said.

"In good time, Harry. Now, I don't want you to miss your plane…" He left the car and headed back to his office.

• • •

Zach Springer spent forty-five minutes following the Mercedes as it slowly cruised through midtown Manhattan, seemingly making turns at random, doubling back at times. Finally, it returned to 14 West 57th Street, where Julian Mellow got out and walked quickly into the building. The Mercedes pulled away with the senator still in the back, and Zach followed it to LaGuardia, where it stopped in front of the Delta terminal. The senator got out, looking far grimmer and more tired than even the prospect of flying commercial to Washington would normally engender.

Zach drove slowly back to Manhattan, fighting the letdown he always felt when his pursuit of Julian Mellow led, invariably, nowhere. Senator Lightstone had accepted a ride on Mellow's jet. Assuming he reported the trip to the feds (and Zach would definitely follow up on this), he'd done nothing illegal. The fact that Mellow and Lightstone had met in the privacy of the Mercedes was promising, as was the fact that Mellow had left the meeting with a smile on his face while Lightstone had entered the US Airways terminal looking…well, terminal. Something was up. But none of that added up to a plausible justification for wasting half a day. He'd call that contact of Sarah's principal as soon as he got home. But as long as he had another ten minutes in the car, he might as well be productive. He took out his phone and dialed the pilot's number.

"Yeah, it's Zach again. Did the senator happen to mention why he was coming to New York?"

He heard Charlie chuckle. "I'm just the lowly pilot, my friend."

"Okay, I tried."

"He seemed extremely agitated. The flight attendants said he jumped out of his seat the moment we turned off the seatbelt sign and got himself a vodka."

"Did he make any calls?"

"Nope. But I did get one bit of information you might be interested in. That guy we flew out this morning, the one who never says much, never gives his name? Our flight attendant heard him ordering a car service on his cell in San Francisco after we landed. He gave his name as Billy Sandifer, had to shout to be heard and ended up spelling it twice."

"Billy Sandifer." The name was vaguely familiar to Zach, but he repeated it twice to make sure he didn't forget.

Perhaps the day hadn't been a complete waste after all.

## THURSDAY, NOVEMBER 4

# CHAPTER 7

Sophie DuVal stopped just two feet in front of the menacingly large but bored-looking guard standing at the entrance to the Sacré-Cœur prison. At five nine she was a head shorter, but she forced herself to look confident even as the guard absently massaged one of the two pistols holstered to his belt. They spoke in French, the official language of Kamalia, which was once part of France's sub-Saharan African empire.

"I am here to see André Mansard."

"Do you have an appointment?"

"No, but I—"

"Then I cannot let you inside."

"Do you know who I am?"

"How could I, when you have not introduced yourself?" he said with something of a leer.

Sophie looked up into the guard's eyes. The motivations of people, native Kamalians like herself, who did the bidding of the government always mystified her. The guard, for instance. Did he take pleasure in denying her entry to the prison, where most of the inmates were held without trial by the fascist regime of President Boymond?

"I am Sophie DuVal, an attorney. My client is André Mansard." Two years ago Mansard was the minister of development for Kamalia. He'd been imprisoned for nearly two years without so much as a hearing. She was there to reassure him that she and others were still working to get him released. Reassurance was about all she had to offer him. "He has had no contact with the outside world since the coup."

"Then how can you be his attorney?" One edge of his lip curled upward as his eyebrows arched. If he did recognize her, then he knew she was not an attorney. But the lie had seemed necessary to gain access.

"I have represented him for two years, first when he was in the government, later when he was in charge of the Front Populaire."

"He has made life hard for Kamalians. First he pushed the old government for more freedoms—"

"How can there be too much freedom?" And what was she doing, having a political discussion with a prison guard?

"For Kamalians, there *can* be too much freedom."

Two centuries of French colonial rule had given the Kamalians a massive inferiority complex. Freedom was for other people: Americans, Europeans, the more developed African nations that surrounded tiny Kamalia.

"Now we have no freedom," she said. "Can you at least agree that there can be too *little* freedom?"

"You had the freedom to come here to talk to me. We are talking freely. In some countries women cannot even show their faces in public. Or their bodies." He gave hers a leisurely perusal.

She had dressed with deliberation that morning. She was not averse to using physical charms to get what she wanted, so long as it served the larger purpose. Today, that purpose was getting inside Sacré-Cœur to see André Mansard. Sometime soon she would use whatever modest gifts she had to help overthrow the repressive and illegitimate government of Laurent Boymond, known as "Le Père."

"And if I am refused entry to this prison, to see a client? That will bring attention."

"You can send a letter to the American newspapers."

She'd sent innumerable letters, written dozens of articles. The United States government cared nothing about wrongfully imprisoned black people in central Africa, and the newspapers had long since stopped publishing her articles and letters. Kamalia was old news. She too was old news, a former model in New York and Paris, at nearly thirty-one getting too old for the runway…but perhaps not too old for the guard. She placed a hand on his upper arm. "Please, I just need to speak to my client."

He flexed his biceps to demonstrate where true power lay.

"No one is permitted to enter without an appointment."

She let her hand fall to her side. "Are you familiar with the May 25th Orphan's Society?" So many children had been left without parents following the coup that an organization had been formed to ensure that the overflowing orphanages had sufficient food and blankets.

"Everyone knows of the Societé," he said.

She opened the satchel that served as her purse and briefcase and took out her wallet. "Perhaps you could make a donation in the name of a loved one." She handed him a hundred-franc bill, enough to buy food for him and his family for a month. He snatched the money and shoved it into his pants pocket. "I will see that it goes to a worthy cause." The by-now familiar leer made her want to take the money back from him, but she calmly walked around him and into the prison.

• • •

# CHAPTER 8

Zach heard Sarah enter the apartment. He checked his watch—five thirty—logged off the internet, and joined her in the small foyer of their apartment, arriving at the same time as a panting Guinevere, who always greeted Sarah's arrival as an utterly unexpected, life-saving event. Sarah was one of the fortunate few who managed to look lovelier as the day wore on, no matter what difficulties it brought. In Sarah's case, this meant a roomful of third-graders, some very bright and demanding "enrichment," others having trouble keeping up and demanding extra attention, the majority somewhere in the middle and at constant risk of getting lost in the public school shuffle.

"Hello, Miss Pearlman," he said in a child's singsong. "You're a sight for sore eyes."

She smiled a touch wearily as she took off her jacket. "Did you bike today?"

"Nyack. Almost." He saw a shadow of disappointment fall over her eyes.

"Did you call that contractor?"

"I left a message," he lied. If she knew how he'd actually spent the day she'd probably leave the apartment and never return, and he wouldn't blame her.

"I'm glad. You want a glass of wine?"

"Maybe later," he said, thinking, as he often did when she returned from a long day at school, that his life, in contrast to hers, added nothing of substance to the world, or even to their own little corner of it. He pulled her toward him and kissed her briefly on the lips.

"You know what, Zach?"

"What?"

"You stink. Eau de bicycle."

"Oh. I was about to wash off."

"Maybe I can help you."

They showered together and made slow, early-evening love, and all he could think of was how little it took to reassure her, how little he would need to do to become the man she wanted him to be—and how impossible that was for him. Later, she brought two glasses of white wine to the bed, which they sipped in comfortable silence.

"Do you know the name Billy Sandifer?" he asked after a while.

"Should I?"

"I Googled him. He was a fairly well-known radical in the nineties antiglobalization movement. Spent a bunch of years in jail for blowing up a building in Boston. Killed a night watchman."

"And now?"

"He's been catching rides on Julian Mellow's private jet."

"Oh, Zach." She probably used a similar voice for eight-year-olds who misbehaved after repeated warnings.

"Why is an antibusiness radical flying around the country on Mellow's plane?"

"Why does it matter?"

"Mellow is apolitical as far as I know. He gives money to both parties. It's about influence and access, not ideology."

"Why, Zach?"

"He'd support the devil if he thought he could nail a favorable antitrust ruling on one of his deals."

"Zach!"

"I have to, Sarah."

She left the room. He heard her call Guinevere to the kitchen for dinner. He drained his wine and fell back on his pillow. He'd worked for Mellow Partners for ten years, beginning right out of Wharton. He'd toiled for low wages in publishing for a while before heading to b-school in Philadelphia, and he'd planned to return to the media business in some managerial capacity, armed with a business degree. But then Mellow Partners offered him a salary that was three times what he'd earned in publishing, with the promise of even larger bonuses. He'd interviewed with Julian

Mellow himself, who was just starting out on his own after walking away from a lucrative partnership at Goldman Sachs. Mellow had been laconic but memorable.

*Why work* in *the media when you can* own *it? Why be an* employee *when you can be an owner?*

He signed on. Over the next decade he'd been Julian's trusted sidekick, helping to engineer buyouts of dozens of companies, including, as promised, several media concerns. He'd grown rich in the process, raking in seven-figure bonuses year after year. Every penny of which was gone.

"I just need to see this through," he told Sarah in the kitchen, where she was assembling a salad for dinner. It looked to be a salad for one.

"See *what* through? What possible outcome can there be that would satisfy you? Julian Mellow is a horrible man, I get that."

"He destroyed me."

"No, he didn't. You're thirty-five, you're healthy, and you're in a great relationship, or you would be if only you could get over him."

"I have no career."

"No career in *finance*. There are other ways to make a living."

"I can't forgive him."

"No one's asking you to. You just need to move on. What do you think you can gain by tracking his every move?"

"He fucked up on the Finnegan deal and pinned it on me. He's bound to fuck up somewhere else, only next time he won't have me to take the fall."

"He's too rich to go down, Zach. Too well connected."

"But he's greedy for success. You have no idea how the need to end up on top drives him, even now. That's why he bought those shares in Finnegan. He made a five-million-dollar profit. For a man like Mellow, that's like ten bucks. He risked everything for ten bucks. He'll do it again."

Zach could talk easily about Mellow's greed, and yet it still astounded him, how stupid the whole thing was. Mellow Partners had been in a fierce bidding war for Finnegan Industries, a Cleveland-based electronic components manufacturer. The company was 30 percent owned by the grandchildren of its founder, one of whom ran it, and had been underperforming its competitors for years—in short, perfect bait for Mellow, who routinely bought such companies, streamlined operations, then took them public at stupendous profit. But the potential profits in acquiring Finnegan had been a bit too obvious, and several private equity firms and leveraged buyout shops had bid its price up. Julian abhorred losing even more than he loved making money, and when he heard through his vast web of contacts that a new entrant in the bidding war was going to make an offer at least 10 percent above his highest and final offer, he publicly announced that he was backing down and then purchased call options on Finnegan through a numbered account. The new entrant's offer tripled the value of those options overnight, netting Mellow a five-million-dollar profit. When the SEC came calling, he produced a document showing that Zach had purchased the options, not him—for his own account. Zach never understood how Julian had been able to forge his signature on those trade confirmations, but what had really mystified him, and still did, was how a man who had been like a father to him, albeit a rather remote one, a man whose vast wealth he'd helped to create, could have turned on him so quickly. Zach had spent half his savings on lawyers, who worked out a deal by which he forked over most of his remaining assets to the government and was barred for life from the securities industry. Julian emerged unscathed, his reputation and wealth intact.

"You could spend the rest of your life trying to bring Julian down. And then what?"

He'd been so caught up with trailing Mellow's every move that he'd never stopped to consider what life would look like if and when he managed to bring down his nemesis.

"And then I'll move on."

"If it's not too late."

He went to the bedroom and fired up the computer, which

had become his prime weapon in an admittedly lame campaign to destroy Julian Mellow. He had bought at least one share in every public entity in which Julian Mellow had an interest, an expensive proposition given the web of holding companies and joint ventures and equity funds he controlled. As a shareholder he received not only annual reports but quarterly filings and proxies—none of which had yet yielded anything that could possibly compromise Julian. But he never gave up hope.

Though he'd been barred from the securities industries, he was free to buy and sell stocks for himself. Still, he didn't want Julian to know that he was monitoring him, and he knew that Julian employed software that continually checked for cross-ownership of his myriad holdings. Meager as Zach's "holdings" were, they could well turn up on a short list of investors that could draw Julian's attention—and perhaps incite some sort of retaliation. So he'd acquired a new identity for the purpose of becoming one of Julian's investors: Arthur Sandler, a combination of his father's first name and his mother's maiden name.

Becoming Arthur Sandler had been no small undertaking. In order to open a brokerage account, he needed a social security number and some sort of established credit. A web search had led him to an organization that provided social security numbers by mail for $50. As far as he could tell, the organization, Eden Services, was a group of antigovernment "bureaucracy" haters. He forced himself not to think about where his $50 was going as he typed in his phony date and place of birth, both of which, he learned, determined the range of numbers on the social security card. Once Arthur Sandler had acquired a social security number, Zach returned to the site to order a driver's license and found that it no longer existed. Instead, he found a single page with a short statement: "We have been forced to decamp to another site to avoid the predatory tentacles of the federal government." He thought of those peddlers of stolen and counterfeit goods who would set up shop on a Manhattan street corner one day, do a brisk business for a few weeks, then disappear, only to turn up on another corner in another neighborhood a few days later.

Hours of online searching led him to an email conversation with a man in Washington Heights who said he could provide the documents Zach needed. He spent a long afternoon in a tiny, dark apartment on West 185th Street as a man who identified himself only as Joey painstakingly created a New York State driver's license containing the photo that Zach had brought with him. Joey employed an impressive array of materials and tools: computer, scanner, Photoshop software, rubber stamps, sheets of Dura-Lar film, X-Acto knife. He deployed these implements with silent, surgical precision.

Armed with a social security number and license, "Arthur Sandler" walked into a bank with a thousand dollars in cash and opened a checking account. He gave as his address a mail drop on Columbus Avenue. A credit card came next, which he used to buy various research reports and other documents concerning Julian's companies. Finally, he opened an online investment account and began buying shares, transferring more and more money from his real account to Arthur Sandler's account to pay for them. It was an unintended but not unwelcome consequence of this activity that, in the year since Arthur Sandler had begun buying shares exclusively in companies controlled by Julian Mellow, his investments had increased by more than 40 percent, even in a flat market. Julian, it seemed, had not lost his touch.

Zach had not told Sarah about his alter ego, nor about his investments. The ease with which he concealed so much from the woman he loved was almost as disturbing as the ease with which he'd created an entirely new person, a person with a growing investment portfolio, no less.

Earlier, when he'd Googled Billy Sandifer, he'd found twelve pages of links. He'd only gotten through the first two pages, which were mostly links to sites selling self-published books about the evils of globalization. He continued working his way down the links until he came to an article from the Williston, New York, *Courier* from four years ago.

### EX-RADICAL RELEASED FROM WILLISTON
### AFTER EIGHT YEARS BEHIND BARS

*William "Billy" Sandifer, a former leader of the anti-globalization movement, walked out of the Williston Correctional Facility after serving eight years of a fifteen-year sentence. Mr. Sandifer ignored the presence of several reporters gathered outside the front gate of the prison and got into the back of a waiting Lincoln Town Car.*

*Mr. Sandifer was convicted of masterminding the 1998 bombing of the headquarters building of the Starret Corporation, a target of the anti-globalization movement because of its ties to allegedly repressive governments in Central America. Roger Morrison, a night watchman, was killed in the bombing. Two other members of the loosely affiliated protest group, which has no name and no centralized organization, were charged with the crime but were never apprehended. Sandifer never spoke publicly about the incident, neither taking nor denying responsibility. His attorneys argued that the bomb was never meant to harm anyone.*

*As an inmate, Sandifer largely disappeared from the public eye and then briefly reappeared during the 2005 uprising at Williston in which three guards and four inmates were killed. The hostage takers wanted to draw attention to what they considered inhumane conditions brought about by the "privatization" of the facility by the Acorn Correctional Corporation, which purchased Williston from the federal government. Sandifer emerged as a spokesman and negotiator for the inmates, although he was never implicated in the uprising itself. The incident lasted four days. At hearings held afterward, inmates contended that the deaths had resulted from a desire for revenge on the part of the guards, who had already regained control of the facility, and not from self-defense. Sandifer testified at the hearings that he had not seen the killings.*

*It is not clear where Sandifer will reside following his release.*

Zach himself had helped engineer Julian's takeover of Acorn, a three-billion-dollar operator of formerly government-owned facilities, including veterans' hospitals, government cafeterias, and correctional institutions. Acorn had been one of Mellow Partners' largest acquisitions, but far from its most successful. The uprising at Williston had drawn attention to the fact that Acorn tended to skimp on such niceties as sanitation and food quality in order to fatten its margins. Julian had been unable to work his usual cost-cutting magic on Acorn and so had never been able to sell it back to the public for his usual stratospheric return.

Acorn *had* to be the link between Mellow and Sandifer. Questions remained, of course: how had the two men connected? Mellow had not been personally involved in the negotiations during the uprising. And what was the enduring connection, a link that had placed Sandifer on Julian's Gulfstream jet on the very same day that Senator Harry Lightstone was also a passenger?

## FRIDAY, NOVEMBER 5

# CHAPTER 9

Julian Mellow walked to Harry Lightstone's townhouse on East 68th Street, between Fifth and Madison, just a few blocks from his own apartment. It was a glorious fall day, the crisp air sweetened by the moldering leaves, the stylish young women heading to work wearing short skirts and light sweaters for perhaps the last time for many months. On such a day the city seemed not only beautiful but governable, as if the clear sky and warm temperature imposed an obligation to behave civilly. At Madison Avenue, he dropped the "burner" phone Billy Sandifer had sent him into a trash can. It had served its purpose: that call from Danielle in San Francisco. He rang the doorbell at number 21. Marcella Lightstone answered, as he'd earlier requested on the phone. No doubt she had a small army of servants on staff, but he thought it best that their first face-to-face meeting take place without observation.

"Julian, how nice to see you," she said, gesturing for him to enter.

The senator's wife was a tall woman of about forty who could most charitably be described as striking. Her face was long and narrow, as was her nose, giving her an equine look that was at once aristocratic and faintly ridiculous. She was very thin, almost gaunt, coiffed and dressed with enough talent and expense to lend her an air of confidence and polish that, in combination, approximated elegance. She ushered him into a small room off the first-floor hallway. It was paneled in dark wood and filled with antique furniture and dark European paintings. Like Marcella, the room felt expensively put together and faintly ridiculous in its pretensions.

"You probably don't remember, but we've met," she said once they were seated on facing sofas. "A cancer benefit, I think. Or a museum. About a year ago, you—"

"I don't remember." He unzipped his laptop case.

She smiled uncertainly. "I could run upstairs for some coffee." She sounded doubtful that she could execute such a mission on her own. Her grandfather, Kenneth Kollan, who'd fled the pogroms in Russia for western Pennsylvania, had founded an electronics company and sold it to General Electric, forty-five years ago, for half a billion dollars. It was possible that Marcella Kollan Lightstone had never made a cup of coffee in her life.

He ignored her as his computer booted up, then he double-clicked on the video icon on his desktop.

"You need to see this," he said. She looked curious but made no effort to get up.

He waited her out. After a few seconds voices could be heard from the laptop's small, built-in speakers.

"That's Harry's voice," she said, a touch nervously. A moment later, with a faint sigh, she joined him on the sofa. They watched in silence as Senator Lightstone slowly undressed the San Francisco whore. She showed no reaction as the senator got over his initial shock and resumed active, even gleeful participation in what evolved into a very different scene from what he'd been expecting. And she remained silent once the clip ended and Julian returned the laptop to its case, recrossing the small room to the facing sofa as serenely as if she'd just dutifully viewed pictures of a guest's recent vacation.

"I take it your husband hasn't mentioned the video."

"What do you want?" she said in a composed voice.

"I want your husband in the White House."

"He hasn't even announced for the Republican nomination. Isn't it too late to—"

"He will."

"Has Harry seen…that?" She thrust a long, French-manicured finger at the laptop, as if at a mongrel dog.

Julian nodded. "He'll announce his candidacy later this week. I imagine he's putting his speech together as we speak. Haven't you two been in touch?"

She smiled wanly. Everyone knew the Lightstones lived apart, the senator in Washington, Marcella in New York. They came together occasionally in Pennsylvania, to remind the voters there that Harry Lightstone represented their interests, and at major social events in Washington and New York and whenever their two sons, deposited in a New England boarding school, had a birthday or other milestone that demanded parental participation.

"He may have mentioned it." The smile warmed a bit. "You do realize that four candidates have already announced."

"We have a lot of work to do."

"We?"

"We both want the White House, but neither of us wants to sit in the Oval Office. Real power doesn't reside there, anyway."

"Paul Nessin would disagree."

"No one understands the limits of the federal government more acutely than the president himself. New York is the center of power in this country. Washington is a branch office."

Her lips parted. Though she clearly appreciated his arrogance, she was not quite prepared to smile. Still, her desire, her *hunger*, was evident. Julian suspected that she had no interest in politics, and even less in the prestige of being First Lady. Her Jewish grandfather and parents had never been fully accepted by Pittsburgh's business and social elite. She'd had it much easier. From birth, precious few things had been beyond her grasp. The White House was one of them.

"How can you help Harry?"

"I can get him elected."

"Do you really…" She couldn't finish.

He nodded. "But I'll need your…" He'd never asked for help from anyone. "Your input."

"What can I do?"

"Keep Harry in line."

"That's never been a problem." She smiled demurely. "In any case, he wants this as much as I do."

"Not true. There are limits to his ambition. Men with limits can be dangerous. I prefer to deal with ruthless men, men who will do anything to get what they want. You always know where men like that stand, what buttons to push. Men with limits are harder to control. You never know how hard to push, or where. That's where you come in. You have no limits."

She leaned forward, prepared to protest, then sat back and crossed her legs. "Harry and I celebrated at a restaurant in Pittsburgh the day after he won election to the House. He raised his glass—I think there were tears in his eyes—and said he wanted nothing more from life than what he had: a family, a seat in Congress. I almost spat champagne at him. Even after five years of marriage I had no idea our dreams were so different." Her mouth puckered in disgust. "But you figured it out right away."

"My real talent is sizing up people, not companies."

"I still don't understand why," she said. "If New York is where power lies…"

"*Why* isn't important," he said quickly.

"You can get the president on the phone any time you want. What difference does it make to you if it's Paul Nessin or Harry Lightstone?"

He said nothing.

"Is it about some company you own? No, you're beyond needing favors on taxes or antitrust. It can't be about kicking Nessin out of office; you've never been considered particularly political, and in any case, there are safer bets than Harry."

He waited her out in silence.

"Although you probably think you can control Harry more easily than the others. Is that why you settled on him?"

He considered answering, then thought better of it. He'd chosen Lightstone because there had been no other choice. The Democratic incumbent was beyond even his reach. The Republican frontrunners had turned up depressingly clean, despite the relentless and well-compensated efforts of Billy Sandifer to uncover something useful. Lightstone had the tax-cutting, family-values, antigovernment bona fides that a Republican needed to get the nomination, and there was an approachable, just-folks aura to him that took the edge off what was really a fairly radical ideology. And there was something else: Lightstone was weak, which made him a risky bet, but also controllable. "I think Harry will make a fine president," he said.

Her eyebrows arched ever so slightly. "How did you find out, by the way, about his proclivities?"

He offered the tiniest of shrugs.

"He likes me to stand on a chair when we kiss." She smiled, almost warmly. "A lot of wives put up with much more."

Julian stood up. "It's important we not be seen together," he said, taking a card from his suit pocket. "This is my cell phone number. Use it to contact me."

"I'm not sure I completely understand my role."

"You will."

She stood up, face suddenly flushed with anger. "Let's be clear about something. I don't need this."

"No, but you want it."

She opened her mouth but said nothing. Julian picked up his laptop and left her.

# CHAPTER 10

Zach waited until Sarah left for work to begin Googling. He quickly found a reference to a speech Senator Lightstone had delivered at the Saint Francis Hotel to an association of manufacturers. There was nothing more about the speech, but he spent some time clicking around various San Francisco sites and stumbled on a story about the murder of a prostitute in the Castro district. Halfway through the story he came across a paragraph that drew his interest:

> *The victim was last seen leaving the Saint Francis Hotel on Union Square at approximately ten o'clock last night. A hotel security official confirmed that the victim had been seen by several people leaving the hotel through the Post Street exit. He refused to comment on the possibility that the victim had been engaged in prostitution with a guest of the hotel. He did, however, confirm that the hotel has provided a guest list to the San Francisco police.*

The prostitute had been in the hotel at the same time as the senator. Zach printed the article and placed it inside a folder that he labeled *Lightstone*. He called the American Association of Manufacturers and was eventually connected to a friendly-voiced woman who identified herself as Peggy Lustig, director of conferences and events.

"I'm putting the final touches on an article for the *Chronicle* about the conference earlier this week at the Saint Francis," he told her.

"Fantastic. We certainly appreciated the small item in yesterday's edition, but obviously a more thorough piece would be great. I wasn't aware that the *Chronicle* had sent a reporter to cover the event."

He charged ahead. "Do you happen to recall what time Senator Lightstone finished his address?"

"I'm not sure of the exact time. It was after dinner…about nine thirty."

"And did he leave the ballroom right away?"

"As I recall he had coffee and dessert and then spoke to our national director for a few minutes."

"So he left the ballroom at about ten o'clock?"

"That's probably correct."

This was vaguely disappointing but hardly surprising. If Lightstone left the ballroom at ten, then he wouldn't have had time for a liaison in his room, since she left the hotel at about the same time. Then again, he was looking for the connection between Lightstone and Julian Mellow, not between the senator and a murder victim. The notion that Sarah was right, that his obsession with Mellow had spun out of control, was beginning to look depressingly credible.

"I hope you're planning to emphasize that the senator was very emphatic in support of additional tort reform. Capping damage awards and limiting class actions, while a good start, is only—"

"Yes, I definitely picked up on that point."

"That's great. Because a reporter from a trade publication was insistent that the senator was less than firm in his support of additional reform. He pestered us all the way to the hotel exit and I practically had to restrain him from following the senator out the door."

"The senator left the hotel?"

"He was staying elsewhere, the Fairmont, I believe."

"He left the hotel at ten o'clock?"

"Give or take. Why is it important when the—"

"You've been very helpful, Peg, thanks a million."

He hung up and made a notation on the cover of the senator's folder: *Exited Saint Francis same time as hooker who was murdered next morning.* Still no obvious connection to Julian Mellow, or to Billy Sandifer for that matter. But conspiracy theories were built on thinner stuff than what he had. He added the folder to the "active" pile on his desk and changed into biking gear.

## TUESDAY, NOVEMBER 8

# CHAPTER 11

Sophie DuVal shifted into low gear as the green Renault wagon lurched to the top of the mountain. The car was ten years old, practically brand-new by Kamalian standards, and badly in need of a tune-up. The engine began to wheeze and buck as the incline steepened.

"Come on, we're almost there." She goosed the gas pedal. Moments later she crested the mountain, one of the smaller peaks in the Saint Eustace chain that formed Kamalia's eastern border. In the distance she saw a crowd of guards patrolling the border crossing. When Kamalia's government was involved there were always more men than necessary—it was President Boymond's one effective strategy for countering Kamalia's crushing unemployment rate. Since nationalizing the country's major industries, unemployment had soared from an already burdensome 10 percent to close to half the population. So every government installation swarmed with uniformed men standing around trying halfheartedly to look occupied. At least twenty men guarded the border, as if anyone would want to enter Kamalia. Leaving was strictly forbidden under Le Père's regime, but you didn't need twenty men to enforce that. You'd think Boymond would encourage emigration, given the lack of jobs and food. But a flood of emigration would look bad, would spread the word that this once progressive country, rich in minerals, a beacon of hope to the rest of sub-Saharan Africa, had squandered its potential.

She turned off the main road a few miles from the border onto a rutted dirt road, which she followed for several spine-rattling miles. Dense brush crowded the roadside, forming an impenetrable wall. Long branches and hanging vines slapped the car's windshield and front bumper, testament to the small volume of traffic the road saw lately. Hundreds of such roads crisscrossed the landscape of eastern Kamalia, hacked out from the brush to allow smugglers access to the country's interior, where they had once made a thriving market in small appliances, blue jeans, and other luxury goods brought in from Europe and America. Now there was no money even for such duty-free imports and the jungle was gradually reclaiming the largely unused roads.

The jolting ride felt endless, and she was beginning to fear that she had turned onto the wrong road when it opened up to the right, revealing a ramshackle hut in a small clearing. She parked the Renault in front and got out.

"*C'est moi*, Sophie DuVal," she called out with as much force as she could muster. She felt small and vulnerable in the isolated clearing, and she knew she was being watched. A few moments later the hut's only door opened and a man stepped out. He was short and thickly built, covered head to foot in denim, the ultimate status symbol. He wasn't a Kamalian, she guessed, and not just from his clothes. Kamalians tended to be taller than their neighbors, their skin darker. But they exuded an air of resignation in the slump of their shoulders, the tired, cynical squint of their eyes, the shambling way they walked, as if no destination could possibly be worth serious effort. Poor Kamalia, once the shining star of the continent, a magnet for the world's economists looking to analyze and replicate its remarkable turnaround. This man coming toward her, his stride purposeful, his expression one of easy confidence, was no Kamalian.

"We were beginning to worry," he said as two more men, both short and stocky, emerged from the hut. They held rifles.

"My car was just barely up to the task. I don't know how we're going to make the return trip loaded down."

"You are alone?"

She nodded. Nevertheless, his eyes continued to move, taking nothing for granted.

"You have the money?"

She walked back to the car and returned with a canvas bag, which she handed to him. "Forty-five thousand dollars, American dollars, all twenties," she said.

He thrust his hand into the bag, and for a moment she feared he was going to count every bill, which could take forever. Instead, he took a long, deep breath, savoring the sensual pleasure of so much American cash, and removed his hand.

"The weapons?" she said, eager to be gone. She had come to this place for a cause, a good cause; he'd been driven there by greed, and the difference in their motives made her uncomfortable.

He signaled to the two men behind him, who withdrew into the hut and reappeared moments later carrying armfuls of AK-74 assault rifles. She opened the back of the wagon and they began loading.

"How does a beautiful Kamalian get her hands on this much cash?" the leader asked her. "Twenty families in Kamalia could live very comfortably on what you have given me."

"I don't ask where you get the rifles."

"As long as you have a reliable source…"

"I feel the same way. Can't your men move faster?"

"They were not counting on having to load the car themselves."

She frowned and followed one of the men into the hut, where she looked around and estimated that they had loaded half the rifles. Stacked by the door were several boxes of ammunition. She was about to pick up a box when one of the men stepped directly in front of her. He was a head shorter, and sweating heavily at his brow and armpits.

"Move," she said firmly.

He didn't budge. The other man appeared in the doorway,

took in the situation, and smiled broadly as he left the hut empty-handed.

"I asked you to move."

He touched her arm and with his other hand began massaging his crotch. When she stepped back he moved closer. He smelled mushroomy, damp and earthy. She moved to her right but he blocked her escape, edging closer to her. He placed a hand on her right shoulder and let it slide down to her breast.

"One last time, back off," she said, swatting away his hand.

He slowly shook his head as his eyes roved up and down her body. In one fast moment she reached to her left, grabbed one of the rifles the men had been carrying when they first appeared in the doorway, and jammed the barrel into his abdomen, forcing him back several steps. Then she aimed the rifle at his chest.

"Load the car," she said. "Now."

His lips curled into a leering smile as he stepped closer to her, absently pushing the rifle to the side as if it were a large purse. His breath warmed her neck as he touched her waist. She lowered the gun and fired, hitting him in the shin. He crumpled to the floor, shrieking. Almost immediately the other two men stormed into the hut. The leader took in the scene and reached for his fallen comrade's loaded rifle, which was leaning against the wall. She pointed her rifle at his chest.

"Don't touch that," she said. He froze, arm outstretched. "You see what I'm capable of." They all regarded the writhing figure on the dirt floor, blood oozing from his right leg.

After a few tense moments the leader let his arm fall to his side.

"Idiot," he sneered at his wounded comrade. "You want to ruin this for us?"

"Now you will have to help load the car," Sophie said to the leader. "This other one won't be of much use." She nodded to her moaning victim.

The loading went much faster after the shooting. Soon, Sophie was on her way back to Villeneuve. But a hundred yards down the dirt road she stopped the car, leaned her head against the steering wheel, and began to hyperventilate. That morning, picking up the cash from a courier in the capital, she'd sensed that she was setting in motion a course of events that would gather momentum until she could no longer control it, and this thought had terrified her to the point of nausea. That Julian Mellow had somehow managed to move so many dollars into one of the most restrictive countries on the planet had emboldened her, however. He wouldn't desert her, she felt certain, not after what had been done to his son. Julian had never liked her—too political, too Third World, too black for his son, the crown prince of American finance—and he had blamed her for luring Matthew to Africa. But since his son's death he'd done whatever she asked.

She couldn't imagine herself actually using the weapons she bought with his money. She'd simply deliver them to the small band of comrades in the Front who, like her, were committed to overturning Boymond's hated regime. But that animal in the hut had touched her, the first touch by a man in over two years, since Matthew. Firing the rifle had felt so right, *so easy*. It was that thought, that she might be capable of much more than shattering the leg of a despicable dog of a human being, that made her gasp for air, unable to drive.

What else was she capable of?

# CHAPTER 12

Zach Springer scrambled into a taxi at San Francisco International Airport and gave the address of the Mission police station. The trip to San Francisco, booked at the last minute and therefore exorbitantly expensive, represented a sort of turning point. Heretofore, his determination to bring down Julian Mellow had taken the form of computer searches, a few phone calls, the close reading of dozens and dozens of business and finance publications for morsels of information, potentially damning but inevitably innocuous, about his nemesis. He contributed his share of monthly expenses from his dwindling savings and spent little on himself. Now, with the trip to San Francisco, checking in at JFK as Arthur Sandler, paying for the flight with Arthur Sandler's credit card, he'd crossed a line, investing serious money in what Sarah considered, not without merit, a destructive obsession. He hadn't told her about the trip—the credit card statement would be sent to Arthur Sandler's mail drop on Columbus Avenue. He'd be back before bedtime, the six-hour return flight offering plenty of time to make up an alibi for his whereabouts.

He'd made a few phone calls before leaving and found out that the investigation of Danielle Bruneau was being handled by a Detective Stephen Flaherty. He asked for Flaherty at the front desk of the modern, red-brick Mission station and, since he hadn't called ahead, was pleased to be led back by a uniformed policeman to a room full of steel desks.

"Steve, you have a visitor," his escort called across the room. A burly man, about fifty, wearing a white shirt, sleeves rolled up, collar open, and a dark blue tie, stood up and approached. "He says he has something on the Bruneau case."

"Thank you for seeing me," Zach began, sitting on the wooden chair next to Flaherty's desk. "I know you're busy and—"

"What do you have?"

Zach took a deep breath, aware that he was crossing another line by sharing his obsession with someone other than Sarah—with a law enforcement official, no less. He reached into his Hermès briefcase, a $1,800 indulgence from fatter days, now badly scuffed, and took out one of the photos of Billy Sandifer that he'd printed from the internet. It showed him leaving prison.

"This is actually a few years old, but I'm sure you can—"

"Who is this?" Flaherty took the photo.

"His name is Billy Sandifer. Back in the nineties, he was involved in the antiglobalization movement."

Flaherty dropped the photo on the desk. "Doesn't ring a bell."

"Well, his past isn't really why I'm here, in fact I don't exactly understand what the antiglobalization movement has to do with Danielle Bruneau."

"Dan Bowdin."

"I beg your pardon?"

"It's officially the Dan Bowdin murder investigation. That was his real name. Danielle Bruneau was…I guess it was his professional name."

"Oh. Well, as I was saying, I don't know what Billy Sandifer has to do with…Dan Bowdin."

"Yesterday we had more than twenty so-called tips about Danielle or Dan or whatever he or she was called. A parade of freaks through this station, each one of them with a story. So I'd be grateful if you'd get to the point."

"Right. You see, the night she was killed, Danielle was at the Saint Francis Hotel."

"Which we know."

"And so was Harry Lightstone, Senator Harry Lightstone."

"You mean that guy?" He nodded across the room to a television set on top of a filing cabinet. Zach squinted to make out the picture and felt a creepy sense of unease. Lightstone was speaking before Independence Hall in Philadelphia, his wife at his side. The volume was turned down, but the crawl at the bottom of the screen announced his candidacy for president.

"Your point?" the detective said.

Zach turned away from the television. "They left the hotel together. I checked with a representative of the organization the senator was speaking before."

"Are you suggesting that the senator murdered Danielle?" His smirk suggested that this was the freakiest theory he'd heard yet.

"Have you talked to the senator?"

Flaherty stood up. "I need a transfer out of this station," he said to no one in particular, then looked directly at Zach. "Yesterday we had a guy—and I use the term loosely—come in claiming he saw a dwarf entering her apartment at the time of the murder. A dwarf strangled a six-foot trannie with a belt. Right. But I'll take a killer dwarf any day over a candidate for president."

Zach stood and picked up the photograph. "This guy, Sandifer, flew to San Francisco the morning of the murder on the private jet of Julian Mellow." Mellow's name evoked no reaction from Flaherty. "He's one of the richest man in America. In the world, in fact."

"Oh, so *he* killed her?"

"That same morning, just a few minutes after Sandifer got off the jet, Senator Lightstone got on it and flew back to New York, where he met with Mellow in the back of a car."

"And the connection to Danielle-slash-Dan?"

"The senator leaves the hotel at the same time as a murder victim. The next morning, he flies to New York on a jet that has just deposited a convicted felon in this city."

"Wait a minute, convicted felon?"

"Sandifer spent eight years in Williston."

Flaherty took the picture from him and studied it. "What for?"

"He blew up an office building in Boston."

"Nice. But I still don't get the connection." He handed Zach the photo.

"If you just ask around…"

"No one saw anyone coming or going that morning."

"But what was he doing here? On the same plane as the senator. A private jet."

"Let me get this straight. The senator, the billionaire, and the radical, they all three killed her…him?" Flaherty regarded him with the combination of pity and exasperation usually directed at children with behavioral problems. Or the certifiably insane. Zach considered reciting the facts again, but he was beginning to wonder if in fact he wasn't beginning to lose his grip on reality. The image of Lightstone on TV across the room only added to his sense of unreality.

"Should I leave the photo with you?" he said.

"Sure, we'll add it to our files," Flaherty said.

"Thanks for making the trip worthwhile," he said, and snatched back the photo.

• • •

Fifteen minutes later, Zach stood in front of the house where Danielle Bruneau, née Dan Bowdin, had been strangled. He had no idea what had drawn him there other than a vague sense—make that desperate hope—that her death was somehow connected to Julian Mellow in the person of an ex-con radical. In one hand he held a photograph of Billy Sandifer. He had planned to show the photograph to passersby and perhaps even ring a few neighborhood doorbells. But he felt his spirit flag, and the sudden recognition of the absurdity of his presence in the Castro on a Tuesday afternoon made him at once heavy-footed and lightheaded. In any case, there were few pedestrians on Church Street. He walked slowly back to Castro and stopped into a coffee shop. He bought a bottle of water and while paying he showed the photograph to the cashier.

"Never saw him, but you can hang it up there."

He pointed to the wall adjacent to the front door on which were taped hundreds of cards and flyers advertising concerts, massage therapists, sublets, tattoo artists, and music lessons. He borrowed a pen and tape from the cashier and, in large block letters, wrote *Have you seen this man?* along with Arthur Sandler's email address. He hung up the photo, momentarily energized by having accomplished something, however trivial, and left.

# CHAPTER 13

With Independence Hall as a backdrop and his equally imposing wife by his side, Senator Harry Lightstone announced his candidacy for the Republican nomination for president.

"The policies of the current administration are the policies of the past," he shouted into a microphone. "A tax system that unfairly punishes enterprise and savings alike. Schools that are failing our kids, even after four years of steadily increasing budgets. A healthcare system in which universal coverage has led to universal confusion and higher costs for just about everyone. Embryos murdered in the name of scientific research that has led to no so-called cures. In short, freedom run amok. I say to the people of this great country, get ready for the future!" Lightstone nodded and mumbled his gratitude as he waited for the small crowd to quiet down.

Julian Mellow, watching the live broadcast on a small television in his office, considered the irony of Lightstone announcing his candidacy in front of a building named for independence.

"We can no longer tolerate an administration that sends tens of billions of dollars to foreign countries when our own infrastructure is literally crumbling around us. I say to the people of America, get ready for the future!"

Julian sighed as the crowd began chanting "Light-stone, Light-stone, Light-stone." He hoped Lightstone wasn't considering "Get ready for the future" as his campaign slogan. And "freedom run amok" might play to the Republican hardliners, but it was a bit too memorable and would not play well to the more temperate public who voted in the general election. Even more disturbing was the isolationist message, which he'd have to nip in the bud before it sank in with voters. He was going to invest far too much, take too many risks, to have Lightstone screw up things this early. All of the Republican candidates were railing against foreign intervention, returning to their isolationist roots after the Iraq debacle. Lightstone would have to take a strong and ostensibly principled stand in favor of opposing repressive regimes. It would set him apart from the other candidates, and while it would initially cause him some problems, eventually, if Julian had his way, it would propel him into the lead.

It was time to make his influence known. He dialed Marcella Lightstone's cell phone number and was gratified to see her glance at her purse, right there on the steps of Independence Hall. He couldn't hear the ringing through the television, but the senator must have: he stumbled over his words and shot Marcella an angry look before regaining his composure. Her voicemail picked up after four rings.

"Tell the candidate to tone down the isolationist message. In fact, I'd like him to call for a more proactive role in world affairs. If I hear a shift in this direction in his public statements over the next few weeks, you won't hear from me."

He clicked off.

# PART II

# CHAPTER 14

"In the future, use the service entrance. I'll come down myself and open the door."

Senator Harry Lightstone raised himself to his full six foot two inches. "I will come through the front door or not at all."

Julian closed the door to his apartment and led the senator into the library. "Plenty of politicians have come here, all of them looking for money. But if you make a habit of it one of the doormen might contact the press. It's no secret that in buildings like this some of the staff are on the payroll of the tabloids. A presidential candidate repeatedly visiting the apartment of a well-known Wall Street figure would be a big story. They might even send a photographer to stake out the place."

"I have no intention of *repeatedly* visiting this place."

"We'll see. Have a seat. Drink?"

He saw the senator take in the room before sitting: burled walnut cabinetry, acres of leather-bound books, a genuine Aubusson rug. Lightstone was no stranger to such rooms, thanks to Marcella's inheritance, but even he did a double take when he spotted the Picasso.

"*Boy with Mandolin*," Julian said. "Picasso's rose period."

"I suppose that makes it more *valuable*." Lightstone's voice was laced with contempt.

"It certainly made it more expensive."

In fact, the Picasso was the most valuable painting he had in the apartment, which also contained a dozen impressionist oils. The real jewels of his collection, of course, at least in his mind, if not on the Sotheby's auction floor, were the portraits in the private gallery off his office on 57th Street. The Monets, Renoirs, and even the Picasso he thought of as merely decorative. "I offered you a drink."

The senator shook his head and sat on the sofa. Julian sat on a wing chair. "Congratulations on Iowa," he said. Lightstone had come in third, which, given his late entry into the fray, was being described as a victory of sorts. Only in politics could a third-place showing be considered a victory; in Julian's world, third was a disaster. Still, Lightstone was given virtually no chance of winning the all-important New Hampshire primary. Since meeting in the back of his car the day after Lightstone's encounter with Danielle Bruneau, Julian had made no effort to contact the senator directly. With New Hampshire looming in just two weeks, that had to change.

"What is it you want from me? You know I have no hope of winning. There are four other men in the running, at least two of whom have a better chance than I do of getting the nomination. And none of us stands much of a chance of winning the general election."

*We'll see*, Julian almost said, but thought better of it. True, there was a sense of complacency in the national air. Paul Nessin— bland, almost phlegmatic, a former Midwestern governor—seemed to have adopted a "first, do no harm" policy that played well with the general electorate.

"This is what you've always wanted, isn't it?" Julian asked. "I just accelerated your timetable."

Lightstone stood up and crossed the room to the Picasso. He stared at the painting for a long while. The young boy seemed to return the gaze with what Julian thought was a vaguely sardonic look, his half smile inscrutable, eyes narrow and doubting. Had Picasso deliberately painted the boy's expression that way to mock future admirers of the work, a succession of plutocrats who the artist must have sensed, even in 1905, would bid up the value of the painting to absurd heights? Or had Picasso merely captured what the boy actually looked like? It was a great painting, truly, the only one in the apartment Julian could stand to look at for any length of time.

"I suppose I knew going in that politics was all about compromise," Lightstone told Picasso's boy, as if justifying himself to a young constituent. "I think they even teach you that in Poli Sci 101." Lightstone turned away from the Picasso. "But I never quite realized just how many compromises there would be, one after another."

Beginning, Julian suspected, with a loveless marriage to the astonishingly wealthy Marcella Kollan.

"I don't think I've made a purely disinterested decision since I first ran for the House. Every issue comes freighted with a quid pro quo."

"Don't tell me you entered politics to change the world."

"You'd probably laugh if I said I did." Julian said nothing. "Yes, I did think I could change the world," Lightstone said. "It's true. A government that worked *for* the people, not against them. A country where the markets, not Washington hacks, determined the course of events. And yet a fairer America, where everyone's interests were acknowledged and respected. I grew up in the sixties, as you did. Some of my colleagues turned against the ideals of that age; if anything, they became more hardened in their beliefs. But for me, the sixties were about self-expression, individual possibilities. I didn't share the ideologies of the protesters and hippies, but I caught their idealism, their passion."

"Did Marcella share your passion?" He couldn't quite keep the sarcasm out of his voice.

Lightstone moved toward him. Julian could see the conflicting forces inside him, contorting his otherwise handsome if bland face into something tense and throbbing and almost ugly: one force urging him to take a swing at Julian, the other urging restraint. Restraint won out, as Julian knew it would. He'd never invest in a loose cannon.

"It was a different decade for her," he said in a tight voice.

"What drew you together, then, if not ideals?" Julian had no

71

interest in the answer, which he already knew, but he anticipated the discomfort the question would cause, and it was important for Lightstone to understand who held power in their relationship. Lightstone seemed about to speak but then didn't. His face went slack, his shoulders sagged. Julian had succeeded in degrading him a bit, but while he felt a sense of victory he had no taste for it. It was as if he'd answered a deep hunger with bad food. His mind flashed forward nine months, to after the election. Would he feel nourished then?

"Is something the matter?"

Julian looked up to find Lightstone standing inches away, looking down his long nose at him. He'd almost forgotten he was there.

"Yes, everything is fine."

"You looked like you were going to be sick."

He stood up and felt momentarily dizzy. "I want you to adjust your foreign policy message," he said when he felt steadier.

"What?" Lightstone wheezed, imbuing the word with gallons of Wasp indignation.

"All the candidates are talking an isolationist game, including the president. I think you can make a mark by raising the possibility of a more fully engaged America."

"That's utter nonsense." More Wasp indignation. "The reason no one's talking about an activist foreign policy is because the voters have no stomach for it. Not since Iraq, Libya, Syria."

"The situation in Kamalia, for example."

"What about it?"

"Laurent Boymond is a monster. Why isn't anyone speaking out against him?"

"The world is full of monsters."

"And I want you to speak to the voters about this one."

"I can't believe I'm hearing this. You want me to make a campaign issue about Kamalia? Do you think there are ten voters in this country who even know where Kamalia is? Let alone care about its tin-pot dictator."

"His prisons are overflowing with dissidents who are routinely tortured. Thousands of innocent people have disappeared in the two years since he took power. Illegally took power. He nationalized every major industry and is diverting every cent they produce into his own accounts."

"Do you propose that I advocate *invading* Kamalia?" Lightstone's lips curled into a smirk.

"Of course not. I want you to talk about Kamalia as part of an overall policy. Zero tolerance for despots, something like that."

"I'll be laughed out of politics."

"You'll be laughed out of politics if the public sees you and that giantess in a San Francisco hotel room."

Lightstone considered him for a moment, his face as red as Picasso's mandolin boy. "This is about your son," he said quietly.

Julian angled around him and headed for the door. "It's late. You know what you have to do."

"Jesus Christ, I get it now. This is about your son. He married that black model. She was from Kamalia, wasn't she? And he was killed there. I'd forgotten that."

"I hadn't."

"My God, this whole thing, that…that person in San Francisco…announcing my candidacy…it's all about *him*?"

"What it's *about* is getting you elected."

"Julian, none of this will bring your son back. You *do* understand that?"

His sympathetic tone brought Julian to the point of retching. "Go home to your wife."

"I don't have a prayer of getting the nomination, don't you see that? And it wouldn't matter anyway, because nothing I do will make a difference to your son."

"You can let yourself out. And remember to use the service entrance next time."

Julian left the senator in the library. As he crossed the long front hallway, or gallery, as it was invariably called in real estate listings, he saw Caroline standing just outside the dining room. She looked stricken and disapproving.

"Don't do this," she hissed. "You'll bring us down. You'll destroy everything."

"Nothing will be destroyed," he muttered without stopping to look at her. He walked directly to their bedroom, then to his bathroom, where he closed the door behind him. He leaned against the sink and stared at the mirror.

"Matthew," he whispered, for it was his son's face he most often saw when he looked in the mirror, as much as he saw his own. And in the image he saw reflected back at him, young and idealistic and bright with hope and love—all the qualities he'd lost, if he'd ever really had them—he found all the encouragement he needed for the greatest, grandest, most audacious transaction of his long and illustrious career.

# CHAPTER 15

Billy Sandifer threw his toolkit over the chain-link fence that "protected" the hangar area of the Barrie, Maine, airport, and then climbed over it. There were no commercial flights into Barrie, and most of the small planes that used the single runway were worth less than a two-year-old SUV, and less useful. Billy had flown commercial to Augusta from LaGuardia, rented a car, and driven about an hour south to Barrie. It was dark when he landed, and he didn't see many lights on the side of the road as he drove, underscoring the sense that he had traveled to the end of the earth.

He quickly found what he was looking for, the Beech King Air 200, a twin-engine turboprop. Parked next to a dozen or so two-seaters, the Beech looked like a large bird surrounded by bugs. He zigzagged toward it, hiding behind the smaller planes in case anyone was there. The hangar was closed.

He had to crouch to fit under the Beech. At the back of the plane he found what he was looking for: a small metal inspection plate. He took a screwdriver from the toolkit and unfastened the four screws that secured the plate. He shone his flashlight into the opening and made out the stainless steel cable that ran through the fuselage, connecting the elevator control system to the flight deck.

He shifted the flashlight until he found the bellcrank that connected the cable to the elevator controls. A guy at Williston named Max had been a pilot for the Medellín drug cartel, ferrying coke from Colombia to makeshift airstrips in Florida until he'd been forced by bad weather to land on Key West, where DEA agents had taken him into custody. Drug running was the least of his offenses, it turned out; Max was wanted for a drug-related murder rap in Brooklyn. When Billy had met him he was six years into a life sentence without parole. They'd had many angry discussions about the evils of global corporations and the country's unfair drug laws. Lifers always appreciated visitors, the more unexpected the better. Max had been very happy to see Billy last week and had enthusiastically suggested several ways to sabotage a small plane when Billy told him about the "corporate pig in Texas" whose unspecified company plane needed to go down. Billy had liked the elevator controls angle the best, since, unlike fucking with the electronic controls, it didn't involve breaking into the plane itself. Max had even sketched the bellcrank mechanism for him.

He found the point where the bellcrank was attached to the cable with a castellated nut secured by a cotter pin. He used a pair of pliers to pull out the cotter pin and then loosened the nut almost to the end of the bellcrank. It would hold during takeoff, but the vibration of the plane in flight would quickly cause it to drop off entirely, at which point the pilot would be unable to control the pitch of the plane. He quickly resecured the inspection plate, switched off the flashlight, and moved out from under the Beech. Before climbing over the fence he turned back to look at the plane. It appeared to glow in the faint moonlight, giving off a solid, almost arrogant sense of security. By tomorrow it would be scattered in pieces across the White Mountains.

• • •

WEDNESDAY, JANUARY 21

# CHAPTER 16

Julian Mellow was watching the Knicks on television when news of the crash came through on the bottom-of-the-screen crawl. Caroline was next to him on the bed, focused on *Interpersonal Foundations of Psychopathology*, typical bedtime reading for her. He switched over to CNN and saw live footage of smoke spiraling up from the wreckage of a plane. It seemed to have lodged on the side of a forested hill. The anchor sounded appropriately somber.

"Preliminary reports from the Barrie Airport, where the Beech King Air jet took off only minutes before the crash, indicate that there were four people on the plane, including one pilot. We emphasize that these are preliminary reports. While we *can* confirm at this point the identity of the passengers on the plane, we cannot confirm that anyone has died, although it doesn't appear from this vantage point that there are any survivors. There are at least two or three ambulances standing by, but as of now they haven't left the scene."

"Would you mind turning it down, Julian?" Caroline said without looking up from her book. He ignored her and focused on the television, which continued to broadcast a live feed of the crash site, with voiceover commentary from a CNN anchor.

"One thing is clear. If Senator Moore was on the plane, then this crash is both a personal tragedy for Charles Moore and his family and a game-changing disaster for the Republican Party. Senator Moore was widely regarded as the frontrunner for the nomination, the man with the best chance of unseating Paul Nessin."

Caroline laid aside her book. "*Senator* Charles Moore?"

He nodded and they watched the broadcast in silence. Sometime after midnight CNN confirmed that the senator had been one of the four people on the plane, and that there were no survivors. Julian used the remote to turn off the television. He'd been wondering how this moment would feel. He closed his eyes and focused inward, which he rarely did, trying to detect something that felt like remorse or guilt or perhaps even fear. He found none of it. True, there was no trace of exultation, either. Just the gratifying sense that things were progressing according to plan, not unlike the feeling of bland satisfaction he felt in recent years when a deal went as planned—documents filed on time, decisions made at appropriate points, funds transferred smoothly into the proper accounts.

"Tell me you had nothing to do with this," Caroline said.

He turned to her and detected a vulnerability he hadn't seen in many years, other than in the months following Matthew's death—and that had been grief and despair more than weakness. Her eyes looked plaintive, needful, the way they'd looked when they met twenty-five years ago, when she was as insecure as she was ambitious.

"Tell me you had nothing to do with this," she repeated with a very slight trembling in her voice. He pulled the covers off her. She had on a short dressing gown, essentially a white T-shirt, but it had doubtless cost several hundred dollars. At fifty-one her body was still nearly flawless. He ran a hand along her thigh, pushing up the dressing gown. He'd forgotten how soft her legs were, how firm. They felt expensive, like fine cloth. He'd barely touched her since Matthew's death and hadn't, until that moment, realized how much he'd missed it. She turned away.

"Not until you talk to me," she said.

He angled himself on top of her and yanked the nightshirt above her waist.

"Answer me, Julian. Tell me—*stop that.*"

It was over in less than a minute.

She turned her back to him the moment he moved off her and it occurred to him that the plane crash had affected him more than he suspected. How else to explain the sudden, urgent need, dormant for two years? He detected a slight vibration on the bed. Caroline was crying. When he placed a hand on her shoulder she shrugged it off. He reached around her and pulled her to him, gently pressing her into his chest.

"It will be all right, Caroline," he said softly. She shook her head. "I've never failed, you know that. I've never failed at anything."

She pulled away, eyes swollen and red with tears.

"Matthew," she whispered.

Was she reminding him of his one failure, a catastrophic one? *Was* Matthew's death his failure? Or was she merely suggesting that some things were beyond his control? He didn't want to contemplate either possibility, so he pressed her face into his chest in a pantomime of comfort giving.

• • •

Harry and Marcella Lightstone heard the news while watching CNN in the bedroom of their suite at the Manchester, New Hampshire, Radisson. There was a debate tomorrow at which the presence of the candidates' wives was all but mandatory, which explained the rare presence of both of them at the same location. There would be a lot more togetherness in the coming months, and if he won the nomination—a remote possibility, even with, as of that evening, a somewhat narrowed field—there would be even more togetherness afterward. They were mostly silent as they took in the news that Senator Charles Moore was dead, along with his pilot and two campaign aides. Harry felt paralyzed by conflicting emotions: the loss of a friend and colleague, the sudden promotion of his own candidacy, the inevitable delay of the debate, and the too-awful-to-consider notion that the crash was no accident.

"The race has narrowed to four candidates," said a political commentator on CNN. "But in a sense it's narrowed even further. The conventional wisdom is that Harry Lightstone and Gabriel Rooney will fight over the far-right block that Senator Moore had locked up, leaving the other two to duke it out for the party's moderate center."

"Conventional wisdom," Harry said, turning to Marcella. "He's been dead less than an hour."

"You'll need a statement."

"I'll have Michael draft something in the morning." Michael Steers, his communications director, would find the right combination of remorse and inspiration.

"No, I think we need to get something out tonight."

He looked at her. Marcella's profile could not be described as attractive, but she had grown into her looks in the eighteen years of their marriage, from a young woman unable to find a style that suited her to a confident woman of forty-two with a sense of style and a presence that evoked words like "handsome" and "striking" in press coverage. He considered telling her about Julian Mellow, about his suspicions about the crash. But she'd never had much respect for his fortitude, and she'd think him even weaker and more craven than before, first for what he'd done in San Francisco, then for what he'd agreed to in New York, and he couldn't take that added burden just then. Then again, perhaps she wouldn't care. She wanted the White House far more than he did.

"It's nine at night," he said. "What good will it do—"

"We need to be first. By tomorrow morning all the candidates will have a statement out. If we act quickly we'll have the eleven o'clock news to ourselves. Get one of the media girls up here." The campaign employed two full-time media relations professionals, both women in their thirties, both staying at the Radisson.

"Charlie Moore was a friend of mine." His voice broke, as much in response to her coldness as for Charlie. "One of the finest men I knew."

She stood up and crossed to his desk. "Excellent, we'll use that." She began tapping out a statement on his laptop while he sat there, staring at live footage of the smoking wreckage in Maine, wondering in a halfhearted way if he wouldn't be better off where Charlie was at that moment.

"This is why we worked so hard to get your campaign infrastructure up and running as quickly as possible," she said as she typed. "So we wouldn't let opportunities like this one slip by. I'll email the statement down to the girls, who'll send it to the networks, but you should prepare some off-the-cuff remarks for a live broadcast. Maybe something from the sidewalk in front of the hotel; that'll give the impression of impromptu honesty. I think I can get at least one news crew over here, a local Manchester station, but they'll upload it to the networks if it's any good. Try to dig up some anecdotes about Charlie, personal stuff, and don't forget to mention his wife and kids. This could be an important night for us."

. . .

Billy Sandifer was in the visitors' lounge of the Newman Center when the news came through. Rebecca was next to him on the sofa, brushing the hair of her doll. There wasn't much hair left to brush; she went through dolls every few months, and usually he remembered to bring her a new one when he visited, always the same one, from American Girl, the Felicity model in colonial frock and hat, her eyes as blank as Rebecca's. It had to be Felicity. He'd been distracted lately and forgotten the doll. Rebecca was fourteen, and though breasts had appeared over the past year, her face looked much younger. Autism had that effect, preserving a kind of physical innocence, but she still looked too old to be fussing over a doll's hair, and the breasts were something he couldn't quite get used to. Did all fathers feel that way about their daughters' breasts, or was it the doll and the sweetly blank face and the fact that she'd never be womanly in any meaningful sense? She wore a very loose cotton T-shirt and baggy cotton sweatpants, always the same outfit, which she had in multiples. Shortly after he left Williston, when they'd briefly lived together, Rebecca had squirmed and squealed whenever he forced a pretty blouse or sweater on her, then scratched her arms and shoulders raw until he let her take it off. Most clothes felt like sandpaper on her skin, according to one of the earliest therapists he had consulted. His beautiful daughter could not bear the touch of wool or silk or synthetics of any kind. Or him.

Some of the residents at Newman seemed more engaged than Rebecca, and sometimes he blamed himself for this, wondering if perhaps he might have forged a closer bond with her if he'd been around for her earlier years. Mostly he knew it wouldn't have made a difference. In addition to being on the autism spectrum, Rebecca was "functioning in the mentally retarded range," as one specialist had put it. The center had done wonders for her, making her more independent, self-reliant. But there was nothing they could do about making her the daughter he wanted. Not an intelligent, vivacious, achieving daughter—he'd long since given up on that. But a daughter who smiled when he entered the room, responded to his touch without flinching, offered something, when he left her, to encourage a return visit.

He watched TV for a few moments as the bodies were removed from the wreckage, the cameras keeping a respectful distance. Four people on the plane, the announcer said. Billy had figured there'd be at least that many and was vaguely relieved that there hadn't been more. An attendant entered the room and, speaking slowly and quietly, said that visiting hours were over. The sound of her voice caused Rebecca to start, and it was a few seconds before she stopped shivering. A car alarm from the parking lot could cause her to clasp her hands over her ears, as if an air raid siren had gone off inches away. Her father's voice, however, had virtually no impact.

He placed a hand on Rebecca's shoulder. She didn't exactly squirm or pull away, but she didn't exactly look at him either. Her indifference felt worse than rejection; he never got used to it. She stood up and walked directly to the attendant, a pleasant, plump, gray-haired woman. That's what a hundred grand a year bought—friendly, grandmotherly attendants instead of the surly prison wardens he'd seen on tours of state institutions. He looked back at the screen in time to see two policemen carrying a black, zippered body bag from the fuselage. Something else a hundred grand a year bought: a dead senator, a dead pilot, and what was presumed to be two dead campaign aides.

"Goodbye, sweetie," he said to Rebecca in the hallway. She hugged her doll to her chest as the attendant led her back to her room.

# CHAPTER 17

Since his trip to San Francisco, Zach had forced himself to put the Julian Mellow–Harry Lightstone–Billy Sandifer connection out of his mind. Sarah had not found out about the trip, but she'd become more and more insistent that he find meaningful work. He'd been trying. And in truth, he hadn't been able to dig up anything more on the connection. He scoured the internet, read every financial report he could lay his hands on, but the three men never appeared in articles together, never attended the same events—sometimes he wondered if he had fabricated the links among them, imagined them out of some need to make his nemesis even more sinister than he really was.

That night, after Sarah fell asleep, Zach felt a surge of restlessness. He quietly got out of bed and went to the living room, where he turned on the computer and navigated to the *New York Times* site, where he learned that Senator Charles Moore had died in a plane crash ten minutes after taking off from a landing strip in Barrie, Maine. He flicked on the television, turned the volume down, and watched with grim interest as various experts assessed the new political landscape now that one of the lead players was off the field. Where did these pundits come from on such short notice? Did the networks keep them in some sort of holding tank behind the studio, on the off chance that disaster might strike? Did they sleep in their suits, fully made up, just in case a plane crashed, a car skidded off an icy road, a heart gave out? It seemed monstrous, somehow, to so quickly and dispassionately piece together a new landscape around the sudden and tragic absence of one of its inhabitants. Harry Lightstone and Gabriel Rooney were now the frontrunners. In fact, there was Senator Lightstone in front of a hotel in Manchester, sending his condolences out to "the family." He sure as hell hadn't wasted any time, though he looked genuinely distraught, despite vows to continue his campaign for "the very values that Charlie fought for his entire career." Standing just behind Lightstone was his wife. Her face was frozen in a mournful frown, but something about her eyes, the way they seemed to be looking past the scene at hand to that new landscape the pundits were talking about, made her appear more calculating than dismayed. Zach had never much admired Harry Lightstone, or Charles Moore, for that matter.

He clicked to the Arthur Sandler email account and encountered the usual profusion of spam. He worked his way down the list, deleting pitches for penis enlargers, Viagra prescriptions, and porn sites, until one email got his attention. "Yes, I've seen this man," read the subject line. The sender's Yahoo address was LoveHaight. Zach opened the email.

> *Hey. Yeah, so I saw this note you tacked up on the board at Castro Coffee, must have been there a long time because half of it was covered with more recent stuff. I'm at the place right now.*

Zach had forgotten about the photo he'd taped to the wall. In the months since his trip to San Francisco he hadn't received a single call or email.

> *Anyway, I saw the guy in the photo. Billy Sandifer, used to be this major anti-globalist back when. We all were. Protesting trade talks, that kinda shit. Billy would hook up with me when he came to SF. Later I read he went to jail for blowing something up, I don't remember what. I was never into politics much then, but he and I did ludes together in SF when he was in town. Guy was seriously off the wall.*

*This one time? We were looking to score some weed in the Tenderloin and this black dude pretends he's gonna sell us a dime bag or something and ends up pulling a gun on us and taking every cent we had. I thought it was all over and when he took off with our cash I figured that was the end of it. Not Billy. He takes off after the guy, tackles him, and starts beating the shit out of him. I kicked the gun out of his hand and got our money, but Billy wouldn't let up, he would've killed the fucker if I hadn't pulled him off. Mr. World Peace, right? Mr. I Just Wanna Help the Kids. I don't think he gave a shit about workers and trade. He just needed to make trouble. A freak, you ask me. Anyway, yeah, I saw him last November, in the Castro, a Wednesday morning, I think. Walking fast down Church Street. I was heading to a job, I do renovations, probably worked on half the Victorians in the Castro, and it wasn't until after he passed me that I realized who it was. I called his name but he kept walking. I know I had the right guy because he started walking faster after I called his name, which kinda confirmed it for me. Anyway, don't know why you want information about him, but that's as much as I know. Don't try to contact me, by the way. Won't work. I opened a Yahoo Mail address to send this. I put that period of my life, drugs and shit, behind me a long time ago and I don't need trouble. And Billy, he scared me. I don't need that shit now. I just thought I'd write and let you know that I had seen him. Last person I thought I'd see in the Castro, you know what I mean? Straight as an arrow, least he was in those days. But who knows? Peace.*

Zach reread the email, then found some paper and began making notes. Billy Sandifer had flown to San Francisco on Julian Mellow's jet, gone more or less directly to Church Street, where, within a few hours, Danielle Bruneau had been murdered. At the same time, a parallel story was taking place: minutes after Sandifer got off the jet, Senator Harry Lightstone got on. The night before,

Lightstone had been seen leaving the Saint Francis hotel a few steps ahead of Bruneau.

Zach put the pen down and considered what he'd written. As he saw it, Harry Lightstone and Billy Sandifer were connected in two ways: by Danielle Bruneau (or Dan Bowdin) and by Julian Mellow. It didn't exactly make sense, but it couldn't be pure coincidence either.

And now the senator was associated with a second tragic death, this time of his political rival.

"With the New Hampshire primary just two weeks away, it remains to be seen if the Moore campaign will officially lend its support to another candidate," a pundit was saying.

*Remains to be seen?* Smoke was still swirling up from the wreckage. Zach used the remote to turn off the TV and was about to log off the computer when he had a thought. He Googled "Barrie, Maine" and found the town's official site. The private airstrip was noted, but the nearest commercial flights came into Augusta. He found the phone number he needed on another site and called the sole airline that connected the New York area with State Airport in Augusta. A reservation clerk picked up almost immediately.

"Yes, I was scheduled to meet a passenger arriving from LaGuardia earlier today, a William Sandifer. I was told he got on the plane but I never saw him. Can you confirm that he was on the plane?"

"Which flight was that?"

Zach had to guess. "The ten fifteen."

"No, I'm sorry, there was no one by that name confirmed on the ten fifteen."

"Maybe that was the problem; he took a later flight."

"Let me see…I can check the one thirty for you."

"That would be great."

He heard her typing, then her voice. "Sorry, he wasn't on that flight, either."

"I wonder if I could have gotten the day wrong. Could you check yesterday's flights?"

More typing, then she chuckled. "Looks like you got your wires crossed, sir. Mr. Sandifer was on the one thirty flight yesterday. I hope that helps."

Instead of elation, Zach felt a sense of dread fall over him. It was one thing to draw dotted lines on a piece of paper between Danielle Bruneau in San Francisco, a nineties radical, and a ranking member of the US Senate. Even he thought it was all a bit too loony to be credible. It was another thing to act on a stupid hunch only to learn that your most paranoid fantasies were in fact grounded in reality.

"Zach, what are you doing?"

He almost jumped out of the chair.

Sarah stood in the doorway to the bedroom.

"I thought you were asleep," he said.

"The TV woke me up."

"Senator Moore's plane crashed. He's dead."

"That's horrible."

Every instinct told him to leave it there, but he couldn't. "Sarah, I got an email tonight. This guy in San Francisco, he saw Billy Sandifer on the street where that prostitute was killed, remember I told you about her? Billy Sandifer and Harry Lightstone were on Julian Mellow's plane together. Well, not together, but the same day. And Lightstone and the hooker were at the same hotel together. So anyway, when I saw the news tonight about the crash, I don't know, it just seemed too weird that Lightstone was involved with—or, not involved with, but in contact with two deaths. I called the airport nearest where his plane took off, Senator Moore's plane, not Julian's. And guess what, Billy Sandifer flew into that airport yesterday afternoon. I'm going to check with the car rental agencies up there in Augusta, just to confirm, but I'd bet you anything he rented a car, and maybe someone spotted him heading south, or near the Barrie landing strip, that's where Moore's plane took off…" He checked his watch. "Five hours ago."

She just stared at him, arms folded across her chest.

"It's Julian, Sarah. I know it. He's what connects all of this: Sandifer, the prostitute, Lightstone, now Moore."

She blinked as tears spilled from her eyes. Then she went into the bedroom and closed the door behind her.

## SATURDAY, JANUARY 24

# CHAPTER 18

Mark Verbraski lived in a large, 1960s-era center hall colonial on the outskirts of Williston, New York, if a town of ten thousand residents could be said to have an outskirts. Zach parked in front and went slowly up the front walk, which was being reclaimed by crabgrass and weeds. He'd called ahead and been told by a groggy-sounding Verbraski that he was not interested in discussing the prison uprising, which had occurred when he was warden. Zach had decided to make the two-hour drive from Manhattan anyway. Now, looking up at the peeling paint, grimy windows, and sagging gutters on Verbraski's home, he wondered if he'd made the right decision. On a street of nearly identical houses, all of them in good condition with well-tended lawns, Verbraski's house looked almost sinister in its decrepitude. He rang the doorbell and a few moments later the front door opened.

Verbraski was as unkempt as his house. He appeared to be about sixty, with a pale, unshaven face and blue eyes that seemed dimmed from overuse. Tall and thin, he had on a white T-shirt and baggy khaki pants, both in need of washing, or perhaps replacement.

"What do you want?" His voice was gruff, with a liquid undertone, as if he were gargling.

"I called you yesterday. Zach Springer?"

"Not interested." He started to shut the door. Zach placed a hand on the knob and pushed his way in.

"It's important."

"How many books about Williston does the world need? How many articles? We've had two documentary films already. You think we need another one?"

"I'm not writing a book or making a film, I told you that yesterday."

Verbraski squinted, as if trying to recall a conversation held decades earlier. "Then what do you want?"

"Can I come in?"

Verbraski hesitated, then turned and headed into the house. Zach followed him through a dark hallway, past a living room empty of all furniture except a huge flat-screen TV on a pedestal and a leather armchair positioned directly in front of it, past a completely empty dining room, and into the kitchen. Verbraski sat on one side of a built-in breakfast nook. A half-full tumbler of clear liquid was waiting for him on the table.

"My wife took everything that wasn't nailed down." He patted the table. "Thank God this was nailed down. I keep meaning to buy some new furniture," Verbraski said, as if in response to a question. "But I can't seem to find the time." He took a long sip from the tumbler and sighed, sending a vodka-scented breeze across the table.

Zach had read about the hearings online. Three weeks of testimony by inmates, guards, and Verbraski himself before a blue-ribbon panel appointed by the governor. In the final report, which ran over seven hundred pages, Verbraski had not been charged with complicity in the bloody outcome of the Williston prison uprising, but he had been held accountable for the inhumane conditions that led up to the riot. He was fired by Acorn, the company that had bought the prison from the government, and was denied his accumulated pension benefits.

"The hearings must have been tough for you."

Verbraski's rheumy eyes expressed how far short Zach's assessment fell. "Yes, very tough indeed," he said with a phonily prim voice. "You want something to drink?"

Zach shook his head. Verbraski reached for a nearby bottle of Absolute and refilled his tumbler. His wife and pension and furniture were gone, but he wasn't skimping on quality booze.

"When you were warden at Williston, the prison was owned by Acorn Corporation, which was controlled by Julian Mellow."

"What exactly is it you want from me?"

"I'm looking into the connection between Julian Mellow and an inmate from the time of the uprising, Billy Sandifer."

What little color there was in Verbraski's cheeks drained away.

"You know, I've had twenty or twenty-five people stop by to interview me about that time, and I've turned them all down. But none of them ever mentioned those two names in the same sentence."

"What's the connection?"

"Connection? One owned the prison. The other lived inside it."

"That's it?" When Verbraski didn't reply, Zach decided to try a different tack to keep him engaged. "The commission report stated that Acorn put pressure on you to cut back on things like sanitation and food service."

"I worked at Williston my entire career, worked my way up from night shift guard, did you know that? I was warden when the state decided to privatize the place." The way Verbraski drew out the first syllable of *privatize*, it sounded both silly and sinister. "When you work for the government, you don't exactly have a blank check. But I never knew cutbacks like the ones Acorn had me make. It started with small stuff, like less chicken in the Sunday stew, less cleaning fluid in the mop pails. Then it got more serious, like clean inmate uniforms every two weeks instead of twice a week, smaller food rations, longer shifts for the guards, which didn't exactly make them more kindly toward the inmate population. You know, if we hadn't had that prisoner uprising, I sometimes think the guards might have rioted."

Zach remembered running the numbers on Acorn, which had fallen far short of its promise following the buyout by Mellow Partners. His job had been to do the financial calculations and

projections while Mellow communicated with the management
teams of the companies he controlled, including Acorn. He hadn't
known that the numbers he had blithely calculated back then had
resulted in conditions at Williston so dismal that riots had ensued.
Then again, he hadn't asked.

"Weren't there state inspectors?"

"'Course there were. And they reported to officials over in
Albany who liked their golf outings and Caribbean vacations, all
courtesy of the Acorn Corporation. Hell, I went on a few of those
outings myself. First class all the way." He raised his glass to toast
the memory.

"Did Julian Mellow ever contact you personally about
cutbacks?"

"Does God speak directly to his flock?"

"Some people think he does."

"Well, God never spoke to me, and neither did Julian Mellow.
Some guy who reported to some guy who reported to some guy
who reported to Mellow would call me and tell me we had to cut
expenses another 5 percent. That's how it worked."

"So you never met Mellow."

Verbraski hesitated before shaking his head.

"You *did* meet him."

"Do I look like I hobnob with his sort? And why do you care,
anyway?"

Zach switched gears. "Tell me about Billy Sandifer."

"He was an inmate. Had a hard-on for free trade or something. Blew up a building in Boston." His voice had tightened, and
he began shifting his tumbler across the tabletop.

"You seem uncomfortable talking about him."

"Yeah?"

"Tell me what you know."

"What I know…" He raised the drink and, finding it empty,
reached for the vodka bottle. But he changed his mind and put it
down. "You want to hear what I know? Billy Sandifer is an animal."

"He protested for the rights of poor people in Third World countries, children working in sweatshops."

"He set a bomb off in a building and killed a man."

"No one was supposed to get hurt."

"That's what he said. Sandifer was bad, just bad, one of the worst I ever met, and I worked in a prison most of my life. He didn't believe in anything except making trouble. Blowing things up. Hurting people. Free trade? Ten years earlier it would've been Vietnam, or hell, civil rights. Any cause would do, so long as it gave him cover to cause mayhem."

Zach tried to square Verbraski's description of Sandifer with what he'd read about him: the high school dropout, globetrotting protester, articulate spokesman for a cause who wanted only to give the poorer countries a fair shake.

"He negotiated between prison management and the inmates during the siege," Zach said. "He got time off for what he did."

"Yeah, he really saved the day. Five inmates and three guards killed."

"That wasn't Sandifer's fault, he was seeking a peaceful resolution. The National Guard killed them."

"Funny that the five inmates who were shot just happened to be the ringleaders. There were fifty-three inmates and twelve hostages in the cafeteria, and the National Guard somehow managed to shoot the leaders. After that, the surviving inmates basically caved."

"Someone on the inside tipped off the National Guard?"

Verbraski shook his head.

"Then how—"

"Sandifer."

"Let me get this straight—Sandifer told the National Guard who the leaders were, and where they'd be in the cafeteria once the siege started?"

"That's one theory. But you know, it went off too cleanly, you know what I mean? Even knowing the lay of the land, how do you pick off five men, dressed identically, in a room of fifty-three?"

"What's the other theory?" Verbraski just stared, waiting for him to figure it out.

"Sandifer *killed* them?" After a beat Verbraski nodded very slowly.

"None of the inmates knew, but some of the guards suspected. Nothing was ever proven. The National Guard had orders to fire at the ceiling unless they were directly attacked. The inmates had knives and a few rifles, taken from the hostages, that's all. Somehow, five inmates were shot."

"And the three prison guards?"

"Had their throats cut. Practically decapitated. Happened while the National Guard was storming the prison. Supposedly that's why they fired, seeing the bodies like that. But we never found one inmate who saw anyone slit their throats. Nobody knows who did it."

"What's your theory?"

"Sandifer. He set the whole thing up. One of the ringleaders survived long enough to tell us that Sandifer got the inmates to kill my three men, to justify the open-fire order. But we never had proof beyond the words of a dying man."

"The other ringleaders?"

"None of them survived. Ballistics showed that two were killed by the National Guard."

"The other two?"

"Killed by rifles taken from the hostages."

"In other words, killed by their fellow inmates."

"By Sandifer, you mean." When Zach started to say something, Verbraski held up a hand. "There's no proof, okay? But the whole thing was too neat. No witnesses to say who killed the guards, other than the one inmate who talked in the ambulance and died before he got to the hospital."

"Sandifer had less than three years to go, and was up for parole in a year. Why would he risk that?"

"A few murders for a year of freedom. People have done more for less." But Verbraski sounded unconvinced.

"There must have been some other incentive." Verbraski reached for the bottle and this time he poured. "Who did Sandifer negotiate with?"

"Couple of guys from the governor's office, National Guard big shots."

"You?"

He waited a beat, then: "Sure."

"Did someone tell him to kill the inmates?"

"I didn't. And I sure as hell wouldn't have told him to kill my own men, slit their throats. We're talking longtime employees, family men." His voice faded to a whisper. "Friends."

"But someone did. And they offered him more than a few months' jump on his parole."

"I don't know."

"Was Julian Mellow involved in negotiations?"

"God doesn't negotiate. He sends his apostles."

"I worked for him at the time. Believe me, he was very close to the situation. It killed him to see one of his investments blowing up like that. And I don't recall anyone being *sent* by him to negotiate."

Verbraski's eyebrows arched. "You work for Mellow?"

"Used to. Every day the siege at Williston continued, he was on the front page of the tabloids, the evil financier mistreating inmates to fatten the bottom line. It ate him up. He wanted the takeover ended at all costs."

"Obviously you were closer to the situation than I was," Verbraski said with undisguised irony.

"Why did Sandifer kill the prisoners and guards?"

"To end the standoff. It worked."

"Who told Sandifer to do it?"

"I got stuff to do." Verbraski stood up and walked unsteadily across the kitchen. He stopped in the middle of the room and turned. "You're asking questions about two of the most dangerous men I ever met, and I was a prison warden."

"Why is Julian Mellow dangerous?"

"Because he hates to lose. He'll do anything, and I mean fuckall anything, to avoid it."

"How do you know that?"

"He owned the company that owned the company that owned the prison I used to run."

"But you said you had no direct contact with him."

He headed for the back door. "Just leave it alone, whatever it is you're looking for." He walked outside, brushing the frame of the doorway on the way. Zach followed him. The backyard was, if anything, more disheveled than the front, the grass having gone to seed, twigs and leaves and bits of garbage littered about. Verbraski picked up a rake from the ground and began running it across a patch of crabgrass. He seemed neither capable of nor interested in the task.

"I lost everything," he said. "My wife, kids, every cent I had. I think of those guards sometimes, the ones with their throats cut, and I try to remind myself that compared to them I'm a lucky guy. But that only goes so far, you know?"

Zach didn't see the point in pressing Verbraski further.

"Here's my card, if there's anything else you want to tell me." He placed his old Mellow Partners card, with everything crossed out but his name and cell number, on a dilapidated lawn chair. As he circled the house he passed the garage, which was open. Inside was a gleaming silver Escalade. He stopped. The flat-panel TV in the living room must have cost at least a few thousand dollars. The vodka was forty bucks a bottle, not the brand you'd expect a penniless drunk to swill. And now the car, eighty grand at least.

"Nice car," Zach shouted from across the yard.

After a long silence, Verbraski looked up at him through milky, bloodshot eyes. "You have no idea what you're getting into," he said. "You think you know, but you don't."

He got up and tottered back into the house.

• • •

# CHAPTER 19

Julian Mellow watched a recording of the previous day's Republican debate, fast-forwarding through most of it. None of the four candidates had managed to make much of an impression, he thought. Certainly not Harry Lightstone. Everyone, even the two most conservative candidates, wanted to carve out the largest segment of the party, the centrist, moderate segment, and so refrained from saying anything that could be construed as controversial. The only time any of them sounded remotely passionate was when they talked about the incumbent president. Without a compelling agenda of their own, their best hope for energizing the electorate was to attack Paul Nessin. Gabe Rooney, a ten-term congressman from Missouri and the frontrunner by a large margin, managed to get particularly worked up over the president's tax increases, designed to relieve the gargantuan federal debt inherited from his predecessor. "You can't tax your way out of debt," he said, reiterating the theme of his candidacy. "We have to grow ourselves out of debt." In contrast, Lightstone seemed almost conciliatory, refusing to endorse a blanket repeal of Nessin's tax increases, which was fine for the general election but a guaranteed ticket to oblivion in the Republican primaries. One exchange did, however, give Julian hope.

The moderator asked about foreign policy differences with the current administration, and the first three candidates to answer, including Rooney, replied with bland observations about the importance of European allies and the need to build consensus while not caving to foreign interests. The public showed little interest in foreign policy, other than its impact on homeland security, and candidates rarely mentioned the world beyond the nation's borders. Then it was Lightstone's turn.

"This administration has a disgraceful track record of cozying up to foreign dictators in return for economic benefits. To my way of thinking, this is a devil's bargain and cannot be tolerated." Lightstone waited for applause from the audience, and when it wasn't forthcoming he cleared his throat and plunged ahead. "In Kamalia, Laurent Boymond brutalizes his own people, imprisons thousands without trial, and yet the Nessin administration remains completely closemouthed. In fact, we continue to grant Kamalia trade benefits so that the flow of copper and cobalt to this country remains uninterrupted. That's a devil's bargain, to my way of thinking, and in a Lightstone administration it will not continue. The people of Kamalia deserve freedom and it is our obligation as the most powerful country on earth to nurture that freedom, not continue to do business with a corrupt, oppressive regime like that of Laurent Boymond."

The moderator signaled for the next candidate to begin. Governor Alex Fortune from New Mexico, whose sole advantage in the race was that his mother had been born in the Dominican Republic, thus making him a potential favorite among Hispanic voters, was caught staring at Lightstone with open-mouthed incredulity, as if his opponent had launched into a tirade against pet ownership or Fourth of July parades and not a rather tepid call for a new policy toward an obscure African dictatorship. He regrouped quickly and launched into a dissertation on the importance of improving relations with countries like Mexico and Venezuela, places at least some Americans could locate on a map.

Julian noted with some frustration that Lightstone's pitch-perfect enunciation of Laurent Boymond—"Lore-unh Bouy-monh" made him sound effete and out of touch, while Fortune's fastidious pronunciation of the two Latin American countries made him sound like a man of the people. So much about Lightstone was just plain wrong, and yet he had seemed, and still seemed, like the best bet. The senator had a lot of work to do to educate the country about a place that few Americans had ever heard of. And he'd have to find a way to get the senator more animated about the topic. If Lightstone couldn't get excited about the plight of Kamalian dissidents, how would the general population?

• • •

# CHAPTER 20

There were nearly four million people in Kamalia, half of them in Villeneuve, the capital. But as Sophie DuVal navigated the narrow streets on the outskirts of the city toward the house of Rémy Manselle, she worried that she might be recognized, even behind the dusty windows of her Renault, even with a black silk scarf tied around her head. Kamalia was the kind of place where everyone knew everyone else's business. In New York City, where she'd lived for five years, anonymity was easily acquired, even during her modeling days, when her image had appeared on innumerable magazine covers, even for a black woman who moved in largely white circles. In Kamalia she blended in more readily, a tall black woman in a country of tall black people, yet she felt watched at every turn. She'd grown accustomed to attracting attention from the years with Matthew—whites always stood out in Kamalia, but a white man and a black woman together might as well have had a spotlight trained on them. Even with Matthew gone she felt watched. There was a pervasive watchfulness about Kamalians— the result, she suspected, of centuries of tribal warfare, seventy-five years of colonial rule, a brief period of democratic self-government, and then the current regime. The person passing you in the street might be just a neighbor or visitor, he might be a spy of Le Père, or he might be an important person in the next regime, whenever that arrived. In Kamalia, paranoia was a survival mechanism.

Rémy Manselle lived in one of the poorest parts of Villeneuve, which was saying something. Stucco houses lined the unpaved roads; though very small and only one story high, they looked in danger of collapsing. Shutters were closed against the midday sun, adding a deeper shade of gloom to the neighborhood. Rémy's house was no better or worse than its neighbors, but it had one amenity, a rare one, that made it a perfect place for Sophie's mission: a garage.

As arranged, the garage door was open when she pulled up. She drove the Renault inside, got out, and shut the door. She left the garage through the back and banged on a wooden door at the rear of the house. A few moments later it opened.

"What time is it?" Rémy looked and sounded groggy.

"Almost noon." She tried not to sound censorious but feared her disapproval had come through.

He glanced skyward, as if to confirm the time. "I forgot to set the alarm," he said, and waved her inside.

"Don't you think we should unload first?" She had a trunk full of AK-74s in the garage.

"Coffee first. Come in."

She watched him make coffee in the tiny kitchen of the tiny house, heating a small saucepan of water on the propane stove and then pouring the water into a mug that he'd emptied of yesterday's dregs. He dropped in two teaspoons of instant coffee. "Want some?"

"No," she said quickly.

He was tall and broad-shouldered, with big, soulful eyes and flaring cheekbones that made him look both reflective and proud. She'd known him slightly at college, when half the girls at the Polytechnique, the only institution of higher learning in Kamalia, had been in love with him. Later he worked for Amalgamated Cobalt, the company Matthew ran, representing employees on the management board. Julian Mellow had bought the company on a bet that cobalt prices would rise as the worldwide economy improved and in particular as military spending in the Middle East increased, once the United States had vastly reduced its presence—and influence—there. Cobalt, a byproduct of nickel, Kamalia's primary natural resource, was used in high-temperature applications like jet engines and in high-abrasion-resistant steels. Julian had been right about the price of cobalt but not about the political situation in Kamalia. When the government nationalized Amalgamated, Julian lost his investment and his son, and Rémy Manselle was fired. She'd lost touch with him, but they'd reconnected later, on the circuit of covert meetings of antigovernment dissidents that had formed two years ago. Every so often he made it clear to Sophie that his considerable charms were hers for the asking, and she always politely turned him down, to his profound amazement.

"Did you hear the news from America?" he asked between gulps of coffee. "One of the candidates for president actually mentioned us in a speech."

"Le Front Populaire?"

He scoffed. "*Kamalia.* He used Kamalia as an example of the kind of repressive regime that America should not associate with."

"Well, that's something. Most Americans have never heard of us."

"This could be very important. A candidate for president interested in Kamalia. Perhaps we are not as isolated as we think." Sophie didn't have the heart to point out to him that, given that it was only January, the candidate had to be running for the Republican nomination. She'd lived in the United States long enough to know that there were invariably many candidates for a party's nomination, and that the more they spoke about something as obscure as repression in Kamalia, the less likely it was that they would be elected.

"Our cause is known throughout the world," she said. "As for America, we already have at least one friend there."

He nodded, drained the mug, and led her back to the garage, where he pulled aside a large, square, wooden plank on the floor, revealing a concrete staircase. "We'll keep the guns in the *cave des vins*, where they can age in a cool, dark environment." Together they unloaded the car and brought the cases of AK-47s into the cellar.

"When will we have enough?" Sophie asked. Cases of rifles and boxes of ammunition were already stacked along two of the walls.

"We have almost one hundred people on our side, dedicated people, and many thousands more, a hundred thousand, perhaps, who will support us once we begin. But if we don't have the necessary arms, we are doomed."

"But we have at least a hundred rifles, and enough ammunition to kill the entire government six times over. Not that we are planning to do that," she added quickly.

Rémy shot her a look that was hard to read before climbing the steps to get the next load. Sometimes she wondered if what really animated him wasn't idealism or even politics but a primal urge for blood revenge.

"Every day another political prisoner is tortured or killed. Every day we wait is a death sentence for someone."

"And if we move too soon, it will be a death sentence on us."

"How will you know when the time is right?"

"The Council will decide."

The Council was six people, including Rémy and herself. In procuring the weapons and serving as the public face for the opposition, Sophie risked more than any of them, yet she'd had to fight to get invited onto the Council. Kamalia was a resolutely patriarchal society; even revolutionaries had little tolerance for a woman's voice. Democracy first, *then* feminism, she told herself at least ten times a day.

"They don't let me into the prison to meet with our comrades any more. The other day, for the twelfth time at least, I tried to see Roger. I bribed a guard to get inside but I never made it past the warden's office. I sense that things are getting worse, not better."

"Be patient, Sophie," he said in a patronizing voice, as if she were eager for a baking cake to be done. "I am crossing the border tomorrow night for reinforcements. That's progress, right?"

Reinforcements—cash from America, smuggled back across the border, used to buy weapons. Sometimes she feared the whole effort had become an end in itself, a self-perpetuating means of generating cash in a poverty-stricken country. Perhaps Kamalia would be better served if they just distributed the money to the hungry and sick.

"I suppose it is."

"He must have loved you very much," Rémy said, his eyes roving slowly down her body, as if to confirm what Matthew Mellow had seen. "His father, too, to continue to send so much money two years after Matthew's death."

"His murder," she said sharply. "And the father couldn't care less about me. He never approved of our relationship, in fact I think it embarrassed him. He wants revenge against the Boymond regime, that's all. I'm a convenient channel for that, nothing more."

He'd never called after Matthew's murder. Two men had broken into their home in Villeneuve and shot Matthew in the head while he slept in their bed next to her. She awoke at the muffled *pops* of the silenced guns to find them leering at her, making no effort to disguise their identities. *Don't worry, pretty lady, we were told to spare you.* They began rooting through her drawers and jewelry box, taking anything of value, to make the murder look like a robbery, or perhaps just to secure a small bonus for their labors—there would be no investigation. And sure enough, the local paper and even the international press covered the incident as a robbery, typical of the anarchy in that godawful part of the world. She'd written to Julian Mellow with the truth but had not heard back.

Until she'd begun to make a name for herself as a dissident. He'd contacted her, by phone, a year after Matthew's murder, when she'd been on a rare trip out of the country, to Paris, trying, without success, to raise funds for the insurgency. His voice had been clipped and unemotional. *Whatever you need, just ask.* He did not inquire about the circumstances of the murder, whether his son had suffered, how she was doing. She hadn't asked how he'd known she was in Paris, though she was gratified that he hadn't risked calling her in Kamalia. She wondered if the loss of the company, one of a hundred he controlled, wasn't the most painful loss of all. But she'd taken him up on his offer, enlisting Rémy to move back and forth across the border to retrieve the funds.

"Who is it you see when you pick up the money?" she asked him.

"A manager at a bank, no one of significance. I sign a few

papers, he hands me the bills. I don't think Julian Mellow has ever set foot in Africa, if that's what you mean. Except for a safari, perhaps." He grinned.

"Of course he hasn't. I just want to know how this works."

"That is not really your concern," he said, again with an infuriatingly patronizing tone.

"I risk my life for the cause. Of course it's my concern. I started this movement two years ago. Now I am kept in the dark about the financial arrangements, talked to like a schoolgirl. I could get on a plane tomorrow for New York or Paris and spare myself this crap."

"But you know we need you here, in Kamalia."

Did they? She'd created something that now had a life of its own, a life that didn't depend on her. The last coup, the one that had ended with Le Père in power, had been accomplished with fewer than fifty well-armed men. Power in Kamalia was pathetically easy to take, and equally easy to lose. She doubted that Julian Mellow would stop the flow of money if she left. It wasn't about her. It never had been. But her influence in the Front rested on her connection to Julian Mellow; she must not squander that.

"Julian Mellow is concerned that things are not moving forward," she lied. She had never talked to him about plans and logistics, nor did he inquire. When the movement needed money she placed a classified ad in *Aujourd'hui*, Kamalia's only newspaper, a disgraceful organ for the Boymond regime. "Seeking employment. Household work, child minding, light cooking." Those exact words, followed by a made-up phone number whose first five digits represented the amount of US dollars she was requesting. He'd never quibbled over that number, which she'd increased over time. "He wants to see some sort of return on his investment."

"Tell him he will see a return soon enough," Rémy said as he opened the garage door. As she backed her car out he knocked on the driver's window, which she rolled down. "Tell Julian Mellow we are risking our lives to avenge his son. Tell him that."

• • •

# CHAPTER 21

"Rooney picked Stephen Delsiner as his running mate."

Marcella Lightstone put aside Trollope's *Barchester Towers* and glanced up at her husband from the fireside wing chair. They'd finished their dinner and retired to the library of their Georgetown townhouse. Harry was home to vote on an appropriations bill; otherwise he spent all of his time in New Hampshire. The petty intrigues in Barchester, sparked by the appointment of a new bishop, seemed an apt guide to the current presidential campaign. Though the players talked about big issues—God and morality in Trollope, the economy and healthcare in Washington—the driving force was far more personal: jealousy, suspicion, ambition.

"Delsiner will deliver Missouri in the primary," she said. "Two terms as governor, one as senator."

"I don't approve of selecting a running mate before winning the nomination. It's grandstanding." He took the poker from its stand next to the fireplace and prodded a burning log. "The entire party should have a say in who is chosen."

"That's naïve, Harry. Do you really think Gabe Rooney cares about principle? He wants the Republican nomination and he knows that with Delsiner on his side he'll have a better shot. He'll look like a winner, and the Republicans want a winner more than anything else."

"I still disapprove."

She sighed. In Trollope, Harry wouldn't stand a chance. In life, he had her, and that had made all the difference. And now he had Julian Mellow.

"We need a strategy for dealing with this," she said. "We could pick our own running mate, but that might look derivative. In any case, the best man has been taken. Perhaps you could take a principled stand, along the lines of what you just said…the party needs to build consensus on a running mate, the presumption of choosing before the first primary has taken place, blah, blah, blah."

His expression of paralyzed indignation made her want to throw the Trollope at him. And the desultory fire had not benefited from his ministrations.

"You can't just stand by and do nothing, Harry. Rooney already has momentum on his side, he's already taken Iowa, though not decisively, and he has a ten-point lead in the New Hampshire polls. Now, with this, he'll get all the media coverage he wants, plus his campaign will have two people making appearances in the time left before New Hampshire. Then in South Carolina…"

"I'll prepare some remarks."

"Call Fred," she said. Fred Moran was Harry's campaign director. As with vice presidential prospects, the best guy had been taken by Rooney. Moran had run several successful Senate races, but never anything on the national level. Still, he'd been the best available.

"It's ten at night."

"Tell him I want a strategy, not just a speech. I want a full message platform around this issue, mapped to every demographic in New Hampshire and beyond."

"He's my campaign manager, I think he knows what he has to do."

"But you're the candidate."

"Am I?" Their eyes locked for a moment. Harry still didn't realize that she knew about Julian Mellow. Some instinct told her that she should keep this to herself, that her influence with Harry would wane once he realized that she knew the shoddy underpinnings of his "principled" campaign.

"You're the candidate and you need to set the direction of the campaign, not Fred. Call him."

He hesitated just a moment. "I have an early flight to Nashua tomorrow morning. Will you be accompanying me?"

"No."

He seemed about to pursue this, then shrugged and left the

room. She waited to hear his footsteps on the staircase and picked up the phone.

"It's Marcella. Have you heard the news about Rooney and Stephen Delsiner?"

"I have." Julian sounded untroubled, infuriatingly so.

"A brilliant move." She tried to keep the anxiety out of her voice. "A preemptive strike. He was already the frontrunner, now he looks like the one man who has at least a prayer of winning in the general election. They like winners in New Hampshire."

"Perhaps Delsiner isn't the asset to the campaign that he appears to be."

"Missouri is a swing state and a key primary, even the garbage men in New Hampshire know that, and they want someone who—"

"Shut up, Marcella."

She gasped and stood up abruptly, as if preparing to defend herself physically.

"How dare—"

"Leave this to me."

"But—"

"Do you want the White House?" he asked lightly, as if mentioning a new car model. He didn't wait for a response. "Then let me handle this."

"Goodnight, Julian."

"Marcella?"

"Yes?"

"I want you in Nashua tomorrow."

"But I have—"

"I want you at your husband's side."

The line went dead, and for a few moments she was dead, too, standing paralyzed in front of her reading chair, still clutching the phone. She was unused to taking orders, unused to being interrupted, unused to compromise. With sufficient money, you avoided all three. And she sensed strongly that this was only the beginning. Was it worth it? Did she really need this? A smoldering log in the fireplace shifted with a hissing spit, startling her. She turned, picked up her book, and headed upstairs.

She had packing to do.

# CHAPTER 22

Zach Springer carefully read the *Times* article concerning the latest development in the Republican nomination battle. Gabriel Rooney had selected Stephen Delsiner as his running mate, which seemed kind of presumptuous, given that he hadn't even secured the nomination. Sitting in his car outside a Gold's Gym outlet in northern Westchester County, he scanned the entire first section of the *Times* and found not a single mention of Charles Moore. Less than a week after his tragic plane crash the remaining players had regrouped. A few days ago his widow had briefly made headlines when she announced that she would not endorse a candidate despite the considerable pressure on her to do so. She had been dignified and resolute following the crash, and her endorsement would have been political gold. In fact, there was a brief flurry of rumors that Elisa Moore herself might run, but while widows picking up their late husband's mantle worked at the state level, it wouldn't fly in a presidential campaign, or so the pundits theorized.

A woman walked in front of his car. He checked the photo he'd printed from the internet and decided it wasn't her. Then he checked again and decided it might be—something in the mouth, locked in a disappointed frown. He got out of the car.

"Francesca Garamondo?" he shouted as she was entering the gym. She turned and watched as he approached her.

"I'm Zach Springer. I'd like to ask you a few questions about Williston."

"For Christ's sake, enough about that."

"Just a few questions."

"There was a hearing. Google it."

"That's how I found you."

"My address isn't—"

"No, but you came up as a trainer here."

She looked away and slowly shook her head. "I moved a hundred miles from Williston, I lost fifty-five pounds, got in shape, even made a career of it. And I still can't get away from that place."

"I'd say you're a long way away." He handed her the old photo, which she stared at for a few silent moments.

"I don't know this person."

She'd been plump and matronly then, thirty-six years old with shoulder-length dark hair. The fingers on her right hand, raised to take the oath, were thick and stubby, with rings embedded in the soft flesh. Now there didn't appear to be any fat on Francesca Garamondo: her face was narrow to the point of gauntness, but her shoulder muscles bulged against taut skin, her arms revealed long, ropy muscles, and her thigh and calves stretched a pair of black, ankle-length spandex pants. Her hair was cropped short and dyed white-blonde. The transformation had been remarkable but perhaps counterproductive, for it had added several years to her appearance, and those years looked hard.

"Ten minutes," he said. "That's all I need."

"Sorry, I stopped talking about Williston fifty pounds ago."

"Don't you owe it to your husband to get to the truth?" Her husband, Jim Garamondo, had been murdered in the prison uprising.

"Where the fuck do you get off telling me what I owe my husband?" Angry veins rose to the surface of her neck. "And since when does anything about Williston have to do with truth?"

"It's the lies I want to hear about."

"Get lost." She entered the gym and let the door close behind her. He followed her inside.

"I want a training session."

She turned around. "Like hell you do."

"One hour."

"Gil, which trainers are on the floor today?" A beefy blond man behind the reception counter consulted a datebook.

"No, I want you."

"I'm booked."

"Actually, your ten o'clock just called to cancel, Frankie," the blond guy said. The veins in her neck looked ready to burst.

"You're not dressed to work out," she said, taking in his oxford shirt and jeans. At least he had sneakers on. He walked over to the counter.

"I'll take one T-shirt, size large, and a pair of shorts, also large."

"It's seventy-five dollars for the hour," she said.

As the blond man rang up the purchases, Zach imagined what Sarah would do if she could see him blithely dropping two hundred bucks on a training session. Throw him out of the apartment seemed a reasonable guess. He paid with Arthur Sandler's credit card.

"The locker room is that way," Francesca said. "I assume you know how to use a locker room?"

He changed quickly and met her on the gym floor.

"We'll start with legs," she said and directed him to a Cybex leg press. Once he was angled onto the machine she set the weight at 35 pounds, the lowest amount possible. He reset it at 150 and pushed out twelve reps.

"You've done this before," she said.

"I'm a biker," he said, trying to ignore the screaming pain in his quads. "Now, about Williston. I'm looking into the involvement of one of the inmates, Billy Sandifer." He saw the name register. "Tell me what you know about him."

"Give me another set."

He managed ten reps, wishing he hadn't set the weight so high.

"Jim hated him, even before the riot. Sandifer was a celebrity, you know. Reporters would show up now and then to interview him. He never talked to them, but I used to hear that he was a hero to a lot of people, you know, hippie types who hated oil companies and Walmart. Jim could never get over the irony of that."

"Irony?"

"That this so-called people's activist was such a freak."

"In what way a freak?"

"Like, an inmate said one thing wrong, or touched him the wrong way, he'd lash into the guy. And not in the way prisoners do, you know? It wasn't shoving or talking trash. It was mean stuff."

"What kind of stuff?"

"Like a guy's wrist would be broken—not just broken, flattened back against his arm, or every front tooth would be knocked out of his mouth. Everyone knew to stay away from him, but sometimes a new guy would step over the line in some small way. And there were never any witnesses, no proof, so he got away with it. Jim said shit went on all the time at Williston, only that Sandifer took it to an extreme. You want to do another set?"

"No," he said quickly. "Maybe a cup of coffee, though." She frowned and led him to the small juice bar overlooking the parking lot, where he bought two cups of coffee.

"Why are you interested in Billy Sandifer?"

"He may be connected to a guy I used to work for." Zach knew this sounded vague, perhaps even evasive, so he changed the subject. "I called a few of the guards who survived the riot, but they wouldn't talk."

"So you figured you'd try a widow."

He shrugged. "You were closest to where I live, in Manhattan."

"So I guess you know that Sandifer was the intermediary between the government and the inmates."

"Why was he chosen, given his background?"

"He chose himself, as far as anyone could tell. He was *high profile*, don't forget. A man of principles. I think he knew he'd get time off for good behavior if he helped contribute to a peaceful resolution. I remember when they told us, me and the other wives—we were holed up together in a bus outside the prison—when they told us it was Sandifer who was going to be the go-between we couldn't believe it. But we were so desperate to get our men back we forgot what we'd heard about him and just prayed he'd do a good job. And you know what was really sick? In most people's eyes, he did a good job. The uprising ended within twenty-four hours."

"With eight dead."

"Three guards and five inmates. Not bad for a day's work." Her hand shook, threatening to spill hot coffee. Gently, he took the cup from her. "I'm sorry," she said. "I've changed everything about myself, where I live, how I look, but talking about it takes me back there. The other two wives, they had children, deep roots in Williston. They couldn't leave. I suppose I'm lucky, no kids, no family up there. You know, I never planned to become like this." She ran a hand along her right deltoid, which flared from her shoulder like an epaulet. "I started working out for something to do and I couldn't stop."

"At least you found something..."

"The funny thing is, I don't think Jim would have liked me this way. We were only married a year. I was heavy when we met, fat, really, and he never complained."

He gave her a few moments before talking.

"Billy Sandifer was regarded as a hero after Williston," he said. "The prevailing thinking was that, bad as the uprising ended, without Sandifer it would have been a lot worse."

"You're talking to the wrong person if you believe that."

"There were never any specific allegations against Sandifer."

"None. Matter of fact, the state shortened his sentence by almost two years. There were eight guards held hostage. Five came home. That's five happy endings against three tragedies. I'm surprised he didn't get the medal of honor or something. And then there's his daughter."

"Daughter?"

"Yeah, she was born right after he went in. Major problems, I think she's retarded or autistic or both. He made a big deal with the parole board that he's her only family."

"The mother?"

"Flew the coop after the daughter was born, or after she was diagnosed. Nice, huh?"

"What happened to the daughter?"

"He testified at the parole hearing that she was in some sort of state institution. Horrible place, the way he described it."

"Does the name Julian Mellow mean anything to you?"

"He owned Acorn, which owned Williston."

"Did he have any direct contact with Sandifer?"

"I don't think he wanted to dirty his hands."

"Then who was Sandifer's contact with the state negotiators?"

"He met one-on-one with the warden. Just the two of them."

And yet Mark Verbraski denied ever meeting with Mellow during the negotiations. So how did Sandifer hook up with him?

"Everyone stayed away," she continued. "We kept waiting for the governor to get involved, the president. Conditions were awful at Williston once Acorn took over, and not just for the inmates. The guards took a 10 percent pay cut the year before the riot, they had their benefits cut back, their hours extended. You can only do that so many times before something happens. Jim used to say it was only a matter of time before someone rioted—the inmates or the guards. So I guess we were stupid to expect the governor to get involved, after he'd basically ignored all the problems at Williston. One time, about four days into the uprising, this huge helicopter came down not far from the main gate. We thought for sure it was the governor or maybe even the president. Stupid us."

"Who was it?"

"Someone from Acorn, I guess. We weren't allowed close enough to see who it was. One guy got out, I do remember that. But it was dark and I didn't see his face."

"This was four days into the negotiations. Wouldn't everyone important enough to arrive by chopper be there already?"

"Hey, we asked who it was, but it was all hush-hush."

"How long was the helicopter there?"

"Less than an hour. That same guy got back in, at least I assume it was the same guy. Trust me, it wasn't a good moment for us, watching the helicopter leave. I mean, we all felt abandoned before, but watching that helicopter disappear into the night was a low point."

It was Julian in the chopper, he'd bet his life on it. Julian was notorious for squeezing every dime out of his portfolio companies—none of his executives had access to private helicopters. But Julian kept one on call at the heliport on the East River. He'd swooped in, made some sort of deal with Sandifer, either directly or through Warden Verbraski, then left. The next day the standoff ended. Verbraski lost his job and then his family but somehow had enough cash for a brand-new Escalade and top-shelf vodka. Sandifer flew around the country on Julian's jet. Somehow it all connected back to Williston.

"You never did tell me why you're interested in Billy Sandifer," she said.

"I said it was about my former employer, Julian Mellow."

"But why?"

"An old score, I guess." She stood up and tossed her coffee cup into a nearby can. He rose and extended a hand. "I know it's not easy talking about this."

She took his hand, shook it, but didn't let go. Her hand felt small and hard.

"Since you prepaid the training session, and we only worked out together for, like, a minute, I feel I owe you something."

"You've already given me a lot of good information."

"Here's something else. Whatever it is you're doing, give it up. It's not worth it."

"But you don't even know what I—"

"I can see it in your face, in your eyes, the way you get almost breathless when you start talking about Sandifer and Julian Mellow. It's the way I was two years ago, convinced that there was some avoidable mistake or grand conspiracy that killed my husband. It's like a hunger you can never satisfy. It grabs you from the inside. But eventually, if you're lucky, you realize two things. First, you're never going to figure things out, they're much too big—too big for you, at any rate. And second, it wouldn't make a difference anyway. Jim is dead, he's going to stay that way. I'm lucky because I figured that out, and because I found this." She ran a hand down her flattened chest and across her taut midsection. "You seem like a nice guy, and by the way, your legs are fucking amazing. I hope you find something else, Zach, before you've invested so much in this search of yours that you have nothing left over for anything more constructive."

"Good advice."

"Which you've heard before."

"Thanks for the information *and* the advice," he said, and she released his hand.

# CHAPTER 23

"Mr. Mellow? I have a Mark Verbraski on the phone."

When Julian didn't reply immediately, Stacy Young added, with a touch of nervousness, "He says it's important."

"Put him through," he said.

"Yeah, Mr. Mellow? It's Mark Verbraski, I was the—"

"I know who you are." Or were.

"So, how've you been, Mr. Mellow?" He sounded drunk, so Julian waited him out. "Okay, well, listen, you've been very generous, Mr. Mellow. I don't know what I'd do without the money you sent."

If he was calling to demand more money, he was wasting his time. One untraceable deposit in a numbered account two years ago was the first and last payment. That had been agreed upon.

"What do you want?"

"And the best part? My wife doesn't have a clue about it." His voice wavered in volume and tone. Julian hated drunks: under the best of circumstances, their lack of control was offensive; with Verbraski, it was potentially dangerous. "She took everything, every stick of furniture, even the microwave oven. What kind of person takes a built-in microwave oven?"

"I have a meeting to attend. Please don't call again."

"Wait! Wait. There's a reason I called. I called because I…" While Verbraski tried to work out why he'd called, Julian recalled their one and only meeting two years earlier, in Williston. He'd taken the chopper upstate, landed near the prison at night without tipping off the swarms of reporters, and met with Verbraski in a small conference room. That's where the deal had been struck.

Verbraski cleared his throat and coughed, bringing Julian back to the present.

"What is it you want?"

"This guy came to see me, Zach something-or-other."

"Zach Springer?"

"That's him."

Julian felt the muscles in his chest constrict. What the hell did Springer want with Verbraski? What possible connection could there be?

"What did he want?"

"He asked a lot of questions about back then, you know, about the riot."

"What kind of questions?"

"He wanted to know if I ever met you."

"What did you tell him?"

He heard Verbraski take a big swallow of something that was probably not orange juice.

"I told him we never met."

"Then there's no problem."

"I just thought you'd want to know."

"You did the right thing. Call me if he makes contact again, otherwise—"

"He asked about Billy Sandifer."

"What did he want to know about Sandifer?"

"About him and me." He heard liquid being poured into a glass, then another noisy swallow. "And him and you."

"And what did you tell him?"

"Nothing. I told him nothing."

"Good. As far as Zach Springer is concerned, you and I never met, and I never met Sandifer."

"No problem."

"Is there anything else?"

"Well, yeah, one more thing." Julian braced for more bad news. "You've been very generous to me in the past."

He actually felt relief that it was only money. "You want more money?"

"My wife, she took everything, and I—"

"I'll arrange for a transfer to my Swiss account and then move the funds into your account. You can draw down on it in three days or so. What amount were you thinking?"

A long silence. He could practically smell booze and greed through the phone line.

"I was thinking about…ten—no, fifteen thousand."

Julian had already resigned himself to sending ten times that to buy his silence. He had nothing but disdain for men who left money on the table. "That shouldn't be a problem. Let me know if anyone else contacts you."

"You got it," Verbraski said.

Julian hung up and felt uncharacteristically overcome. Zach Springer was a name he never expected to hear again. He'd assumed Zach had moved on. What was he doing, nosing around Williston? What had he learned?

Julian got up and walked to the gallery door. He looked into a small lens, which scanned his left retina and compared it to scanned images in a database of authorized visitors. There was, of course, just one authorized visitor in the database. The steel-reinforced pocket doors slid open.

Slowly, he strolled up and down the long, narrow gallery, feeling a sense of security return in the presence of old friends. Back then, when Zach still worked for him and Matthew was still alive, people often intimated that Zach was his surrogate son, and he'd always hated that. He had a son, albeit a son who chose not to work for his father, at least directly, which was hardly a sin. It was true that Zach had been an extension of him, in a way, scouting acquisition targets, evaluating offering documents and prospectuses—a second pair of legs and eyes. Perhaps a second brain. And Zach's parents were both dead, which added to the appearance of a father-son relationship. Zach hadn't ever been truly indispensable, though he may have thought so, but it was undeniable that Julian couldn't have risen so far, so fast without him. Still, he hadn't hesitated to frame him for the Finnegan scandal. It had to be done. Someone needed to take the fall, and it certainly wasn't going to be Julian.

He hadn't really known himself until the Finnegan scandal. Before that, his life and career had been all about making the right decisions, hiring the right people, buying the right companies, making the right exits at the right time. Then he'd done something stupid, bought a pitiful six million dollars in Finnegan stock, acting on nonpublic information and the petulant desire for revenge, and suddenly the skills and habits that had made him a success were irrelevant. Judgment, financial acumen, psychological insight, timing—they would not keep him out of jail. So he'd turned on Zach and realized, to his complete but not unhappy surprise, that he had another useful skill: the ability to disengage from relationships, cut people free, even destroy another person without self-recrimination. It was a skill he doubted he'd ever use again—he rarely got personally involved with people in the first case—and then Matthew had been killed and he'd had to draw on it once more.

So he hadn't given Zach Springer a moment's thought since that time, not a single moment, until the call from Verbraski, whom he hadn't thought of since transferring five hundred thousand dollars to a numbered Swiss account. It seemed to violate some fundamental law of nature—*his* nature, at least—that Zach should have resurfaced. He'd obliterated him from his mind—and in some absurd but quite real way it seemed wrong that he hadn't been obliterated from the world as well.

Julian considered Memling's Italian nobleman, part of a diptych; the other panel, showing his wife, was in the Metropolitan Museum, which he could see from his office window. His half of the diptych was thought to have been destroyed a century ago in a fire in a manor outside Bruges, and in fact there was evidence of charring on the back of the panel. It pleased him, knowing that the nobleman was alive and well while the art world continued to mourn his passing.

He left the gallery, picked up the phone and dialed Billy Sandifer.

"Write down this name," he told him. "Zach Springer. Here's what I want you to do."

## TUESDAY, JANUARY 27

# CHAPTER 24

Marcella Lightstone dialed Fred Moran's number from the jet that was flying her back to New York from Concord, New Hampshire. The ten-year-old Falcon 50 EX felt cramped and a tad jittery, so she decided to focus on business, which then, as always, meant Harry's political life.

"It's Marcella," she said to the young-sounding woman who answered at Lightstone headquarters in Pittsburgh, no doubt a volunteer. "Get Fred."

"Oh, Mrs. Lightstone, wow, that was a really excellent appearance in Concord, we were all watching it on C-SPAN, and we all thought—"

"I'm in a hurry."

"Oh, right, okay, hold on."

The line went dead. Furious, she pressed redial. "*Please* put Fred on the line."

"Oh, Mrs. Lightstone, I'm sooo sorry, I thought I had pushed—"

*"Please?"*

This time she managed to put the call through.

"Hello, Marcella."

"Concord was a disaster," she greeted him. "I counted twenty-nine people there, Fred. Including the reporter. From the University of New Hampshire *Gazette* or whatever the hell it's called."

"It's the *Eagle*, and a lot of its readers are first-time voters, many who—"

"To hell with first-time voters. Do you have any idea what it was like to give a prepared speech to what amounted to a cocktail party?"

"Harry gave the speech, Marcella."

"I was up there with him, at your insistence."

Fred Moran had been Harry's choice to lead the campaign. The universally acknowledged number-one manager, Alonzo Maddigan, had been scooped up by Gabe Rooney nearly a year earlier, with predictably stellar results. She hated settling for second best. But Harry had liked Fred. Harry always opted for the unthreatening alternative, and Moran—late fifties, avuncular, soft-spoken—was anything but threatening. Which, she found herself thinking, made Harry's taste for Amazonian women all the more puzzling.

"Marcella, did you want something?"

"How about a strategy, a plan? Rooney is destroying us."

"We're in second place, which isn't bad considering our late start and the field includes four candidates."

"Second out of four—is that your definition of success? And we're third if you count undecideds. *We're behind undecideds!* We need to win New Hampshire or at least come in a very close second, which is not happening. Without that momentum we don't have a prayer in South Carolina, we won't even make it to Super Tuesday."

"I'm doing the best I can. Everybody is."

She thought of Julian Mellow. Everything she knew about the man told her he would never bet on a losing proposition. Would he allow Harry to fail in New Hampshire? Was it within his power to affect the outcome? He couldn't very well hand out cash to likely voters, like Rockefeller distributing dimes to children, though he could afford to. It seemed hopeless.

"How could you let Stephen Delsiner slip through your fingers?" she said, and then, before Moran could answer, she added, "Who are we going with for VP?"

"You'll have to ask your husband," he said. When people referred to Harry as her husband they always did so with a slightly ironic edge.

"He looks to you for political advice." She added in a drier voice, "We both do."

"Choosing a running mate is a very complicated process. Each candidate has to be extensively vetted, which can take months. We've only been in this race a few months. Choose the wrong guy, a guy who turns out to have a skeleton in his closet—drugs, women, *boys*—and you look like an incompetent, a man who'll put the future of the country in the hands of a junkie or adulterer or pederast."

The New York skyline came into view out the port side of the jet. She had climbed to the top of that skyline, figuratively speaking, of course, salting a dozen top-drawer charities with her father's money, befriending the right people (which also involved money, more often than not), joining the right boards and committees (also a question of money). Now, thanks to Julian Mellow, she was having to shimmy up another slope, this one leading to the White House, a far steeper incline. There'd never been a Jewish president. She doubted she'd live to see that. But a Jewish First Lady…the first Jewish First Lady, that would be a climb worth making. Still, the White House wasn't the Upper East Side. There were limits to what she could spend in the campaign, and spending limits represented a new and unwelcome concept.

"We're landing any minute," she told Moran midway through his boring and condescending lecture on the vice presidential selection process. She hung up.

"We'll be experiencing some minor turbulence on the way down, Mrs. Lightstone," the pilot twanged over the intercom.

Well of course we will, given the tin crate they were flying in, not nearly as sturdy as her own, larger and newer jet, which the campaign had forbidden her to use. Bad optics. She tightened her seatbelt and wondered if there weren't some way to neutralize Stephen Delsiner and his Missouri influence, or perhaps bring him over to their side.

# CHAPTER 25

Senator Stephen Delsiner left the Equinox Sports Club on 22nd Street off M Street at eight forty-five, right about when he always did. Delsiner was a man of rigidly kept schedules, a fact that was well known not just among members of his staff and family but to members of the press, several of whom had had interviews canceled as punishment for arriving a scant minute or two late. Voters in Missouri liked the fact that they could depend on Delsiner not just for punctuality but for a predictable, if rather unexciting, overall performance. He was a centrist Republican, popular on both sides of the aisle, as he never failed to point out in speeches and mailings, a happily married father of four, and a regular at the Equinox, where he exercised most evenings from seven thirty to eight forty-five. Workouts were among the few times he had to himself; on the Hill he was surrounded by aides and colleagues, and since he'd been picked as Gabe Rooney's running mate, at least one reporter accompanied him wherever he went in New Hampshire, where he was spending most of his time. But when in DC, where he'd returned the night before for a key budget vote, his trips to the gym had so far been undiscovered. If he and Rooney nailed the Republican nomination, which seemed likely, given the latest New Hampshire polls and strong momentum elsewhere, he'd have

Secret Service protection around the clock, which would include gym time. So he relished his remaining moments of privacy.

Carrying a small gym bag, the senator walked to his car, a politically correct white Ford Fusion. He had just unlocked the door with the remote button on his key chain when a figure stepped toward him. Delsiner moved back, shoulders hunching instinctively in a protective shrug.

"Hey man, 'sup?" said the stranger. He was several inches shorter than the senator, which put him at about five nine. Delsiner, in a suit jacket, body molded by regular gym visits, looked bigger in every way than the stranger, who even in the darkness seemed gaunt. In one hand he carried a large envelope, badly wrinkled.

"Excuse me," Delsiner said as he tried to step around the man to get to the front door of his car.

"Look, man, I could use some cash," the stranger said without budging.

"Find an ATM."

"'S'funny. 'S'really funny." The man's voice was full of cigarettes and sarcasm. "I mean it, I need money."

"There are numerous programs in this city for homeless people where you can get a bed and a warm meal."

"Did I ask you for a bed?"

"Step aside, please."

"Anyway, who says I'm homeless?"

"Am I going to have to call the police?" Delsiner took a cell phone from his coat pocket.

"You don't want to do that, *Senator.*"

Delsiner lurched backward, as if shoved. Being recognized added a new level of menace to the situation. "The District police will be here in a flash if I call them," he said, a bit of a tremor evident in his voice.

"Well of course, you're a big shot in this town. I'm well known too, in my own way."

Delsiner squinted at the man. "I doubt that very much."

"Sure you don't recognize me?" After a beat the senator shook his head. "'S'great, just great. See, whenever I see you on the news, or in the papers, about your perfect family and your perfect career in politics and your perfect credentials for vice president, I always figure you for a big phony, major league bullshitter, ya know? I mean, at heart I figured you were a drug-addicted scumbag, same as always, only you just pretended not to be. But maybe you really have changed, if you don't remember me for real."

"My substance abuse issues are well known. If you think you can extort money from me for—"

"Substance abuse issues…that's good. You were a fucking oxy freak, *Senator*. Hillbilly heroin."

"Voters understand what I went through, beginning with my back injury, and they appreciate that I have reformed my ways."

"The straightest arrow in Washington." His voice dripped sarcasm. "Only, what did a bad back have to do with cocaine, Senator? Did you rub it into your spine?"

"One addiction leads to another, it's well documented."

"You took to coke like a fucking duck to water."

"Get out of my way." Delsiner pushed the man to the side.

"You weren't exactly eager to get rid of me back then. Don't you remember, Senator?"

Delsiner turned and edged toward the man. He stared at him for a second or two, then stepped back. "You're Cody."

"Kobe, like the Laker, but close enough."

"What do you want?"

"Funny, hearing that from you. Used to be I was the one asking what you wanted. Week's supply, two weeks."

"That was a long time ago. And in Saint Louis. What are you doing here?"

"I get around."

"Well, continue traveling. I need to get home." He opened the back door of the Ford and tossed in his gym bag.

"A man of regular habits now, isn't that right?"

"Get out of my way." He started to shut the door, but Kobe stopped him.

"Look, I took a shitload of heat once you got clean and made yourself into some kind of born-again virgin, reporters all over me, trying to get me to rat you out."

"I made no secret of my past."

"Yeah, well, that didn't stop the press vultures from wanting shit on you. I gave them squat, you might recall."

"It wouldn't have mattered. I was honest with the public about my painkiller addiction and the steps I took to get beyond it. So if you want to get paid all of a sudden, forget it."

"I don't want a lot. In here…" He held up the big envelope. "Photos of you and me doing business. Clear as day."

"Are you blackmailing me?"

"Whatever. Hundred bucks and they're yours."

"No deal. As I said, everyone knows what I went through back then."

"But they don't have pictures, Senator."

"You followed me here, from Saint Louis, to sell me pictures for a hundred dollars?"

"Like I said, I travel a lot. I could use the help."

"You don't look strung out." The senator considered him closely. "You don't look like you're on anything."

"Times are tough. Look, all I want is a hundred bucks for this and you'll never see me again."

The senator hesitated, then reached for his wallet. "Something about this isn't right. I don't recall anyone taking photos. And your being here, wanting a hundred dollars, you're positive that's it?"

"Never been more sure of anything in my life."

"Here." Delsiner counted out all the cash in his wallet and handed it to him. "Eighty-five, it's all I have," he said.

Kobe hesitated, took the money, then handed him the envelope and gave the senator a thumbs-up with a big, phony grin. "Give me a thumbs-up, Senator." When Delsiner looked puzzled and started to get into his car, Kobe grabbed the door. "Thumbs-up, Senator," he said.

The senator sighed and gave him the high-sign, then got into his car.

• • •

Kobe watched the senator drive off, then walked to the edge of the lot. "How'd I do?" he asked.

"You did fine," Billy Sandifer said as he reviewed the video on his phone. "I'll have to do some editing, but it's all there."

"I delivered the money shot, right? I mean, he bought the whole photo thing. Like I actually had someone taking pictures back then."

"You're Marlon Brando. The thumbs-up was a nice touch. Here." He handed Billy a wad of hundred-dollar bills through the passenger window. "Get in," he said. "You don't want to miss your plane." He put the car in gear. "Oh, I almost forgot. I brought along something to celebrate with." With his right hand he opened a small plastic bag and removed two bottles of Corona.

"Awesome," Kobe said as Billy handed him a bottle.

"I even have an opener." Billy handed him his Swiss Army knife and focused on the road as they left the Equinox parking lot.

Billy knew Washington well, having spent countless weeks in the capital during the nineties, mostly organizing protests, knocking off the random convenience store or townhouse when no one was looking. As long as you hitched your wagon to a cause you could get away with almost anything on the side.

Kobe had already chugged half the Corona before Billy turned off Massachusetts Avenue onto a sunken bypass that traversed Rock Creek Park, connecting the lush, elegant, embassy-studded northern section of the District with downtown.

"Don't you want any?" Kobe asked, his voice slurred, the Anectine in the beer already working. He guzzled most of the remaining beer. "Hey, this don't feel like the way to the airport."

Billy pulled off the main road onto a dark service road.

"Why are we stopping? This isn't…shit, I don't feel so…something in my throat."

• • •

# CHAPTER 26

It took Zach just under three hours to bicycle from the Upper West Side to the Newman Center in Tenafly, New Jersey. Combining his exercise routine with his pursuit of Julian Mellow made the day seem less of a waste of time, one activity giving cover, in a sense, for the other. The winter air was unusually warm for January but still chilly, the wind biting into his face as he sped northward along Route 9. He turned off at Closter Dock Road and followed the directions he'd memorized. In the parking lot of the Newman home he put on a pair of jeans and an oxford shirt he'd brought with him.

A friendly receptionist looked puzzled when he mentioned that he was there on behalf of Ms. Sandifer.

"You mean Rebecca Sandifer?"

Excellent, a first name. "Yes, Rebecca. She's my niece."

"Our visiting hours are—"

"I don't want to see her," he said quickly. "I'm concerned about her financial situation."

"Financial situation?"

"Her fees and so on."

"Would you like to speak to our bursar?"

"That would be great, thank you."

A few minutes later a pale man of about forty appeared in the reception area. "I'm Jay Forsling," he said. "You have a question about fees?" Officious and a bit tense, he seemed inclined to hold what he expected to be a very brief conversation right there in the lobby.

"My niece, Rebecca Sandifer, is a resident here and I—"

"Rebecca Sandifer," he said quickly. The name appeared to thaw him a bit. "Why don't we talk in my office?" He led Zach down a long hallway lined with small offices. "Would you like coffee? Water?"

Zach declined and they turned into one of the exterior-facing offices, with a view of the parking lot and, beyond it, a large, well-tended lawn. Forsling sat behind his desk, which was covered with neatly stacked papers. Zach sat opposite him.

"You said you were Rebecca's uncle?" Like his desk, Forsling was neat and unrevealing; he was slight, with pale skin and small features, a mole of a man.

"She's my sister's child," he said.

"I wasn't aware that the mother had any involvement in the financial arrangements."

"Well, that's really what I'm here about," Zach said. "My sister doesn't have a lot of financial resources. Her husband, my brother-in-law, William Sandifer, isn't wealthy, either. Fortunately, I'm in a position to help out, but neither my sister nor Billy will even listen to my offers of assistance."

"I'm not sure I understand," Forsling said, pushing his glasses up his nose.

"They're proud people. I think they believe that if they were to accept help from me it would mean—"

"But surely they told you…" He shook his head and neatened a pile of reports.

"Told me what?"

"This is really a private matter."

"We're talking about the long-term care of my niece. If there's any possibility of her not being able to remain here, then it's very much my business."

"But you must know that's not even remotely an issue."

"Why is that?" Another anxious shake of the head, another pile of printouts squared. "Look, Billy Sandifer isn't exactly wealthy," Zach said. "And this place isn't exactly cheap, so if there's a problem, I'd like to know about it. I'd like to know in advance so that my niece will not have to suffer."

"Rebecca Sandifer will never have to leave the Newman Center."

"How do you know that? What if her fees aren't paid, what then? We're talking, what, a hundred grand a year?"

Forsling stood up. "All I can say is, there is no problem, now or in the future. She will be a part of our community for as long as she, for as long as her parents want her to be."

"But how—"

"That's all I can say. I suggest you take this matter up with your sister, Mr....did you tell me your name?"

"Who's paying the tuition for Rebecca Sandifer?"

"I'm sure you understand we can't divulge the identity of... well, it's quite confidential."

*The identity.* Would he have used that phrase if the fees were being paid by the girl's parents? Zach stood up.

"How long has Julian Mellow been paying Rebecca Sandifer's fees here?"

"I can't tell you that," Forsling said, circling the desk. "Which isn't to say that he *is* paying the fees. In fact, that was rather a 'When did you stop beating your wife?' type of question. Quite unfair. I have things to do," he said, pointing to the hallway outside his office. "If you'd like to visit with your niece, I'm sure it can be arranged."

"It's not visiting hours."

"Yes, well, I think we can make an exception just this once."

"Because of Julian Mellow?"

"Because we're a caring institution," he said through gritted teeth. He nudged Zach out of his office and closed the door behind him.

Zach felt that he'd found a key link in the chain that connected Julian Mellow to Billy Sandifer, the reason the ex-business basher was working for the ur-capitalist. On his way to the lobby he saw a long hallway leading away from the office area. It looked like a corridor in an upscale hotel. Patients' quarters, he assumed. It occurred to him that he hadn't seen a single resident or even an attendant since arriving at the Newman Center, but that was probably part and parcel of being in a top-of-the-line facility: the sense of privacy, the impression that this was a resort. Despite everything, he felt a momentary pang for Billy Sandifer, who seemed to have changed so dramatically, compromised so much, to keep his daughter in such a place. Then he saw the plaque, just to the right of the entrance to the long corridor. WELCOME TO THE NEWMAN CENTER'S MATTHEW MELLOW CHILDREN'S WING.

# CHAPTER 27

Kamalia had become almost entirely isolated from the outside world since the coup. Major industries had been nationalized, causing most foreigners, who had once either controlled or worked in these industries, to leave. That had been the case with Amalgamated Cobalt. The government had tried to retain top managers after absorbing it, including Matthew Mellow, but without a strong profit motive (all profits went to Laurent Boymond and his cronies), few remained. There was still a sizable contingent of Americans; those not associated with the embassy were mostly engineers, who were paid substantially more than they could make in the States to keep Kamalia's mining operations running smoothly. Mercenaries, is how Sophie viewed them. But the Americans kept to themselves, most living in a gated community on the outskirts of the city. Matthew had stayed on because he'd felt obliged to fight for the rights and safety of the company's fifteen thousand employees, and he'd paid with his life when Boymond decided he was one corporate asset that could be safely liquidated.

As Sophie DuVal waited in line at the central post office in Villeneuve (home delivery of the mail having been curtailed shortly after the coup, an attempt to limit the flow of information as much as to reduce the national budget), she noted that at least two-thirds of the light bulbs in the overhead fixtures were burned out, casting a jaundiced gloom over the large, high-ceilinged room. Isolation was driving Kamalia into the past, a kind of reverse evolution. The pace of modernization that had once made Kamalia a model for the rest of Africa had at first slowed following the coup, then stopped altogether, and then started to creep in reverse. Electrical outages were an almost daily occurrence, so that people had begun to cook on wood fires in their yards, sometimes even when the power was still on, rather than risk disruption midpreparation. With little input from other countries, there was a sense that history had ceased: world leaders had changed since the coup, fashions had come and gone. But Kamalia was largely oblivious to it all.

During the interminable wait she read *Aujourd'hui*. She trusted not a word it contained, but scanned it most days to find out what the government wanted her to know. Online, she tried to read American newspapers, though most sites were blocked. A US candidate for president was mentioning human rights abuses in Kamalia in his speeches. That Kamalia had become a topic in the US election, at least for one long-shot candidate, was of course not mentioned in *Aujourd'hui*. Instead, the news for several days running was all about Claude DuMarier, or General Claude DuMarier, though it was unclear when or where or in what military he had ever served. DuMarier had long been a close friend of Le Père Boymond and, following the coup, had been appointed the head of Amalgamated Cobalt, effectively becoming Matthew's boss. He knew nothing about running a business and, after Matthew's murder, had taken Amalgamated from a profitable emblem of Kamalia's future to a money-hemorrhaging symbol of its demise. As a reward for this performance he was being made head of "government security," which meant, Sophie intuited from the elliptical and poorly written article that covered most of the paper's front page, that he was in charge of protecting the presidential palace and all its occupants, including Boymond and his family. There was a large photo of DuMarier and Boymond on the front page, both dressed in ceremonial uniforms that bespoke a glorious military past that had never existed.

She tossed the paper into an already full garbage can and waited another forty-five minutes. Finally, she gave her name to the teller and was handed a small packet of mail. A letter from a childhood friend, who lived an hour away and used to communicate via telephone or email, back when such services were reliable. A few letters from friends in New York, all of them showing signs that they'd been opened. Her incoming mail was read by the government, she being a well-known "agitator," the term applied to her and likeminded Kamalians by *Aujourd'hui*. It was ironic, really, since her American friends wrote about nothing weightier than the latest couture collections in New York, Paris, and Milan, about whose contract with which modeling agency or cosmetics firm had been renewed or dropped, about what new restaurant or club they'd been to. There was always an expression of concern at the situation in Kamalia, and an entreaty for Sophie to leave—but even the paranoid Boymond regime could find nothing sinister in that. And then there was her copy of *Fashion Week*, the bible of Seventh Avenue. Indispensable news of the rise and fall of hemlines and the hot color for the next year, photos of designers and models and fashion executives at shows and parties: it seemed a missive not from another place but from another time or even planet. It was the one foreign publication she subscribed to that the government didn't bother to confiscate. She had no interest in it, of course, in fact it depressed her, since it reminded her of a time when clothes and parties had been the most important things in her life, and she missed that time—she mourned it, in fact, for it felt dead to her, long gone. She read *Fashion Week* because its owner, Pretium Publications, a group of dozens of very profitable trade publications, was owned by Masters Media, a conglomerate that included the largest collection of network-affiliated television stations as well as a film production company and numerous local newspapers, which in turn was owned by Mellow Partners, which was owned, of course, by Julian Mellow, who sent her a complimentary subscription.

She took the mail to a coffee bar on the rue de la Paix, the city's grandest boulevard, lined with multistory apartment houses and limestone mansions that were once home to French foreign service officers and their families. Later they housed a wide range of foreigners who flocked to Kamalia following the end of colonial rule. Since the coup they were occupied mostly by Kamalians, but this wasn't the happy ending it might have seemed, for the mansions and apartments had been chopped up into tiny apartments, most with shared bathrooms, and already a lack of maintenance in the tropical Kamalian climate had caused their facades to crumble and peel. Most of the nearby shops were boarded up.

At least the bar/tabac on the corner of rue Lafayette had survived. In fact, it was crowded at ten in the morning, filled with workers on a coffee break and the unemployed enjoying an affordable indulgence, a cup of espresso costing only ten francs—Kamalian francs, each worth about a US penny.

She ordered a double espresso and took an inside table under a large, anemic ceiling fan. The news from friends in New York was predictably upbeat and irrelevant. Was there really a place where clothes and makeup and getting into the hottest nightclub was so important? Had she really lived in such a place? Her grade-school friend, in contrast, wrote of shortages and strategies for dealing with them, and reminisced about happier times. Finally, she opened *Fashion Week*, turning immediately to the last page, the employment ads. She scanned it quickly, expecting, as always, to find nothing relevant, and almost dropped the tiny espresso cup when she came to the small ad in the lower right corner:

> *Position available immediately in Paris. Candidate must have substantial fashion experience. English and French speaker required. Apply by January 31. Qualified candidates will be contacted. MM Enterprises. Care of this paper, box 77949988.*

She was being summoned to Paris. With her mail intercepted, her phone calls, when they miraculously got through, tapped, and email mostly nonexistent, the employment page of *Fashion Week* was the only reliable and secure way to contact her. Each week for two years she'd dutifully waded through the publication; only twice before had she actually received a message, each time a summons to Paris. Travel to and from Kamalia was virtually suspended, but there were still daily flights to Paris, and the government allowed them since it needed some channel for currency exchange, and because the French government was, shamefully, a backer of the corrupt Boymond regime. This time she was to be there on January 31, where she would dial a specified number. The call would be answered by Julian Mellow.

## THURSDAY, JANUARY 29

# CHAPTER 28

"Why aren't you in New Hampshire?" Julian said as Marcella Lightstone was shown into his office. Those were the first words from his mouth, and his none-too-subtle humiliation of a society grandee and, more recently, potential (if unlikely) First Lady, in front of his assistant, Stacy Young, had its desired effect. Her face, porcelain pale and preternaturally unwrinkled, flushed a livid crimson, and her monied voice, once the office door was closed, grew uncharacteristically strained.

"I've left a number of messages with your girl," she said.

"Stacy is my secretary, not my 'girl.' And 'assistant' is even more appropriate."

As she cooled her heels in front of his Josef Hoffmann desk, Julian once again marveled at what money, if judiciously spent, could do for a person. He liked self-created women. Caroline was one. Marcella was another. She'd had no lack of funds from the beginning, but she'd not been blessed with Caroline's beauty or charm, and so had to recreate herself using not only inherited wealth but a resolute belief in herself and a bracing dose of discipline. He knew all about self-creation, and admired it in others, particularly women.

"Harry has to be in Washington today for an important vote. If he misses it the negative publicity will be horrendous for him."

"The Arms Appropriations Omnibus Bill. The vote is expected to be very close."

"Whatever. I'm not happy about—"

"Nevertheless, your presence is not required in Washington. I think Harry can figure out how to vote on his own."

"You'd be surprised," she said without cracking a smile, and he felt a sexual stirring. Her ruthless objectivity was breathtaking. He glanced away from her. "This is a losing proposition," she went on. "Rooney's a shoo-in in New Hampshire next week, and after that it's all over. I don't plan to break my neck campaigning in South Carolina just to show that we're not giving up. I detest that sort of pointlessness and hypocrisy, smiling bravely and saying things like 'Our cause is not over' and other banalities. I won't be part of that."

"You're not the one running for president."

"Neither are you, Julian. This Kamalia nonsense you insist on Harry spewing, it's making him a laughingstock. I understand your son died there, but—"

"He was murdered."

"I'm sure you could pay someone to go over there and kill whoever was responsible. Wouldn't that be easier?"

As if a single death would balance the scales. He wanted—needed—much more than that.

"You always assume there's someone you can pay to do whatever it is you want," he said.

"It's been my experience, yes."

He sighed. "What is it you want now, Marcella?"

"We need something dramatic to turn the tables. I want

Harry to announce that Constance Strickland is his choice for vice president."

"Out of the question."

"She's wildly popular with women, she'll help to temper his abortion and gay positions, which are perceived as extreme."

"I had no idea you were so politically oriented."

"I despise politics. As do you. I want the White House."

As if it were a piece of art being auctioned, or chairmanship of a top-drawer charity dinner.

"Congresswoman Strickland has not been vetted."

"We can have her *vetted* in twenty-four hours."

"We're not talking about hiring a new maid."

"Maybe someday you'll explain the difference to me."

"If we bring Connie Strickland on board, and she turns out to have a skeleton in her closet—perhaps she neglected to pay the social security taxes for *her* maid, or burned her bra in the sixties, or Googled something inappropriate—it will sink Harry's chances. It's the biggest decision of the campaign, and it has to go perfectly."

"I don't see that we have anything to lose," she said. "All this nonsense about Kamalia…we need a dramatic gesture."

"Leave the drama to me."

She studied him for a few moments. "You're planning something," she said. Julian shrugged. "You wouldn't get into this without some sort of plan."

The phone console on his desk chimed and he gratefully picked up the receiver.

"I'm sorry to interrupt you, Mr. Mellow, but you asked me to tell you when Mr. Franklin called."

"Yes, thank you."

He hung up and engaged his private line, the number of which not even Caroline had. He held a finger up to Marcella, and dialed Billy Sandifer's cell.

"Mr. Franklin, this is Julian Mellow," he said when Billy answered.

"Yeah, so listen, I got a call from the Newman Center today."

Julian felt a tightening in his abdomen, his inevitable response to impending bad news. "What about?"

"This guy, the bursar? He says my brother-in-law showed up asking about how Rebecca's fees are paid. Thing is, I don't have a brother-in-law."

"Did he give you a name?" He ignored a long, aggrieved sigh from Marcella.

"He didn't remember, maybe he never gave him a name. A guy in his thirties, athletic, dark hair."

"Zach Springer."

"The guy you told me about, the one asking questions upstate about Williston?"

"Yes, him."

"You want me to take care of this situation?"

"Not just yet." First he needed to know what Springer had found out, whom he'd told, and what he planned to do. "Keep an eye on him. Let me know where he's living, who he talks to."

"No problem, but I gotta tell you, this guy makes me nervous. I could handle him nosing around Williston, but when my daughter's involved…"

"He won't be a problem. Now, did you send the package we discussed?"

"Yesterday morning."

"Good. Keep me informed about the other matter." He hung up. "Is there anything else?" he asked Marcella, to her visible consternation.

"Just remember, ours is a mutually beneficial relationship. You need me as much as I—or Harry—needs you." She stood up. "I saw Caroline at a luncheon yesterday, a benefit for some sort of psychiatric charity."

"You should have been in New Hampshire."

"She really is a beautiful woman. I don't understand why she works as hard as she does. No one does. Does she know what you're up to?"

"That's no concern of yours."

"No, I suppose it isn't. Still, I would think even a man like you would need someone to confide in, someone to share with."

"Goodbye, Marcella."

She considered him for a long, uncomfortable moment. "I pity you, Julian. To be so alone."

After she left he entered his private gallery and closed the door behind him.

# CHAPTER 29

Harry Lightstone was enjoying the morning working at his desk in the Russell Office Building. Since announcing for president three weeks earlier he'd been there only once. True, his staff—a secretary, a speechwriter, a press aide, and two interns—kept things going in his absence, sending him whatever reports and correspondence he needed to see. But he missed the place. His private office was crammed with a lifetime's accumulation of books and photographs and framed commendations. It was messy and homey and haphazard, the antithesis of his homes in Georgetown, New York, and Pittsburgh, which Marcella had decorated (well, had paid someone else to decorate) with a studied elegance that always seemed impervious to human touch, *his* touch. In contrast, his office was an extension of him, a validation, in a way. The photo of him at eighteen shaking hands with a smiling, retired Dwight Eisenhower in Gettysburg. There he was with Daniel Patrick Moynihan—a Republican's Democrat, he'd always thought—touring a Pittsburgh slum. Laughing it up on a fishing trip with Dick Russell himself, another Democrat who knew how to play well with others, the senator's senator, as he was known. And a hundred more like them, tokens of a full, important life.

He liked his desk, a partner's desk, it was called, with knee openings on both sides. What a perfect symbol for how he liked to operate—a fact that was noted in most of the longer profiles of him. He liked the carved wood mantel over the fireplace, the big, inevitably dirty windows facing Constitution Avenue. Once, Russell had been so crowded that the original suites had to be divided into tiny cubbyholes—he'd been a lowly congressman then, but had visited Russell many times. With the opening of a third Senate office building in 1982, many of the original suites had been recombined for the thirty-six senators assigned to Russell. The accommodations might be fresher in the other two buildings, but he liked the musty sense of history in Russell, and he never failed to get a kick out of riding the private underground subway that connected it to the Capitol, a kick far more bracing than the one he got riding in Marcella's Gulfstream. He even relished the piles of papers and reports waiting for his attention, dealing with matters weighty and mundane. And the stacks of letters from constituents, mostly heaping praise on him but often enough lobbing complaints. People were paying attention, those missives told him. The work he did mattered.

He should never have entered the goddamn campaign. He was a shoo-in for reelection in two years, reelection to the world's best job, as he'd always thought of it: United States senator. And not from just any state, but Pennsylvania—big, populous, historic, urban-and-rural, usually-but-not-always-Democratic Pennsylvania. Senior senator from Pennsylvania.

That fucking video. That devil Julian Mellow. Even Marcella came in for some vitriol, as he sat there in his office cocoon, silently brooding. Wife of the senior senator from Pennsylvania wasn't good enough for her. Nothing was. Well, he was going to lose anyway, next week in New Hampshire would end it for all practical purposes, and then he'd be back home—well, back in Washington. He thought briefly, guiltily, of the seven million dollars in campaign funds he'd blown through, much of it raised in hundred-dollar increments over the internet. Who were these people? What could possibly have encouraged them to enter their credit card number and expiration date on Lightstoneforpresident.com? He'd staked out no original or compelling positions, had failed to rise to any oratorical heights that might have inspired such generosity. The fat cat donations he could understand: even if he lost in New Hampshire—*when* he lost in New Hampshire—he'd still be one of the most influential men in Washington. But these anonymous donors, thousands and thousands of them…who were they, what had they seen in him…what were they expecting? Could they all be abortion-hating zealots? Gay bashers? Was his campaign being underwritten on a tide of anger and hate? Did they see him as one of them? Because he wasn't, really. He'd had to shimmy far to the right to be taken half seriously in New Hampshire, becoming a caricature of his old, more temperate self.

"Senator," came a female intern's high, nervous voice from the doorway to the outer chamber. She was young and pretty, Ivy League-brilliant and eager to please. He could have had a fling with her, have it videoed and distributed to the media, and *still* win reelection. An intern was acceptable every now and again in the new political climate. But that…person in San Francisco? "There's something happening downstairs in the mailroom. The supervisor called and asked you to come down."

He stood up and put on his jacket. He was the top-ranked Republican with an office in the Russell Building. Duty called. "Did he say what it was?"

"No, but he sounded upset. You want me to come?"

"That's okay, wait here." He registered her disappointment—interns rarely got to leave their desks except to fetch coffee—and headed off along the interminable second-floor corridor. He took the stairs to the basement, where a small crowd had already formed outside the entrance to the mailroom. It parted obligingly as he approached, but a man in a dark suit held up a hand to stop him from entering.

"Dick Shelton, FBI. I can't let you in there, Senator Lightstone."

"What's happening?"

"At ten fifteen, give or take five minutes, a Senate postal worker doing a routine mail scan uncovered a suspicious package."

"Bomb?"

"Anthrax."

Harry shook his head. Five years ago, while serving on the Senate Arms Service Committee, he'd signed an appropriations bill that had authorized the installation of automated anthrax detection systems in all congressional office buildings. The system collected air surrounding mail-handling equipment and used polymerase chain reaction analysis to look for anthrax DNA, returning a result on sampled air in as little as thirty minutes. But the equipment was a bit too sensitive, generating innumerable false alarms, each one disrupting work at great cost.

"It's the goddamn equipment," he said. "We haven't had one legitimate anthrax case since we installed it. Thank God for that," he added quickly.

"Can't blame the equipment this time," the agent said. "One of the mail handlers felt a powderlike substance inside an envelope, and there was some spillage on the outside."

"Jesus, do you think it's—"

"Unlikely, but we're taking no chances. The handler is in quarantine, on his way to Bethesda Naval."

"Well, it sounds like you have it under control. Do what you have to do."

"Yes, sir. The press may be here later, and they may want a statement. That's why we thought you should come down."

"Press? This is what, the third incident in a year? We've never had press."

"But this particular package is addressed to Stephen Delsiner. Marked confidential."

*Shit.* The Rooney-Delsiner campaign would get miles of publicity out of this, and if it turned out to be an actual anthrax attack, they'd not only get the nomination by a landslide, they'd get Purple Hearts. Losing in New Hampshire was one thing, a humiliating loss quite another.

"Has Senator Delsiner been alerted?"

"He has, sir. He's in New Hampshire."

"Good. Call me the moment you have a read on the powder.

And let me know if the press needs a statement." The crowd parted again to let him pass. Upstairs, he entered his office suite through the public door, rather than the private door that opened directly from the corridor. That meant walking through a series of chambers occupied by his staff, which he liked to do every so often, stopping to talk business or inquire about a sick relative or recent vacation, just to keep morale up now that he was away so often. As he passed through his press aide's office he saw Stephen Delsiner on the always-on television in the corner.

"What this shows," Delsiner was saying, "is that we live in a dangerous world. We need to strengthen our defenses even in a time of peace..." He stood in front of a colonial-era house, no doubt somewhere in New Hampshire, enhancing his brand-new image as a fearless battler of tyranny.

"You know it's baby powder," his Senate press aide, Ramona Carson, said. She'd been largely marginalized since he'd announced for president, replaced by a media professional picked by Fred Moran. Soon enough she'd be back in charge. "I mean, he's talking as if being senator is a daily act of courage."

"Still, you can't buy this kind of publicity," he said and headed for his office. It would all be over in a week, he told himself. His new mantra...*all over in a week.*

# CHAPTER 30

Billy Sandifer waited across from the apartment building on West 82nd Street until a man he assumed to be Zach Springer emerged at ten fifteen. It had been a long and tedious morning, watching a parade of well-dressed men and women emerge from the unimpressive building. Fancy clothes, shabby building...Manhattan in a nutshell. The man he thought was Springer had a bicycle with him, a sleek model that looked like it weighed less than an empty briefcase, and he was decked out in a tight-fitting shirt and shorts, with clip-on bike shoes that Billy heard clicking on the sidewalk even from across the street. Good-looking guy, obviously fit, his hair a bit stragglier than his neighbors'. He didn't appear to be a person who was looking forward to a little exercise, some fresh air. In fact, as he put on his helmet and fingerless gloves, he looked preoccupied, his mouth locked in a frown, his forehead creased—a fighter pilot suiting up for what he sensed would be a doomed mission. Well, it was a cold day, though mild for January. You had to be a little obsessed to be biking on a day like this.

Springer pedaled off to the west. Billy waited a few minutes, just in case, then walked across the street. He found Springer's name on the buzzer panel, handwritten next another printed name, S. Pearlman. Roommate? Lover? Wife? He pressed the buzzer for 6D, waited, pressed it again, waited some more. No answer. He then pressed a few different buzzers until someone answered.

"Who is it?" came a woman's voice through the small speaker in the buzzer panel.

"Con Ed, I need access to the basement."

"I didn't call Con Ed."

"It's a building-wide issue, m'am," he said.

"See the super," was the response. Then silence. He tried a few more apartments and had one hand in his jacket pocket, ready to take out his pick set, when someone buzzed him in without questioning.

He took the service stairs to the sixth floor to avoid running into anyone. Apartment 6D was protected, if that was the word, by a single tumbler lock. He removed a leather pouch from his jacket pocket and selected a medium-gauge pick and tension wrench. He'd had the set since he was a kid in Canarsie, a gift from an older friend who was heading off to prison on an assault charge. The passing of the torch. Before he'd come across the antiglobalization movement as a focus for his general restlessness and occasional rage, he'd been a bad kid, breaking into neighborhood apartments and stores. Thank God for global trade and child labor, he'd often thought. He and his pals used to break into the mansions of CEOs of global companies when no one was home and loot the places. They'd spray paint walls (*$1/hour for children in Haiti...how do you sleep at night?* was a favorite in master bedrooms), slash paintings, break china...occasionally take something back as a souvenir and reward. Stupid stuff that rarely made the papers but always made them feel good.

He first inserted the tension wrench, then slowly pushed the pick all the way into the cylinder until it hit the back, simultaneously twisting the wrench a bit to force the shaft against the pins, forming an edge for the pins to press against. Next he raised the pick to the top of the cylinder and dragged it to the first pin, twisting it side to side to lift the pin up and out of the cylinder, where it rested on the edge made by turning the cylinder with the tension wrench. A small but very satisfying vibration and an almost imperceptible click told him that the pin was released. He repeated the process, working quickly but deliberately, until all five pins had been raised, then turned the cylinder all the way around using the tension wrench and the pick. When the deadbolt gave way he felt the tiny click travel down his body in a shiver of satisfaction. He opened the door and entered the apartment.

. . .

Marcella Lightstone was outside a strip mall near Nashua, shaking hands with strangers, hands slippery with sweat and no doubt teeming with bacteria when a campaign aide tapped her on the shoulder. "You gotta see this, Mrs. Lightstone," he said. "There's a TV in the deli over there."

She was grateful beyond measure for an excuse to take a break. While it was depressingly true that her appearances at strip malls and coffee shops and ghastly "warehouse" stores the size of stadiums hardly caused stampedes, they were exhausting and vaguely humiliating. How often could she drone the words "I hope you'll come out for Harry next week" without feeling stupid? Her jaw muscles ached from smiling. And then there was the futility of the thing. Harry was still down ten points in the polls. Why bother?

She followed the young campaign aide, who looked like an idealistic volunteer but was in reality on the payroll, like most people connected to the campaign—Harry didn't inspire volunteers, and wouldn't unless he began to look like a winner. Inside the deli, a small group was staring up at a television mounted above the cash register, where Stephen Delsiner was addressing a gaggle of reporters in front of what looked like a school building.

"It is utterly ridiculous, outrageous, in fact, to suggest that I in any way asked for or requested or solicited that cocaine," he was saying. In his open-collar white shirt, blue blazer, and pressed gray slacks, he looked as likely to use drugs as break into a freestyle rap. But the geniality that had made him one of the Senate's most popular members and a hit with voters in New Hampshire had deserted him, she could see right away.

"Look, anyone can send illegal drugs to anyone, and that's what happened here. Someone sent me a quantity of cocaine, knowing it would be picked up in the Russell post office because of its resemblance to anthrax. It was meant to embarrass me, perhaps to chase me out of this race. But I will not be scammed into withdrawing. My problems with drug abuse are well documented, as were my successful efforts, over a decade ago, to take them out of my life."

Several reporters shouted out questions. One voice rose above the rest.

"Senator, has Gabe Rooney asked you to step down?"

"He has not."

"Has he contacted you today?"

"We speak every day, several times a day, actually."

"And did you discuss the cocaine?"

"In passing. Now, if you don't mind, I'd like to spend some time with the good people of New Hampshire." He walked off camera amid a pelting of questions.

"The Xavier School, where he's appearing, is just a mile or so down the road," someone in the deli said. "Maybe he's on his way here for some munchies."

"Cocaine doesn't make you hungry," someone else said. "It takes away your appetite."

Marcella wondered if the cocaine delivery was what Julian Mellow had in mind when he told her to *leave the drama to me*. It seemed a rather feeble gesture, unlikely to do much, if any, damage.

"Do you think this will hurt him?" she asked the young campaign aide.

"Nah, looks like a hoax. I mean, who has coke sent to their office? With his approvals, he'll probably come out of this looking like a victim, which could even *help*."

Damn Julian Mellow. Did he really think it was so easy to sink a campaign? The cocaine package barely rose to the level of high school prank, hardly the sort of thing to change the course of an election. She needed this, all of this—the sweaty handshaking, the nervous speechmaking, the cheap charter flights, the jaw-numbing smiles for the ever-present cameras, most of all the disruption of what had been one of the great lives, *her* life—she needed this like a fucking hole in the head.

"Mrs. Lightstone?"

"*What?*"

The campaign aide flushed and took a step back. "I'm sorry, I just thought—I mean, as long as we're here—I thought—"

"What is it you want me to do?"

"There's a diner about a mile from here, it fills up about now and so I figured we might as well—I mean, if you don't object we could—"

"Let's go," she said and walked quickly out of the deli.

• • •

Billy Sandifer had a flashback to a time when his after-school activity had been breaking into neighborhood homes to pilfer loose change, the occasional portable radio, small, usually worthless jewelry that he'd give to his girlfriends. Nothing really valuable or obvious—if he'd showed up at home with a television or stereo Freddie Sandifer would have beaten him senseless, something he did frequently, anyway, and he'd had no idea how to fence stolen goods back then. What took Billy back to those times was the sense of extraordinary peace and stillness he felt in someone's else's home. It was like entering another dimension altogether, as if you weren't breaking a law of man but some fundamental law of physics. As he moved around Zach Springer's small apartment, he felt invisible, impervious, safe, which was an odd way to feel, given that what he was doing could get him sent back to jail for a very long time. But that's how he'd felt back then, in Brooklyn, and perhaps that's why he'd done it, to live in someone else's world for a few minutes, undetected in a place that had nothing to do with him or Freddie Sandifer.

The kitchen yielded nothing of interest, other than the identity of Springer's live-in girlfriend, which he wrote down on a small pad he'd brought with him. While inspecting the refrigerator just for the hell of it he heard something from the bedroom. He took his blade from his pocket and recrossed the living room. Standing in the doorway to the bedroom, he almost laughed out loud. A big dog—sheepdog, he guessed—was cowering in the far corner of the room, whimpering.

"Some fucking guard dog you are," he said, then proceeded to go through every drawer in the bedroom while the big, stupid dog looked on. He learned that Sarah Pearlman was a size four, wore a 34C bra, and, judging by the photo of her and Zach on top of a dresser, was hot in an intelligent, class brain kind of way. As for Springer, his wardrobe was mainly bike clothes, jeans, and polo shirts, although there were a bunch of very expensive suits in a back corner of the single bedroom closet. In a nightstand drawer he found a sheaf of condoms, some half-burned candles, a book of matches, and a clutch of photographs. He pocketed a snapshot of the two of them—at someone's wedding, it looked like.

Back in the living room, he turned on the computer, which sat on a small table in one corner. A nice room, he decided as the machine fired up, definitely decorated by a woman with a limited budget but a good sense of how to make a space feel comfortable and happy. Deep sofa, cushiony chairs, Oriental rug, thick red drapes. The tiny, dark studio he rented in the West 40s, with the tub in the kitchen and the kitchen in the living room, would never feel like anybody's home.

He turned his attention to the manila files on top of the make-shift desk. The handwritten labels were like chapter titles in what appeared to be a major obsession. "Mellow: Recent Deals" was the thickest folder, crammed with newspaper clippings and print-outs from internet stories about the doings of Mellow Partners. "Mellow: Social" contained a collection of stories and pictures of Julian and his wife at various fundraising events, most of them for psychiatric-related charities. He worked his way through "Mellow: Art Collection" and "Mellow: Son Matthew" and "Mellow: Press Interviews" (a very thin folder) until he got to one that sent his insides tumbling: "Mellow: Billy Sandifer." Inside were a few arti-cles printed from the internet, most of them having to do with the uprising at Williston and his release two years earlier. Nothing incriminating in itself—in fact, nothing in the file connected him to Mellow, but he hated seeing his name and Mellow's on the same folder. And the next folder, labeled "Mellow: Lightstone," wasn't exactly comforting. Inside were articles on Charles Moore's plane crash, airplane schedules to Portland, Maine, an article about Lightstone's speech at the Saint Francis in San Francisco, another one about the murder in San Francisco—*fuck*, what were all those articles doing in the same file? And then there were dozens of lined pages torn from a notepad, covered in handwriting, much of it unreadable. Springer did a lot of diagramming, connecting names (Mellow, Sandifer, Lightstone, mostly) with long lines interrupted by question marks and exclamation points and accompanied by scrawled notations. The scribbling of a lunatic, except a lot of it happened to be true.

He checked out the sites Springer had recently visited. Most of them had to do with Mellow or Lightstone. Springer had a major hard-on for Julian Mellow, that much was clear, and he'd somehow managed to uncover at least the outline of what was going on. If he were able to connect a few more lines to a few more names—and all the information he needed was basically in those files—then he'd know everything. And what flashed through Billy's mind just then wasn't an image of being taken back to Williston but of Rebecca being led out of the Newman Center and dumped into the state institution from which he'd rescued her two years earlier.

He gasped, having forgotten to breathe for a good minute, and found himself panting, as if he'd just run up several steep flights of stairs. He would never let that happen to Rebecca. Her mother had deserted her, and he'd been unable to help her for so long. She was never leaving the Newman Center. He'd made a pact with himself, and with Rebecca.

Footsteps, outside the apartment's front door. Probably headed for another apartment, but with only four units to a floor...the jangling of keys, the unmistakable sound of a single key sliding into the lock of apartment 6D. He held in the on/off switch of the computer until it shut down—five seconds that felt like five hours—then crossed the living room to the closet just inside the front door. He squeezed into the closet just as the front door opened, crouching under hanging coats and jackets, gripping the edge of the door with his fingertips and pulling it almost shut.

He heard footsteps crossing the living room, then the sound of the dog running to greet the new arrival. He took his switchblade from the inside pocket of his jacket. Had Springer cut short his ride? Too cold even for him? He could kill Springer now, remove the files, and Rebecca would be safe. There would be an investigation, of course, and the connection to Mellow, whatever it was, might surface, but so what? As long as the connection between Mellow and himself was never revealed, Rebecca was safe. Springer was a few inches taller, and in shape, but he had the element of surprise in his favor, and he had experience in this line of work.

Suddenly a voice, a woman's voice. "Hello, Guinevere. How's your day been so far?"

So it was the size-four girlfriend, not Zach Springer.

He ran his thumb over the switchblade release button, gently enough to keep from ejecting the blade. What would be gained by killing her? Nothing, and it would potentially alert her boyfriend that his amateur investigations had been discovered. A shame, because killing her would be easier than waiting in the closet, his knees already throbbing with pain from maintaining a crouch.

A sudden noise—from the living room television, he quickly realized—startled him back to the moment. His legs still throbbed but now he felt a tingling in his feet and hands, which had lost sensation. Then something in the newscast caught his attention.

"…political analysts doubt that this will derail the Rooney-Delsiner campaign," a male voice was saying.

"Has the Lightstone campaign issued a statement?"

"Senator Lightstone said, through a spokesperson, that he has no reason to doubt Delsiner's sincerity," came the male voice. "Remember, Delsiner has made no secret of his past problems with substance abuse, and he has used his back-from-the-abyss story to great advantage. A lot of voters relate to his life, particularly the role of Christian faith in his recovery. And let's not forget what we're talking about here, a quantity of cocaine mailed to the senator. There is not a shred of evidence that the senator requested the drug."

"Thank you, Bill. In other news, President Nessin appeared in Canton, Ohio, today, widely regarded as a pivotal state for both parties in the upcoming…"

Billy felt a small sense of satisfaction that his parcel had been detected in the Russell Building mail room. Julian Mellow was clever, no doubt about it. No wonder the man was worth a gazillion bucks. He was looking forward to seeing how the whole thing played out, since Mellow kept him pretty much in the dark about the bigger picture. He liked the whole idea of a born-again holy-roller type getting nailed on a drug charge. Before he knew it the TV was off and he heard her heading into the bedroom.

"Ready for a walk, Guinevere?" The dog panted its enthusiasm.

She'd be leaving soon. He flicked open the switchblade and slowly cracked the closet door. There was no rationale for what he was about to do, other than that he needed to do it. He was crossing the living room when he heard a toilet flush in the bathroom, which was off the bedroom. A second later he heard a cell phone ringing, and then her voice.

"Hi, how are you?" she said, and then, after a pause, "I'm walking Guinevere."

He didn't want to surprise her while she was on the phone. Whoever it was would call the cops and that wouldn't leave time for what he had in mind. In an instant he calculated and recalculated his options. He heard the sink turn on while she continued to talk, then it was turned off and her voice grew louder as she left the bathroom, still talking. He was frozen at the center of the living room, paralyzed by conflicting desires. He'd wait till she was off, assuming she hung up before leaving the apartment. He entered the small kitchen and opened what he thought was a closet but turned out to be a tiny service bathroom. He closed the door behind him and waited.

She was still on the phone when she left the apartment, the dog in tow. He left the bathroom and crossed the living room to the window, which overlooked the street. A minute later he saw her leave the building with Guinevere. He raised the window and leaned out, following her down the street as she continued to talk on the phone. When was the last time he had a conversation that long? Had he ever? What did he have to say that needed five, ten minutes? What person would he say it to? He envied her for the long, comfortable conversation and for a thousand other things. He hated her, too, for the easy confidence in her voice, the way her ass swayed ever so slightly as she walked, for the easy intimacy she shared. He hated her because he hadn't fucked her or run his knife across her throat and because she would never see the inside of the Newman Center or its unspeakable state counterpart. When she turned onto Amsterdam Avenue, disappearing, he stood up, grabbed the fancy red drapes and pulled hard, tearing the supporting hardware from the wall. Let them try to figure out what had happened, he didn't give a fuck. He went back to the kitchen and opened a few drawers until he found what he was looking for: a spare key. He used it to lock the front door behind him and placed it in his pocket for future use.

# CHAPTER 31

Julian Mellow approached the receptionist on the forty-third floor of 1222 Avenue of the Americas, a building he controlled through his 51 percent interest in Sundian Real Estate Investment Trust (he'd divested the other 49 percent in a public offering, netting just north of $540 million), and asked for Simon Avery, the chairman and chief executive officer of Masters Broadcasting, the nation's largest group of network-affiliated local television stations. He controlled Masters through a 100 percent interest in its parent company, Masters Media.

"And your name?"

"Julian Mellow."

"I'm sorry, you said Junior Moody?"

"Mellow," he said. *Spelled O-W-N-E-R,* he almost added, but he was in fact pleased that she recognized neither his face nor his name.

"Is Mr. Avery expecting you?"

"He is not."

"I'll call his assistant," she said warily. "Why don't you have a seat?"

He was still standing less than half a minute later when Simon Avery bustled into the reception area.

"Julian, what a pleasant surprise."

They both knew the surprise was anything but pleasant. Masters Broadcasting had been a lackluster performer since Mellow Partners' takeover three years earlier. Avery, who had been head of affiliate relations at one of the big networks, had been brought on board soon after the buyout, when the entire senior management team had been shown the door, with the mandate to turn the ship around so that it could, in a leaner, meaner, more profitable incarnation, be sold back to the public in an IPO at a substantially higher price. So far, he'd underperformed.

"Can I get you some coffee? Water?" he asked as they walked back to his corner office. Avery was a fleshy fifty-year-old who regularly showed up in the society columns, schmoozing with a broad cross-section of New York's media establishment. With his luxuriantly thick, bluish-white hair, pink complexion, and preference for foppish bowties, he, unlike Julian, was no doubt recognized by most receptionists in town, as well as the maître d's at the better restaurants.

"Nothing," Julian said.

When they were seated in Avery's office, across from each other in matching wingback chairs, Avery jumped right in. "I'm guessing you're here about the fourth-quarter numbers. I was as disappointed as I'm sure you were that we didn't make our goals, but I think in this environment, with what's happening over at the networks, a 4 percent increase in overall audience—which translates into a 6 percent increase in gross margins, by the way—is an impressive performance." Avery let out a long, slow breath and crossed his meaty legs. A fine line of sweat glistened on his brow. His performance stank—did he really think Julian was unaware that competitor affiliate groups had turned in double-digit growth figures?—and a personal visit from Julian was certainly bad news. Mellow Partners had six managing directors who oversaw its investment portfolio, and it was these men (all were men) who had direct contact with the operating company CEOs. Zach Springer had been his first managing director, and the most capable, even as the organization expanded and additional high-performance

MBAs were brought on. It would have been his job, or that of one of his successors, and not Julian's, to grill an anxious CEO about his numbers, his goals, his strategies. Julian swooped in only for the most important events, such as planning divestitures and "bolt-on" acquisitions. And high-level firings, of course.

"I'm not here to discuss the numbers," Julian said. The darkening of Avery's complexion indicated that he feared the worst. "It's about a news story, actually." He handed Avery a flash drive. "There's one file on this. Play it."

Avery let out a long, slow breath and hoisted himself from his chair. He plugged the flash drive into his computer.

Julian stood behind Avery as he watched.

"What is this?" Avery asked.

"Wait."

A minute or so later a figure approached a car.

"That's...Stephen Delsiner," Avery said, turning to Julian, who nodded and pointed at the screen. Avery tried to turn up the sound, but there was none.

Before Delsiner got to his car a second figure appeared on screen.

Five minutes later it was over.

"Where did you get this?"

"It was emailed to me. Anonymously. An accompanying note indicated that man with Senator Delsiner in the video is Christopher Ruben, known as Kobe, a drug dealer from Missouri."

"Do you have the note?"

"No."

He could see the frustration mounting in Avery's expression.

"Why you? Why was this sent to you?"

"I own the largest group of network-affiliated television stations."

"But why not send this to the networks themselves?"

"Our local stations have wider reach than any single network, and we're affiliated with all of the networks anyway. Plus, I think whoever sent this realizes that the networks might not show it."

"We don't run anonymous tips, either."

"Is there something about this video that strikes you as inauthentic?"

"It certainly *looks* like a drug deal, and after the cocaine incident at the Russell Office building, this would almost certainly destroy him. Which is why we can't run this without knowing where it came from, who shot it, what the circumstances were…"

"I told you, I received it anonymously." Julian returned to his seat.

"We can't run it, Julian."

"You will run it, *Simon*."

They locked eyes. Avery turned away first. "This violates a cardinal rule of journalistic ethics," he said without looking at Julian. "Interference with the news operations by corporate management is unthinkable. I won't do it."

"Your performance as head of this group has been very disappointing to us." Avery watched with fresh alarm as Julian reached into his briefcase and removed a multipage document, which he tossed onto the coffee table between them.

"What is that, my resignation? I won't sign, you'll have to fire me."

"It's a three-year contract, with a 20 percent raise included as well as various performance bonuses built in. It also provides for equity participation when we take the company public."

"Is this a payoff?"

"An acknowledgment of your superior performance." Julian emitted a tight smile.

"And if I don't sign it?"

"You will be replaced."

Avery's eyes unfocused as he took this in. A droplet from the line of sweat on his forehead broke free and ran down the side of his face.

"Why, Julian? Why is this so important to you?"

"It will be a scoop. Our ratings will go through the roof. It will put our news operation, which hasn't exactly been your strong suit, on the map."

"For a day or two."

"Given the performance of this company, even a day or two of improved ratings will be like a blessing." He allowed another tight smile as Avery slowly shook his head.

"I can't do it. A dubious video from an anonymous source. If we had more time to investigate…" The New Hampshire primary was in four days, he might have said but didn't. Instead, Julian took the contract and stood up. "Goodbye, Simon," he said as he left the office. "And good luck." He walked quickly to the elevators and had just pressed the down button when Simon appeared.

"You're positive you have no idea where the video came from."

"Absolutely."

"Can we at least have a few days to verify that it's authentic?"

"It must run tonight, on the evening news, in every one of our stations. You'll want to check out the identity of the other man. Kobe Ruben, from Saint Louis."

"You mentioned equity participation," he said. "Will those be restricted shares, and what about the lockup period?"

Julian handed him the contract. "I'll look for the story on the news tonight." He stepped into the elevator but held open the door with one hand. "It has occurred to me that we need to beef up our foreign coverage."

Avery blinked as he took this in. What little foreign news his stations ran came from pickups of wire service stories.

"We have no budget for foreign news, you must know that."

"I think we can find a few dollars for important stories. The situation in Kamalia, for example. We should have a reporter there."

"Kamalia? But that's—"

"I'll look for your recommendations early next week on how you want to proceed with the Kamalia story," he said, and let the elevator close.

• • •

# CHAPTER 32

"What happened?"

Sarah crossed the living room to the windows, where the red drapes lay in a heap on the floor.

"Jessica called me about this," Zach said. "She said they were fine when she left to walk Guinevere. When she got back they were on the floor."

"But I had them professionally installed."

"The plaster must have given out."

He had almost screamed when he first saw the drapes after returning from a long, cold ride up the Hudson to Nyack. All that red fabric heaped on the floor had at first looked like a body, and it still had a sinister, portentous appearance.

"I'll call the place that installed them tomorrow," Sarah said. She went to the bedroom but returned a moment later to stare at the drapes, as if they were evidence of a crime, or an omen. He could see that she was upset. The apartment was very much her creation, an extension of herself, a zone of comfort and familiarity in a tense world of noisy, demanding children and anxious, demanding parents. He hugged her for a few moments. She felt rigid, her arms at her side.

"Any progress today?" she asked.

"Not much," he removed his arms from her. She seemed about to pursue this, then took a sip and went to the bedroom.

He made pasta that evening with tomato sauce from a jar that he enhanced with whatever vegetables and herbs he could find in their refrigerator. While waiting for the water to boil he turned on the television with the remote in time to catch the beginning of the local news.

"Our top story this evening concerns the campaign of Senator Stephen Delsiner, the designated running mate of Gabe Rooney, who is seeking the Republican nomination for president. Accu-News has obtained an exclusive look at a video in which Senator

Delsiner appears to be purchasing drugs from a man who law enforcement contacts have confirmed is alleged to have ties to the drug world in Saint Louis..."

Zach walked over to the TV and watched the short, grainy video. It certainly looked like Senator Delsiner was buying something. If the other man could be confirmed as a drug dealer, Delsiner was finished. He'd easily survived the incident involving the package of cocaine sent to the Russell Office Building. But there was no way he could explain *two* incidents, both involving drugs. And if he went down, so would the man who had chosen him, Gabe Rooney, leaving Harry Lightstone the likely winner in New Hampshire next week.

Harry Lightstone. Once a dark horse, now the likely frontrunner. A passenger on Julian Mellow's private jet, someone connected to the murder in San Francisco, perhaps through a former inmate whose daughter's long-term care bills were being handled by Julian Mellow. Everything came back to Julian Mellow.

He glanced at the fallen drapes, then walked quickly to his desk. All of his files were still there. Zach decided to go online for more information about the latest turn of events in the campaign, but when he turned on his computer he got a message indicating that, because the machine had been improperly turned off, it would perform a routine check of backup systems.

Zach glanced back and forth between the drapes and his computer. Had someone broken into the apartment? Then he heard the pasta pot boiling over and ran to the kitchen to turn down the heat.

"It's ready," he called out later. Sarah joined him in the kitchen.

"I'm not hungry."

"But you haven't—"

"This isn't working," she said.

He glanced at the bowl of pasta, stupidly hopeful that she meant the meal.

"I'll fix the curtains tomorrow," he said, though he knew it wasn't the curtains either.

"I can't live with you anymore. I can't watch you destroy yourself with your stupid obsession with Julian Mellow. With the past. You're pulling me down with you. I won't let that happen."

"I'll make some calls tomorrow."

She shook her head. "It won't make a difference because you don't want to move on. When I saw the curtains on the floor, it felt like everything we built together is wrecked. We can't help each other. I've tried, but I can't." Her voice was flat, but tears were spilling down her cheeks. "I want you to leave, Zach. As soon as you find a place of your own."

"But I—"

"By the end of February. Please tell me you'll be gone by then. I need to feel that there's movement, some sort of progress."

"I'll get a job, anything to contribute. Bike messenger, waiter."

"Just be out of here by the end of next month." Her voice had weakened to a whisper, but her expression was resolute. "Promise me you'll be out of here, Zach. Please?"

He felt his throat constrict. Words were impossible, so he nodded, almost imperceptibly. She turned, walked to the bedroom, and shut the door.

## SATURDAY, JANUARY 31

# CHAPTER 33

The Galérie Saint-Estèphe, on the rue de Lisbonne in the 8th Arrondissement, was an unprepossessing establishment that catered to wealthy tourists and snobbish arrivistes eager to hang something "original" over their sofas and mantles. It sold near-worthless prints churned out by brand-name artists and sloppy oils by deservedly obscure, long-dead painters. Julian Mellow always spent a few minutes with these dreadful pictures before heading for the back room where his real business was conducted. It was useful to be reminded of the difference between talent and genius.

"Monsieur Mellow, how delightful to see you." Claude Suisse crossed the large gallery with an outstretched hand. He was a small, elegant man whose impeccable dress and manners and facility with multiple languages were very reassuring to the culture vultures who strolled over from the nearby George V looking for something authentic to complement their living room décor back home in Chicago or Tokyo or Bahrain. "You look well, my friend."

Julian doubted that he looked any such thing, having just landed at Charles de Gaulle after an overnight flight. Even on his own jet, with a comfortable double bed in the rear cabin, he found it hard to sleep while hurtling through the ozone at five hundred miles per hour. The two scotches he had taken to induce sleep had only succeeded in making him woozy upon arrival the next morning. But he had changed into a fresh suit, a silky pinstriped Brioni, and put on a crisp white shirt and tie, both from Sulka, so perhaps he did present an acceptable appearance, although it wasn't Suisse he had come to Paris to impress.

"Would you like a coffee, perhaps?"

Julian nodded and an assistant was summoned from across the gallery with a snap of Suisse's fingers. She was a head taller than her employer—her slender, miniskirted legs alone seemed longer than his entire figure—and unselfconsciously chic in the way of even homely French women. She was far from homely.

"*Un espresso pour Monsieur Mellow. Rien pour moi.*"

She disappeared through a door behind the receptionist desk.

"*Allons*, enough of this wallpaper," he said, casting a dismissive hand at the artwork surrounding them. "Let us visit the true purpose of your journey."

He led Julian to his office, a small, windowless room behind the gallery cluttered with stacked canvases and piles of paperwork. He waited until Julian was seated, then picked up a small oil painting of a harbor scene in an elaborate gold-leaf frame.

"A beautiful Monet," he said. "*N'est-ce pas?*"

"Only if Monet had a blind younger brother."

Suisse laughed warmly. "Do you know, I could get ten thousand euros for this travesty, even in a new frame. It is old, after all, and the red sky from the sunset, it will match perfectly the leather settee." As he spoke he pressed his fingers into the canvas, pushing it out of the frame by its edges, gradually working his way from one side to the next. There was a quiet knock at the door and he quickly put the painting facedown on the desk in front of him.

"*Entrée.*"

The leggy assistant entered and placed a tiny cup of espresso before Julian, then retreated under the close scrutiny of her employer.

"Monique has been very good for business. She intimidates the clientele with her long legs and long nose, and that makes them eager to please her, especially the Japanese. They will pay handsomely to win her approval."

"You were in the middle of something," Julian reminded him.

"*Eh bien.*" He picked up the frame and within a few minutes had loosened the entire canvas.

"It is good you are sitting down," he said, then pulled away the offending landscape. "Voilá."

Julian rose to his feet, an involuntary movement. As his eyes took in the canvas, every muscle in his body tensed. After a long silence he forced himself to take a deep breath, sat down, and nodded at Suisse—authorization to speak.

"Hans Holbein...the Younger, of course. *The Lady Ratliffe.* Late 1520s. She was lady-in-waiting to Jane Seymour, the third wife of Henri the Eighth."

"I've seen the drawing in the British Museum, but I assumed..."

"Yes, the preparatory drawing in chalk for the portrait, which everyone assumed was missing forever."

"Where did you find it?"

"Ah, that I cannot reveal. The seller is from one of those very old and very aristocratic and, alas, very poor English families, and he is not eager to pay taxes. He wants only a private sale, funds deposited in a Swiss account, and, of course, a significant discount if the buyer does not publicly display or reveal the source of the picture."

"How much?"

"Ten million US dollars."

"That doesn't sound like much of a discount."

"At an auction this would bring in at least fifteen, perhaps twenty million. There has not been a Holbein English portrait on the market for two decades."

She stared forthrightly from the canvas, her head swathed in an elaborate Tudor headdress, an unusual pose for a Holbein subject, who more typically were depicted in profile, or three-quarters view. Her eyes were slightly too far apart, which gave her unsmiling expression an uncomfortable hint of omniscience, and her thin lips were neither disapproving nor sensual, just disturbingly noncommittal. She had a thin neck, well suited for the Henrician chopping block, though that had not been her fate, and a tiny, birdlike torso that looked not quite up to the task of supporting a head so intelligent and unwavering. Julian leaned forward and gently touched the Lady Ratliffe's forehead with a finger, half expecting her to flinch at his inappropriate gesture.

"Eight million," he said.

"My client is quite determined to—"

"There are perhaps a hundred collectors in the world who can afford this. Fewer than a dozen of them are drawn to Renaissance portraits. Of those, I can think of just one other person who has no need to display his acquisitions for the world to see and admire and covet. Two collectors. This is not what economists call a liquid or efficient market." He stood up and started for the door. "I have an appointment."

"Monsieur Mellow."

He turned back and was almost astonished that the Lady Ratliffe had not moved.

"I may be able to persuade the seller to accept your offer."

Julian suspected that Suisse had already bought the picture from the impoverished aristocrat, and for substantially less than eight million dollars.

"My plane leaves Charles de Gaulle at noon."

"If the purchase comes through, and I think it will, I will have our lady friend on that plane, with the proper paperwork, of course."

The *proper paperwork* would indicate a near-worthless landscape with a value of perhaps ten thousand euros. While US customs inspectors always trudged out to his plane when he arrived from overseas, they never had the temerity to inspect his luggage. Perhaps there was some sort of list or database of large contributors to the president's reelection campaign—he didn't know and didn't care. He only knew that the proper paperwork would not, more than likely, be necessary.

"Excellent," he said, and actually smiled at her, the lady-in-waiting, confident that she would cross the Atlantic with him that afternoon, to take a place of honor in his private gallery, his first Holbein lady, his new favorite.

• • •

Julian saw Sophie DuVal the moment he entered the Hotel George V. Tall, black, possessed of an aloof, forbidding beauty, she would stand out anywhere. But in the near-empty lobby of the George V, all gilt and crystal and intricately patterned rugs and drapes, she looked like a work of art from a different century, a time that valued simplicity and clean lines rather than rococo excess.

She recognized him immediately, too, and stood up. He saw her expression darken as he approached. He too felt a heavy curtain of sadness fall over him as he took in her white T-shirt, dark slacks, and heeled sandals, an unexceptional ensemble that, on her, looked impossibly chic. He thought: *This should be Matthew, not me, crossing the lobby of the best hotel in Paris to meet the most beautiful woman in France.*

He kissed her cheek and momentarily lost his bearings when she presented her other cheek, which he eventually kissed as well. When they stepped apart he saw that she was crying.

"I'm sorry," she said. "I forgot…I…"

He nodded as she reached into her purse for a tissue. She'd forgotten how much he looked like Matthew.

"Do you want coffee or some breakfast?"

"Yes, but not here," she said, waving an arm to take in the preposterous excess of the George V. They left the hotel and turned right on the Avenue George V.

"It's hard enough to be in Paris, after Kamalia. Somehow you never quite remember how beautiful it is. It seems wrong, so much beauty and contentment."

Her accent was French, with a subtle lilt that he assumed was Kamalian.

"Is it terrible?"

"Some days it's the poverty that infuriates me. We were never a rich country, but we were on our way, and now it's gotten much worse than it ever was. People's diets have gotten so bad, you see it in their faces, drawn and drained of health. Other days it's the political repression, the lies in the newspaper, the friends and comrades who disappear one day and are never heard from. Other days it's the apathy of the Kamalian people, who seem to feel that there is nothing they can do because in some way they think they deserve everything that has happened to them."

She was his height almost exactly, but her legs were longer and she walked the way she talked, fast and with an angry resolve.

"And we had come so far," she said, her voice faltering. "What Matthew did with Amalgamated, it was a model for all of Kamalia. Employees treated with dignity who delivered higher productivity. Although never enough productivity to satisfy you."

"No, I…" He saw that she was smiling, softening her face, opening it up. On magazine covers and cosmetics ads she had glowered and pouted like an insulted high priestess. Her smile rendered her accessible, which was perhaps why it had rarely made it into print.

"Matthew never minded," she said. "Everyone thought he was this raging reformer, some sort of dangerous radical, but he understood business very well, he always knew that we had to do well to do good. He was your son, after all."

Julian had tolerated Matthew's African adventure, but never approved of it. Amalgamated Cobalt had come to Mellow Partners as part of a much larger acquisition; he had never wanted to get into the mining business and certainly not in Africa. But by then Matthew had met Sophie, and the opportunity to use Amalgamated to transform the homeland of the woman he loved had fired his romantic imagination.

At the corner of rue François 1er they turned to the left and found a small café, where they sat outside on rattan chairs, facing each other over a small, pink marble table.

"I should have been more supportive," he said.

"Amalgamated was doing fine, we—"

"No, I mean of you and Matthew, your relationship."

"Oh." She bowed her head as a waiter appeared. "Do you want an espresso?" she asked. He nodded. "A croissant?" She turned to the waiter and ordered in French, then looked back at him. "I never resented you. In your eyes I took Matthew away from the life you had built for him, I took him to a terrible, uncivilized place. I was black…"

"No, no, that—"

"Don't defend yourself. All parents want an easy life for their children. Mixing the races is never easy. It's complicated at best."

"I could have been warmer to you, when we met in New York."

She shrugged. "I don't think warmth is your strong suit, Monsieur Mellow. I never expected it and…" She looked down.

*And neither did Matthew.* He glanced over her shoulder at the seventeenth-century facades of the *hotels particular* across the way, an unexceptional Parisian street yet exquisitely, painfully beautiful.

Too beautiful. They should have met in the cold fluorescence of the airport.

"And what you've done since Matthew's death has been extraordinary. Your money is all that is keeping the movement alive."

"My money," he muttered as the waiter placed cups of espresso and two croissants on the table. Matthew's death had taught him the infinite value and terrible limitations of his money.

"Just knowing that you're out there, thinking of us, this great capitalist, this world-famous businessman." She touched his arm. "Everyone expresses themselves the way they can. This is your way."

"No!" He flung off her arm. He would not be placated. He would not settle for absolution.

"Monsieur Mellow, please. Matthew's death must stand for something," she said in her gentlest voice. "If I thought it didn't, I would, well...I would go insane."

He nodded but looked away. The poor girl, she really thought that making a cause of Matthew would ease the pain of his loss. Matthew was worth twice that whole pathetic country, *Kamalia*. He was worth more than the entire continent of Africa. Did she think seizing power from a tin-pot dictator would balance the scales? Could she be that naïve? It would take more than *regime change* to fill the awful void of Matthew's absence from this earth. To avoid saying something intemperate, something hurtful, he turned to the business at hand.

"I wanted to meet you because there has been a development," he said. "I couldn't take the chance of calling. Are you aware of Claude DuMarier?"

"The new minister of security."

"He is a friend of mine. And now, of course, of yours."

"DuMarier is a thug. His reward for a lifetime of brutality is handling personal security for Le Père. Do you know what that involved?"

"That really doesn't interest me, I—"

"Friends of mine, men and women committed to nonviolent

protest against this regime, simply vanish one day, never to be seen again. We think they are being held in prison, but we don't know. We hear reports of torture and forced confessions that are later printed in the paper as evidence of our treason. DuMarier is the man responsible for this, all in the name of protecting a single person. How can you call him a friend?"

If smiling lent her face an unfashionable warmth and accessibility, anger brought out the sharp lines and shaded contours that photographers and advertisers had loved.

"You will never succeed in overturning the Boymond regime without help from inside the government." When she started to speak he raised his hand. "That is reality. Once you have regained power, you can do with DuMarier what you please. For now, working with him represents your best chance of success."

"How…"

He could sense her awe at the reach of his influence. DuMarier had been on his payroll since Mellow Partners acquired Amalgamated Cobalt. When the company needed something from the government—a permit, an export license, that sort of thing, DuMarier had been only too happy to arrange it, for a small fee. Matthew had known nothing of the arrangement. It would have offended his sense of propriety. Treating workers with dignity wasn't nearly as productive as he had thought; inevitably, you had to grease the right palm. Matthew had died an innocent, in a way. Julian had kept DuMarier on the payroll since Matthew's death, making regular deposits in Swiss accounts and communicating through diplomatic pouches routed through the French embassy.

"*How* is not important," he said. "What is important is this. When you are ready, DuMarier will make sure that the government is not. He will tell you when it is safe to make your move."

"*He* will tell *us*."

"He will ensure your success."

"I can't meet with such a man."

He stood up and placed several euros on the table.

"I thought you were realist enough to know what had to be done. Dreamers, idealists never succeed."

"Is that why Matthew died?"

He could easily have reached across the table and strangled her for that. Instead he called his driver and gave his location.

"That was wrong, to use Matthew's name like that," she said. "But he *was* a dreamer, you know. An idealist. We both were. He thought he could use his incredible gifts—not his wealth but his intelligence and passion—to make the world better. I know that that sort of idealism is unfashionable, perhaps even embarrassing. But that was Matthew. He believed. And I know that you want the world to be a better place, too."

He nodded, but the gesture was a lie. He wanted the world obliterated, sucked into a black hole along with every single human being who had lived while his son had died.

"I only want justice," he forced himself to say. The words tasted sour on his tongue. "Will you meet with DuMarier?"

"In the interests of the cause, and only because—"

"Will you meet with him?"

"Yes," she whispered.

"Fine, then you will be contacted. Do as he says, and trust him. Your interests are aligned, however unlikely that may seem from your perspective."

His hired black Renault with tinted windows pulled up to the curb.

"Can I drive you somewhere?"

"No, thanks. I think I'll walk around a while, just to put everything in perspective. A few minutes in the Faubourg should get my blood back to boiling."

"I hadn't noticed that you'd cooled down."

He extended a hand but she leaned into him and hugged him.

"*Merci, Monsieur Mellow,*" she whispered moistly. "*Vous êtes notre ange.*"

An avenging angel, perhaps, he thought as he gently extricated himself from what he suspected would be an uncomfortably long embrace.

As his driver closed the back door of the Renault, she gave a small wave and said, "For Matthew."

He nodded. She was right: in different ways, with very different goals in mind, they were both working for Matthew.

# CHAPTER 34

Senator Harry Lightstone stepped behind a podium at the front of a meeting room in the Nashua Crowne Plaza and addressed a crowd of reporters—and through them, the country.

"First, I would like to extend my sincerest support to Stephen Delsiner and his family at this very difficult moment in their lives. I have known Steve for almost a decade and I am confident that with the help of Sally and the children, he'll pull through."

Marcella, almost lost in the crowd of video cameras, had worked with Michael Steers to draft the opening, and she thought it worked. Harry always came off best when expressing regret or conveying comfort; he was a kind of national uncle, always there with a steady, consoling hand on the shoulder, a proffered tissue. If he came off a bit wimpy, well, in times of peace, his avuncular qualities played well.

"I am sorry to see Steve leave the ticket," Harry said. "He added a note of vigor and a new voice to the contest. Marcella and I wish him well on this next journey of his."

Delsiner had not only resigned from Gabe Rooney's ticket, he had left his Senate seat as well, succumbing to the uproar from voters in Missouri, who had elected him precisely because he'd put his drug problem behind him and campaigned so fiercely as a born-again crusader against the evils of narcotics. But *had* he slipped? He looked as vigorous as ever, on TV at least, and his denials struck her as plausible. However, the polls, which had magically appeared moments after the scandal erupted, the way they always did, like rainbows after a storm, showed that Americans didn't believe him, by a margin of almost two to one. He almost certainly would have survived the cocaine in the letter sent to his office, but not the video. Though the provenance of both the letter and the video were rather fuzzy, one seemed to support the veracity of the other. In any case, Delsiner was damaged goods and had to go, that much was clear.

Marcella listened closely as the all-important segue to the top of the ticket arrived.

"But even as we wish Steve well, we have no choice but to question the judgment of Gabe Rooney in selecting him as his running mate. This is the most important decision a candidate makes, perhaps the most important he'll ever make, whether he wins office or not. There is no margin for error. With so much information coming to light about Stephen Delsiner's background, we must ask: how thoroughly was he vetted? Did political considerations trump concern for national security? What did Senator Rooney know, when did he know it, and when was he planning on sharing this information with the American people?"

The not very subtle echo of Watergate had been her idea. Harry needed to find his edge, at least in public, and feeding him time-tested barbs like "What did he know and when did he know it?" seemed like as good a way as any. She'd have to talk to Julian about the Kamalia nonsense. No one could get worked up over a small African country that fewer than 10 percent of the population could find on a map. All that talk about human rights abuses in Kamalia made Harry sound a little potty, and bored his audiences half to death in the bargain. Since Iraq and the rash of homegrown terrorist incidents, the country had become Fortress America; no one cared what went on over the walls. It was too bad about the son dying in Kamalia—or had he been murdered?—but a campaign for president was no place to work out personal grievances. Whenever Harry called for more stringent antiterror measures his numbers trended up. President Nessin's obligatory (some said deeply felt) references to civil liberties made America nervous, and him appear weak.

Suddenly, with Delsiner's fall, what had begun as a quixotic shot in the dark was looking like a horse race. Rooney's numbers had plummeted, according to a private poll commissioned by Fred Moran. Rooney and Lightstone were in a dead heat, and all the momentum was on Harry's side. For the first time since this strange journey began, she would find herself imagining, in the rare quiet moment, life in the White House, wondering if she'd find it comfortable. It had always struck her, during the occasional state dinner or luncheon, as sort of cheesily down-to-earth, everything resolutely American, with no real personality or point of view, a least-common-denominator of a house. She'd worked with the greatest interior designers in the world, acquiring masterpieces of furniture and art, regardless of where they came from or whose sensibilities they might offend. French antiques from the eighteenth century were her favorites, but she doubted she'd be able to bring them with her to Washington. People were still so stupid about the French, she doubted she'd—

"Mrs. Lightstone?"

Her mind required a few moments to travel back to New Hampshire from 1600 Pennsylvania Avenue.

"Yes?" she managed to say with a smile. Harry had finished, apparently, and was talking to a small group of reporters.

"Do you have any comment on the Delsiner situation?" a reporter asked her as several others listened in. Microphones were thrust into her face like ugly bouquets from scruffy suitors.

*Well, you might be interested to know that it was probably all set up—somehow, miraculously, incredibly—by Julian Mellow, the financier. You might want to look into that! And while you're at it, check out Senator Lightstone's proclivities for very tall women. There are scoops here for all of you!*

"My heart is with the Delsiner family," she said, forcing her lips into a sympathetic frown. "My heart and my prayers."

• • •

"Mr. Mellow, there was a message. The caller said it's urgent. He didn't leave a number."

Julian's housekeeper, Inez, handed him a piece of paper in the foyer of the apartment on Fifth Avenue. He'd just returned from Paris and felt more unsettled than tired. Private jet travel had that effect. It spared such inconveniences as check-in and baggage claim but its very seamlessness induced a sense of disorientation. He placed the Holbein, swathed in bubble wrap and encased in stiff cardboard, against a wall and read the note.

*Mr. Franklin needs to see you. Four o'clock.*

He checked his watch—three forty-five. He closed his eyes for a moment, shook the fatigue from his body, and took two long, deep breaths. Then he left the apartment.

# CHAPTER 35

Though Central Park was just across Fifth Avenue from his apartment, Julian rarely ventured into it, content with the view from eight floors up, where it looked as orderly and peaceful as a Dutch landscape. But as he headed to the bandshell for his appointment he regretted not taking advantage of the park more often. The sense of oasis, especially in winter, when the walks were nearly deserted, was almost palpable.

He arrived at the bandshell at noon. He'd read somewhere recently that the Parks Commission wanted to tear it down, but that the family that had donated it and whose name was etched in the limestone structure was asking the courts to prevent such a desecration. *Sic transit gloria*—those should be the only words etched in building walls. Or perhaps, *Vanity of vanities, vanity, all is vanity.* Attempts at immortality were all futile, for even granite buildings eventually outlived their usefulness. He gave tens of millions of dollars away every year, to museums and hospitals and universities and medical research organizations, yet Julian Mellow's name was found above no door or gallery or hospital wing, was never listed in event programs. He'd allowed Matthew's name to grace a building of the private school he'd attended, and a wing at that kid's nursing facility in New Jersey—he wanted Billy Sandifer to have an unmissable reminder of who was keeping his daughter out of a state institution each time he visited her. But it would have depressed him to see his own name etched in granite, for he didn't care what he left behind, and attempts at immortality struck him as pitiful and small and ultimately, of course, ·pointless. After he died the world could stop spinning for all he cared; he would leave nothing behind that meant anything to him.

"Mr. Mellow?"

He turned and for a few moments didn't recognize Billy Sandifer. They'd met only once, just after Sandifer's release from Williston. Warden Verbraski had set up the meeting once Julian had begun to form his plan and realized that he'd need a front man, as it were. He'd already proven himself useful during the prison takeover. Back then, Sandifer had looked sickly, his skin sallow, shoulders hunched, eyelids drooping with defeat. He hadn't yet shaken the aura of confinement. The man before him looked far more robust. His hair was longer, and he seemed to have added weight and confidence along with it; even his voice sounded deeper than Julian remembered. Sandifer, wearing a gray sweatshirt over black jeans, was a good-looking man in his forties, athletic and healthy.

"Let's walk," Julian said, and immediately headed west, toward the carousel.

"I was afraid you hadn't gotten my message."

"Clearly I did get it." They'd arranged a while ago that a request for a meeting with "Mr. Franklin" meant the bandshell in Central Park. This was the first such request.

"It looks like the Rooney-Delsiner ticket is over," Sandifer said. "Mission accomplished."

"Yes."

"I saw a poll this morning on the news. Lightstone pulled ahead by a few points. An upset in New Hampshire would mean the nomination is basically his. It's all about expectations these days."

The last thing Julian wanted was a political discussion with Billy Sandifer. With anyone, for that matter. Getting to the point was a sacred policy of his, and any endeavor in which doublespeak and obfuscation and the endless repetition of platitudes held sway—politics, religion, much of business—made his head ache with restless contempt.

"You wanted to see me?"

"I checked out Zach Springer. I entered his apartment when he was out. He has these folders, all about you."

In retrospect, he shouldn't have been surprised to learn that Zach was doggedly following him. He'd been almost obsessively thorough in checking out acquisition targets, not content until every aspect of a company had been vetted, from the market share trends of its least important product to the peccadilloes of its chief executive officer. It had been Zach who'd kept him out of the superficially appealing but ultimately worthless technology stocks, sparing Mellow Partners billions in losses. Now he'd turned his zeal for due diligence to his former employer.

"He and I had a falling out. I'm not surprised that he's keeping track of me."

"These files? They have labels like 'Mellow and Lightstone,' 'Mellow and Sandifer.'"

Instinctively, he looked around, reacting to a sudden chill of vulnerability. Was Zach out there, following them? Was there someone else?

"Do you think he told anyone?"

"Can't say. He lives with a chick…"

Julian had met the *chick* a few times, a public school teacher. He'd always assumed that Zach offloaded his residual idealism onto her so he could help his employer gobble up half of corporate America, and implement the inevitable layoffs and benefits cutting, with a free conscience. If Zach suspected that he was involved in something, especially something that involved politics, he would certainly share it with the schoolteacher.

"Did you take the files?"

"That would have tipped him off. You want me to go back in and copy them?"

"It doesn't matter what's in them." Just the names, together: Lightstone. Sandifer. Mellow.

"You want me to take care of him?"

Julian felt himself gripped by something new and disturbing: indecision. The correct thing to do was never a mystery to him. Then why the hesitation? He'd done so many things in the past month, or authorized them to be done. But he did not want Zach Springer killed. *Why?* He would slaughter an army, level a city, to get what he wanted. Was it because he owed Zach so much, he who owed nothing to anyone?

They approached the carousel, which was not open. Its brightly painted horses and carriages had a sinister air under the darkened roof, as if they'd been abandoned and forgotten. He and Caroline had often brought Matthew there when he was a boy. How many times had he hoisted Matt up onto the biggest horse, it always had to be the biggest horse, then stood at a discreet distance, holding onto a pole, ready to catch him if he fell off as the carousel began its gentle turning? He'd been a good father, despite having never had an example of such a person in his own life. He wondered sometimes: what if he'd been taken to a carousel, or a movie, or a parade? Would he be a better man? A less driven, less successful man, almost certainly, but also perhaps a man who could look at an empty carousel on a cold January afternoon without the paralyzing desire to order its destruction, or tear it to splinters with his own hands.

"Make it look like an accident, or a robbery, I don't care," he said softly as he gazed at the darkened carousel. For one awful moment he thought he saw it start to turn.

"What about the girl, she might—"

"Her too," he said, then turned and walked quickly away.

• • •

To the west of the carousel, the terrain gradually rose to a stand of oak trees, now bereft of leaves. Behind one of these oaks, Zach shielded himself from the two men standing by the carousel. With the New Hampshire primary three days away, he'd grown desperate to prove the connection between Julian and Harry Lightstone. And the red drapes heaped on the floor of the apartment—he couldn't shake the suspicion that someone had broken in. And then there was Sarah. They hadn't spoken since her ultimatum. If he could prove that his pointless obsession, as she saw it, was grounded in reality, perhaps she'd reconsider her eviction order.

So he'd found himself standing across Fifth Avenue earlier, staring up at the eighth floor of Julian's building, as if he could tele-pathically intuit what was going on inside, when Julian's Mercedes had pulled up. Julian got out and disappeared inside the building. Zach stood there for a few minutes, frustrated that his nemesis was so physically close and yet completely off limits. He was about to walk away when Julian reemerged, looking concerned, and headed across Fifth Avenue and into the park. At the bandshell he met Billy Sandifer, whom Zach immediately recognized from photos he'd seen online. They stood and talked for a bit and then walked, Billy looking relaxed and comfortable, Julian stiff and aloof. They stopped at the carousel. Zach used his cell phone to snap a picture of the two men. It wasn't the clearest shot, but it did reveal an unexpected sight: one of the world's richest and most powerful men standing shoulder to shoulder with a violently antibusiness ex-con. Who knew when such a photograph might prove useful?

## TUESDAY, FEBRUARY 3

# CHAPTER 36

The mile-long ascent from the road that paralleled the Hudson River up to Route 9 in Closter, New Jersey, was something of a legend to the serious cyclist. Neophytes liked to boast about which gear—never the lowest—they used to get to the top, or how they never resorted to standing up on their pedals. For veterans like Zach, the climb was the closest thing the route offered to a challenge, and it was all about maintaining a nice, even speed, finding the groove and staying in it.

He was almost halfway to the top, feeling good. He'd stopped noticing the biting wind miles back. Sometimes he liked to clear his head before a major climb, the better to focus on each turn of the pedals. Other times he let thoughts fuel his efforts, and that was the case just then. He sensed that he had most of the key pieces to a puzzle that, when complete, would take down Julian Mellow. The photo of Julian and Billy Sandifer together in Central Park was hardly sufficient proof to derail the Lightstone campaign or destroy Julian—his real objective. But he felt fortified with a print of it tucked in his wallet—the only concrete evidence he had that he wasn't entirely insane. He'd tried showing it to Sarah, but she wasn't interested. In fact, their only conversation over the past few days had been about the Craigslist ads she'd forwarded to him for tiny apartments all over the city, including one in Queens, a forty-five-minute subway ride from their current place. Still, he felt sure he was getting closer to figuring things out, that soon Sarah would understand too, and that thought pumped strength into his legs, even if he didn't know how everything fit together. Three hundred miles to the north, the polls were due to open in one hour for the New Hampshire primary. Harry Lightstone was the unlikely frontrunner, and if he pulled it off he would more or less coast to the Republican nomination. Julian was somehow connected to Lightstone, and Zach had a strong feeling that the more prominent Lightstone became, the harder Julian would fall.

He hadn't left the apartment on Monday, watching televised news reports of the impending Republican primary and reviewing his files, hoping to stumble on a missing link that would lead, somehow, to Julian's downfall. But that morning he'd gotten up early and needed exercise, needed to get out, needed to focus on something other than Harry Lightstone and Billy Sandifer and Julian Mellow.

He heard a car downshifting behind him as it, too, struggled with the climb. To his right the hillside plunged down to the Hudson River along a steep embankment dense with trees and rocks. He edged very slightly to the side to let the car pass—you didn't want to get too close to the edge, even on the ascent. Drivers were used to sharing the road with cyclists in this part of Bergen County.

He was in a nice rhythm, legs pumping smoothly, fingers loose on the handlebar. Julian was going down, he was sure of it, and then he would move on, he and Sarah together. He'd been successful once, he would succeed again.

The car, a dark four-door sedan, pulled next to him and slowed. *Move on, asshole,* he wanted to shout, feeling pinched between the car to his left and the steep embankment to his right. He stole a glance to his left but before he could make out the driver the car jerked to the right, toward him, and the next—and last—thing he noticed was a swirling mass of green coming at him as he hurtled down the hillside, detached from his bike, detached from the earth, wondering if this was how it would end, thinking of Sarah, wanting to tell her something—wanting to tell her that he was thinking of her, just her—not Julian Mellow, not New Hampshire, just her—as he tumbled.

# CHAPTER 37

Entering Zach Springer's apartment the second time was a cinch. After buzzing apartment 6D from the ground-floor vestibule to make sure no one was home, Billy Sandifer used one of the keys he'd taken during his first visit. He also remembered to bring snacks for the big sheepdog, who offered a timid whine from the bedroom before succumbing to the cookies. He'd hoped to take care of Zach and the girl, Sarah Pearlman, on Monday. Sarah had left for work at eight, but Zach had stayed inside all day. She'd come home for lunch and to walk the dog, left again, then come home for good around five. Billy had kept an eye on the building from either end of the street, pacing back and forth to keep from going insane, but Zach had never emerged. This morning, Tuesday, he'd gotten lucky. Both of them had left the building, Sarah at seven thirty, Zach, on his bicycle, at eleven.

He decided to make himself useful while he waited for Sarah to come home for lunch and to walk the dog. He went right to the desk in the living room and took all the files he could find bearing the name Mellow—including the one that made his stomach muscles clench, the one with his own name on it—and stashed them in a leather satchel. He turned on the computer and nosed around for a few minutes. He found only one item of interest: an icon for a picture file on the desktop labeled *Central Park, 1/31*. He double-clicked on it: he and Julian were standing close together, as if whispering secrets. Nothing illegal in that, but it might raise questions: for one, what was a convicted felon doing chatting with a multibillionaire in the middle of winter in Central Park? He closed the photo and deleted it. Zach's internet history indicated that he spent most of his days visiting sites about Mellow and his companies, but that would only lead cops, if they looked into his computer, to conclude that Zach Springer had been pathetically obsessed with the man who had fired his sorry ass a few years ago.

Now there was nothing to do but wait for her to come home for lunch, as she had when he'd broken into the apartment that one time, as well as the day before, when he'd stood across the street, watching. It was convenient, working with people who kept regular schedules. Zach, for example, left on his bike rides at about eleven in the morning, heading up the West Side and over the George Washington Bridge. He took the same route every time, so it had been a no-brainer to wait until Zach left his building that morning, then drive ahead to Jersey and wait for him at the bottom of the steep hill that led up from the Hudson in Jersey.

A sharp jerk to the right—he'd felt only a slight jolt from inside the car, like fender-tapping when parallel parking—and suddenly the road was empty. No way Zach would survive a fall down that hillside. No way he'd ever again visit the Newman Center, sticking his nose where it didn't fucking belong. Of everything he'd done for Julian Mellow, jerking his steering wheel a few inches to the right that morning had been the easiest. A pleasure, almost.

But where was the girl? He estimated that Zach's body wouldn't be found for hours, perhaps days. Even so, if Zach was going to be a suspect she would have to die sometime before…he started to check his watch but stopped when he heard a key in the front-door lock. He hurried to the bathroom off the master bedroom, almost tripping over the stupid dog, which had jumped to its feet at the sound of door opening.

"Guinevere!" she said. "Ready for your walk?"

The dog panted its enthusiasm.

Holding a switchblade in his right hand, he started to leave the bathroom to intercept her when he heard footsteps heading to the bedroom. A moment later he saw her, back to him, just a few feet away, idly looking at the pictures on the dresser, all of them of her and Zach. Sentimental, and just as well for her—her last images would be happy ones. In one swift movement he stepped into the room and reached around her shoulders with his left arm, pulling her back to him. She had just enough time to gasp, but no time to protest or even, he guessed later, to take in what was happening. He drew the blade across her neck and felt a rubbery bit of resistance as it severed her trachea. She stood there, leaning against him, for a long moment, as if her body were trying to gauge the severity of the injury and the appropriate response. Then he felt her go limp and he let go. She fell to the floor in what was already a small pool of blood.

Guinevere the sheepdog stood in the doorway, watching. Billy lifted Sarah's arm and took her pulse, or rather confirmed the lack of one. With luck the police would suspect her boyfriend—unemployed, depressed, a self-admitted perpetrator of securities fraud…

he'd killed her and fled on his bike to establish an alibi, then either thrown himself over a cliff or gotten careless and died.

*Without* luck there might be an investigation into the improbability that two people living together had died on the same day, though twenty miles and a river apart. It seemed highly unlikely that either death would be connected to Julian Mellow, and virtually impossible that he, Billy Sandifer, would be involved.

He took the file folders and gave Guinevere a pat on the head.

"It's going to be a long, lonely night," he said. Then, just before leaving, he dug into his pockets and gave her the rest of the cookies he'd brought with him.

• • •

Julian Mellow's phone rang at nine o'clock, just as the polls in New Hampshire closed. It rang twice, then stopped. A minute later it rang twice again, then stopped. Two rings, twice. Two people dead. The prearranged signal at the prearranged time.

"Aren't you going to answer?" Caroline said from her side of the bed.

He ignored her. Instead, he searched inside himself for some nugget of remorse and was deeply relieved not to find one. In the park, with Sandifer, his reluctance to authorize what he knew needed doing had alarmed him. There could be doubts, no second-guessing. The stakes were already high, and getting higher.

He aimed the remote at the TV and upped the volume.

"In New Hampshire, in what will surely be regarded as one of the most bizarre and unexpected primaries in history, Pennsylvania senator Harry Lightstone has been declared the winner of the Republican primary by a comfortable twelve-point margin."

"Are you happy, Julian?" Caroline asked, putting down her book. "I don't know what you've done, I don't *want* to know. But I do know you had a hand in this." She aimed a long, elegant index finger at the screen. "So my question is, are you happy?"

He looked at her and saw that she was genuinely curious, perhaps even concerned—but for whom? For him, or for the life she'd built for herself? A shroud of chilly isolation fell over him and all he could think to do was move over to her side of the bed and pull her toward him.

"Are you happy, Julian?"

He pushed her nightgown up over her hips and forced his right hand between her thighs. She sighed irritably as he worked his hand up, but in a few short moments he felt her legs relax, and then the rest of her seemed to give way as well.

*A statement from Senator Lightstone is expected in just a few minutes.* "Answer me, Julian. Are you happy?" she whispered in his ear as he entered her.

*The magnitude of senator's victory here in New Hampshire makes him all but a shoo-in for the nomination. It also promises to bring the issue of global human rights to the forefront.*

"Whatever it…it is you're…doing…has it…it made you happy?"

He thrust harder, then harder still.

"Are you happy, Julian?"

"Not yet," he whispered, bracing himself on his hands and thrusting so hard Caroline's head rammed the headboard. Crack. Crack. Crack. He thought he heard her protest, or was she moaning with pleasure? It made no difference to him.

*Here comes the senator now, accompanied by his wife and campaign aides.*

He thrust harder, faster. *Was* he happy?

Crack. Crack. Crack.

"Julian, stop, you're…"

He covered her mouth and continued the assault, then answered her question, but silently.

*Was he happy?*

Not yet.

# PART III

# CHAPTER 38

They met in the dining room of the senator's Georgetown townhouse, the group charged with putting Harry Lightstone into the White House. Harry had called the meeting the evening before, and the eight assembled people, himself included, had scrambled from wherever they happened to be to show up. An aura of stifled dread filled the room. It was as if they were all moving in slow motion, unable or unwilling to summon the energy for decisive action. Handshakes were just shy of firm. Porcelain coffee cups, filled by the Lightstones' butler, were raised to mostly silent lips, then lowered without a sip. Voices were muted, but out of weariness, not respect. It was the second week in October, the convention over, the vice president selected, the debates come and gone without any serious embarrassment to either side. The polls, even those conducted by Harry's own people, indicated that the chances of a Lightstone victory in two and a half weeks were close to nil.

"I want to thank you all for coming on such short notice," he said, then decided to cut the campaign speech bullshit, which lately sprang from his lips as easily as *please* and *thank you.* "We have to turn this dog around. If Nessin beats us on the issues, so be it. The country has spoken. But I'm reading in the *Times* and the *Post* that we're running the most inept and uncoordinated campaign in recent history. There was an hour on Fox devoted to our incompetence. On Fox! I don't want to lose because we can't get our goddamn act together."

He was gratified by the uncomfortable shifting in seats, the discreet throat clearings.

"Fred, speak to me."

Fred Moran tilted back in his chair but he appeared anything but relaxed. The campaign had taken a toll on his face, which only a few months ago looked younger than his fifty-five years, handsome in an approachable, CNN-ready way, and now looked tired and older and a touch bitter. He'd gotten three governors elected against all odds over the past decade, but he seemed to have lost his touch. Or perhaps he wasn't up to the rigors of a national campaign.

"We have three challenges," he began in the slightly nasal voice that had once seemed to reflect a cynical insider's perspective on politics but now suggested nothing more than a chronic sinus infection. "First, we haven't identified a compelling issue to claim as our own. The economy is stalled in low gear, but people seem okay with it, or at least they haven't responded to any of our proposals for improving it. Health insurance is still a problem, but no one believes our plan will work any better than the last one, or the one before it. No one believes we're serious about lowering taxes, even after sixty-five million dollars in ads focused specifically on that issue. There's nothing in the foreign policy arena to get people excited. Every month that goes by without a terrorist incident the president's poll numbers go up a percentage."

"Jesus Christ!" The outburst came from Martin Selkirk, the vice presidential candidate. "Why don't we all just go home now. If we can't find a single goddamn issue that gets people excited let's just pack it in."

At sixty-three, Selkirk was the oldest person in the room by several years. He'd been selected for his Southern bona fides—as a four-term governor of Georgia he added "balance" to the ticket, not that anyone seriously expected the Peach State, or any other Southern state, to go to the Democratic incumbent anyway. But it had seemed important to counteract Lightstone's reputation for Northeastern frigidity with some plain-talking Southern warmth. Selkirk was reassuringly plump, with a full head of gray hair always in need of a trim, and a kindly face that made a lot of voters think of their beloved grandfather. He was happily married, the father of three, and grandfather of many more than that. After the Stephen Delsiner disaster the Republican faithful craved normality, and Selkirk was nothing if not normal. He seemed too un-self-conscious to be devious or dishonest, and that's just what the country wanted. If he struck some as not the sharpest tool in the shed, well, men without intellectual credentials had made successful presidents in the past, and Selkirk was only running for veep, after all. He was the do-no-harm choice, just the ticket, as the saying went.

"Mother of God, we've got a trillion-dollar deficit this year, maybe more. I bring up the deficit and the crowds go apeshit."

"Those are our people, Marty," Moran said. "You're preaching to the choir. The rest of the country knows there are only two ways to deal with the deficit. Cut spending, which means social security and Medicare, or raise taxes. Political death, both of them."

"Well, we're already dying here. We could go out speaking the truth at least."

Harry saw Moran make eye contact with Hugh Jamison, the campaign's lead pollster. Expressions of principle made them uneasy.

"You mentioned three challenges," he said.

"Number two is white men," Moran said. "They're usually our bread and butter, but they're not buying what we're selling. We've got the values vote—abortion, family, indecency on TV, the usual crap. But values are a women's issue, and we never get above 45 percent of the women. For men it's the economy, and they want a balanced budget and lower taxes, which in the current circumstances are mutually exclusive."

"But that hasn't stopped the other side from offering both," Lightstone said with a sigh. He'd had this conversation a thousand times in the last few months.

"We used to own lower taxes and a balanced budget, but we blew that with Bush Two. Now we're blamed for jacking up the deficit by blocking spending cuts, which means we can't cut taxes. We talked about coming out with a spending freeze proposal, but that turns off women and minorities, and we've been making head-way with minorities."

"A modest tax increase for the top 1 percent and a big cut for the rest—"

"Would be political suicide." Moran glanced around the table, challenging anyone to contradict him. "No one ever got elected president promising to raise taxes, even on the top 1 percent."

"That's because half the country thinks they're in the top 10 percent," said Jamison the pollster.

"We're supposed to be the solution," Martin Selkirk said in his trademark gargling-with-nails drawl. "Problem is, we don't have a problem people can get excited about."

"Number three?" Harry said quietly.

"Kamalia." Moran let the word hang in the air for a few moments.

When Harry couldn't take the disapproving silence any longer, he asked: "What about it?"

"Nobody gives a rat's ass about some two-bit African hell hole. Shit, nobody cares about foreign policy, period. Since Iraq, Afghanistan, they want a wall around the country, nobody comes in, nobody leaves, except for sightseeing trips to Europe, which no one can afford anymore anyway."

"Torture, human rights abuse…none of this is important?" Even to his own ears Harry didn't sound passionate on the subject.

"They could dismember every man, woman, and child in Kamalia, do it on the evening news, and it wouldn't get you one single vote," Moran said. "Unless it's Americans getting killed, nobody cares."

"I care," he said as convincingly as he could.

There was silence, punctuated by shifting in chairs and muf-fled coughs. Personal convictions, when the election was two weeks away and the polls were against you, were not acceptable fodder for polite discourse. Jamison finally broke the awkward silence.

"Our latest tracking poll shows that Kamalia is the issue most connected with you, Harry. That's a disaster. Voters hold one or two impressions of a candidate, that's all. Fifty percent of your reputation is tied to a place most people can't spell. We can't afford that."

"Hugh is right."

All heads turned to Marcella Lightstone at the far end of the table. She never sat in on strategy meetings, even when they were held in one of the Lightstone homes. This one she'd insisted on attending. *I never asked for this,* she'd told Harry that morning. True enough, but he strongly suspected she wanted it. *I had a great life, one of the greatest lives on this planet. Now I can't walk down the street without a thick-necked Secret Service agent two feet behind me and people coming up to me and touching me with sweaty hands, and God forbid I refuse to shake them, the papers make me out to be some sort of "Let them eat cake" ogress. I knew it wouldn't be easy. But this? We need a way to win this thing. I won't have it be a waste of time.*

At the end of the table, Marcella projected a surprising gravitas, given the infrequency of her appearances at strategy meetings, her diminutive size, and the fact that, even after a well-received speech at the convention in July, she was still not associated with a single issue or cause other than getting her husband into the White House. She was something of a cipher to the electorate, in fact, but that didn't seem to be having an impact on the polls. She simply wasn't in the political equation at all, and given the *sturm und drang* surrounding past First Ladies, that didn't seem like a bad thing at all.

"Our platform is weak to begin with," she said in an upper-class lockjaw that, in small gatherings like the present one, verged on ventriloquism. "The last thing we need is to distract voters with a silly issue that they have no interest in."

"The arrest and torture of thousands of innocent people is hardly silly, Marcella, in fact—"

"Kamalia is off the agenda."

No one gasped at this wholly unexpected and entirely inappropriate exercise of spousal authority, but they might as well have. All heads turned slowly to Harry, like turrets atop a flotilla of gunboats.

He waited until he felt he could speak with a steady voice. "Hasn't our polling shown that the 'We deserve better' theme is working?" He didn't wait for Jamison's answer. "Eighty-plus percent recognize that line, and most of them agree with it. Let's figure out a new creative strategy. Same message, new execution. Get some fresh blood around it. And we'll go negative at the same time; I know that makes everyone at this table happy."

After a tense silence, Jamison spoke. "What about Nessin's son?"

Peter Nessin had recently made headlines after a consulting firm that he'd built, largely on his father's name and connections, declared bankruptcy.

"He's off limits."

"We don't have to name names," Michael Steers said. "We compare and contrast." The campaign's chief spokesman glanced from Harry to Marcella and back.

"No, the boys are off limits." Since the convention, Alan and Brian had been back at Saint Andrew's, out of the public eye. They would not be paraded in front of the press to demonstrate Lightstone family values. He stood up. "I need to prepare for a briefing with the *Times* editorial board tomorrow, and then a speech to the Roundtable. Let's see some new ad concepts by tomorrow afternoon."

"And Kamalia?" Moran asked.

"Kamalia stays on the agenda."

• • •

"You have no idea what this is really about," he shouted at Marcella when they were alone in the library. "You have no goddamn idea what the pressures are on me, so I'll thank you to keep your mouth shut."

"Don't shout," she said calmly, pointing to the door, behind which stood the inevitable Secret Serviceman. Even after eighteen years surrounded by Marcella's army of servants, eighteen years in which the two of them had very rarely had one of their several homes to themselves, he still could not get used to the ubiquitous Secret Service, with their undertakers' suits and bird-furtive eyes and subtle suggestion of inappropriate knowledge.

"I'll do whatever I want in my own goddamn home." But he had lowered his voice, and sat down in one of the leather wing chairs on either side of the fireplace.

"Doing what you want is *not* what this is about." Marcella took the facing wing chair.

"Well, I'm tired of taking advice that gets me nowhere."

"That's not what I meant."

Their eyes met for a long moment.

"You know."

She nodded slowly.

"How long?"

"From the beginning."

He'd never told her about Julian Mellow, had never been tempted to, not once, during the long primary season following the New Hampshire upset, when things were going well, during the leadup to the convention in Dallas, when the momentum from the uncontested primaries carried him forward, nor since Dallas and the disappointing debates, when the momentum behind the campaign seemed to be leaking like air from an old tire. It wasn't the San Francisco video so much as not wanting her to know that the whole colossal enterprise, which had already burned through $635 million, a sum that even the daughter of Kenneth Kollan could appreciate, employed several hundred paid experts and thousands of volunteers, had attracted hundreds of thousands of donations from supporters rich and poor on the internet, had eaten up countless of hours of air time and thousands of square feet of newsprint—that this whole enterprise was built on nothing more than a personal humiliation.

"I'm sorry," he said softly. She shook her head, but the apology wasn't really to her—or to her alone. No sooner had the words left his mouth than he felt a lightening of the weight he'd shouldered for nine months.

"After Iowa, which was inconclusive, you were thinking of getting in anyway," she said, which was part truth, part historical retrofitting. "Julian gave you the encouragement you needed."

There would be, he realized with relief and, surprisingly, some ill-defined disappointment, no discussion of the video itself.

"Since then, he's stayed out of your way, so I really don't think there's anything to be embarrassed or concerned about."

She smoothed the skirt of her pale blue suit, one of many cheerfully bland ensembles she'd purchased for the role of candidate's wife. Once he'd been safely defeated she'd revert to black couture.

"He's stayed out of my way because I mention goddamn Kamalia in every speech. And what about Delsiner?" he practically whispered.

Again, their eyes met, a rare occurrence after eighteen years of marriage. She looked away first.

"The man did have a drug history. In any case, *we* had nothing to do with that."

"And Charles Moore?" he said even more quietly.

"An accident," she said without taking her eyes off the carpet. "Small plane crashes are an occupational hazard of politics. The NTSB report blamed the failure of the plane's elevator controls, whatever that means."

"At night, I dream about them, Delsiner and Moore. If I thought—"

"Well, don't think," she said. "Don't think. They're taken care of, whether by fate or God or Julian Mellow we don't know and we never will, not if we know what's good for us. We have the future to think about."

*Fate or God or Julian Mellow.* He could only nod. Her conviction was bracing and unsettling. For a moment there he'd briefly looked forward to sharing the burden of what he knew, and what he suspected, but he now knew that they shared nothing. Remorse and guilt and even uncertainty were alien to her—he'd always known that, but he felt disappointed nonetheless.

"About Kamalia."

"Julian insists that I—"

"I know what Julian insists. But we have to draw the line. It's bringing down the campaign. You're the candidate now. He wouldn't dare release that video at this point. It would destroy him as much as you. You're your own man now, Harry."

He shook his head.

"It's the one thing he wants from me. I don't feel comfortable defying him on this."

She stood up and stepped toward him.

"Listen to me, Harry. You are your own man." She placed a hand on his shoulder and squeezed it. "You're bigger than Julian Mellow now. You're the candidate. He can't control you."

He took her hand off his shoulder and held it. It had been a mistake, keeping so much to himself. She couldn't share his guilt and doubts. But she could help him know what to do.

"You're right," he said. "I'm bigger than Julian Mellow."

"Good. Now, not a word about Kamalia in tonight's speech. Let's show Julian just where he stands."

## THURSDAY, OCTOBER 15

# CHAPTER 39

Receptions at the American embassy were as glamorous as things ever got in Villeneuve, Sophie thought. Everyone dressed up. The Americans tended to overdo the British Empire bit, the men sporting blue blazers and even khaki safari jackets, ties resolutely knotted despite the stifling humidity, the women donning straw hats even after sundown, all of them sipping gin and tonics from sweating highball glasses and smoking Rothmans and talking wit-

tily about their previous postings. Well, you couldn't blame them
for trying to inject some dignity into what had to be a very unde-
sirable posting. Rich American and European campaign donors
or Presidential roommates got Paris or London or even Pretoria.
Career diplomats without the right pedigrees or connections got
dusty Villeneuve. The locals in attendance—business and government leaders and their wives—also tried to rise to the occasion,
but even their best clothes looked at once painfully bright and
badly faded, relics of better times. Sophie wore a short white dress
that Calvin Klein had given her after she'd modeled it at one of his
shows, and high-heeled sandals, relics from her past.

The day before, a handwritten note from Claude DuMarier
had been slipped under her front door, inviting her to the affair.
The US embassy was an unsurprising place for them to meet. The
Boymond government still kowtowed to the Americans, even as
it plundered the companies once owned by US investors, and she
was considered an honorary American, having spent so many years
there. She was also, she knew, the closest thing Kamalia had to a
homegrown celebrity, at least in the eyes of Americans. In truth,
most Kamalians had no idea who she was.

She arrived a few minutes after the party's seven o'clock start
and immediately procured a glass of white wine. The first sip nearly
brought tears to her eyes, it tasted so cool and expensive—like her
old life, she thought, forcing herself to drink slowly. She made her
way across the crowded patio to DuMarier.

"I am—"

"*Je vous connais*," he said with what he must have thought was
charming insinuation. "You look fantastic, Sophie. Your photographs do not do you justice at all."

Her last modeling gig had been three years earlier. Had the
government been photographing her since then?

"I was surprised to learn that you are interested in helping us,"
she said. "There are reports of an escalation of arrests in the name
of state security."

"Do not believe everything you hear."

"You are head of Boymond's security, so you tell me, then. Is it true?"

"In Kamalia, truth is a moving target."

He smiled, as if he'd said something original. Tall and well fed, DuMarier had a fleshy face that almost obscured his small, round eyes and a tight, teeth-concealing smile. He was in full military regalia: a white jacket with a row of five straining gold buttons and covered with medals and ribbons commemorating service in imaginary battles.

"Why are you sympathetic to us?" she asked him.

"Who told you I was sympathetic?"

Best not to raise the name Julian Mellow. "I was led to understand that you would help us."

"Ah, help you, yes. Sympathetic, no."

It was about money. How stupid of her, to imagine that principles might be motivating him. Whatever the government paid him, Julian Mellow was paying him more.

"You wanted me to come here," she said, suddenly impatient to be away from him.

"I want you to look around, get to know this place. If things should go badly for you and your friends, you can come here. You will be safe here, legally we are really on American soil."

"I have been here before." When Matthew was alive, they'd been frequent guests of the ambassador and his wife.

"I know that," he said with a creepy lift of his eyebrows. "This time, I want you to notice the back gate, the one the servants use. I do not suppose you have entered through that gate before." Another insinuating eyebrow lift. "It will be left unlocked at the critical moment. If you need to seek sanctuary, that is."

"Critical moment. When—"

"You and your comrades will decide when. I, however, may be able to let you know when vulnerabilities are apparent."

It was horrible to be dependent on such a man, who so smoothly sold out his government, however corrupt, for personal gain.

"Will these vulnerabilities be *apparent* anytime soon?"

"Very soon. Be ready. Ah, Madame Albertson," he said, directing his tiny fish eyes over Sophie's shoulder. "How nice to see you." He nodded at Sophie and made his way to a matronly white woman, whose right hand he kissed with a ceremonial bow.

She wandered through the ambassador's residence, a low, white building full of immaculately maintained 1960s-era furniture. The embassy had been built during the brief Kennedy administration, when Kamalia, sensing the optimism spreading across the United States, had encouraged the Americans to construct a bigger, more elegant embassy, something more appropriate to the great things the two countries would do together. And indeed, a period of major economic expansion had followed, fueled by new American-financed factories and cobalt mines. The embassy hadn't changed much since then, and neither had Kamalia. The factories had been nationalized by the Boymond regime, and there were frequent threats from Washington to close the embassy in protest, but so far it remained open, though thinly staffed. As she made her way through the crowded public rooms, she thought it looked like a marooned ocean liner, a bit too grand, too carefree, for the land on which it had washed up.

"Sophie!"

The two Knapp girls, Sally and Julia, daughters of the ambassador, ran up to her. She'd met them at various events over the years.

"How pretty you both look." She leaned over and kissed them both twice, in the French style, which they always enjoyed. "And you've grown! How old are you two now?"

"I'm seven," said Sally.

"I'm five," said Julia.

She asked them about their classes at the International School, about their dolls, about their last trip back to America, while they stared up at her with adoring eyes. They knew she'd once been a famous model.

"Do you know what I've always wondered?" she asked them. "Where your groceries come from. I can't believe that deliveries are allowed through the front gate."

The girls shook their heads solemnly.

"Never," said Sally.

"There's a back entrance," said Julia.

"Really! I've never seen that."

"Would you like to see it now?" Sally's eyes widened, as if proposing a daring adventure.

They led her through the vast embassy kitchen, where it felt ten degrees warmer and a small army of sweating Kamalians were assembling canapés, then along a back hallway and out into a small concrete yard.

"That's the gate," Julia said triumphantly. She pointed to a forbidding-looking metal door in a concrete wall that had to be ten feet high, topped with razor wire. The front of the embassy faced the rue de la Paix, the grandest boulevard in Villeneuve, and was just one block from the president's palace; it declared America's august stature and welcoming disposition (though two armed Marines stood by the gate at all times). The back projected a much less friendly demeanor.

"There's a buzzer," Julia said.

"And intercom."

"What in the world are you doing here?" Paula Knapp stood in the back door, arms pressed against the jamb, as if she alone were holding up the entire edifice. Tall, thin, and blond, she looked like the house itself: not fashionable but expensively put together, and not quite bearing up under the stifling and humid heat. Her husband, Ray, ten years her senior at age fifty, had worked his way up through the State Department; Kamalia was his "reward."

"Hello!" Sophie said as cheerfully as she could.

"It's nice to see you, Sophie," Paula said a bit icily. Sophie hadn't been on the official party list, and in fact hadn't been invited to the embassy since the Boymond takeover, when she'd become controversial. She wondered how DuMarier had arranged for sanctuary in the embassy, given the official American neutrality to the dissidents' cause.

"Your beautiful daughters were giving me a tour," she said.

"She wanted to see where the groceries get delivered."

Paula Knapp flashed her a look of hostile skepticism.

"We were talking about all the food for the party and…" Sophie shrugged.

"Come, let's rejoin the party. People have been asking for you, girls. Let's not disappoint them." She shot Sophie a *don't rock the boat* look as they all reentered the house. Sophie wondered if she'd thaw at all if she and her comrades were forced to take refuge in her home, and she wondered how soon DuMarier would signal that certain *vulnerabilities* had become apparent.

# CHAPTER 40

Harry Lightstone's address before the Business Roundtable was covered live by C-SPAN. Julian Mellow watched it from the library of his Fifth Avenue apartment. Lightstone wasn't a bad public speaker, but neither was he very exciting; he tended to impress the policy wonks more than the people, with his somber delivery and habit of explaining things in a pedantic singsong more appropriate for an audience of middle school students. It had been the same in the debates: the "experts"—professors, former campaign advisers, columnists—had declared him, not Paul Nessin, the winner of all three, but every poll showed that voters gave higher marks to the president. Likability was far more important than intelligence in US elections, and Lightstone had a rather chilly demeanor in public, while his opponent, with a slippery grasp of the issues even after four years in office, looked like the kind of guy with whom you'd be comfortable sharing a beer and football game. The incumbent was the nation's buddy, the challenger its school principal.

Julian watched the speech with rising irritation. Lightstone hit the usual issues the audience of CEOs wanted to hear, presenting himself as both business friendly and a champion of the middle class. He touched on foreign policy only briefly and said nothing about Kamalia. Perhaps he'd come back to it. He moved on to education, fighting terrorism, scientific research, trying to sound distinctive but basically parroting the incumbent's policies. He closed with a reaffirmation that big business would have a champion in Harry Lightstone.

Julian stood up and went to his desk, where he picked up the phone. Lightstone would be kissing CEO butt for another hour at least. He couldn't wait that long.

"What the hell was that?" he said after Marcella Lightstone answered her cell phone.

"Hello, Julian. I thought he did well, didn't you?" He caught the insolence in her voice.

"Where was Kamalia?"

"Where it's always been—in Africa. Nobody cares about Africa and nobody cares about Kamalia. There will be no further mentions of Kamalia, Julian. The entire staff agreed." She pronounced *staff* as if referring to her household help.

"That's bullshit."

"That's reality. Now, kindly stay out of the campaign, and do not contact me or my husband again. Goodnight, Julian."

He stood there, phone in hand, for a few paralyzed minutes. Power had shifted—she knew it, and he knew it. The video he had was worthless now that Harry had won the nomination. Releasing it would doom his candidacy, but from the Lightstones' perspective it was already doomed. And if things got ugly, and it appeared that they had nothing more to lose, they might implicate the source of the video. If Harry should achieve the Oval Office, the video would reacquire value—at that point Harry would have everything to lose. But for now they were calling his bluff and he needed to play with a different hand.

He dialed a second number.

"Mr. Franklin?"

"I'm sorry, you must have the wrong number," Billy Sandifer said before hanging up.

An hour later, at the bandshell in Central Park, beneath a dark, starless sky, Julian gave his instructions.

"I'd like you to take a ride up to Saint Andrew's tomorrow, first thing," he began. "I believe you know the place."

## FRIDAY, OCTOBER 16

# CHAPTER 41

Back when Billy Sandifer used to hurl rocks and bottles at policemen during demonstrations, it was images of places like the Saint Andrew's School and all that they represented that fueled his anger. Not that the poor cops he assaulted had any connection to an elite boarding school, but in Billy's mind they were part of a long and sinister chain-link fence drawn around the privileged elite of America, keeping low-born types like him out. Since Rebecca had been diagnosed his anger had turned at once specific (toward anyone or anything that stood in the way of his caring for her) and amorphous (toward fate, life, biology, God, the gods). As he walked around the brick-and-ivy Saint Andrew's campus, twenty miles west of Hartford, he realized that it felt good, after all those years, to carry an anger that was bigger than him but still aimed at an actual, reachable target. The young faces he passed beamed with privilege; they shone with a confidence in the future that only those sheltered by money and pedigree and history could possibly possess. He hated them, every single one of them, hated their school, their parents, their ancestry, the elite colleges they would attend, the investment banks and law firms they would join, the privileged children they would spawn, their pasts and their futures. He hated their country.

He'd been to Saint Andrew's several months ago, before the New Hampshire primary, at Julian Mellow's behest. Lightstone had had no Secret Service protection then, and neither did his two sons, Alan, an eleventh-grader, and Brian, a freshman. It had taken a few hours of asking around to locate "his nephews'" rooms, and then he'd broken into them while the entire dorm was at class. Brian's room hadn't yielded anything of interest, but Alan's had.

He found the dorm he was looking for, climbed the stairs to the third floor, and knocked on a door at the end of a long corridor.

"Hold on," came an adolescent's croaky voice. He knocked again, only louder. "I said, hold on!"

Spencer Thornburgh was a pale, scrawny kid, wearing a white T-shirt and boxers covered in Red Sox logos. His hair was greasy, red pimples covered his cheeks, and his eyes glistened with a rheumy unhealthiness. Still, the way he looked at Billy, at once fearful of an adult's unexpected presence and utterly confident that nothing, in the long run, could harm him, suggested that Spencer Thornburgh was no scholarship kid.

"Spencer Thornburgh?"

"Yeah..." His hand never left the edge of the door, as if he were prepared to slam it shut. Taking no chances, Billy stepped forward, forcing the hand off the door by pressing his body into the boy's arm.

"Hey, what the—" Billy slammed the door behind him and shoved Spencer Thornburgh across the small, cluttered room and onto his unmade single bed. "What the hell do you want?"

Billy began opening drawers and tossing out their contents. Clothes, papers, condoms, cigarettes.

"Get up," he said, and when Spencer, eyes wide with fear, did nothing, he grabbed him by the shirt and flung him onto the floor. Then he lifted the mattress and tossed it against the wall.

"Not very original, Spence."

Lying on top of the bed's platform were about ten or twelve small bags of white powder, as well as what looked to be several thousand dollars in cash, neatly rubber-banded into wads of twenties and tens.

"It's not mine," he said quickly. "I had no idea that was there. Seriously, I don't know how that—"

"*Shut the fuck up.*"

Still sprawled on the floor, Spencer skittered a few feet away.

"Why do you do it, Spence?"

"I told you, I…"

Billy reached down, grabbed a fistful of white shirt and jerked Spencer to his feet. Then he slammed him against the wall, feeling the kid's warm breath gust out of his mouth.

"Why do you do it?"

"You have to believe me, I—"

Billy pulled Spencer toward him, then slammed him back into the wall.

"A simple question…"

"For the money, okay? For the money." He started to cry.

"Your father is a partner in some big-ass law firm in Boston, Spence. Plays golf with the mayor. You need money?"

"You know my father?" A new depth of terror had taken hold.

"Old man doesn't pay you enough, is that it?"

"You try living on a hundred bucks a month." Resentment added some vigor to Spencer's voice.

Billy looked around, taking in the new, top-of-the-line MacBook, the iPad, the Bose speakers, the big-screen television, the multiple pairs of $300 sneakers strewn across the floor. Killing Spencer at that moment would have been the easiest thing he'd ever done.

"Don't your folks wonder where you get this stuff?"

"Like they visit?"

Billy released the kid's shirt. Warily, Spencer circled him and sat on the bed.

"You a cop?"

"Not important. There's something I want you to do for me. Do it, and you'll never see me again. Don't do it, and your father gets a call."

"You want money? Coke? Here." Spencer grabbed a few wads of bills and an envelope.

Billy swung at his face, remembering at the very last instant to open his fist. Nevertheless, the slap sent Spencer onto his side, and when he righted himself he was sobbing. "What do you want from me?" he wailed.

"Tomorrow, I want you to sell some of this shit to Alan Lightstone." Spencer started to say something, then his mouth slackened. Billy could see it suddenly dawn on the kid that he'd gotten himself into something way bigger than selling drugs to friends to satisfy his electronics and footwear cravings.

"But he's the—"

"I know who he is."

"Anyway, he doesn't use this stuff."

Billy had found evidence to the contrary on his last visit to Saint Andrew's.

"I don't like it when people lie to me, especially rich punks like you."

"Okay, maybe once in a while. I mean, why are you…who are you…"

"Not your concern. Your concern is doing what I say and staying out of trouble."

"But Alan—Al, he's my friend, and his father…"

"You'll call him, tell him you have a new shipment, make him an offer, a good offer. Something he can't resist. And I want you to make sure he samples the goods."

"And then what, you're going to bust him or something?"

"Don't worry about me. And you won't be involved in whatever happens. Just set it up."

"I can't do that." His face was a mess of tears and snot.

"Come here," Billy said in a gentler voice. He took the boy's hand and pulled him off the bed. "Look, I understand that this isn't easy for you," he said gently when Spencer was standing. Then he bent back the index finger on the boy's left hand until he heard it snap. "But you'll find a way."

The boy howled as he danced from one foot to another.

"You'll need to see a doctor about your finger. Here's my cell number." He handed him a slip of paper. "When you have an appointment with Alan...*Al*...you'll call that number and tell me when and where. I want at least a few hours' notice. Make it for today or tomorrow. No later."

He walked toward the door but turned back just before leaving. "If you say anything to anyone, or fuck this up in any way, telling your father that young Spencer is a drug dealer will be the least of what I do. A broken finger will feel like a mosquito bite. You understand that, Spence?"

His face was so wet and mucusy it looked battered. He was staring at the broken index finger, transfixed.

"I asked you a question, Spence." Billy moved toward him.

"Yes, I understand," the boy whispered.

Billy opened the door, found the hallway deserted, and left.

## SATURDAY, OCTOBER 17

# CHAPTER 42

Emerging from the small, dark house into the harsh Caribbean sunshine was always a shock, physical and mental. The eyes felt the assault first, then the skin, and quickly even the nose picked up the dry, vaguely sinister scent of heat. But it was the mind that had the hardest time adjusting, even after nine months on Saint Sebastian. The astonishing aqua blue of the sea, framed by tall, arching palm trees on either side of the cove and by a sky whose blue was an embarrassingly pale cousin to the water below, was something you never really got used to. There was no tone in the mind's palette that came close to such brilliance.

Or perhaps it was simply the shock of remembering, each morning, after a dreamless tropical sleep, where he was. Zach Springer stood before the small, dark house and let his eyes adjust to the light. Then he did what he did every morning. He walked thirty yards from the house to the edge of the water and let the small waves lap over his bare feet. Yes, it was real. He was there.

Each morning, even after all these months, he had to trace the course of events that had brought him there, just to reassure himself that he hadn't been washed ashore from a passing freighter—or dropped from above by a spaceship. It always began the same way, with a tap on his rear bicycle tire, then a plunge down a cliffside that never ended, as far as he could recall, an onrush of green that grew thicker and denser and finally darkened to black. He'd awakened in a hospital room, one arm in a cast, bandages covering cuts on his face and legs, but otherwise okay. Then the call on his cell from Sarah, her voice almost unrecognizable.

"Zach, someone killed Jessica, Jessica Winter, in our apartment, she was in our apartment to walk Guinevere, and someone killed her and now the police—"

He became aware of a deep pain at the very center of his brain. It took everything he had to stay focused. "Where are you, Sarah?"

"In front of our building, they won't let me up, they thought it was me, they thought I was the one who was...where are you, Zach?"

"Listen to me, Sarah. You need to get out of there. Walk away, just walk away."

"There are police everywhere, they want to talk to me, they thought I was the one up there, in the apartment."

"Sarah, listen to me. Someone tried to kill me. The same person tried to kill you, too, only he got Jessica. When he realizes you're still alive he'll come after you again. You have to get out of there."

"Someone tried to kill you?"

"I'm all right, Sarah. But I'm not safe, and neither are you. You need to walk away from there." He gave her the address of the man in Washington Heights who'd helped him create Arthur Sandler. She'd need to become someone else too. "Just meet me there," he said when she started to ask why.

"The police will protect me." She sounded more scared than convinced.

"Not for long." He briefly thought of going public with what he knew, but he'd sound like a lunatic, accusing the richest man in America and a candidate for president of some ill-defined conspiracy that began with the murder in San Francisco. Besides, Julian Mellow *owned* the media, or a big chunk of it. They needed to disappear, at least for a while.

"Go to Washington Heights, right now."

There was a pause, then: "What about Guinevere?"

"She'll be okay," he said. "She'll be taken care of. We'll be back soon, Sarah, I promise, as soon as I have a plan, but right now we need to get away."

"Soon" had turned into nine months, and his "plan," if you could call it that, was to wait until the election was over and then resurface. Or maybe never go back. Arthur Sandler's checking and brokerage accounts contained about twenty-five thousand dollars, which went a long way on Saint Sebastian. The tiny house they rented on the island, where they'd vacationed five years earlier, was a few hundred a month. Eventually they'd need to find work, perhaps waiting tables at one of the island's two small resorts. Maybe he could work on a fishing boat. Would they ever feel safe anywhere else? Saint Sebastian was five miles long and less than a mile wide. In their short time there they'd gotten to know just about every inhabitant, who knew them as Arthur and Alison Sandler from Chicago. No one remembered the handsome vacationing couple who'd taken the ferry over from Saint Thomas five years earlier, happy to find an out-of-the-way, untouristed, somewhat down-at-heel refuge from the pressures of New York. At the time, he hadn't had a vacation in almost five years, and had walked out of a closing meeting after announcing to all assembled, including Julian Mellow, that he would be incommunicado for a week. He'd broken down only once, calling the office to find out if the deal has closed as expected. As punishment, Sarah had withheld sex for twenty-four hours.

"Some days, all I want to see is a cloud, one big, fluffy white cloud." Sarah stood next to him, wearing the swimsuit top and sarong that had become her uniform. He put his left arm around her bare middle, which felt smooth and warm and firm. Saint Sebastian's lone doctor had removed his cast nearly eight months earlier, but his left shoulder still felt stiff when he raised his arm. "Do you miss clouds, Zach?"

"Sometimes."

She nodded slowly. Sarah missed their old life more than he did. The apartment, her kids at school, Guinevere. She'd called her parents from the airport and told them that she and Zach were all right, that they were going away for a while. Nothing more, despite her parents' anxious pleas for information. That had been a tough phone call for her. For Zach, it was the lack of people to call that he'd felt the hardest. His parents were long dead, and he'd devoted himself so fanatically to Mellow Partners, and later to bringing down Julian Mellow, that he'd never developed a network of friends.

The newspapers kept the story of their disappearance alive for a week or so. The lurid slashing death of Jessica Winters, her body discovered when the braying yelps of Guinevere had caused an upstairs neighbor to call the police. Their disappearance had quickly pointed suspicion at them. The gist of the newspaper stories was always the same: Zach, the disgraced former investment hotshot, had killed his neighbor and dog walker, perhaps after his sexual advances had been rebuffed, then taken his bicycle to New Jersey, perhaps to establish his alibi, where his anxiety over being caught had caused him to lose control, sending him over the cliff. Or had it been a suicide attempt? Sarah's disappearance had puzzled the police. According to newspaper accounts, it was feared that Zach had killed her, too, but there was that phone call to her parents, assuring them that she was okay. Was she perhaps standing by her man, despite his misdeeds?

The story gradually retreated into the nether regions of the New York papers before disappearing altogether.

Sarah's rage had taken longer to subside, and had never completely gone away. At the forger's apartment in Washington Heights that first day: *You put us in danger, you almost got us killed, you got Jessica killed, now what are we going to do?* He'd been unable to take even the smallest consolation in the fact that now, at long last, she knew that his theories about Julian were not obsessive fantasies.

Every day on Saint Sebastian for at least a month: *Don't talk to me. Don't touch me. You were supposed to leave. Instead you put us at risk, put me at risk.*

And then, after that awful first month: *How do we get out of this place? When will we be safe?*

Several thousand dollars in cash, a credit card, their driver's licenses, were in a safety deposit box in Saint Thomas. They'd brought only what they absolutely needed to Saint Sebastian. No one knew where they were, but Zach had learned the importance, the absolute necessity, of having a Plan B. Their Plan B was that small steel box in Saint Thomas. Sarah wore the key on the chain around her neck that had formerly held the silver heart he'd given her two years earlier.

They'd grown close again, perhaps inevitably, given their isolation. Most days he convinced himself that their relationship was better than it ever had been, but he also knew that she was suppressing anger and fear and that these would never go away as long as they remained on the island. She'd lost everything because of him. Everything *except* him. Until they were back home, and safe, she'd never truly forgive him, if then.

"Well, less than three weeks and we can go home," she said. When he didn't respond she said, more emphatically, "Three more weeks until Election Day, and then we can go home."

"I still think I should do something."

"Listen to me, Zach. There is nothing you can do or say about the election that will change anything, other than get us killed."

She needed to believe that after Election Day it would be safe to return to New York. The president was holding on to a 10 percent lead in the polls, which was a landslide by modern election standards. So Harry Lightstone would fail, Julian Mellow's dreams of pulling the Oval Office strings would be thwarted, and they could resume the life they'd left behind last spring.

Only he sometimes wondered if they ever would be safe. If Julian knew that Zach had discovered the connection between Harry Lightstone and Senator Moore's plane crash, the death of that hooker in San Francisco, would he leave him and Sarah alone? And Zach was the prime suspect in the murder of Jessica Winter. Still, they couldn't stay on Saint Sebastian indefinitely, or at least Sarah couldn't. So he'd convinced himself, more or less, that after Election Day they could return. He'd have to convince the police that he hadn't killed Jessica—Sarah would back him up. And he would find a way to confront Julian directly with what he knew. He'd deposit a written account of everything he knew with attorneys, perhaps, who would release it to the press if anything happened to him or Sarah. Maybe he'd even be able to get some money from Julian.

"After Election Day," he said, trying to sound as if he meant it.

## SUNDAY, OCTOBER 18

# CHAPTER 43

The envelope was dropped off by messenger and brought up to the master bedroom by the Lightstone's New York maid. It was marked "Urgent," but the hour of its delivery, just after nine in the evening, made the case for urgency just as well. Marcella opened the envelope and took out a thumb drive and a handwritten note: *Include in tonight's address: "Withdraw the Kamalian embassy and all American nationals to protect their safety. Any other course irresponsible."*

There was no signature, nor was one needed.

"Absurd," she muttered—to herself, for Harry was campaigning in Seattle, where she was to join him tomorrow for the first day of a final swing by bus (bus!) across country, west to east. "Time to move past your son's death, Julian," she said to no one. "The campaign is in enough trouble as it is."

Nevertheless, she put the thumb drive into her laptop, made herself comfortable on the bed, and clicked on the only file that appeared, expecting to see images of Kamalian rebels or political prisoners or perhaps Julian himself, arguing the case for making Kamalia a campaign issue, which he was never going to win. His influence over the campaign was nonexistent.

But it wasn't Kamalia, unless Kamalia was a country of white-shuttered brick buildings covered with red and brown ivy. How odd. As the camera jerked its way from one building to another she slowly recognized Saint Andrew's. She sat up and increased the volume, but all she heard was footsteps on a leaf-strewn path. The camerawork was jerky but the focus was quite clear.

After what amounted to a guided tour of the beautiful Saint Andrew's campus the screen went momentarily blank, then came to life again on two people, at first blurry. After a few seconds the image focused and she saw Alan and another boy, standing next to what looked like the back of a building, another brick building. Alan had on his uniform, a blue blazer with the Saint Andrew's crest on the front pocket and gray slacks. His blue tie hung loosely over an untucked white shirt. The boy standing with him was not quite as tall as Alan, and much scrawnier. He wore an identical uniform, and when he moved she noticed a flash of white on his left hand, a large bandage or perhaps a splint. The video was now perfectly still, as if the cameraman were using a tripod.

Again, she upped the volume; this time she managed to make out voices.

"No, you have to try this shit."

"I trust you, Spence. I got calculus in ten minutes."

"One hit, seriously, Al, it's fucking amazing."

She now saw that the other boy, Spence, held a very small clear bag in this right hand.

"What happened to your hand?"

"Long story short, I fell on it."

"Asshole."

"One hit, that's it." She saw Al take the plastic bag from Spence. It was one-fourth filled with what seemed to be, even in the grainy video, white powder.

"Fuck!" she said as she pulled the laptop screen closer.

Al dipped his index finger into the bag and pressed it to his nostril. His entire torso distended as he sucked in the powder. For a long minute the two boys just stood there, glancing about somewhat awkwardly. Then Alan's face slowly relaxed into a smile, and he let out a long, audible sigh. "The fuck am I going to concentrate on calculus?" he said.

"Good stuff, right? Take another hit." He held out the bag.

Alan snorted a second dab of powder.

"This is the purest cocaine I've had in, like, a year," Spence said.

There was something artificial in the way he uttered the last line, as if he were reading from a script. The use of "cocaine" rather than "coke" sounded off, for example. His diction felt stilted. She recalled hearing about all sorts of drugs being used at the best boarding schools, including cocaine and even heroin, but it had never once occurred to her that her own son would be tempted. He was a straight-A student, on the varsity lacrosse team.

"How much?" Alan asked after two more hits.

"One twenty-five."

"What?"

"It's practically pure cocaine, Alan." Again, his voice sounded forced, lingering on the words "cocaine" and "Alan."

She saw her son reach into his pants pocket and pull out a clump of bills. He counted out several and thrust them at Spence, who handed him the plastic envelope.

"Man, you were right, this shit is unreal, I think I'm gonna cut calc, I'll get the notes from someone. Or maybe I'll send one of those goons the feds keep around to protect me. You think the

Secret Service can do calculus?" Alan found this very funny, but not Spence, who glanced around anxiously.

"Speaking of Secret Service, you're sure they're not—"

"Watching? They're under orders to stay a hundred yards away from me and Brian, unless I'm attacked."

"Yeah, well, I got a class."

"Great, I'll walk with you."

As they moved off camera she heard Spence tell Alan to "be cool," and then the screen went black.

She sat on the bed for a while, immobilized by rage and sadness, unable to choose between two opposing impulses: walk three blocks up Fifth Avenue and claw out the eyes of Julian Mellow; or drive two hours north and throttle Alan. Instead, when she was able to move, she reached for the bedside phone and dialed. Fred Moran answered.

"Get Harry."

"He's putting the finishing touches on tonight's speech to the Coalition for Families, Marcella. I don't think it's a good idea to—"

"Get him!"

A moment later a tired-sounding Harry asked her what she wanted.

"Tonight's speech—you need to make a small change."

# CHAPTER 44

Julian Mellow watched the address on the television in his study. Most of it was familiar and uninteresting, though it had to be acknowledged that Lightstone had improved his delivery. Another six months or so and he might actually be a viable candidate. As it was, with less than two weeks to go, he was stalled at 10 percent behind Nessin, which meant it would take a miracle to turn things around.

"When Americans are in harm's way, the buck stops in

the Oval Office," Lightstone was saying to the fifteen hundred "family advocates" gathered in Seattle for their annual boondoggle. Middle-aged, middle American, and virtually all white, they were united by a few simple beliefs that Lightstone had already touched on. "As president I will take personal responsibility for every American posted abroad, whether in our armed services, in our diplomatic service, or in the service of our great global economy. I do not sense the same resolve in my opponent. Why else would he allow more than fifty US nationals to continue to reside in Kamalia, including our ambassador and his young family, when intelligence reports clearly indicate that this is a volatile situation that could erupt into violence against Americans at any time. I call for the immediate evacuation of every American from Kamalia. I say to the president, do not wait for the election to do the right thing. Let's take politics off the table. Protect American citizens by getting them out of Kamalia!"

The reaction from the family advocates was underwhelming, to say the least. There was some tepid applause, which Lightstone's impassioned delivery all but required, but as the C-SPAN camera panned across the audience, the expressions were more puzzled than convinced. Apparently family values didn't extend to protecting families, even American families, in Africa. Julian turned off the TV. They would all know soon enough that miracles did happen. Puzzlement would turn to conviction soon enough. He left the room.

"You look upset," Caroline said when he entered the bedroom. She was reading on the bed.

"Do I?" He went to her dressing room and looked into the large mirror over her vanity. It was true that he'd lost what little summer tan he'd acquired, and he'd lost weight since the campaign—his campaign—began, which perhaps made his face look a bit drawn. Well, he felt stressed. All of the work he'd been doing for nine months was coming to a head—the next two weeks would determine if he'd acted in vain. A part of him yearned to tell Caroline what he was doing, but she'd be more appalled than supportive, he guessed. Worse, she would remind him that even if he succeeded, nothing would change.

Everything was falling into place, so why the obvious stress? He had assumed that his little victory that night in the power struggle with the Lightstones would relax him a bit. It hadn't. For almost nine months, since the New Hampshire primary, one fact had tormented him every waking hour and even in his dreams.

Zach Springer was alive.

Zach Springer, unlike Caroline—unlike anyone except perhaps Billy Sandifer—knew what Julian was doing, or knew enough to be dangerous. Where had he gone? And the girl was with him… how could two people disappear without a trace? A week of lurid headlines had completely unsettled him: "West Side Woman Murdered: Disgraced Banker Suspected" was typical. He'd been called by a dozen papers, as Zach's last employer, the head of the firm he'd betrayed. The "surrogate father," he'd been labeled. He'd had no comment, of course, but each call carried with it the threat of discovery. The calls and the headlines had trailed off with lack of fresh news, but anxiety had taken root like a dull, persistent ache. Nothing in his life was ever left to chance.

He got into bed, closed his eyes and drifted into a light, restless sleep. But all night, like every night for six months, he woke frequently with one question on his mind: *Where were they?*

When threatened, people run to the familiar—so where would Zach run? He'd had Billy Sandifer, whose carelessness had created this situation, check customs records, local hotels, phone records of every place Zach had ever been for business or pleasure. Nothing. Billy Sandifer had even staked out Sarah's parents on Long Island. Nothing.

Sleep came in small, unsatisfying segments, filled with troubling dreams. He tried to focus on Lightstone's speech, and what it would mean to the campaign, but any small satisfaction he felt was pushed aside by thoughts of Zach Springer. The references to his "surrogate son" were particularly galling. Zach had never meant a fraction of what Matthew had. True, he had spent far more time with Zach, an employee, than with Matthew, who'd spent his last years an ocean away. And even before Kamalia, Matt had felt the need to go his own way, forge his own identity. But what son didn't feel that need? They'd been close, very close.

Or had they? Dark thoughts of Matthew, stirred up by memories of another young man, haunted his waking moments. He'd worked so hard, all those years when Matthew was growing up. Had he ever been there in the mornings, before school? How many nights had he come home after Matt's homework was done? Well, it wasn't about the amount of time spent together but the quality. They'd taken trips together, box seats at Yankee Stadium—once they'd played golf in Connecticut. And he'd often told Matt that he loved him.

Or had he? Over the past two years he'd silently whispered those words to Matt so often that they had become memories of conversations that may or may not have taken place. So many long, sleepless nights, silent whispers telegraphed across time.

And then, as the faint, yellowy light of dawn began to creep around the edges of the bedroom drapes, he had a thought. A memory. He crept from the bedroom to his study and dialed his secretary's home phone number. After three rings Stacy picked up.

"I need you at my office," he said.

"Now? But it's—" She paused, no doubt consulting the bed-side clock. She was paid $250,000 a year to do what he asked without question, to be available whenever he needed her, so her next words came as no surprise or even comfort to him. "I'll be there in half an hour."

MONDAY, OCTOBER 19

# CHAPTER 45

At six in the morning, faint light from neighboring skyscrapers, just detectable through the south-facing window, cast an eerie glow over the Mellow Partners reception area. Stacy Young stood just inside his office, dressed for the day in a conservative blue suit, her hair neatly pulled back in a discreet ponytail. Only the dark circles under her eyes indicated that this was not the start of an ordinary workday, which for her typically began at eight o'clock.

"How far back do we keep phone logs?" he asked her.

She took a deep, disappointed breath at his failure to acknowledge her early arrival. "Five years, sometimes longer, depending on the deal."

As he'd expected. Every bit of paperwork connected with an acquisition was retained in the event of a shareholder suit or SEC investigation, which were rare but unpleasant potential side effects of any transaction in the current environment. Typically, the paperwork, including phone messages, was kept several years after a company had been divested, just in case. Emails were stored on remote servers.

"Good. Get the phone records for the Alden deal, all of them." Alden Industries was one of the world's largest manufacturers of office furniture. Mellow Partners had acquired it after a very intense, three-way struggle five years earlier. It had been Zach Springer's last deal before the Finnegan fiasco, and he'd performed magnificently, crafting and recrafting strategies for outmaneuvering the other two bidders, working round the clock. Then, hours after the other two players conceded defeat, he'd charged into Julian's office to announce that he was leaving for vacation, his first since joining the firm. "What if I need you?" Julian had asked. "You won't, it's a done deal." He'd reminded Zach that no deal was ever "done" until all the paperwork was finalized. "It could still fall apart," he said. "It won't," Zach had insisted. Even Julian had to concede that Zach looked exhausted, his handsome face wan and drawn, his frame more spindly than lean. And though he'd never been a toady, a quality that had made him unique within the Mellow organization and especially valuable to Julian, his willful, almost insubordinate insistence on a vacation indicated that he had reached the end of his rope. "Okay, then. Leave a phone number with Stacy in case there's no cell service," he'd said as Zach headed for the door. "No, Julian, I need to go somewhere where you can't find me," Zach had said as he left.

*I need to go somewhere where you can't find me.* He'd refused to leave a number, so while Julian had suspected he might return to wherever he'd gone, he had no idea where that might be. Then last night, a memory.

"This is everything," Stacy said, entering his office with a pile of folders.

"I want phone messages, phone bills…"

She plunked the pile on his desk and selected two files. "These are the incoming messages, and this file—"

He grabbed the first file. Inside was a wire-bound notebook, each of its hundred or so pages containing three carbon-copied phone messages, the originals having been placed by Stacy on his desk and then discarded by him. He had no voicemail, insisting that callers leave word with Stacy, who more often than not could redirect their calls to someone else in the organization. He flipped quickly through the notebook: messages from investment bankers, from the CEO of Alden, from attorneys at the three firms he'd retained to advise him, from the head of the investor relations firm that had handled the media. You could read the entire history of the contentious transaction from those messages, some marked "urgent," some containing bits of information (*Suggests increase in cash portion of offer; please advise ASAP*). And then, just two pages before the end, the message he'd been waiting for.

*Zach called for status of Alden deal.*

Yes, Zach had needed to get away, but he couldn't resist calling in to see if the deal had closed. Why had it taken him so many months to recall this single fact? You couldn't turn your back on three months of grueling work and more than three and a half billion dollars, no matter how exhausted you were. If Zach needed to escape again, and in a hurry, it made sense that he'd return to a place he'd already been, a place he didn't think anyone else knew about.

"Stacy!"

She hurried back into his office. He read her the phone number on the message. It looked like an American exchange.

"Find out where this call came from," he said. She left and returned a few minutes later.

"It's in the US Virgin Islands," said the ever resourceful Stacy. "As best I can tell, it's a tiny island off Saint Thomas called Saint Sebastian."

"Shut the door on the way out," he said. As soon as she was gone he picked up the phone and dialed Billy Sandifer.

# CHAPTER 46

Sophie DuVal woke up with the sun, as she always did, and after a quick cup of coffee she spent thirty minutes exercising in the living room of her tiny house near the center of Villeneuve. There were no health clubs in Kamalia, just a handful of dingy, poorly equipped gyms, none of which welcomed female members. After stretching she went through her usual routine: a variety of sit-ups, then push-ups, and then, using heavy books, she improvised a few resistance moves: lunges, squats, curls, raises. Midway through her regimen there was a knock at her front door. She opened it a crack and then almost fell backward when someone pushed it in. A moment later Claude DuMarier was standing inside her living room.

"Who the hell do you think you are, shoving your way in here?"

"I am head of the secret police of the Republic of Kamalia," he said without smiling. His eyes appraised the tube top and spandex shorts she had on, relics from her membership in a posh gym in New York.

"I cannot be seen standing outside the front door of the house of a known insurgent," he said as she went to her bedroom and put on a sweatshirt, though it was hardly chilly. "It was necessary to enter as soon as possible."

She knew better: petty displays of pointless power were a mainstay of the Boymond regime, which felt puny and impotent on the global scene, even in comparison to its African neighbors, and so lost no opportunity to flex its near-atrophied muscles before its powerless citizens.

She nodded to the sofa, the best she could do in the way of hospitality. After a moment's hesitation he sat down.

"To what do I owe the honor of a visit from such a distinguished member of our government?"

He patted the sofa next to him. She took a chair across the room. Frowning, he began to speak. "One week from Saturday, at noon exactly, there will be a small ceremony at the presidential palace. His Excellency has called the entire cabinet and all the generals together."

"The three-year anniversary…"

"Of our glorious revolution, yes."

She had to glance away. The *glorious revolution* had taken Matthew and transformed her from a complex person with interests in many things—art, music, politics, sex—into a one-dimensional radical.

"There will be no public celebrations, like last year." A year earlier, a ragtag group of protesters had tried to disrupt the anniversary ceremony, a pathetic little pageant held in front of the palace and attended by high-ranking government officials. Security forces had turned on the unarmed protesters with semiautomatic weapons, killing three young men and arresting dozens more. Sophie had not been among those arrested, but the debacle had been a turning point for her, convincing her that organized, armed conflict would be the only way to bring down the Le Père regime.

"Wise decision," she said.

He acknowledged her sarcasm with a small nod. "At twelve fifteen I will arrange to have the palace guard assemble on the west lawn for a training exercise. There will be no men at the south gate, which will be unlocked. Even so, I trust you could handle a small contingent of guards, given the contents of your armory."

She felt a shiver of vulnerability—how much did he know about the group's weapons?

"Once you are inside the walls," he continued, "you will proceed across the courtyard to the bronze doors. These doors are six inches thick and quite impenetrable. Inexcusably, someone will have left them unbolted. You will open these doors and proceed up the staircase, which you will see directly in front. This will take you to the long second-floor hallway. The first door on your right—"

"Is the presidential reception room. I have been there many times." She and Matthew had been invited to numerous official events under the old regime.

"There you will find the entire power structure of Kamalia. Perhaps one or two personal bodyguards, but nothing substantial. I trust you will be merciful."

"We do not plan to kill anyone unless we have to. They will be arrested and afforded all the rights they have denied to the people."

"That is very noble of you. Personally, I would kill them all."

"How much is he paying you?"

"Paying?"

"Julian Mellow."

"Enough to start a new life in France. An apartment in the *huitième arrondissement*, perhaps the *seizième*, something small but comfortable in the south, perhaps the Riviera, perhaps Provence. I am accustomed to a warm climate. And of course there is the pride in knowing that I have helped to restore *democracy* in my country." He pronounced *democracy* with a slight upturn of one side of his mouth, as if it were a quaint custom he was helping to bring back.

"You are certain that things will unfold as you have said?"

"Completely. You only have to show up at twelve fifteen exactly. How many men—excuse me, *people* will you have?"

"We will be at least a hundred," she said, though in fact she suspected that no more than seventy-five would heed the call to arms.

"That should be sufficient. Once you have the generals in custody, the soldiers will head home. Many of them have not been paid in months, they stay only out of fear. And of course you will have no problems with the palace guard. If something does go wrong—and it won't—I have arranged to have the service gate of the US embassy left unlocked, as we already discussed. You and your comrades will be safe there."

He stood up and she did the same.

"I will be assured passage out of this hellhole at the earliest possible time," he said.

"I cannot offer you that assurance," she said. "Once we have control, we—"

"No, no," he said with a patronizing smile. "Arrangements will already have been made."

"No doubt that was part of the agreement."

"Perhaps you will join me?"

"You have a wife," she said, although his having a wife was the least of his detractions.

He sighed heavily. "Matthew Mellow was a lucky man."

"Hardly."

"Oh, yes, I see," he said with a chuckle. "Lucky in love, though." He extended his hand and, forcing herself to concentrate on all that DuMarier was doing for the movement, never mind his motives, she took it.

"Until next week," he said, then let himself out.

## TUESDAY, OCTOBER 23

# CHAPTER 47

Mellow Partners occupied the fifty-ninth and sixtieth floors at 14 West 57th Street, a small amount of space considering the large swath of the world economy the firm controlled. Maintaining a lean operation had always been important to Julian Mellow. He acquired companies that were undervalued, which more often than not meant that their management teams were bloated and incompetent. Once he had control he cleaned house, employing legions of lawyers to unravel the employment contracts that rewarded second-rate performance, and installed his own team of executives, incentivizing them with employment contracts that, if they achieved the ambitious financial goals he imposed on them, and only if they achieved them, would make them fantastically wealthy. They almost always got fantastically wealthy. He believed in hiring the best and then leaving them alone—thus, the small scale of the home office.

He preferred to communicate by email and phone, even with managers who worked down the hall. He wasn't much of a "people person," that awful phrase; in fact, he sometimes felt that his inability—or perhaps unwillingness—to relate on a personal level to business associates was what had made him successful. He could evaluate anyone with a dispassionate eye, and he never mistook greed and ambition for loyalty—the downfall of many people in business. His phone calls were always taken at the highest levels of business and government, even if he never asked about this one's battle with cancer or that one's daughter's college choice.

So he wasn't the least bit surprised to see a look of both astonishment and alarm come over the face of Grace Carr when he walked into her office. In the six years since he'd hired her to manage Mellow Partners' technology infrastructure, he'd never once set foot in her office, with its view across 57th Street of the midtown Manhattan skyline.

"Mr. Mellow, how are you?" she said. "I mean, come in, please, have a seat."

Given her extensive expertise in the latest networking and data storage technologies, Grace Carr was unexpectedly frumpy. At fifty-six, she had short, salt-and-pepper hair and carried an extra twenty pounds or so on her small frame. As proficient as she was with technology, she was hopeless with makeup, slathering far too much foundation and eyeliner on what would otherwise be a rather sweet, accessible face. The credenza behind her desk held framed photographs of her two sons, both in college, and her husband, who had been laid off six months ago by the insurance company he'd worked for since college. He knew all this because earlier that day he'd asked Stacy to update him on Grace's life. A newly unemployed husband could be useful.

"I'm here about Searchlight," Julian said as he sat across from her. "It's come to my attention that there may be some irregularities concerning certain investments they've made."

"I see," she said, smiling faintly.

Searchlight Investments was an asset management firm that Mellow Partners had acquired several years back when the mortgage meltdown led to the collapse of the stock market. Searchlight had made its mark with shrewd investments in bank stocks and had branched out into unrelated sectors, attracting billions in capital from pension funds and wealthy individuals who were drawn to its successful track record. But when banks fell into a slump, the firm found itself facing massive withdrawals, and had turned to Mellow Partners. Julian had played hardball, purchasing Searchlight for about twenty cents on the dollar.

"You handle the email accounts for all of our investments," Julian said.

"That's correct."

"If I wanted to monitor the email activity of key Searchlight executives, you could get me into the system?"

"That would be unethical." Her right hand began to fiddle with her mouse.

"It's ethics I'm concerned about. There have been insinuations that some of the firm's funds have been traded for the personal gain of the principals."

"Then perhaps an investigation firm should be—"

"This cannot leave Mellow Partners," he said slowly. "I won't allow it to. You are aware that Searchlight's investors include many prominent people."

"Including the vice president's blind trust."

Evan Smith had placed roughly half of the twenty million dollars he'd made in the construction business into a blind trust managed by Searchlight. To avoid potential conflicts of interest, he was given no information about where his money was invested, and was not allowed to direct Searchlight investment managers on where to invest.

"Precisely. If there were the slightest hint of a scandal it could bring down Searchlight. I would like to monitor the email of the top two or three executives to determine for myself if there is cause for concern. Can this be done?"

"Yes, of course it *can* be done; it's not a question of *can* but of *should*."

"Actually, Grace, it's a question of *when*."

Her eyes glanced ever so briefly at the photo of her family. "Please don't ask me to do this," she said quietly.

"I have no choice. Just as you have no choice about paying tuition bills."

She waited a long moment before speaking. "What exactly are you looking for?"

"It's best that you don't get any more involved in this than you already are. I need to monitor several email accounts. I'll provide you with the names. I would also like to be able to send emails under the names of these individuals."

"But that's completely—"

He stood up. "Please arrange for this by end of day. I'd prefer you stop by my office with the details. The less we commit to writing, the better. Email isn't nearly as secure as it would seem, is it?" In fact, at financial institutions, every email sent or received was archived in remote servers, in case the SEC or some other regulator came calling. "I'll see you later, then."

Her face, already pale behind all that foundation and eyeliner, had lost every trace of color.

• • •

# CHAPTER 48

The chartered Challenger 300—two pilots, one passenger—touched down at Saint Thomas's Cyril E. King Airport at noon. Billy Sandifer checked his watch. His goal was to take the plane back to Teterboro, then a quick visit with Rebecca, then home. Travel always made him want to see her. As the plane taxied to the terminal, he felt trapped in an alien world in which people looked forward to swimming in warm blue water, dining by candlelight, sleeping late next to loved ones. He'd forgotten such a world existed—or had he ever known?

He deplaned, walked quickly across the airport, and jumped in a taxi, which he directed to the Red Hook marina. There, he hired a small, rundown charter boat outfitted for deep-sea fishing. He offered the captain double the usual rate for the entire vessel, on the condition that he be allowed to take the boat out on his own. When this was met with understandable resistance he offered him ten times the usual charter, which was probably not far short of what the boat was worth, and they struck a deal.

Saint Sebastian was roughly twenty miles south of Saint Thomas, a three-hour trip across calm turquoise waters. Billy had downloaded a nautical map off the internet. There were only two hotels on the island, he'd learned; both relied on a scheduled ferry to transport guests from Saint Thomas. There was no one registered at either place under the name Springer, though he doubted Zach would use his own name. He also doubted that Zach had the cash to stay at a hotel for six months. He was probably renting a place, assuming he was even on the island.

Billy did his best to ignore the spectacular seascape around him, aqua water dotted with tiny, lush green volcanic islands. Beauty so insistent was an affront, it enraged him, and rage was a distraction he couldn't afford. He briefly wondered if the plutocrats whose homes he had trashed, first for the fun of it, as a kid, later in the name of protest, vacationed in places like Saint Sebastian while children stitched their sneakers and backpacks and T-shirts for pennies an hour across the Caribbean in Central America. He forced such thoughts from his mind. He needed a clear head. The three hours felt like three long days until he finally put in at the small marina on the eastern edge of Saint Sebastian. On the map the island looked like a football, fat in the middle and tapering off at the ends. No more than five miles long, it rose spectacularly from the sea, a mass of craggy green mountains ringed by narrow white beaches, all deserted.

A handful of boats bobbed in the marina, all of them small and none in very good repair. After tying up, Billy put on a pair of over-sized dark sunglasses and approached the first and only person he saw, a dark-skinned black man sitting in the bow of a small sport fishing boat. He showed him a photo of Zach and his girlfriend, clipped from an article in the *New York Post* about Jessica Winter's murder.

"Everybody know them," the man said, and Billy felt an enormous relief. "Art and Alison. We don't have too many white folks here, besides the tourists at the hotels, and they don't come here to this side of the island much."

"Yes, Art and Alison. Did they ever mention their last names?"

"No," he said, and squinted at Billy. "Why you want them people?"

"They're old friends, from New York."

The man looked him up and down. He would be an important witness, as would the charter captain in Saint Thomas and perhaps the crew on the jet flying down. But he hadn't needed a passport to enter Saint Thomas and had no reason to think his true identity would ever be associated with a killing on a remote Caribbean island. Only Zach Springer and his girlfriend would know why he was there.

"Can you tell me where to find them?"

"You see this road?" He pointed to strip of pitted asphalt a few yards from the end of the dock. "You take this road, going west. First, it snakes around that large white house with green shutters."

"They live there?"

The man gave a big laugh. "No, man, that the governor's house. Your friends live two houses down, on the beach side."

"How long a walk is it?"

"Long walk, fifteen, twenty minutes."

"Can you give me a lift?"

"Of course I can, if I have a car!"

"I'll walk, then."

"You ride a bicycle?"

Five minutes later and ten dollars poorer, Billy Sandifer set off, his small leather bag, which contained a Japanese Arisaka sniper rifle, with muzzle, disassembled in five parts, looped over the handlebars.

• • •

Zach lay down on the warm sand in front of their small house, still wearing the T-shirt, shorts, and sandals he'd put on for the walk into town, where he'd bought provisions for the day. He closed his eyes against the brutal, early afternoon sun. Perhaps he should join Sarah, who was snorkeling above the reef fifty yards offshore. She often spent an hour or more floating in the warm water over the colorful reef, letting the gentle current move her slowly east, toward the governor's house on the other side of the small peninsula that jutted into the sea. But the walk to town and hot sun had drained him of the energy required to stand up and amble the twenty feet to the water's edge. He'd take a short nap instead—he napped a lot on Saint Sebastian—and when he awoke perhaps then he'd join her.

But a faint rustling pulled him back from the edge of sleep. A lizard skittering through the brush at the edge of the beach, probably; they had a way of intruding at the worse possible moment. Last night—or was it the night before?—one had scuttled across the wall next to their bed just as their lovemaking was reaching its climax; Sarah, who had never quite gotten used to the tiny lizards, among other tropical vicissitudes, had gasped and rolled off him and, after he'd made a valiant but vain attempt to track down the lizard, had begun to press him, as she did most days, about their plans for leaving the island.

So he didn't, at first, pay much attention to the rustling. But a moment later he heard it again, and something about the sound, an unlizardy heaviness, activated a vigilance that had never entirely left him, not even after nine months on the island. He sat up abruptly and turned to face the back of the beach just as an explosion erupted from somewhere in the brush.

He threw himself to the side, away from the sound, even before his mind processed the fact that what he'd heard was a muffled gunshot. He rolled and then crawled quickly across the hot sand toward the stand of palm trees and low shrubbery that separated their small beach from the governor's property.

There was a second explosion and an eruption of sand just to his left. He rose to a squat and sprinted toward the trees like a monkey, hands on the ground stabilizing him as he went. He stood up only when he'd managed to put a slender palm tree between him and the source of the shots, which was still invisible to him. He glanced behind him and saw Sarah floating obliviously over the reef, then back at the edge of the beach, trying to locate the assailant. The absurdly thin palm would offer little protection once the assassin regrouped. None of the trees would save him. His only option was to run through the small palm forest to the governor's house and hope that someone there would let him in before he took a bullet in his back. But what about Sarah? She was in as much danger as he was; any minute she might decide to head to shore, an easy, slow-moving target as she strolled onto the beach.

So he ran for the water, zigzagging as he went. There was another gunshot, this one ending in a dull explosion as the bullet hit a tree. At the water's edge he dove right in, protecting his face from the sand with his outthrust arms but badly scraping his chest and stomach. A bullet pierced the water to his right. He swam underwater as long as he could, broke the surface for a split second to gulp air, then went under again. No gunshot. He managed to reach the reef in only three breaths, and when he touched Sarah she jerked, startled, and started to take off her mask and breathing tube. He put a hand on the top of her head and pressed her back under water. A second later he let her come to the surface. Before she could speak he said: "Gunfire…the beach."

She glanced toward shore. Again, he pressed her head into the water. This time he pulled her in the direction of the governor's house. When they broke the surface for air he managed to say "Governor's house…boat" before once more forcing her face underwater. He had no idea if the sniper could reach them, nor if he even knew which direction they were swimming. What choice did they have? They couldn't head to shore, and the other direction was open sea. Their only chance was to make it to the governor's dock.

They swam as quickly as they could, underwater as much possible. Sarah, with a breathing tube and fins, moved much faster. When she turned to wait for him he shouted, "Don't wait! Go!" He did his best to keep up, only once giving into the temptation to look back toward their beach. He saw the gunman, now standing in the open at the water's edge, peering in their direction. He raised the rifle but didn't fire, apparently doubtful that his targets were within range. Although he could walk faster than they could swim, there was still the possibility that they could make it to the dock before him. For one thing, the road that connected the governor's property to their house (former house, he thought, aware of a sense of regret even as his continued to breaststroke and frog-kick under the water's surface, trying to formulate a strategy) wound inland for several hundred yards before heading back toward the sea, and it took a circuitous path around the governor's property before reaching the tiny marina. The assassin's need to circle the property would buy them precious time.

They rounded the small peninsula between their beach (former beach) and the governor's house, whose dock jutted twenty or so yards into the sea. Two small motorboats bobbed on the side nearest them; on the other side was moored a somewhat larger boat that the governor used to ferry himself and his family to and from Saint Thomas. There was a fourth boat, close in side to the governor's, that Zach had never seen before.

Sarah was a good twenty yards ahead of him, already swimming toward land. But he was gaining on her and he hoped she had enough left to swim the full distance. He had little to spare himself. As exhaustion began to set in, the water, always tropically warm, began to feel cool, almost cold, and he found himself breaking the surface for more and more frequent gulps or air.

"Head for the bigger boat," he managed to call out to Sarah when they both broke surface together. He noticed that the lawn between the governor's house and the water was deserted. There was no beach, just a manmade stone bulkhead that rose about three feet from the surface of the water at high tide.

Several long minutes later Sarah reached the larger boat, which concealed her presence from the shore, and treaded water while waiting for him to catch up.

"Zach, what—"

"I was on the beach...almost asleep...then shots."

"But no one...knows we're here."

"Someone does."

"How?"

He didn't know and didn't have time to figure it out. "Wait here." He swam to the bow of the boat, grabbed onto the dock, and pulled himself up, slowly craning his head around. Still no one on the lawn. He fell back into the water and swam to Sarah.

"Melvin!" he called out. "MELVIN!"

The boat rocked as if in response and a few moments later a large man was peering down at them from the side of the boat.

"My brother," Melvin said. Whenever they met, Melvin always called Zach "my brother." Zach had never asked why he used the vaguely religious address, though he had seen Melvin, dressed in suit and tie and in a state of rare sobriety, attend Sunday services at the island's sole house of worship, a Pentecostal church. And Zach didn't press him for an explanation.

"Help us out of the water!" Zach managed to say as he tried to catch his breath.

"What in heavens you doing down there, man?" Melvin sounded woozy, as if he'd either just woken up, had an early morning drink, or both. He was retained as captain by the governor—an undemanding job, to be sure—because he was somehow related to the governor's wife. On Saint Sebastian, everyone was somehow related to just about everyone else.

"Just get us onto the boat. Please. Alison first."

Melvin shrugged and leaned over, extending a hand to Sarah. He was a powerfully built man and, with Zach helping by pressing her up from her legs, he had no difficulty lifting her into the boat.

"Stay down!" Zach said. "Is there anyone on the shore?"

"No one," Sarah answered.

Zach grabbed the side of the boat and managed to pull himself partway up. Sarah and Melvin reached over the side and grabbed Zach's arms and dragged him the rest of the way onto the boat.

"My brother, you nearly give me heart attack, me thinking the fish are calling my name. Now I see it is a mermaid." He leered at Sarah, who had on a bikini. She was shivering, and Zach realized that he, too, was cold from exhaustion, despite the strong midday sun. He saw a small pile of towels on a bench near the pilot's chair and took two, giving one to Sarah.

"We need to get to Saint Thomas, Melvin. Can you take us there?"

"On the governor's boat? You know that is not allowed, my brother. Only the governor and his family use this boat. And his friends, sometimes." His laugh engaged his entire body in a rocking motion; everyone on the island was a friend of the governor. Everyone, unfortunately, except Art and Alison, who were not only newcomers but had kept resolutely to themselves.

"Please, we have to get off the island," Sarah said.

Melvin gave her shivering body a long, lustful examination and then went into the small cabin at the front of the boat, returning a moment later with a bottle of dark rum.

"Why you in such a hurry all of a sudden?" He took a copious swig of rum and offered the bottle to Zach and then Sarah.

"Once we get to Saint Thomas we can pay you," Zach said. "Whatever you want."

"You think money change my mind?" He frowned and drank more rum. "How much money you got?"

"Just what's in my wallet." Zach patted his back pocket and hoped the saltwater hadn't destroyed the contents of his wallet. Just then he saw a figure emerge onto the lawn from behind the governor's house.

"Now, who is that person there?" Melvin said. "Oh, yes, he leave his boat here earlier." He got up on one of the benches that ran along both sides of the boat. "Hey, my brother," he shouted. "Where is my bicycle?"

The man continued to run toward the dock. It was clear, now, that his right hand was holding a long rifle.

"What is this, a gun?" Melvin mumbled, taking a pull of rum. He hoisted himself onto the dock. "You cannot come to the governor's property with a gun, my brother!" He began to lurch unsteadily down the dock toward the shore.

"Sarah, untie the ropes," Zach whispered as he moved to the boat's small cockpit and scanned the dashboard.

"Don't you think we should—"

"Untie us!"

None of the knobs or levers looked designed to start the boat.

"You cannot have a gun here!" Melvin shouted when he and the intruder were about ten yards from the start of the dock. The intruder stopped, brought the rifle forward, and raised it to shoulder level. Melvin, too, came to an abrupt halt, raising his arms above him.

"Sarah, stay down," Zach whispered as a single shot rang out. Melvin fell with such force Zach could feel it in the boat, all the way at the end of the dock.

Still searching for a way to start the engine, Zach glanced

briefly backward and saw the intruder—the killer—step over Melvin's body. He was running full speed toward the boat.

Damn, where was the ignition? He began jabbing at buttons and turning every knob, but nothing happened. The boat had begun to drift away from the dock. Sarah scrambled to the bow.

"I can't start it!" Zach cried. "Get inside."

She crawled into the small, low-ceilinged cabin.

The killer was less than ten yards from the boat, which had drifted several feet from the dock. Zach had no alternative but to join Sarah in the cabin, close the flimsy wooden door, and hope they drifted far enough from the dock to preclude the killer jumping aboard. He squatted and heard a bullet shatter one of the glass dials on the dashboard in front of him. As he scrambled the very short distance to the cabin he saw a small key on the underside of the instrument panel. He turned it to the right. The engine fired up as a second bullet pierced the fiberglass outer wall of the cabin. Still crouching, shielded only partially by the captain's stool-like chair, he reached up and pulled down the accelerator handle.

After a terrifying, one-second lull in which the engine seemed determined to stall, the boat lurched forward. At the very same moment the assassin sprang from the dock and leaped onto the boat. It took him a few seconds to regain his balance on the narrow ledge that circled the seating area, time enough for Zach to recognize the face, older and more hardened than in the photos of protests and, later, of the Williston riot. As Billy Sandifer raised the rifle and simultaneously started to step down from the ledge into the more stable seating area, the boat now slicing through the choppy water, Zach jerked the steering wheel to the right. Sandifer got off one shot, which landed somewhere in the water, before being thrown to the left. He hit the boat's port edge with a distinct thud and, Zach thought, a cracking noise, perhaps a broken rib. Before Sandifer could regroup, Zach grabbed the rifle and pulled it from his grip. With one hand he reached behind him and pulled down the lever. The boat lurched to a stop.

For a moment they just stood facing each other, speechless.

The sudden silence was as disorienting as the insistent rocking motion of the choppy sea. Then Sandifer spoke.

"You gonna shoot me?" He sounded more curious than alarmed. He looked older than Zach expected, even accounting for all the time that had passed since his notoriety after Williston. Though he was quite obviously fit, with broad shoulders, a flat stomach, and a coiled aspect that suggested speed and danger, there were lines across his forehead and running down from the edges of his mouth, dark circles under his eyes. But it was the eyes themselves, the emptiest eyes Zach had ever seen, that suggested a life lived long past the point of caring. That absence of all desire, evident in his eyes, in his voice, in the way he stood on the deck, hands casually on hips—he wanted nothing, not even to live, so what power did Zach have, even with a rifle in his hands?

Nevertheless, Zach kept it trained directly at Sandifer's chest, his finger on the trigger.

"Shoot him, Zach," Sarah whispered, crawling from the cabin.

"*Shoot him,*" Sandifer said, mocking her urgent whisper.

Zach tensed his trigger finger. "No, I want him to explain to the police, to the FBI, what he and Julian Mellow have been doing," he said.

"Don't do this to us. Don't do this *again*. Shoot him! *Now!*"

"With him dead, no one will know what we've been through, no one will believe us."

"Or are you afraid to shoot?" Sandifer took a step toward him.

"*Shoot him, Zach, do it.*" In a split-second glance at her he saw the eruption of nine months of suppressed rage. "Remember what he did."

"You sold out for money," Zach said.

"It isn't *about* the fucking money." He seemed passionate about the point.

"Why is Julian doing this? He has everything…everything he could ever need or want."

"Except his son."

"This is about Matthew?"

232

"It's always about the children," Sandifer said with a touch of sadness. The boat continued to rock, lapping waves punctuating the vast silence.

"Your daughter, in the home in New Jersey, this is all about—"

"My new cause," he said quietly.

"Zach, the rifle!" Sarah cried.

Distracted, he'd let the nose slip a few inches. Raising it to chest level, he said, "Sarah, you have to steer the boat to Saint Thomas."

"Not with him on board. He's dangerous. I don't trust him."

"She's right, Zach, don't trust me." The cold voice was back. Sandifer took a step toward him, arms still on his hips.

Zach raised the rifle a few inches. "Stop there."

Sandifer took another step, then another. He seemed confident that Zach wouldn't shoot—or perhaps he didn't care.

"*Shoot him, Zach!*"

When Sandifer was within a few feet he reached for the end of the rifle with his right hand.

"*Shoot—*"

Sarah lunged at the rifle, perhaps intending to pull the trigger herself. Zach felt the weapon being yanked away from him—Sandifer had wrapped his right hand around the barrel and was beginning, cautiously, to tug at it.

He fired. The discharge flung him against the captain's chair, and it was a second or two before he could assess what he'd done. Sandifer was gripping his left shoulder with his right hand, blood oozing around it, and staggering back toward the ship's stern. His eyes never left Zach; in fact, he didn't appear to be blinking. Something in the gaze—hatred combined with chilling disinterest—caused Zach to raise the rifle and fire again. But the bullet missed him by at least a foot. He aimed again. Sandifer, still registering no emotion of any kind, casually stepped onto the back ledge and jumped—or, rather, fell—into the water.

"Don't let him get away, Zach!"

Zach moved to the stern. The current was drawing Sandifer

quickly away from the boat, back toward Saint Sebastian. He
didn't appear to be making any effort to swim.

"He has nowhere to go," Zach said. But even as he said it he
wondered why he didn't fire. Because the man's only motivation
was the desire to provide for his daughter? *Was it sympathy?* Or was
he a coward? "We'll call the police when we get to Saint Thomas."

WEDNESDAY, OCTOBER 21

# CHAPTER 49

"I have an important story for you."

Julian observed, with some satisfaction, Simon Avery's face
darken. They were in the European painting galleries on the second
floor of the Metropolitan Museum.

"Why so glum, Simon? The last story I gave you bumped your
news ratings by 15 percent."

"The drug charges against Delsiner have still not been sub-
stantiated, and we've had a team of journalists on the story. But
that didn't help him. He's through."

"Yes, well that's politics. It's not the truth that matters, it's
the perception of truth. What people believe, not reality. What do
you think of her?" He pointed to the Ghirlandaio portrait of an
unknown fifteenth-century woman, one of his favorite paintings
in the Met.

"It's very nice," Avery said warily, as if the anonymous figure
might be the subject of the important story.

They considered the Ghirlandaio for a few moments, like an
awkward couple on a first date, seeking distraction. Julian had
summoned Avery to the Met because he missed the Ghirlandaio,
her golden, ringletted hair, eggshell skin, inscrutably dark eyes,
above all her laudable imperviousness to the parade of visitors who
ignored her as they hurried to this or that blockbuster exhibit. She

seemed more timeless than the emaciated Madonnas and tortured saints that surrounded her in the always deserted gallery, more worthy of worship. He wanted her, wanted to *own* her, but she was forever beyond his grasp, or so he had long thought. He'd offered, through contacts on the Met's board, which he'd been invited to join many times, to buy any number of pictures that had come up for auction and donate them to the Met in return for the Ghirlandaio, a deal that would have cost him tens of millions of dollars. But such a transaction went against the museum's policy. Perhaps if things worked out with Harry Lightstone such a policy might be loosened just once. The promise of National Endowment funds for an upcoming exhibition, invitations to a state dinner or two for a Met trustee, perhaps an overnight in the Lincoln bedroom—even the Met's august and wealthy board members had their price.

Then, too, dragging Simon Avery up to the Met sent a very clear message about who was in control, not that Avery needed a reminder that Masters Broadcasting was controlled by Mellow Partners. It was just that journalists, even broadcast journalists—even executives of broadcast companies—could be tedious about ethics.

"You are aware that I control Searchlight Investments?" Julian said, still staring at Ghirlandaio's anonymous muse.

"Is there anything you don't control?" Avery said with more sorrow than sarcasm.

"Searchlight handles the investments for many prominent people, including Evan Smith." He heard Avery groan at the mention of the vice president's name. "I have in my possession an email message from the chief investment officer of Searchlight, Victor Carron, concerning the vice president. The email directs a subordinate to move all of the vice president's assets out of Searchlight's oil and gas fund and into its media fund at the vice president's request."

"Impossible. Smith's assets are in a blind trust."

"Exactly. Which is why this email is so potentially important."

"How did you get it?" Avery asked.

"Unimportant."

"Not to me. We must know our sources before we run a story. I'm assuming you want us to run a story on this."

"The email was sent six weeks ago. Three things have happened since then. The White House proposed tapping the strategic oil reserve, which immediately drove down the price of oil, which substantially drove down the stocks of oil companies, many of which are held by Searchlight. The White House also proposed further loosening the restriction on cross-ownership of media properties, which drove up the stocks of media companies, many of which are owned by Searchlight. And Searchlight moved the vice president's assets, some twenty-three million dollars, from Searchlight's oil stocks to its media stocks, netting a very impressive profit. This was all done at the specific request of Smith."

"Do you know what you're suggesting?"

"It's an important story, and a coup for Masters Broadcasting."

"I assume you have proof beyond the email message."

"The email is from Victor Carron to one of his subordinates, indicating that the assets were transferred at the request of the vice president."

"Internal email messages don't constitute proof, Julian. I think you know that."

"And we are not arguing this case in court, Simon. I also have an email acknowledgment from Friend to the vice president's chief of staff that the transfers were made."

"But no evidence that the vice president or his staff ever received the email. This entire thing could be a fabrication. Where is the email from the veep's office requesting this reallocation?"

"It was done by phone, apparently."

Simon sighed heavily. "Will Marvin Friend support this story? Will he admit that he moved assets at the request of the vice president?"

"I doubt it."

"Then there is no story."

Julian turned back to Ghirlandaio's serene and patient woman. As always happened with great portraits, she appeared to have changed since he'd consulted her few minutes earlier. Had the right edge of her lips always curled up ever so slightly, as if she knew what Julian was up to, and approved? Could she guess the magic that Grace Carr had worked, backdating emails and cleverly secreting them in the fathomless depths of Mellow Partners' servers? Had she any idea of the cost of college tuition, or what a midlevel executive with an unemployed husband might do to pay it?

"Certain facts will be uncontested. In addition to threatening to open up the oil reserves, the administration, at the urging of the vice president, expanded domestic drilling rights for oil companies, thereby driving down the price of a barrel of oil 10 percent, give or take. Another fact: the vice president has been at the forefront of the movement to further relax the rules that govern ownership of local television and radio outlets, which recently resulted in legislation that did just that. Another fact: Searchlight Investments, just prior to both policy changes, moved all of the vice president's oil and gas assets into media stocks."

"But that could have been coincidence. No, that could have been *strategy.* I'm no expert in investments, but plenty of people were anticipating both the drilling legislation and the new media ownership rules. I'm sure many investment advisers reallocated their funds to capitalize on these events."

"But if you knew in advance that the legislation was going to be proposed, and had a good chance of passing..." Julian stopped himself. He would not be drawn into an argument with Simon Avery. Instead, he handed him a manila envelope. "Here are the email messages and additional background information."

Avery hesitated before taking the envelope, which he regarded as if it might burn his fingers.

"I'll have my news director look this over and—"

"I want the story to run tonight, on every Masters outlet."

"I can't do that."

"The very same new media rules we've been talking about make this a very propitious time for taking Masters public. In fact, this week my staff is working with bankers at Goldman on the deal. One of our biggest tasks will be allocating ownership stakes to Masters executives. If the deal moves forward as we anticipate, several of them will be immensely wealthy the day the company goes public."

"Are you suggesting that—"

"But if anyone should leave before the IPO, well, obviously they will miss out on an extraordinary opportunity. You might want to spread the word, Simon, that leaving Masters at this point in time would be very unfortunate from a personal financial perspective. That would include being fired."

He turned away from Avery and gave the Ghirlandaio a final glance. She looked vaguely disappointed, as if this were just one more illustration of greed and betrayal that she'd had to witness for over six centuries. Nothing had changed since the 1400s, she seemed to be thinking. Today it was about oil and gas and broadcast media, all unknown half a millennium ago. But the motivations, the threats, the compromises, the vanity—these were as timeless as the portrait itself.

"Goodbye, Simon," he said, and walked quickly from the gallery. As soon as he reached the top of the main staircase his cell picked up a signal and vibrated. The LED screen showed his secretary's name.

"I've been trying you for almost twenty minutes," Stacy said when he answered. "Mr. Franklin called."

THURSDAY, OCTOBER 22

# CHAPTER 50

Zach rented a car at the Lambert–Saint Louis Airport and drove out to Ladue, a suburb. He'd managed to sleep for an hour on the flight from Miami, the only rest he'd gotten over the past day or so, and it hadn't done much to relieve either his fatigue or sense of unreality. Had he really been shot at on Saint Sebastian? Had he really ever lived there? Had he and Sarah really witnessed the execution of his "brother," Melvin, and then stolen his boat? But the most surreal moment of the entire day had been in the police station on Saint Thomas, where he and Sarah had gone after docking Melvin's boat at the nearby Crown Bay Marina. While waiting to tell their story they heard two police officers discussing a bulletin that had just come in from Saint Sebastian. An employee of the governor had been gunned down on the governor's dock. Two Americans were suspected, a young couple who lived next door and who had conveniently vanished with the governor's boat.

So much for the police. They were considered armed and dangerous and were to be detained without access to counsel until federal authorities arrived from the mainland.

Zach convinced her to get out of there, arguing that they'd be locked up indefinitely, given what had happened on Saint Sebastian and, earlier, in New York. They emptied the safety deposit box with the key Sarah kept around her neck, took a cab to the airport, where Arthur and Alison Sandler bought two tickets to Miami. At Miami International Airport, he debated with Sarah what to do. She was still in favor of throwing themselves at the mercy of the police. At least they'd be safe, she'd argued. Zach argued that the police would probably lock them up for killing Melvin—Zach was still a suspect in Jessica Winter's murder, after all, and Sarah's sudden reappearance wouldn't help their case—and they were hardly likely to buy his paranoid rant about a plot by a well-known pillar of the investment community to change the course of the upcoming presidential election, just ten days away.

"I need to expose him," he told her at the airport taxi stand. After all that had happened, he was reluctant to even give voice to his nemesis's name. "That's the only way we'll ever be safe." He needed to expose Julian, stop him. He couldn't take the chance that the police would lock him up, potentially until after the election.

"Why didn't you kill him?" she asked in the taxi from the airport. It was the first mention of Billy Sandifer since leaving Saint Thomas. "You let him get away."

"I shot him in the shoulder. I doubt he survived the swim back to shore."

"Doubt? You *doubt* he survived? This is my life you're talking about." Then, in a quieter voice, "Our lives."

He had nothing to say in his defense, so he said nothing. She had stayed behind in Miami, and he had traveled on to Saint Louis. They'd had a difficult farewell.

Stephen Delsiner lived in a center-hall colonial in the upscale Saint Louis suburb of Ladue. Zach recalled that he'd been a lawyer before entering politics, and 33 Winfield Road was the sort of unassertively prosperous home a successful attorney with political ambitions might choose. Had the drug scandal not erupted, bringing down not only Delsiner but the nominee at the top of the ticket, Gabe Rooney, there would probably have been a dark sedan parked by the curb with a pair of Secret Servicemen inside, perhaps a caravan of news vans—assuming Delsiner was home and not on the campaign trail. As he walked toward the front door across the neatly-tended lawn, raked clean of all but a thin scattering of late autumn leaves, Zach sensed something eerie about the quietness of the Delsiner home, as if it had been overlooked or forgotten or even stifled in some way. Or perhaps it was the early morning hour in a sleepy Midwestern suburb that felt strangely quiet to him, after decades in Manhattan and nine months on Saint Sebastian, serenaded by the incessant lapping of the Caribbean.

Delsiner opened the door. At first Zach didn't recognize the former senator. He looked thinner and older, his face darkened by stubble. "Senator Delsiner?"

"Used to live here," he said. "Not anymore."

His voice seemed to lack the energy for irony, let alone humor.

"May I come in, senator? I'm investigating certain events surrounding the current presidential campaign and I—"

"Reporter? I thought you guys had given up on me. The

lapsed ex-drug addict, disgraced former senator. Has-been. You got your story."

"I'm not a reporter."

"Police? Because you're wasting your time if you are. You won't find drugs here, or any information about drugs, or the names of drug dealers, or other drug users…"

"I'm not a policeman. I'm a former employee of Julian Mellow. Does that name mean anything to you?"

"Used to be one of my biggest contributors."

Julian had never expressed a single political view in all the years Zach worked for him, but he had spread money around both major parties, hedging his bets. Nevertheless, it was unsettling, if not surprising, to think that Julian had once supported, however perfunctorily, the man he had later set out to destroy.

"I think he's responsible for…" He hesitated, then figured that neither he nor, judging by his appearance, Delsiner, had anything to lose. "…for your downfall."

"Julian Mellow?"

Zach nodded and waited an eternity for Delsiner to respond. Finally, he waved him inside. "Well, someone's responsible. I might as well hear your theory."

Delsiner led him through an elegantly appointed hallway to the kitchen, where a television was tuned to a campaign appearance by Harry Lightstone.

"I don't know why I even pay attention anymore," Delsiner said. "My wife had it on before she left for the office. You want coffee?"

"Desperately," Zach said.

The ex-senator poured two cups from a coffeemaker and plunked them down on the small kitchen table. He got a carton of milk from the refrigerator and placed that on the table too. He rooted through two cabinets before finding a box of sugar. Watching him shuffle around the kitchen, dressed in a wrinkled blue work shirt and jeans, Zach considered how far Delsiner had fallen. Then again, he'd resurrected himself once; perhaps a second rebirth was possible.

"I don't know how he does it," he said, nodding to Lightstone's image on the screen. "How do you keep up the energy when you know you're going down?" His eyes drifted from the television, perhaps applying the question to his own situation.

"I wouldn't count him out."

Delsiner looked directly at him.

"You get that tan on a beach somewhere? A beach with no newspapers or TV? You can't turn around a national election in twelve days, not when you're double-digits behind."

"I think there's going to be a surprise."

"Ah, the famous October Surprise. Hell, the only surprise that would help Lightstone would be coming up with something original to say, a compelling reason for voters to oust the president. He hasn't done that in ten months, he's not going to do it in ten days."

"What could move a few percentage points over to the Republicans?"

Delsiner sipped his coffee while, on the television, Lightstone segued, awkwardly, Zach thought, from a riff on health insurance to human rights abuses in Kamalia.

"The president could be caught on video fucking a farm animal. That would probably turn a few people off, especially if it's a male farm animal." Delsiner took a deep breath—he'd been caught on video too. "Or something could happen overseas, some sort of war breaking out. When Americans start dying, voters start paying attention."

"So it's scandal or war," Zach said. It seemed a safe bet that Julian was cooking up the former—war was beyond even Julian's grasp.

"And I don't see either coming. Nessin hasn't so much as looked at a woman other than his wife since the day he set eyes on her. And as for war, well, it doesn't look like that's in the cards for the next week or two. Terror attack? Since the Chicago train bombings and the DC ricin scare, it's Fortress America. Nessin inherited that, you can't really blame where we're at on him. Last month we turned away more than twelve thousand people at airports—some of them just for having the wrong name or complexion. 'Better safe than sorry'—they should put that on the Statue of Liberty. Nessin says he wants to roll back some homeland security policies, but he won't do anything about it. No president wants another attack on his watch. Now, you said something about a theory."

Zach launched into his story, trying his best to appear calm, rational, focused—anything but a raving lunatic spinning conspiracy theories. Delsiner listened attentively, revealing nothing about what he was thinking. But when Zach was done Delsiner shook his head, a half smile on his lips.

"Just in case I missed something," he said. "Your man Julian Mellow caused Charlie Moore's plane crash. He set up the so-called drug sale that killed my career. He has something on Harry Lightstone that's forcing him to focus on Kamalia, where his son was murdered. He's got this former radical running around the country killing people, or trying to, including a San Francisco prostitute and you and your girlfriend. Did I miss anything?"

"No."

After a short silence, Delsiner said, "You know, I almost wish it were all true."

Zach felt the air rush out of his chest. "It is true," he said, but the words emerged in a feeble whisper.

On screen, Lightstone had moved on to education, proposing a hodgepodge of tax credits for college tuition and parochial schools and grants to states for new schools and more teachers. He sounded halfhearted, as if even he knew none of this would happen, no matter who got elected. It was pathetic, Zach thought, when the candidates had become as cynical as the electorate.

"Now that I'm out of the game, it all seems so tired," Delsiner said, turning away from the screen. "No wonder it all comes down to who you'd rather have a beer with—nobody really believes that anything's going to change. That's why people like you want to believe in some sort of massive conspiracy of billionaires. At least

SETH MARGOLIS

there's some comfort in knowing that *someone* in this goddamn country can make things happen."

"It's not a conspiracy. It's one person."

Delsiner gave him a pitying look which, given its source—a fallen, disgraced politician—drove Zach to an even deeper level of misery.

"Harry Lightstone has always been one of the luckiest guys in the world, you know that? Born with a face that belongs on a ten-dollar bill, married to a gal rich enough to buy him a seat in Congress, then the Senate, two healthy sons. Next to those advantages, what's a plane crash in Maine and a drug deal in a DC parking lot? More good luck, that all."

"You're saying you really bought the drugs?"

"What's the difference?"

"Because if you were set up, it means—"

"It means shit." Delsiner stood up and refilled his coffee mug, which, after a moment's consideration, he emptied in the sink. "It's all about perception, and the perception is that I bought drugs that night outside my gym. What actually happened doesn't matter to anybody."

"It matters to me, because I believe that Julian Mellow set you up, but if you're telling me that you actually bought drugs..." Delsiner moved aimlessly around the kitchen, as if physically dodging the issue. "Isn't your reputation worth anything?"

"I spent a week last January on every news and interview show in America, claiming innocence. Look where it got me."

"What if I had proof?"

Delsiner stopped and looked at him. His eyes showed a spark of life.

"Where's your computer?"

Upstairs, in a bedroom that had been converted into a study, Delsiner turned on a desktop computer. Zach took control of the mouse and Googled *Billy Sandifer*. Within a few seconds he had pulled up a photograph of Sandifer leaving Williston Prison.

"Did you see this guy outside your gym that night?"

Delsiner drew his chair closer to the screen. As he studied the image, Zach told him everything he knew about Sandifer, including how he'd come to know Julian Mellow.

"No." Zach felt the tension of the past twenty-four hours come crashing down on him. "I didn't see him, but I knew the guy in the video…"

"You knew him?"

"What I didn't know, still don't know, is how he found me. He was my dealer a long time ago, here in Saint Louis. What was he doing in Washington? And where the hell did he go? No one can find him, not even the media." Delsiner got up. "I gave him some money. He seemed kind of manic, which frightened me, and he insisted I give him a thumbs-up, which didn't look good on video. My wife earns a good living as a lawyer. My daughters are both married to good men, they ask nothing from me. I'm getting used to obscurity. There are worse things."

"I don't believe you mean that."

"What you believe doesn't matter. What happened last winter was a fucking nightmare. I won't go back there unless you have absolute proof."

"I'll get proof," Zach said. On the monitor, Billy Sandifer's image appeared to grow brighter, more vivid as they talked, as if he were taking strength from the ex-senator's reluctance to pursue him. Sandifer had to be the link between the drug dealer and Delsiner—Julian would never get involved in something as sordid as tracking down a dealer and videotaping him in a parking lot. Someone, after all, had handled the video recorder. He logged off and followed Delsiner downstairs.

"Julian Mellow," Delsiner said, holding open the front door. "You know, I could always count on him for a big contribution, back before McCain-Feingold. But I always figured him for more of a Democrat than Republican, one of those guys who likes to salt the GOP with cash but basically supports the tax-and-spenders. Never understood rich guys who root against their own interests."

"I never had a single political discussion with him. He thinks he's above politics."

"And how about you?"

"It's not about politics. I don't care who wins. Not anymore. It's about saving my life, my girlfriend's life."

"And about settling an old score."

"It's way beyond that now."

Delsiner nodded. "Well, whatever it is that's driving you, I wish you luck."

Zach started down the path toward his car but turned around.

"You believe me," he said, smiling for the first time in days. Delsiner face remained expressionless, but Zach saw something in his eyes, a spark of interest, of hope. "You believe me," he repeated before turning back and heading for his car.


## FRIDAY, OCTOBER 23

# CHAPTER 51

Harry Lightstone had just finished speaking to an audience of police officers in Gary, Indiana, when Michael Steers tapped him on the shoulder. The tap was not unexpected. His communications director was often on the podium with him, part of the crowd of photogenic "supporters" who could be trusted to clap enthusiastically at appropriate moments. Mike liked to say something encouraging after a speech, "They're eating out of your hand, Senator," being his favorite line. This time his message was different.

"There's good news, Senator," he shouted above the din of applause from the friendly audience. Indiana was a state the Republicans had to win to be in contention, and he was down somewhere between eleven points, according to Gallup, and seven points, according to a *Wall Street Journal*/NBC poll. The bus tour was crossing a number of pivotal states like Indiana, the last stop, to little avail. (The states to the east were pretty much beyond his grasp.) Perhaps Mike had just heard otherwise.

"Let me shake a few hands and then we'll talk," he said.

"No time. We need to react fast."

Normally he liked to walk to the edge of the stage and lean over to press some sympathetic flesh. He was tired of listening to his advisers, who had done little to help his cause, but at least he was being summoned to hear good news. He gave a final wave to the cheering cops who had, as expected, responded deliriously to his call for increased federal funding for law enforcement, and exited stage left, Mike Steers close behind.

"A story just hit the wires about the vice president. Apparently his blind trusts aren't so blind."

Harry felt a small letdown. Wealth was the elephant in the room of the campaign, something that was never mentioned because all four candidates, presidential and vice presidential, were filthy rich. Politics had become a rich man's hobby. If Evan Smith's blind trust was in play, so was Marcella's trust fund, and if the Democrats went there, the Republicans would have to plant stories about President Nessin's dividends from Stellar Corp., the defense contractor he'd briefly headed between stints in Washington.

"Masters Broadcasting is leading with a story tonight that Smith directed his investment firm to move his assets out of oil and gas and into media stocks."

"Jesus, why would he do something so stupid?"

They were leaving the speech venue, a public high school, by the cafeteria door. Harry spent a lot of time walking through kitchens, and each time he thought of Robert Kennedy in Los Angeles and wondered anew why he'd gotten into this game and if he'd meet his end in a cold, sanitized room full of oversized stainless-steel appliances.

"Not stupid," Mike said as they walked through a cordon of Secret Service agents toward a waiting SUV—one of the few overt luxuries, along with a private plane, that candidates were still allowed, indeed expected, to have. "Smith must have known the exploration bill was going to pass. And as for media companies, he was the administration's point man with Congress, so he knew—"

"Stupid because he knew he couldn't get away with it."

They got in the limo, someone closed the back door, and off they went to the airport, a driver and Secret Service agent up front.

"Where his money and his dick are involved, every man thinks he's invincible." Mike checked his watch. "It's just about six. Let's watch." It took him less than a minute to find a Masters Broadcasting affiliate feed on his phone.

"Allegations surfaced today concerning the financial arrangements of vice president Evan Smith. A highly confidential internal email from the head of the investment firm that manages the vice president's so-called blind trust, Searchlight Investments, informs a subordinate that the vice president has requested a shift out of energy stocks and into media stocks. The request came shortly before the administration announced its support of the wildlife drilling initiative, which drove down energy prices, and its support of the media ownership expansion bill, which drove up the value of media companies. With a blind trust, the beneficiary, in this case the vice president, is supposed to have no knowledge or control of the assets under management. They are typically established for politicians who need to avoid conflicts of interest. For more on this story, we go to senior White House Correspondent Al Diamond. Al?"

Harry felt a familiar dread as he listened—though the story, if it had legs, would certainly help his campaign. "Who owns Searchlight?" he asked.

"Julian Mellow. Why?" Mike pointed to the screen, where Al Diamond, his trench coat buttoned to the neck against the October chill, was standing at the end of the long driveway that led up to the Naval Observatory, the official home of the vice president.

"The vice president, through a spokesman, has denied that he ever contacted anyone from Searchlight. Vice President Smith is campaigning in Wisconsin and is not available for comment. His spokesman did say, however, that the vice president's positions on both drilling and media ownership have been well known for a long time and that he in no way sought to profit from what was common knowledge. The spokesman further noted that the email message was not from the vice president himself but was an internal message between Searchlight employees. A representative of the Lightstone campaign, however…"

Harry turned to Mike.

"I had our staff in Pittsburgh provide a statement while you were talking to the cops. Hugh Jamison is constructing a poll to determine how we should play this after today—above the fray or righteous indignation. He'll have his recommendations by noon tomorrow."

Between Julian Mellow's manipulations, including, perhaps, the emerging Searchlight scandal, and the machinations of his own campaign, he sometimes wondered if he couldn't just hole up at his place in Pennsylvania and wait out the remaining nine days, confident that events would churn along without him. Given the criticism of his wooden campaign style, absence of common touch and lack of humor, perhaps it would do his numbers good.

"…has indicated that Senator Lightstone is deeply troubled by these latest allegations, viewing them as one more example of the, quote, arrogance and self-dealing that have typified the Nessin administration for the past four years, unquote. I believe we have a report from Peter Applebaum, our financial correspondent in New York. Peter?"

"Al, I'm standing outside Searchlight's New York headquarters in lower Manhattan." Applebaum was also bundled against the chilly night, black leather gloves holding the microphone and adding a sinister touch to the story. "Victor Carron, the chief investment officer of Searchlight, has denied that he ever sent an email referencing the vice president's account. Earlier we caught up with him as he was leaving this building on Broad Street in Manhattan's financial district."

A small, understandably anxious-looking man emerged from the revolving doors in front of the building, surrounded by several other suit-and-tied men. As he made his way to a waiting car, a mic was thrust into his path. He regarded it like an asp. "Is it true, Mr. Carron, that the vice president asked you to shift investments from energy to media?" He shook his head, continued toward the curb, then stopped and turned. "It is absolute nonsense. I never heard from the vice president, and if I had, I would have immediately notified the Federal Elections Board…" One of Carron's associates pulled him away from the mic and whispered something in his ear, after which he turned briefly back to the camera and said, "No comment."

"He looks like he's lying," Mike said gleefully.

"You always look bad when you're ambushed like that. I've been on the receiving end a few times. From the public's point of view, 'No comment' is like taking the fifth—you might as well announce 'Guilty as charged.'"

Peter Applebaum was back live. "In a Masters Broadcasting exclusive, we have obtained Searchlight's most recent quarterly performance results, which have not yet been sent to clients. According to this report, Searchlight did indeed move funds out of energy and into media stocks. Our own analysis reveals that the vice president's investments surged a whopping 32 percent as a result, or eighteen million dollars, because of the move. Now, this does not mean that the trades were illegal, or that they were directed by the vice president. But they do raise serious concerns about the timing, and whether Evan Smith had any knowledge— or should I say, foreknowledge, of the moves."

"It's an October Surprise," Mike said, reaching for his cell phone. "A fucking October Surprise. I waited my entire goddamn career for one of these. I need to get you some airtime right away."

"I don't want to look like an ass if the story goes nowhere."

"Doesn't matter. We'll run with the drilling-in-our-precious-national-parks angle on the energy side and kowtowing-to-big-media on the other side. They're always so high-and-mighty about protecting the environment and fighting for the little guy. No matter what happens on the blind trust front, we'll show them up for the hypocrites they are. And *oh by the way,* these guys in the Nessin administration have a way of playing fast and loose with our elections laws. This is gold, you can't buy publicity like this."

At that, Harry had to smile, thinking of Julian Mellow.

# CHAPTER 52

Julian Mellow stood in the back of the rec room at the Malcolm X Children's Center in East Harlem, a converted synagogue, of all things. The room was swarming with print journalists, crews from every network news organization, Lightstone campaign advisers, local community leaders and, crowded in the front, sitting cross-legged on the floor before Marcella Lightstone, about a dozen honest-to-goodness children. She was reading *The Very Hungry Caterpillar*, a children's book, in an elegantly fluid voice.

Julian wanted a word with Marcella, who was more accessible than her husband now that the campaign had staggered into its final, blitzkrieg phase. He preferred to speak in person, mistrusting phone lines when national politics were involved, but he didn't want her coming to his apartment or office, nor did he want to go to her townhouse, now that her every movement was shadowed by the Secret Service and, more often than not, the media. A chance meeting at a public event would raise few if any eyebrows.

"Is that Julian Mellow?" He felt a tap on his shoulder. "It's Gordon Lewis, from the *Times*? I interviewed you a few years ago."

He had granted a rare interview to the *Times* during the heated competition for Finnegan. It had been a stupid and desperate reversal of his usual policy, the first of several such moves during the imbroglio, but he had felt Finnegan slipping away from him and thought some publicity might help. Gordon Lewis, he now recalled, had been young and ambitious and had used the interview to probe the entire career of Julian Mellow. Julian had thrown him out after five minutes. Nevertheless, the damage had been done: Gordon was one of the few members of the media who could immediately recognize him in a crowd.

"Don't you cover business stories?" he asked quietly.

"I've been temporarily transferred to the campaign. Covering Marcella isn't exactly going to win me a Pulitzer. But the paper is sending me down to Florida for Election Day, which is a step in the right direction. I'm really more interested in politics, particularly the intersection of politics and business."

"Then I'm sure you're fascinated by what I heard on the radio on my way uptown this evening, about the vice president's blind trust."

"Amazing. The *Times* already has three reporters on it. Unfortunately, I'm not one of them. Of course, we won't run the story. Emails are too easy to fake, and no one involved, or allegedly involved, has admitted anything."

"But you've assigned three reporters."

"To cover the story *about* the story. That's what counts nowadays, not the story itself, which in this case is pretty flimsy, but the tangle of stories that gets woven around it. Who's denying the story—the vice president himself, his campaign manager, a spokesman? We'll run an entire story analyzing the implications of each of these, and soon that *becomes* the story. Nobody remembers or even cares if the underlying story is true or not."

"Do you think this will harm the Nessin campaign?"

"Inevitably. I don't think it's the proverbial October Surprise that going to turn the election on its head, but it's going to tighten things up."

Marcella Lightstone's voice was replaced by a man's, who thanked her for giving so generously of her time and showing support for the after-school programs sponsored by the center.

"Can you believe they held the kids here for an extra two hours without food just to make this appearance happen?" Lewis said. "Someone should call the city's child-abuse hotline. Anyway, I need a statement from Marcella. She's been doing a lot of these kiddie readings lately, trying to soften her image. Her approvals are still half of the First Lady's. Any chance you'll want to sit down for an interview once the election's over?"

"You can call my assistant."

"In other words, no." He shrugged and made his way through the crowd to Marcella. Julian followed her through the throng of reporters and cameramen. He stopped when he had Marcella in his sights and listened to her tell a reporter that the administration's policies had resulted in fewer after-school programs, cutbacks in Head Start, and a drastic reduction in funds for school lunches. She didn't seem particularly passionate about the issue—no doubt Saint Andrew's was unaffected by the budget cutbacks—but she was admirably in control, salting her statement with statistics and the names of congressional bills. Someone had even managed to get her to tone down the East Side ladies-who-lunch look. Her hair, usually swept up into an imperious chignon, hung loosely, more democratically, to her shoulders, and the suit she had on, while it probably cost as much as most Democratic voters made in a month, was less resolutely tailored than her usual getup.

She spotted him and momentarily lost her train of thought, fumbling her words. He watched her recover with impressive speed and then graciously excuse herself to a small group of print reporters, including Gordon Lewis. A nervous-looking man in a gray suit took her arm and escorted her to the door.

"If I have to read that fucking caterpillar book one more time I'll blow my brains out," he heard her whisper to the man.

"The kids love it."

"If a miracle occurs and Harry wins I'm going to insist he have it banned from every library in the country. I'll have him bring back book burnings."

"I hope you don't seriously think that—"

"Shut up, Stuart. I need to have a word with this man." She shook off his hand and walked over to Julian. "Stuart Pearson, my campaign manager. I'm counting the seconds until he's out of my life. Why are you here?" she asked, as if addressing an overly attentive department store salesperson.

"I'll walk you outside," Julian said. After a moment's hesitation she turned and headed for an exit at the back of the room.

A small, painted-over mezuzah on the doorjamb harkened back to a time before Harlem's Jews had decamped for the suburbs. A phalanx of dark-suited men materialized and blocked the reporters from following Marcella.

"Why this place?" he asked as they walked. "I wouldn't have thought New York was in play for the Lightstone campaign."

"It doesn't matter where the hell I read that infernal book, as long as the cameras are rolling. I prefer Manhattan to *Des Moines.*"

"You'll make a very poor First Lady with that attitude, Marcella."

"I have about as much chance of becoming First Lady as Lady Gaga."

"People love her. Your favorability numbers are in the toilet."

She stopped just short of the door and looked at him. "I wouldn't be in this position if it weren't for you. What is it you want?"

He took a piece of folded paper from his jacket pocket. "Some talking points for Harry's final week of campaigning. You'll see that he gets them right away."

She did not take the paper.

"Take it, Marcella," he said, then added with mock sweetness, "For the boys' sake."

"You shit." She grabbed the paper and shoved it into her bag.

"I'll want to see evidence that Harry's read this in his campaign addresses tomorrow. If not, the headlines will be about a handsome but troubled young man at an elite boarding school with a bit of a drug problem."

He held the door open and she hesitated a moment before walking through, as if accepting even that small favor would compromise her.

"What's the point, Julian? You've bet on a losing horse," she said on the sidewalk, where two beefy men stood guard in front of two waiting SUVs.

"Haven't you seen the news tonight?" He smiled enigmatically. "The vice president's in some hot water."

• • •

# CHAPTER 53

At a restaurant in the Lambert–Saint Louis Airport, Zach ordered a Coke and a cheeseburger and watched the vice president's financial scandal unfold on television. The reporters covering the story made no mention of who controlled Searchlight Investments, the firm that handled Evan Smith's blind trust; nor did they mention who controlled Masters Broadcasting, the network credited with breaking the story. Early predictions by a team of hastily assembled pundits were that the scandal, assuming it had legs, would not bring down the administration but would probably tighten the race to within a few points. No one connected to the nascent scandal had a comment, although the Lightstone campaign had already released a statement to the effect that, if true, the issue was a sad commentary on the ethics of the Nessin administration, blah, blah blah. The news report was followed by a fluff piece about the role of the candidates' wives, and ended with a note that, in an effort to soften her image, Marcella Lightstone had taken to reading books to children at carefully selected sites around the country. That very evening she would be reading at a youth center in Harlem.

By the time his plane touched down at LaGuardia it was already too late to intercept Marcella Lightstone in Harlem. Instead he took a taxi to her townhouse on East 68th Street. He asked the cab driver to let him off on the corner of Madison Avenue and walked slowly west, toward Fifth. The street was one of the prettiest in the city, lined with limestone mansions, several still occupied by a single family or, in a few cases, a consulate. He stood across from the Lightstone residence, which was dark. He knew from the news report that the senator was in the Midwest; it looked as if Marcella wasn't yet home. As he waited for her he contemplated his situation: homeless, close to broke, a thousand miles away from the woman he loved, possessed of information that no one in the world believed—other than the people who wanted him dead. Somehow, being back in New York only made his sense of isolation more painful. If he had no friends in New York, what *did* he have?

Two dark SUVs turned onto the street and stopped in front of the Lightstone home. He started to cross the street just as the back door of the first car was opened by a burly, dark-suited man whose head seemed in constant motion, swiveling back and forth, eyes alert. When he saw Zach approach he ordered Marcella back in the car, but she hesitated.

"That's close enough," he shouted. In what felt like a mere second, two other men emerged from the other car. The driver of the first car took Marcella's elbow and began to hustle her toward the front door of her townhouse while the two men formed a human shield between her and the street—between her and Zach.

"Marcella, I need to talk to you!" he shouted.

She started to turn but the three men closed ranks, preventing her from seeing him.

"I know about Julian Mellow! I worked for him! I know what's going on."

Before he was finished she was inside the house. Standing in the center of 68th Street, he saw lights go on inside, first on the ground floor, then on the second. He felt someone clutch his upper arm.

"We'd like a few words with you," said one of the men who'd escorted Marcella.

"Let go of me."

"Get in the car, quietly, and there won't be trouble."

"I'm not getting in any car. *Let go.*"

One of the other men walked over and took out a small wallet, which he flipped open to reveal a badge.

"Secret Service, assigned to protect Mrs. Lightstone."

He felt himself being pulled toward the second SUV. A part of him thought that being in the custody of the Secret Service wasn't such a bad idea—he'd be beyond the grasp of Julian Mellow. Another part of him sensed that once in custody, he'd be treated as a deranged and dangerous mental case and shipped off to wherever they sent such people for a long, long time. As he considered these possibilities he was stumbling closer and closer to the SUV, the back door of which was being held open by one of the men. Should he fight or go along with them? Was there any point to fighting? Perhaps he *was* deranged, stalking the wife of a presidential candidate and shouting conspiracy stories at her.

He was trying to shake off the man's hand, just for good measure, when a woman's voice caused them both to freeze.

"It's okay, he's not dangerous."

Marcella Lightstone stood in the doorway of her home.

"Ma'am, protocol requires us to take him in for questioning."

"I know him," she said imperiously. "He worked for a friend of mine. I'd like to invite him in."

"I'm afraid we can't do that."

"You can make sure he's not armed, if you'd like. And I have my own security, private security, inside."

There were a tense few moments while the agents talked this over, one of them still clutching his arm. Finally, they patted Zach down and, finding no weapon, released him.

He walked unsteadily over to the townhouse, where Marcella greeted him with open arms, pulling him into an embrace.

"It's so wonderful to see you again," she said. "I'm so terribly sorry I didn't recognize you just now. Please, come in and we'll have a drink."

The Secret Servicemen looked put out. One of them spoke up.

"We'll be waiting here if you need us, Mrs. Lightstone."

"Thank you," she said, and led Zach inside, closing the door behind her. He had the sense, as he entered, that he was not only stepping into a building, he was entering new territory—a place where theory became reality, where the dots connected, where he was *believed.*

She preceded him up a grand staircase and took him into a paneled library, where she opened a cabinet door to reveal an impressive bar.

"I'm having vodka. You?" she said, her first words inside the house.

He knew he should answer "water" but, giddy with relief and anticipation, said "Vodka for me too."

He sat on a sofa, where she brought him a crystal glass with vodka on ice. She sat catty-corner on a leather chair.

"Why did you invite me in?"

"You mentioned Julian Mellow. Why?"

He'd seen her image on television and in newspapers and magazines, the heiress married to the rising Republican star. She emitted a pampered vibe, as if everything could be hers simply because she wanted it. It unnerved him, the feeling of being, in some way, at her mercy.

"I think that Julian Mellow is calling the shots in your campaign. I think it began in San Francisco and…" He fortified himself with a gulp of vodka. "And the murder of a prostitute. I think Julian has some sort of information on your husband, damaging information, and that he's using it to direct your husband's campaign."

"Why would he do that?"

"To control the president of the United States."

"To what end?" she asked.

The very question that had puzzled him from the beginning. What could Julian Mellow possibly want that was worth risking everything he had?

"It's about Kamalia."

He detected a very faint coloring of her porcelain skin.

"Where?"

"The election is a week away, Mrs. Lightstone. There's no time for bullshit. You know where Kamalia is. It's been mentioned in every speech of your husband's since the convention. Why?"

"He's concerned about the safety of the Kamalian people, if that's what they're called. And of the Americans living there."

"Bullshit!" He stood up and she flinched. "No one cares about Kamalia except Julian Mellow. His son died there. He's forcing your husband to make intervention in Kamalia a part of his standard campaign speech."

"Why?" she said, and he thought he detected genuine puzzlement.

"You tell me, Mrs. Lightstone." She shook her head. He decided to shift course. "Do you know what Julian Mellow has on your husband?"

"You're spinning some sort of sick fantasy in your head. No one *has* anything on Harry."

"Was it the prostitute in San Francisco?"

"I don't think something like using a prostitute would be enough to get my husband to change his views on foreign policy. The country has grown up in that respect. Perhaps you should do the same." She looked directly up at him and smiled superciliously.

"The prostitute was actually a man. And I don't think we've *grown up* to the extent that murder is no big deal."

After several long moments of silence she said, "I wish you'd sit. You're making me nervous." At least he was having an impact. He sat.

"Your husband didn't want to run for president. He said over and over that he wasn't interested. No 'fire in the belly,' he said. The standard excuse. Then, less than a week after a prostitute is murdered in San Francisco, he announces he's in the race."

"Do you have proof that Harry and this prostitute ever met?"

"She was captured on video following him out of a hotel."

"Hardly arm in arm." Her taut face relaxed a bit. "And let me ask you another thing. You say you worked for Julian Mellow? Have you ever known him to back a loser?"

"No."

"Did he ever make an investment knowing that it wouldn't pan out?"

"No."

"Did you ever know him to take an enormous risk, something on the order of blackmailing a United States senator, when the chances of a payoff were slim to nothing?"

"No, but—"

"Then why the hell is Julian, why the hell *would* Julian Mellow risk everything to force my husband into a race that he quite clearly can't win?" Her voice was louder, and her lower lip was quivering. Zach had the confirmation he'd come looking for—she knew *what* was going on, but not *why*. Still, he had no proof of anything.

"Julian's son was murdered in Kamalia. I think he wants to raise awareness of the political situation in that country."

"*Raise awareness?* Is that what this is about?" She threw her head back and laughed. "He owns half the TV stations in this country. He could produce and broadcast a dozen documentaries to *raise awareness* of Kamalia."

"Look, I don't really care why he's doing this," Zach said. "One of Julian's…associates tried to kill me and my girlfriend. Twice. I just want to save us, that's all. I don't care who wins the election."

"Don't you? Here I thought I had invited a rabid Democrat into my home, someone intent on bringing down my husband."

"It's not about politics, Mrs. Lightstone. This is about me and Sarah."

"You sound like Julian. He has the rich person's disdain for politics. Either they buy their way into the game at the senatorial level or they lavish their money on both parties, which is really the ultimate fuck-you, when you think about it, as if they're above mere ideology, impervious to it."

"So you admit you know Julian."

"Of course I do. At a certain level of wealth everyone knows everyone. Great wealth is the smallest of worlds."

"Other than insisting that your husband focus on Kamalia, is there—"

"I haven't said that he insisted on anything."

"Other than Kamalia, is there anything else he's done to influence your husband's campaign?"

"He has no influence on Harry."

"Then it's about *after* the election."

Her eyes lost focus for a second. "Harry is going to lose

next week," she said in a tense and tired voice. "Then all this will be moot."

"Sarah and I won't be *moot*. We'll still be in danger."

"Are you in love with her?" she said with something approaching tenderness.

"Yes."

"Then don't waste this precious time in your life on politics and conspiracies." She seemed to drift off for a few moments, then resumed speaking in a quieter tone. "Harry and I never had time for ourselves. From the moment we met our lives were public property. We never really learned how to be intimate. Sometimes I think the public knows him better than I do because the man on the podium, bland as he may seem, *is* Harry Lightstone. The man alone with me doesn't really exist, he's nothing without an audience, or at least a reporter."

She reached for her drink but changed her mind and stood up. Without saying anything she headed out of the room. Zach followed like a royal attendant.

"You're a handsome young man," she said downstairs at the front door. "And if you worked for Julian you must be smart, too." She ran a hand along his arm. There was something sad and hungry about the gesture, the way her hand gently squeezed his arm, as if taking his measure. "Forget about all this, for your sake. Go to your girlfriend, let her help you through this. I can arrange for a car to take you to her. Is she here in the city with you?"

"No, she's—" He looked closely into her face. "She's somewhere safe."

She opened the front door and he saw two secret servicemen at the curb. "Goodbye, Zach." She made a show of kissing his cheek for the security detail.

He left the townhouse and grabbed a cab to the hotel near his old apartment on the West Side, where he'd earlier checked in.

• • •

# CHAPTER 54

"There's a lunatic outside my townhouse who says he knows you," Marcella Lightstone said in her fluty, unflappable tenor. The call to Julian's cell phone came just as he and Caroline were settling into bed. "He says he used to work for you, and he's threatening to, quote, expose everything, unquote, unless I talk to him."

Julian knew instantly that it was Zach Springer, and just as quickly he formulated a plan. "Is he alone?" When she answered in the affirmative he said, "Invite him in, find out what he knows, where he's staying, where his girlfriend is. This last point is crucial: the whereabouts of his girlfriend."

"This is getting to be—"

"Goodnight, Marcella." He clicked off.

"You need to tell me what's going on," Caroline said before he'd even put down his phone. Standing by the bed, wearing a floor-length satin robe, her hair pinned up, she looked as beautiful and untouchable as one of the Greek goddesses in the Met across the street. For a moment, a moment of weakness, he wanted to tell her everything, just to offload the burden, but he knew she couldn't help him, and so there was no value in letting her in on his plans. This filled him with a heavy sadness, another thing that held no value—an enemy of value, in fact, in as much as sadness might make him weak or irresolute. So he did the only thing he could do to relieve it. He walked across the library to her and loosened the sash around her waist, exposing her flawless form. He ran his hands along her waist and stomach, noting the smooth, marblelike coolness of her skin, then up to her breasts, even smoother but much warmer. Did her patients imagine the perfect form under the sensible suits she wore to her office? Did they desire her?

"Please, Julian, I'm worried," she said as he continued to trace her sculpted form with his hands. "You're distracted, you're anxious, you're not yourself."

He placed one foot behind her and gently pushed, putting her off balance. He caught her before she fell back and slowly lowered her to the floor.

"Here?" she whispered as he tugged at his belt. He didn't answer.

Minutes later she whispered, "Julian, you're hurting me."

He forced himself to ease up, scrambling to find another image on which to focus, for it had been Marcella Lightstone's lips he'd been kissing, just to stanch that voice that seemed always to mock him, Marcella's breasts he'd been nuzzling, Marcella's body he'd been assaulting.

"Julian, stop."

He ignored her until he had his release, then got up and left his wife on the floor in the study.

## MONDAY, OCTOBER 26

# CHAPTER 55

Victor Carron lived in a grand home about forty-five minutes north of Manhattan. At heart it was a standard suburban center-hall colonial, painted white with black shutters. But like a computer morph of an ordinary home it stretched in all directions, becoming enormous, outsized, monumental. Billy Sandifer, who had parked his rented car a quarter mile away, guessed that it had six or seven bedrooms, and at least as many bathrooms. It was one of about a dozen giant houses in a new subdivision—a down-market term for a string of one-acre, lavishly landscaped plots.

The late morning autumn light was flattering to the neighborhood and to the Carron mansion, surrounded not by saplings but fully mature trees, no doubt transplanted fully grown at unimaginable expense. The fall foliage was on fire, the preternaturally green lawns jangly with red and yellow and orange leaves skittering in the gentle breeze.

Victor Carron, chief investment officer of Searchlight

Investments, had received a call over the weekend from Julian Mellow, telling him not to come to work Monday morning; the publicity surrounding the vice presidential scandal was too intense, so his presence would be disruptive—just stay at home, answer no questions, and sit it out. Carron's wife, Julian had told him, a cardiologist at Mount Sinai Hospital in Manhattan, would presumably not take the day off. But if she did, Julian had wanted to know, Billy would deal with it, right?

Right.

And the two young kids would more than likely go to school, same as always, never mind the scandal. But if they *were* at home, Billy could deal with that, right?

Right.

And if there were household help, Billy could deal with—

Right.

"Don't fuck up again," Mellow told him. Billy rubbed his left shoulder, where the bullet had hit him. Zach Springer had fucked up, not killing him in the water when he had the chance. Now he was back in New York, had even visited Marcella Lightstone. And Sarah was nowhere to be found.

He'd do what he had to, but as he approached the front door of the house, which he was pleased to note could not be seen from the street, thanks to a row of meticulously trimmed hedges, he hoped Victor Carron would be alone. In fact, he was guessing that was the case. The house exuded emptiness, despite the window curtains and shades. For all its grandeur, there was something eerily still and one-dimensional about it, like an exterior set for a movie that could be dismantled in an hour.

He tucked in his shirt and slicked back his hair with his hands, trying to transform himself into a credible emissary from the second or third richest man in America, and rang the doorbell. After a few seconds he rang it again, then again. Had Victor Carron disobeyed the great Julian Mellow and left the house?

"Who's there?" came a man's voice from the other side of the thick wooden door.

"Julian Mellow sent me," he shouted and immediately heard a lock opening.

Victor Carron was a slightly built man, about forty, whose dark, suspicious eyes and beakish nose suggested a wary, predatory intelligence, just the face you'd want on a man who managed your wealth. His still-thick hair, slicked back from his face, was silvering around the edges, which added to the aura of sleek control. He had on a blue-checked flannel shirt, more Brooks Brothers than Land's End, and khaki slacks.

"You're alone," Carron said, disappointed. "When Julian told me he was sending someone I figured there'd be a whole team of lawyers." His eyes ranged up and down, taking in Billy's black sweatshirt, blue jeans, running shoes—not the attire of a lawyer dispatched by a mogul to defend an investment wizard.

"Short notice," Billy said as he stepped inside an airy, two-story foyer dominated by a grand staircase. A lawyer-foyer, it was called, he'd read that somewhere; always double height with some sort of giant overhead lighting fixture and a staircase out of *Gone With the Wind*. He could see similarly outsized rooms opening off the lawyer-foyer and felt angry resentment rising inside him, the muscles in his arms tensing almost painfully, as if they wanted, on their own, without instructions, to tear down the banister, smash the huge globe on the chandelier, rip the face off the lord of this phony-ass manor.

It had been satisfying, back in the day, desecrating the ill-gotten homes of the undeserving rich. It had been fun.

"Are you alone?" Billy asked as casually as he could.

"We thought it was important to maintain as normal a schedule as possible, for the children," he said. "My wife is a cardiologist; she has post-op rounds to make…"

"Servants?" he asked, and could tell from Carron's subtly pained reaction that no respectable lawyer would have used that word. "Household help?"

"We have a cleaning lady, she sleeps out, and we told her not to come today." The phone rang from somewhere nearby. "It never stops ringing. I don't answer it."

"Reporters?"

"Mostly friends. The press doesn't have my landline or my cell. Not yet. Do you want coffee? Let's work in the kitchen, I've outlined a strategy for refuting this whole thing, which is total bullshit, by the way, I assume you understand that going in."

The kitchen was vast and, to Billy's untutored eye, vastly impractical, the refrigerator a long and circuitous trek around a marble-topped center island from the stove, the sink a similarly wasteful journey from the large breakfast table. For some reason Billy found the kitchen's impracticality particularly offensive. The pistol seemed to leave his jacket pocket on its own.

"What the hell?" Carron shook his head, more incredulous than alarmed; perhaps it was the surreal quality of the past day that made the appearance of a gun pointed at his head seem like just one more bizarre and soon-to-be-resolved incident.

"Get your car keys."

"What?"

"Your car keys."

As if in a trance, Carron walked to a drawer near a door at the far end of the kitchen and found a set of keys.

"Which way is the garage?" Billy asked.

"You're not from Julian Mellow." The color had drained from Carron's face.

"The garage," Billy said, and slowly raised the gun to Carron's head. "I'll kill you right here if I have to."

Sweat bubbled up on Carron's forehead as tears began leaking from his eyes. But he seemed unable to move.

"Watch my index finger, Vic." Billy slowly, carefully flexed it on the trigger.

"Okay! Okay. Garage." Carron backed away slowly, then turned and walked to a door at the far end of the room. This led to a laundry room the size of the living room of an ordinary house (more resentment at the obscene waste of space), and then, through another door, to a three-car garage.

"Where are we going?" Carron asked.

Billy shut the door. The garage, illuminated only by faint light through a small window at the far side, contained a single vehicle, a gleaming silver Lexus SUV (gas-guzzling pig car). Billy's finger tightened on the trigger.

"Get in the car," he said.

"Who are you?" Carron's voice was an octave higher, and his face, even in the dusky garage, glowed with perspiration. "Is it money? I can get you what you want."

"Yeah, I see that."

Carron smiled uncertainly. "How much do you want?"

"Get in the car."

"Is this about the vice president?"

"What do you think?"

"But I didn't do anything. I never had any contact with him, no one did. This is a plot." A deeper intensity of terror flashed across his eyes. "Are you with the government?"

"Not the government. Get in the car."

Carron opened the door.

"Now get in and start the engine."

After a brief hesitation Carron used a remote to open the garage doors and pressed the ignition button. Billy glanced around and noted the two concrete steps from the garage to the laundry room door.

"Get out," he said.

"I don't—"

"*Get out.*" Carron's right hand reached for the ignition. "No, leave the car on." Carron got out and stood between Billy and the Lexus. He was several inches shorter than Billy, which was good, but he'd have to be very accurate for everything to work as planned.

"Back in the house," Billy said.

"But the car…"

"I doubt fuel efficiency is something you worry about," Billy couldn't help saying.

Carron smiled weakly and moved toward the door. Just before he placed his right foot on the first of the two concrete steps, Billy smashed the pistol into his right temple. After a long moment in which Carron seemed frozen in a standing position, he crumpled to the floor, his head hitting the concrete with a thud that would have been sickening, if Billy were susceptible to such a feeling.

The garage was already filling up with fumes, so Billy had to work fast. He went back into the house and, in the paneled library, found a wet bar—the rich were so predictable. He donned a pair of leather gloves and took a bottle of vodka, Carron's drink of choice, according to Julian Mellow, and brought it back to the garage. From his pocket he removed a small funnel, which he inserted into Carron's mouth, then filled it slowly with vodka. Blood had begun oozing from the right side of his head onto the battleship-gray floor. Billy continued to slowly fill Carron with vodka. When he'd poured three drinks' worth he capped the bottle and put it down. He lifted Carron's limp body and angled it so his head brushed the top step, leaving a bloodstain on the sharp corner. Then he positioned him so that the scenario would make sense: Carron gets in his car, restless after a morning pent up in his McMansion, unsteady from all the vodka, realizes he's forgotten something and gets out of his car, only to stumble, hit his head on the step, and fall down, unconscious, on the garage floor, where he dies of carbon monoxide poisoning. Or maybe he'd been trying to kill himself—assuage his guilt—and had fallen when the car fumes began to take effect.

Billy reached into the car and pressed the remote to close the garage doors. He reentered the house, closed the door behind him, found a glass in the kitchen that he filled with a finger of vodka, and left the glass and bottle on the counter. He started to leave but had a thought. He took the funnel out, placed the thin end in his mouth, and poured a small amount of vodka—Ketel One, an expensive brand he'd never tried—down his throat. It was good, like burning silk, a realization that angered him as much as anything. It cost twice as much as regular vodka and it really was good. Fuck.

He put the funnel back in his pocket and left the house. By the time he started his own car, several minutes later, he had no doubt that Victor Carron was dead.

TUESDAY, OCTOBER 27

# CHAPTER 56

"We have made the decision to move on Saturday."

Sophie scanned Rémy Manselle's small living room, so crowded it reminded her of a rush-hour subway in New York. All memories of New York felt like bulletins from a life lived in another, distant era by another person; their unreality always disoriented her, like a spell of dizziness. She had to force herself to focus on the moment, on the twenty or so faces, all of them male, looking at her, waiting for instructions.

"We will move on the palace at eight thirty," she said. "From every possible direction. In small groups, no more than two or three, to avoid detection. We need a final head count. Guy?"

"I will have ten with me."

"Étienne?"

"Six."

"Max?"

"Six."

And so on, as she polled the room to determine how many each comrade had managed to round up for their cause. She kept a running tally in her head, and when everyone had spoken she announced the result.

"Ninety-five," she said. "We have more than enough weapons here. Between now and Saturday morning, you are responsible for distributing them to your comrades. Bring a car and drive it directly into the garage. There you will get what you need."

Under Rémy's garage were just over two hundred assault rifles, a king's ransom of weapons paid for by Matthew's father, perhaps the only man who hated the Boymond regime as much as she did. Even her comrades didn't burn with hatred the way she and Julian Mellow did. They wanted freedom and liberty and justice, as did she. They wanted power, which didn't interest her. But she would never have risked her life for such abstract principles, nor would Julian Mellow have invested his money in them. What she wanted was to dig her knife into the heart of Laurent Boymond, to watch his face as she twisted it, to feel his warm blood on her hands. For her, revenge was the least abstract of emotions, the most tactile. Since Matthew's murder, only the image of Le Père suffering at her hand had the power to incite her.

"Do we have a chance?" someone asked, pulling her back into the room. She rubbed her hands together and was almost surprised to find them dry. "They say the palace is guarded by more than two hundred men."

"On Saturday, most of the cabinet will be meeting for a ceremony in the *Chambre d'Etat*. The south gate will have been left open and unguarded. There will be a skeleton crew on duty, just enough to keep the government from noticing that the usual contingent of guards is absent. It is the perfect opportunity. The government does not usually meet on a Saturday, a day when the streets around the palace are empty."

"How do you know about the skeleton crew?" someone asked.

"I have the assurances of one of the top men in the government."

"Who is it?"

"I cannot say."

"Then how are we supposed to trust him, to trust you?"

"He will make it easy for us to gain control of the palace, and therefore the government."

"Why?"

"Yes, why is he doing this?"

"He favors our cause," she said with as much sincerity as she could summon.

Otherwise she would have to explain that Claude DuMarier was being paid by a very rich American to betray his country, having been promised a life of luxury in exile, and she didn't want them to believe, *to know*, that they were risking their lives on the word of a man whose only motivation was greed.

"Hah, no one in the government favors our cause," someone said.

A chorus of agreement filled the room. It was time to retake control.

"If you don't believe in this, leave now," she shouted over the din, which quickly subsided. "I have worked for the past year to make this day happen. I have traveled long distances to make this day happen. I have smuggled arms across the border into Kamalia, risking everything I have, including my life. And I am telling you now, here, in this room, that on Saturday the south gate at the palace will be unguarded, the entire government will be in the *Chambre d'Etat*, waiting for us. If you do not believe this, leave now."

The room went silent, and for a few moments she was back in New York again, lights trained on her face, hair and makeup assistants scurrying around her, a camera clicking away, and all because of her, because she had the power to draw these people with their powerful lamps and huge reflectors and long-lensed cameras, the magnetic center of the universe—that's how she'd felt when the hot lights had made her skin glow like something radioactive, something fearsome. It had lasted only briefly, that feeling of power, fading with the bright lights, but it had felt wonderful. And she felt it in Rémy's living room, the power to move people. Only now it wasn't her almond eyes and sharp cheekbones; it was her words, her conviction.

"Saturday, then," said someone.

"Saturday," someone else repeated, and soon the room was chanting, throwing their fists in the air: "*Samedi! Samedi! Samedi!*"

But Sophie's fists remained at her side as she watched. In her mind's eye her right hand clutched a knife and held it above the heart of Laurent Boymond, a moment frozen in time, the moment she'd been working toward ever since thugs had burst into her home, *their* home, and taken Matthew from her.

# CHAPTER 57

Zach arrived in Washington, DC, by Amtrak on Tuesday morning. He walked quickly through Union Station, content to be jostled by crowds of ambling tourists admiring the magnificent building and by commuters ignoring it as they hurried to their offices. He never wanted to be alone again. The cab ride to the State Department building on C Street took him past several DC landmarks and a dozen or more marble buildings housing government offices, all designed to project solidity and timelessness. They struck him as vain and preening. Real power wasn't contained by marble tombs in Washington but sheathed in gleaming glass and steel 250 miles to the north—in particular, on the sixtieth floor of 14 West 57th Street.

A Google search at the Upper West Side hotel he'd been holing up in had yielded the name he needed, which he gave to the guard on the first floor of the enormous Harry S. Truman Building on C Street, headquarters of the State Department. He'd called from New York to make an appointment, claiming to be a representative of Julian Mellow, a name that opened doors everywhere, even in the State Department's Bureau of African Affairs, which focused on sub-Saharan Africa.

Jackie Yonkus greeted him at a second-floor reception area. She struck him as incongruously glamorous for a policy wonk: thirty-five, he guessed, tall and model-slim, with long, silky blonde hair and pale, delicate features that were in sharp contrast to the drab quarters in which she worked. She wore a pale lavender sweater, black slacks and heeled shoes that brought her up to almost six feet. Zach felt a bit underdressed in her presence, even in the khakis trousers and white oxford shirt he (or rather, Arthur Sandler) had bought that morning at a Gap on the West Side.

She led him down a series of corridors before showing him into a dark, windowless office. Books filled every available surface, and her small desk was covered with neat piles of papers and reports, but otherwise Jackie Yonkus's office offered few clues to her life outside the office: no family photos, no revealing knickknacks, not even a coffee mug or takeout cup.

"I would have thought Kamalia was the last place Julian Mellow would want to be involved," she said from behind her desk. Zach sat in the single visitor's chair across from her. "After you called I sent emails to our Deputy Chief of Mission in Villeneuve, as well as to our public affairs officer, our political officer, and our economic officer. No one has had any contact with Julian Mellow since his cobalt operations were nationalized. I'm sure you know his son was killed there following the coup."

"Matthew was a reformer. I think his father wants to carry on his work."

Her pale blue eyes flashed skepticism. "Julian Mellow, a reformer?"

"Where Matthew is concerned, Julian's not the same man he is in business."

She considered this for a few moments. "Perhaps. West Africa is something of a backwater here at State. And Kamalia is the backwater of the backwater. We get very little attention. Other than cobalt there's nothing much to interest anyone in the place." She lifted a slim manila folder. "This is a file of every article published in the United States about Kamalia so far this year. You see, nobody cares."

"Harry Lightstone cares."

"It's a bit of a surprise, a huge surprise, actually, that Lightstone keeps mentioning Kamalia. In the past month I've had a dozen reporters sitting right where you are, asking about Kamalia. But even they don't end up writing articles. There's not much to say, I suppose."

"What got you into it, then?"

"Why Kamalia?" Her pale skin reddened very slightly. "When I started here there wasn't even a Kamalia specialist. I began on the West Africa desk. I'd joined the Peace Corps after college, went to Ghana, and fallen in love." Her color deepened. "With the country, the region. Everything there is so much more vivid, I thought, at least compared to Greenwich, Connecticut, where I grew up. Everything in Greenwich is tastefully muted, monochromatic—the green lawns, the pastel sweaters, the white skin. In West Africa the colors seemed brighter to me, more varied, the sounds louder and crisper, the issues so much more vital. Here, we argue every four years about *paying* for healthcare. In much of West Africa, there is no such argument because there is no healthcare to speak of."

She was completely flushed, though it wasn't embarrassment but rather conviction. And whatever delicacy he'd read into her face was gone, replaced by a formidable passion.

"Of course, it was never really that simple," she said. "Especially once I got to State, where it's all about nuance. Here it's all about how a 1 percent increase in the export duty in Ghana will result in a 6 percent increase in the cost of cocoa in the US, which will result in a point-zero-three percent rise in the price of candy bars, which will result in a point-zero-zero-three rise in inflation, which is unacceptable, completely unacceptable, never mind that that 1 percent increase in the Ghana export tax will finance a new hospital and three schools. What's a hospital and schools compared to affordable candy?"

"But why Kamalia?"

"It was offered to me two years ago. I was one of the youngest people to be assigned to a country desk, so I took it. It was after the coup, which caught us by surprise, and State hates surprises. They felt they needed a specialist in case the place got hot again. At first I couldn't wait to move on. There isn't much prestige in Kamalia, as you can see." She looked around the small, cluttered office.

"Ghana and Ivory Coast get windows. Not Kamalia." They both smiled. "Have you been there? It's not much of a country, really, Villeneuve doesn't have a speck of colonial charm. Everything is half finished—the roads, government buildings, power plants. Everything stopped when Laurent Boymond took over, so there's a Brigadoon quality to the place, as if any progress at all was just a dream. But when you leave the city and travel up into the mountains, it's the most beautiful place on earth, something about the air fills you with energy, and the sky seems so close, you feel like you're in some sort of magical biodome where nothing bad can happen. The Kamalians feel it, too, even after all they've been through. There's no despair there, just resignation."

"Why is Lightstone talking about Kamalia? Is there really a threat there?"

"Nothing is happening in Kamalia. Le Père Boymond has everything under tight control."

"Lightstone talks about human rights violations."

"Our sources indicate that, compared to other countries in the region, Kamalia is not a human rights concern. Human Rights Watch puts it at number forty-three. For Africa, that's practically nirvana."

And yet Lightstone had made Kamalia a centerpiece of his campaign, devoting precious sound bites to it when he could be talking about issues that really resonated with the public. Would Julian Mellow go to such lengths just to hear Le Père's regime denounced in speeches by a candidate who was sure to lose? Would that be enough for him?

"What about civil unrest, danger to the Americans there?"

"We have intelligence that suggests that there is a small band of insurgents who are dedicated to overthrowing Boymond's regime. They are well armed, but small in number…perhaps a hundred people, mostly in their twenties. They're led by a woman named Sophie DuVal."

"Matthew Mellow's girlfriend," Zach said. He'd met her once or twice, and recalled occasional newspaper profiles of the glam-

orous couple who inexplicably deserted New York for third-world
Africa, where they dedicated themselves to improving the lives of
the people.

"We think she's planning some sort of coup. It will fail."

"Why are you so sure?"

"Le Père's army is loyal to him, his palace is more secure than
the Pentagon, and I don't think the people will rise up in support
of them even if they do make headway. As I said, this is not a
country of activists."

"But you said they are armed."

"AK-47s, mostly. State-of-the-art assault rifles."

"Well…"

"The government has ten times as many AK-47s, and grenade
launchers and tanks. Everything short of nukes. If they had nukes,
I'd have a window."

"If the government has such tight control, where did the
insurgents get the weapons?"

"They must have smuggled them into the country somehow.
And someone's financing their activities. Sophie DuVal occasionally travels to Paris, as recently as four months ago. We think she
meets her backer there, but we have no proof. Is it Julian Mellow?"

"I don't know," he said, though he was quite sure it was. Still,
the question nagged at him: why would Julian back a doomed
coup? It seemed as uncharacteristic as backing a losing presidential
candidate.

"He has the motive. Le Père nationalized his company and
then killed his son."

"So there's no hope for Sophie and her comrades?"

"If they do go ahead with the coup attempt, it will be suicide
for them."

"But Le Père was successful three years ago."

"We assume he had some sort of ally within the former government. If the insurgents have someone inside the Boymond
government helping them, they may have a chance. But our intelligence says there is no such person."

Or perhaps there was. Julian might have arranged for an "ally" within the Kamalian government. He'd recently shown the lengths he would go—the lengths he *could* go—to manipulate events and people.

"And if the coup fails, the US's position on that will be…"

"No position. An internal affair in a sovereign nation."

"But if Lightstone should win?"

"Perhaps he'll deliver another speech on the subject of human rights at a fundraiser. But I doubt anyone will cover it. My message to Julian Mellow would be, 'Stop your support of the insurgents; you're sending them to certain death by encouraging them with money and perhaps a sense that the greater world cares about them.' I don't want to see any more bloodshed in Kamalia. They don't deserve it. Will you send him that message?"

Julian never backed losers. Yet Sophie DuVal and her comrades were doomed to defeat in Kamalia. Why was he supporting them, even if financing a few hundred weapons was, for him, a tiny investment? A sentimental attachment to the woman his son had loved? But Julian had no sentimental attachments. And sending her to her death was hardly a way to honor his son's memory. No, if Sophie was going to lose, then losing, for Julian, was winning. Her defeat would help him in some way, help his cause, which was electing Harry Lightstone to the White House. Sophie would lose—in fact, she was being set up to lose. Of course, her defeat—inevitably bloody—would validate the seemingly out-of-left-field ranting of Harry Lightstone, make him look prescient and perceptive. *Presidential.*

"Will you tell Mr. Mellow that his support of the Kamalian insurgents will only lead to more bloodshed?" Jackie asked.

"I'll do my best," was the only honest answer he had.

• • •

# CHAPTER 58

Julian read the *Times* coverage of Victor Carron's death as his Gulfstream G650 banked over northern New Jersey and headed west. He could just make out Newark Airport to the left, commercial jets lined up on the runway, waiting their turn. He'd be halfway to Chicago before the last one left the ground.

The flight attendant brought him black coffee as soon as the pilot turned off the seatbelt sign. He drank it while reading the paper. Apparently Carron had been asphyxiated in his own garage, according the Westchester coroner's office. He'd slipped and split his head open on a concrete step leading from the garage to the house. One theory was that he'd been headed somewhere, after a drunken morning, turned on the car, realized he'd forgotten something inside the house, and left the engine running when he went in to retrieve it. The vodka-induced fall had not killed him, but it had knocked him unconscious and the carbon monoxide had done the rest. Another theory held that he'd turned on his Lexus to attempt suicide, decided to go back inside the house to get something, perhaps more vodka, or paper and pen to write a note, and, lightheaded from the carbon monoxide, had slipped and fallen.

The death was front-page news. Proponents of the suicide theory, including several Wall Street colleagues, were quoted in one of several *Times* articles on the affair speculating that, after a life of nothing but success, Carron slipped up just once, in agreeing to manipulate the vice president's portfolio, and simply couldn't forgive himself—nor face the prospect of a trial and, potentially, jail. He was a man who allowed himself no flaws, said one associate. With Victor, it was perfection or nothing, said another; faced with a major shortcoming, he'd chosen nothing. That he was guilty of colluding with the vice president was unspoken but understood; his suicide was as good as an admission. Of course, others quoted in the articles, mostly family members and close friends, held to the accidental death theory. But his blood alcohol level seemed to point to a guilty conscience in any case.

Julian put down the *Times* and devoted a few moments' thought to Victor Carron. He tried to have as little involvement as possible with the men who ran his companies. He'd set up a pyramid structure that enabled him to oversee his empire with only five people reporting to him. Victor Carron had not been one of those people. But Victor's boss, who oversaw all of Mellow Partners' financial services investments, had reported to him, and so Julian had not been able to completely avoid meeting him. He recalled that Carron had tried to interest him in joining a board, a disease charity, something to do with children. More than likely he had a child afflicted with that disease, since it didn't sound like the sort of charity you'd join to build business contacts; museums and hospitals were better suited for that. Well, the sick child and the rest of the family would be well provided for. Carron had been paid several million dollars a year and had a generous, company-paid insurance policy.

As had become his custom, Julian searched inside himself for a trace of remorse and failed to find one. Victor Carron was no longer available to refute allegations that he'd manipulated the vice president's investment trust at the veep's request. And his suicide, if that's what it was, seemed to confirm the public's worst suppositions. Julian waved for the flight attendant and asked for his breakfast.

• • •

In Chicago, he was met by a car and driver and taken to the Ritz-Carlton, where a Secret Serviceman escorted him from the lobby to a suite on the top floor, then through a large living room to a smaller sitting room with a view through a large picture window that was all sky and lake, a flat, uninterrupted expanse of pale blue.

"Gentlemen," he said on entering the room.

Four men, huddled around a coffee table covered with documents and newspapers, looked up at him, but only Harry Lightstone showed recognition.

"Julian, good morning," he said wearily. "We were just talking about the suicide, if that's what it was. It's simply unbelievable. Terrible tragedy."

He seemed genuinely saddened, which was almost sweet in a pathetic way, given that Harry had never met Victor Carron and that the election, which would be significantly impacted, in his favor, by the suicide, was less than a week away. It seemed highly unlikely that the vice president would resign, but he had been transformed from a political asset into a serious liability, sucking attention away from Nessin himself.

"Julian Mellow, this is Fred Moran, my campaign manager, and this is…"

"Can we talk in private?"

Lightstone's jaw quivered with indignation, for he correctly saw the waving off of introductions as a humiliation directed at him, not his staff. As Julian expected, the other men recognized the Mellow name, if not the Mellow face, and promptly stood up. Money talked, even in the last, frantic week of an apparently doomed national campaign. Especially then.

"We'll issue a statement," Moran said as he gathered his papers. "Sincere condolences to family, confidence that this had nothing to do with the vice president, importance of focusing on the issues affecting the American people."

"I'll get someone on that right away," said another man whom Julian recognized as Michael Steers, the campaign's communications director. Like Moran, he had the sallow, bug-eyed look of someone riding a sleepless wave of caffeine and adrenaline. All four men hurried from the room.

"A few things," Julian said the instant he and Lightstone were alone. He was shocked by how gaunt the candidate looked. He'd lost a good ten pounds. Didn't candidates usually gain weight? If the election were somehow postponed a month Lightstone might simply vanish altogether. "First, there are reports that money is running short in the campaign."

"You can't simply write us a check, Julian. There are limits, even for you."

"Is it true or not?"

"We've blown through about a billion dollars in total, since the convention. Every penny we have left is earmarked for television ads."

"Is there enough?"

"We thought so. But some of the states we'd assumed we'd lose—Indiana, for example, and Virginia—have tightened up. We've had to divert funds from battlegrounds and Virginia isn't a cheap media market; it's—"

"I'd like a list of states where you need more advertising," he said, cutting off the next president.

"Do you really think you can buy this? Don't you realize that if there's a hint of scandal, you'll blow what little momentum I have?"

"I'd like the list by this evening, categorized by media market."

"If you think you can—"

"Second. Tonight you are speaking before the Veterans of Foreign Wars."

"Otherwise known as my base."

The door opened and Michael Steers stepped in. "Senator, there's a crew from CNN in the lobby, looking for a live statement on the Carron suicide. If we hurry we'll make the morning shows."

"The senator will be available in five minutes," Julian said before Lightstone had a chance to reply. Steers glanced uncertainly at Lightstone and retreated.

"I want you to call for the president to send a peacekeeping unit to Kamalia. Challenge him in front of an audience of aging hawks. Warn the country that there will be bloodshed, American blood, if we don't take proactive measures."

"We're getting no traction on Kamalia. In fact, I look like a jackass every time I mention that godforsaken—"

"Third, I need to locate a person. Somewhere in this country, more than likely using a fake or stolen credit card. I need you to use your government connections to trace this person by whatever means necessary. I need this information immediately, tomorrow morning at the latest." Julian found himself somewhat short of breath; giving orders was easy, but he was unused to asking favors, and the effort taxed him.

"Do you want me to call the CIA? The FBI?" Lightstone was being sarcastic.

"Whatever you need to do."

"This is not Stalinist Russia."

"But this *is* late October, and you can't afford a negative surprise. Neither can your son."

Lightstone's face crimsoned and his jaw quivered again.

"Her name is Sarah Pearlman." He held out a piece of paper to Lightstone. "Here's everything I know about her. It is vital that she be found. Vital to the campaign," he added when Lightstone seemed about to protest. "She could be your October Surprise, and not a pleasant one."

After a long moment's hesitation, Lightstone took the paper.

## THURSDAY, OCTOBER 29

# CHAPTER 59

Zach had slept during most of the overnight flight to Johannesburg and sleepwalked for two hours at that city's airport before catching a connecting flight to Villeneuve. He'd dreamed of Sarah and their beach on Saint Sebastian, a place that had felt like a prison three days earlier and now seemed like paradise lost. He'd called her before he left JFK; she told him she rarely went outside her hotel, feeling vulnerable even on the crowded sidewalks of South Beach. He assured her that they'd soon be safe and hoped that it was so.

There were only a dozen or so passengers on the South African Airways flight to Kamalia, and he was fifth in line to face the single immigration clerk at Laurent Boymond Airport in Villeneuve, who sat rather imperiously on a high chair behind a scratched Plexiglas screen. Nevertheless, Zach waited almost a half hour, ample time to second-guess the trip to Kamalia. Phones could be monitored, he reminded himself. On both ends. Asking about Julian Mellow's role in a planned insurrection on a tapped phone might endanger Sophie DuVal.

The terminal was a plain, nearly deserted building that looked like a converted hangar; one wall was lined with small, unmanned booths for various obscure airlines. The airport had a sleepy, vaguely dejected air to it, reminding him of restaurants in Manhattan just before they shut down, the scattered diners avoiding eye contact rather than acknowledge, through an embarrassed glance or awkward gesture, that they had made a mistake in coming there.

"Why are you visiting this country?" the clerk asked. He sounded more incredulous than suspicious.

"Business."

"What business do you have in Kamalia?"

"I represent American mining companies," was his prepared answer. "We are interested in Kamalia's rich deposits of nickel and cobalt."

The clerk leafed through his passport, which Zach had purchased, along with a burner phone, the day before from "Eden Services," the outfit that had provided his Arthur Sandler identity, including credit card and license, almost a year ago. Now he was yet another person, Richard Legard, who had apparently either died recently or had his passport stolen—the Eden operative would say nothing about the document's source, other than it might not be valid for more than a week or so. The photo looked like a slightly younger version of Zach, which is why the Eden guy chose it from an amazingly large cache of available passports. *Don't shave for a few days,* he'd told Zach. *Study this guy's expression and match it, okay?*

Zach held his breath and tried to look calm as the clerk consulted a stapled sheaf of papers that appeared to contain a list of names, several of them crossed out or highlighted in yellow. He gave Zach only a cursory glance. Finally, he stamped the passport, slid it back under the Plexiglas shield, and slowly, with obvious reluctance, turned to the next person in line.

As Zach headed for the exit, carrying a small gym bag containing a change of clothes, he took out the piece of paper on which he'd written Sophie DuVal's address. Earlier that day—no, it was yesterday—he'd made a list of the top New York modeling agencies. The third one he'd called had been Sophie's former representatives. He'd been connected to someone's assistant, mentioned a large advertising agency, fed her a story about the client, a cosmetics firm, insisting that only Sophie DuVal would do, and was told that she was no longer available.

"But you must be forwarding her residual checks to some address," he'd insisted.

"To Africa," she'd replied. "How bizarre is that?"

A few minutes later, after quite a bit of persuasion, he had the address, which he gave to the driver of the lone taxi waiting outside the terminal. They drove on a long, straight highway into the city. Occasionally the taxi, a battered old Renault, would drift onto the rutted dirt shoulder, causing it to gyrate terrifyingly until the driver managed to regain the asphalt. The dry, scrubby landscape turned gradually more urban as they neared the city, the houses and stores, most of them one- or two-story stucco structures, growing closer and closer together. Finally, they turned off the highway into a crowded residential area. Though the houses lining the streets weren't tall, and the day was sunny, an aura of gloomy twilight cloaked the neighborhood.

"Here," the driver said, pulling up to one of the nicer houses in the neighborhood, a single-story cottage with a tiny but neatly tended garden in front. The stucco was painted a pale tangerine, in stark contrast to the neighboring homes, whose exteriors were a drab oatmeal. He handed the driver twenty dollars in American currency and got out. He knocked on the front door. After a few seconds it was opened.

There was no mistaking Sophie DuVal. He'd seen her face dozens of times on magazine covers and in celebrity profiles, and he'd seen her once or twice in person, but still he was shocked by her stark, sculptural beauty. She was almost as tall as he was, shoulders squared, neck thrust slightly forward, arms at her side and bowed slightly at the elbows, as if frozen between classical dance movements. And that face: it was beautiful but not trite, each feature slightly off—the eyes a bit too large, the nose too sharp, the forehead unexpectedly narrow. Somehow it all came together to form an unassailably stunning whole.

"You must be from Julian," she said, glancing behind him in each direction. "Well, come in, then." She took his arm and gently pulled him inside. The front door opened directly onto a small living room. The furniture was ramshackle, but she'd made it appealing: a silk scarf draped over the back of a sagging armchair, a profusion of bright pillows artfully arranged on the faded sofa, several small, threadbare rugs overlapped just so.

"I have nothing to do with Julian Mellow," he told a half lie.

"But I met you, in New York. Matthew was honored at a dinner, for his work on behalf of Amnesty International, I think. Julian was there, and you were with him."

She was correct. Julian avoided fundraising dinners—disdained them, in fact, as a waste of time and money. *His* time and money. But where Matthew was concerned all the rules changed, and that night he'd made half the Mellow Partners staff attend the dinner at the Waldorf. Sophie had been there, on the dais, between Matthew and his father. He'd almost forgotten that they'd been introduced, perhaps because she'd seemed as remote to him in person as she did glowering from the cover of *Vogue* or *Elle*.

"I worked for Julian, but I don't anymore."

"Then why are you here?" She folded her arms across her chest. Every gesture was an un-self-conscious pose.

"We need to talk, I—"

She raised a hand. "You look exhausted."

"No, really, I'm—"

"I don't want you collapsing in my living room. And you don't want to experience the glories of the Kamalian healthcare system. Sit, and I'll make coffee."

She left him alone. He sat in the armchair and tried to compose his thoughts. She returned after a few minutes, carrying a tray.

"Matthew took his coffee black," she said when he refused her offer of milk. "I always thought that was typical of him, strong and low maintenance."

"I don't know how strong I am, and my girlfriend would probably not describe me as low maintenance."

"We see so few Americans these days, not like before. It's nice to hear English, to speak it, in my own home. It's very nice." Her voice broke over the last few words.

"I can't say I knew Matthew, but I met him a few times. He was…" He tried to summon a word that would express his admiration for Matthew Mellow without sounding trite or hollow.

"He was unexpected," she said.

"Yes, exactly."

"You knew his father, so you know how remarkable it was that Matthew turned out the way he did. Not that Julian is a bad man. But Matthew had a heart. A soul."

Two things missing from the father—neither had to say it.

"Julian is helping you," he said. She shrugged and sipped her coffee. "He's providing money for weapons," he said. Another shrug. "I was at the State Department," he said. "They know that you're the leader of a group that plans to overthrow the Boymond government. They know that you've acquired arms on the international market. Even I know that takes cash."

"I don't know whether to feel comforted or alarmed that the State Department knows what I'm doing. Or thinks it knows," she added quickly.

"They also think you're doomed to fail."

"Then they definitely do not know everything."

He leaned toward her. "Listen to me, Sophie. They have experts on this part of the world. People who devote their lives to it. I'm sure they have access to intelligence reports. They have contacts within the government. They know about you and your comrades. They know about the AK-47s. And they are convinced that you will fail."

"Then I will have to prove them wrong."

He detected no braggadocio, only profound confidence. Was it her personality, or did she know something that even the State Department didn't?

"I think you're being set up," he said.

"The Boymond regime has killed thousands of innocent people, jailed many thousands more without charging them, let alone bringing them to trial. Under the banner of 'native rights' they've nationalized all of the country's important industries, then eliminated jobs and slashed wages in order to collect more money for themselves. We were on the way to becoming a modern country, a beacon of hope for Africa. Matthew and I were privileged to witness this firsthand, to play a small role in helping it along. Now we are moving backward, slipping into the very same darkness we'd almost succeeded in leaving behind. If you could understand the passion that we feel, the need we have to make things right again, then I think you would not have come here to lecture me about risks and danger."

"*Unnecessary* risks," he said. "*Unnecessary* danger."

She shook her head. "No such things. It is all necessary. Anyway, you haven't told me why you are here. For all I know you are working for them." She jerked her head toward the front door and the hostile world outside her charming cottage.

"Julian Mellow is plotting to..." He took a deep breath. It was always difficult to tell the story from the beginning. Even to his ears it sounded incredible. "...to manipulate the US presidential election." He gave her a summary of what he knew.

She didn't interrupt him. She didn't laugh at him. She didn't roll her eyes or shake her head. When he finished she considered him in silence for a few moments, then spoke in a measured, gentle tone. "I don't see why any of what you've told me, whether it is all true or imagined, brings you here."

He collected his thoughts before explaining. "You and your group are planning something in the next few days, correct?"

"You can't expect me to tell—"

"No, I can't expect you to tell me. You and your group are planning to move against the government between now and the American election. The Republican candidate, Harry Lightstone, has made human rights in Kamalia a theme of his campaign."

"It has been very encouraging to us."

"When your uprising fails, and there are bodies in the streets of Villeneuve, he's going to look very smart, so smart he could win the White House. Julian Mellow is using Kamalia to win the White House."

"Do you expect me to believe that Julian would betray his son's lover, his son's *cause* to…to what, to be in a position to manipulate the president of the United States?"

"It would be the ultimate acquisition for him, true power."

"I don't believe it."

"You're being set up. You can't win. The State Department knows it."

"Maybe they don't know everything, maybe we…"

She glanced away, as if afraid to reveal something in a glance.

"What is it?" he asked.

"It isn't always just about weapons or manpower, who has more. It is also about information and timing. It is true that we are outnumbered. But we will prevail. I know more about this country and this situation than you or your State Department."

Her confidence was absolute, and something in her tone indicated that it was based as much on information and strategy as bullheadedness.

"There's nothing I can say to persuade you to call off your plans?"

"I haven't even confirmed that I have plans."

"But you *have* confirmed that Julian Mellow is the source of your funds."

"I do not recall saying that."

"The US election is six days away. Can you at least confirm that you aren't planning anything until after that?"

"No," she said quietly, "I can't do that."

So the uprising would take place before the election, and would have an impact one way or another. A bloody conflict, no matter what the outcome, would vindicate Lightstone's pointless speeches about the Kamalian situation. But would it be enough to swing the election? He found himself staring at her, trying to picture her beautiful form at the front of an angry mob, trying not to picture her gravely wounded.

"I wish there was something I could say that could persuade you to call off your plans."

"Again, I have not mentioned plans. You have."

"Julian Mellow threw me to the wolves to save himself from a financial scandal. I thought at the time that was as low as he could sink. In the past months he's tried to kill me and the woman I love, and I'm fairly certain he's arranged for the murder of several others, including a US senator. I don't think he'd hesitate to sacrifice you, if he thought it would advance his interests."

"You don't know him as I do," she said. "To me, he wasn't the head of a thousand corporations. He was the father of a brilliant young man."

"He is always Julian Mellow."

She stood up and took the coffee mugs into the kitchen. He followed her. It was a cramped room with a tiny sink, two-burner stove, and waist-high refrigerator. A pretty teapot on the stove, a cheerful tea towel draped on the oven handle, a framed print of the Place des Vosges on the wall—these items claimed the space as hers.

"Now I have some advice for you," she said as she rinsed the mugs. "Leave Kamalia. Immediately." She turned to face him and looked intently into his eyes.

"I wasn't planning on staying."

"It is dangerous for you here, and your presence will draw more attention to me, which I do not want. There's a flight out this afternoon. I will drive you."

"That's not necessary, I'll—"

"I want to. It feels good to speak English, like exercising a muscle you haven't used in a long time. I…" She touched his arm, as if making sure he was real. "I miss him so much."

Tears began spilling from her eyes. He embraced her until she stopped trembling. When she pulled away, her face had regained its resolve.

"I'm sorry," she said. "Most of the people here who knew Matthew are either in jail or missing or confirmed dead. I never talk about him." She took a deep breath. "Let's get out of here."

# CHAPTER 60

The call came through on Julian's private office line. Fewer than six people had that number.

"Monsieur Mellow? *C'est moi*, Claude DuMarier."

The connection was poor, even by Kamalian standards. Julian had a momentary and painful memory of similarly fuzzy calls from Matthew.

"Speak English," he said.

"*Oui, bien sûr.* Very well. How are you, Monsieur Mellow?"

"What is it you want?" He hoped it wasn't more money. He would not deposit a penny more than the six million dollars he'd already transferred to Swiss accounts in DuMarier's name, but he was in no mood for an argument.

"*Toujours les affaires*," DuMarier said. "You asked me to contact you whenever Mademoiselle DuVal had a visitor from overseas. She has one today, as we speak. He arrived from New York, via Johannesburg."

"Who is he?"

"His passport says Richard Legard. Do you know this person?"

"Describe him."

"He is white, tall, athletic physique, brown hair in need of a cut."

"He cannot leave Kamalia until we confirm his identity. Take his photograph and email it to me as soon as you can."

"You do understand, Monsieur Mellow, that I cannot go to Mademoiselle's house personally. We have an arrangement concerning this Saturday, and she must continue to trust me. I will send a trusted lieutenant to handle this, with two associates."

"Will your *lieutenant* have a camera?"

"On his cell phone, of course. You will have the photograph immediately. What email address shall I have him send it to, and the phone number, to confirm?"

Julian told him. "If it is the person I'm looking for, he can't leave the country. You will have to stop him."

"I will have him detained at the airport."

"He must not return to this country."

"I can hold him as long as you want. Of course, after our scheduled event I will not be here to see that he remains in custody." DuMarier chuckled.

"*He cannot return to this country.*"

"Then you are suggesting a more permanent solution?"

"Yes."

"*Très bien*, that can be arranged *aussi*. Of course, this was not part of our original arrangement. I will need to take care of a few people. You do not expect me to do this personally, I hope?"

"How much?"

A long, staticky silence. Julian pictured DuMarier rubbing his fat hands in greedy calculation.

"One million dollars."

It was worth ten times that, a hundred, to have Zach taken care of once and for all.

"I will transfer two hundred and fifty thousand dollars into your account once I receive confirmation that the visitor will no longer be returning to this country. Ever."

"Monsieur Mellow, you cannot—"

"I will not negotiate."

Another long pause. "*Eh bien*, I accept. I must move quickly, while he is still chez DuVal."

Julian was about to hang up when he had a thought. "Wait."

"Monsieur Mellow?"

"If it is him, and before you are finished with him, I want you to ask him a few questions."

"My lieutenant will ask him a few questions."

"Yes, yes. Your *lieutenant* will ask the questions."

"Will he want to answer these questions?"

"No."

"Ah, then this is a more complex assignment."

"If you get me the information I need, I will double your fee."

"*Très bien*. What is the information you need?"

"Your visitor, if he is in fact who I'm looking for, has a girlfriend," he said.


# CHAPTER 61

While Sophie retrieved her car keys from the bedroom, Zach considered the futility of his trip. He'd come to convince Sophie to call off the rebellion and to find more evidence of the connection between Julian Mellow and the insurgency in Kamalia. He'd failed at the first and most important aim, though perhaps he'd had some success with the second: Sophie had as much as admitted to an ongoing, possibly financial relationship with Julian—a man who never backed a loser.

"I wish you would tell me what's really going on," he said when she rejoined him in the living room. "You seem completely confident, but you have only a hundred people on your side at most. The State Department is very close to this situation."

"Then how can we lose?" she said lightly. "Come, I want to get you back to the airport as soon as possible." She grabbed her purse.

They were halfway across the living room when the front door exploded.

A large man in army fatigues, who appeared to have simply walked through the wooden door, charged at them, a rifle held before him. Two similarly dressed men were right behind him.

"What are you—" Before Sophie could finish the lead man shoved her onto her sofa.

"*Ne parlez pas,*" he said as the other two men trained their rifles on Zach.

"If this is about me..." he managed to say despite the pounding in his chest. "Don't hurt her; I came because we are friends from New York."

In one smooth movement the lead man flipped his rifle around and swung the butt into the side of Zach's head, throwing him on top of a small end table, which crumpled under his weight. The right side of his head throbbed, and he felt a warm trickle of blood behind his ear.

Inexplicably, the man took out his phone, held it at arm's length in front of him, and took two photos. He waited a long moment or so, then began typing on the phone.

"Have you received the photograph?" he spoke into the phone a minute later. "Good. Will you confirm that this is the man you are seeking? Yes, I have my instructions. *Au revoir.*"

The man hung up and turned to Zach. "Where is Sarah Pearlman?"

Hearing her name, in that house, in that country, from the lips of that man, was surreal and horrifying.

"I don't know who—"

The lead man flipped his rifle back into position and turned it on Sophie, still on the sofa.

"Tell us where is Sarah Pearlman or I will shoot this woman."

"Don't tell them!" she said. "They won't kill me, they can't. I'm too famous."

"Tell us or we will kill her," the lead man said, but a tremor of irresolution had crept into his voice.

"Don't, Zach. They won't harm me. They have had opportunities before and they never did anything. Don't tell them."

The lead man considered her for a beat, then turned to his comrades.

"*Levez-t'il.*"

They each took one of his arms and yanked him off the broken table. The lead man stepped closer to him. His breath smelled of cigarettes and coffee and his eyes seemed not to blink.

"Tell us where is she and we will not hurt her or you," he said.

Zach was trying to weigh his options, to think the situation through, when the lead man put down his rifle and grabbed his left hand. Before Zach could register what he was doing he bent back his pinky and broke it at the first knuckle.

He howled as his legs buckled. The pain burned up through his arm to the rest of his body.

"You have ten fingers. I will break each one until you tell me where is Sarah Pearlman, then I will move on to larger bones." He still held Zach's left hand in his own, much larger hands.

"She's in New York."

"Where?"

"I…don't know, I…"

The lead man gripped Zach's ring finger and started to pull it back.

"Wait! Wait. Okay, I'll tell you. She's at the Apthorp Hotel." It was the name of the hotel he'd stayed in two nights ago.

The lead man took his cell phone from his belt holster. He said something in French—Zach recognized only the words *Apthorp Hotel* and *New York*—and hung up.

"We wait," he said.

• • •

# CHAPTER 62

It seemed safest and easiest to call Marcella Lightstone.

"I'm about to read *The Very Hungry Caterpillar* to a group of six-year-olds in Canton, Ohio. Actually, 'read' is a misstatement. I've memorized the fucking thing. What do you want?"

Her insolence was both offensive and vaguely attractive.

"I need the Secret Service to do a room-to-room search at a hotel in Manhattan."

"What?"

"The Apthorp Hotel. Her name is Sarah Pearlman, but she may be using an alias. A single woman, by herself. I need to know if she's registered there."

"What is this about?"

"This must be done immediately."

"I can't just order the Secret Service to—"

"Tell the head of your security detail that you've received threats from a woman who appears to be registered at the hotel. They'll be over there in an instant."

"Julian, you're going too far, this is—"

"DO IT."

He heard her gasp. She, too, was unused to being contradicted. After a few moments she quietly said, "Give me the details again."

After he repeated his instructions he added one more: "They are to report back to you and only you, and they are not to harm the girl or take her into custody. You, of course, will call me as soon as you know anything."

He hung up and waited.

• • •

Two hours later and half a world away, the leader's cell phone chirped. After a brief conversation in French he hung up and stepped closer to Zach.

"She is not at the Apthorp Hotel in New York City."

He'd been expecting it. The two hours had been endless, throbbing pain from his left hand mixing with confusion and uncertainty and panic.

"She's using another name. I don't know what it is, but she's there."

"The Secret Service searched every room."

*The Secret Service was looking for Sarah? Julian had managed to enlist the Secret Service to his cause?*

The leader took Zach's injured hand and squeezed it, sending spasms of pain up through his arm.

"One more chance. Where is the girl?"

"I told you, the Apthorp Hotel, she—"

He heard the knuckle of his left ring finger crack and then felt the pain surge like molten lead from his hand to his shoulder. He may have briefly lost consciousness because the next thing he knew the two other men were propping him up by the arms, as if he'd fallen to the floor.

"You have eight fingers left," the leader said. "But I think I will proceed with two at one time for the sake of efficiency. Where is the girl?"

"I DON'T KNOW!" he wailed. "I DON'T KNOW WHERE SHE IS. I DON'T KNOW."

The leader shook his head, feigning disappointment, but his unblinking eyes looked eager as he stepped toward Zach, still supported by the other two men.

"Maybe your fingers are not important to you. Perhaps a larger bone." He picked up his rifle, released the safety, and aimed it at Zach's legs.

"I DON'T KNOW WHERE SHE IS," he shouted through sobs. "I DON'T—"

A shot rang out. He braced himself for the inevitable pain, and when it didn't register he thought, for a moment, that he might be dead. Then the leader dropped his rifle and, a moment later, fell to the floor, a red circle on his back. Zach turned to Sophie, who held a handgun in front of her.

"Drop your rifles," she said.

The two men each held a rifle in one hand, Zach's arms in the other. In the time it would take to let go of Zach and raise their rifles, Sophie could easily shoot them booth. Neither moved.

"*Drop them*," she said.

They released Zach's arms but neither man let go of his rifle. Zach, still standing between the men, reached with his unharmed right hand for the rifle carried by the man on his right. Before he could grab it the man raised it in front of him, his finger on the trigger. Sophie shot him squarely in the chest. He got off a shot, which pierced the ceiling over his head, before collapsing. The other man dropped his rifle at once.

"There is rope in the closet in the kitchen—get it," she said to Zach. He did nothing, still trying to take in what had happened. "Get it!"

Less than five minutes later they had the surviving soldier tied up and gagged.

"I need to get you out of the country," she said when they were done. "My car is in front of the house." Before leaving she grabbed some surgical tape, bandages, and disinfectant from a small first aid kit in the kitchen.

Out front, a small crowd had gathered. They emitted a collective gasp when Sophie emerged, and with a white man, no less, having seen the soldiers enter. She walked quickly across the street to a battered old Renault station wagon and got in behind the wheel. He got in next to her.

"*Au revoir, ma petite maison,*" she said quietly as she pulled away from the curb. "I won't be coming back here. Perhaps I will see you again, after..."

His head was throbbing, almost more than his left hand. Every time he tried to speak he found himself choking, as if unable to breathe. He had no idea what her plan was, where they were going, but he felt safe with her. She had just killed two men, after all. She had already saved him.

A few miles outside the city she pulled over and began to bandage his hand.

"This will hurt, but it's important to immobilize the joints." She bound his left pinky and ring finger tightly to his second and third fingers, wrapping layer after layer of tape around them. The pain was exquisite. He forced himself to concentrate on what she was saying.

"In Kamalia, everyone learns to administer their own health-care. I am sorry I couldn't use my gun sooner, I had to wait until all three were distracted. After I'm finished with your hand I will make a phone call to some people I know who will take you across the border, where they won't be looking for you."

"And you?"

"I will stay with friends until…"

"You should come with me."

"You insult me when you ask me to leave. You see that I can take care of myself."

After bandaging his hand, she got back on the road. A few minutes into the drive she made a phone call, talking in French. Zach felt dizzy as he listened to the conversation that he couldn't understand and watched the passing landscape that he didn't recognize—dry, dun-colored hills interrupted every few miles by clusters of small huts and grazing cattle. His heart still beat so emphatically that he found it hard to sit still, and his hand burned as if it had been dipped in hot oil. And yet, sometime later, vaguely aware of the car slowing and then stopping completely, he opened his eyes and realized he'd been sleeping, or unconscious.

"We're at the border," Sophie said. "You slept for almost forty minutes."

They got out of the Renault. A few yards away was a small hut surrounded by dense underbrush. The air was thick with dust and heat and the insistent, kazoolike whining of some sort of cricket. Another car, an old Jeep, was parked nearby. Two men got out.

"These men will take you across the border and to the airport. They do it all the time, though it's usually weapons they're smuggling, and in the other direction."

The two men, dressed in baggy jeans and stained T-shirts, did not inspire much confidence, and their sneering expressions did little to soothe Zach's nerves.

"The last time, she fire at my friend," one of them said in French-accented English. "He is still not walking properly."

"His 'friend' attacked me," she said to Zach, then turned back to the men. "*Alors*, here is the situation. You will take this man across the border and to the airport, make any arrangements you need to ensure he gets onto a flight. When I have received confirmation that he is safely on his way, we will make plans to meet again to give you your second payment. Here is the first." From her pocketbook she extracted a thick wad of bills. "Ten thousand US dollars."

The two men divided the wad and counted the twenty-dollar bills. It occurred to Zach that he was being rescued by money provided by Julian Mellow.

"These men are scumbags, but they will do anything for US currency," Sophie said as they counted. One of the men smiled at her characterization. "You will be safe with them."

"And you? I feel as if I'm abandoning you."

"There's nothing you can do. Things are going to work out well for us." She seemed so confident he could only nod. "Even so…" She looked around, as if seeing the small clearing for the first time. "Even so, the idea that we're standing here, in the middle of nowhere, and that in half a day you will be in New York. It would be nice to see New York again, to be that person again."

"You will. I'll…" He tried to think of something he could do for her in New York that would in some small way repay her for what she'd done that day for him, and failed. "We'll meet in New York."

"Yes, I know we will."

She kissed him on both cheeks and walked quickly to the Renault under the leering eyes of the two men.

"She is a bitch," one of them said, "but a beautiful bitch." His comrade grunted his endorsement and they both headed to their car.

Once again, Zach felt agitated with pain and anxiety as the Jeep bounced over unpaved roads, yet somehow he managed to pass out, waking up just as they pulled into a small airport. If they had been stopped at the border, which he doubted, he had slept right through it. Two hours later he was on the first flight out, to Johannesburg and, after a six-hour layover, also sleep-filled, the long flight to New York.

## SATURDAY, OCTOBER 31

# CHAPTER 63

Julian awoke early Saturday morning, as was his custom. The *New York Times* was waiting for him in the breakfast room, along with a carafe of coffee. The front page of the paper noted that the election was now a dead heat, with the usual disclaimers about margin of error, the importance of turnout, and, he was gratified to read, "any sort of unpredictable event that could tip this close race in either direction." It was also noted that the contest in certain key states was tightening up.

He drank a cup of coffee and, feeling unaccountably anxious, decided to forego his usual second. He never felt such tension. Anxiety was counterproductive; it led to errors of judgment.

At seven fifteen his cell phone rang.

"Mr. Mellow? It's Mr. Franklin. The plane from Johannesburg just landed."

• • •

Zach had downed two vodkas after takeoff from Johannesburg International Airport Friday night and had slept for most of the flight. Earlier, he'd spent hours at the Joburg airport, dozing on and off while waiting for his flight to New York. As the plane made its slow descent into JFK he formulated a plan, which began with a visit to an emergency room to have his left hand looked at. Then he was going to take what he knew about Julian Mellow and the presidential election and go public. He'd start with the *New York Times*; he had a vague recollection of a business reporter there who would probably give him a hearing based on his former relationship with Mellow Partners. If he couldn't get the *Times* to listen—or believe—he'd move to broadcast networks. He'd distribute leaflets on street corners if he had to. His motivation wasn't to derail Julian; it was to protect himself and Sarah. Once he'd gone public with his information he'd cease to be a threat to Julian. He'd be safe, in fact. Once the world knew what he and Sarah knew they would be safe—it didn't matter if anyone believed him or not.

He joined a long line at US customs, praying that Richard Legard would not be stopped at passport control. He'd take a cab directly from JFK to an emergency room, in Queens, perhaps, then he'd go right to the *Times* on Eighth Avenue. A scoop on the reclusive Julian Mellow would lure any journalist to the office on a Saturday, particularly one who—

He felt hands clutching both arms. On either side of him stood two men in dark suits. He didn't recognize them but easily guessed who they were.

"Secret Service. Please come with us," one of them said quietly.

They didn't wait for him to answer, practically lifting him from the floor and half dragging, half carrying him away. They took him to a small, windowless room that contained a table and four chairs, shoved him into one of the chairs, and left him. He immediately got up and tried the door, which was locked. Several minutes later the door opened and Billy Sandifer walked in.

"You're in luck," he said. "The Secret Service is releasing you. I told them they had the wrong guy."

Zach headed for the door, but Billy grabbed his arm before he got to it. "You're coming with me."

"Like hell."

"We have Sarah."

Zach froze. He hadn't spoken to Sarah since leaving for Africa. Could they have found her? How?

"I don't believe you."

"Then walk out of here." Sandifer shrugged. "You'll never see her again."

"What do you want?"

"Mr. Mellow wants to speak to you."

"Prove to me that you have Sarah."

"Mr. Mellow will give you proof. I can't."

"Tell *Mr. Mellow* to call me."

"I don't tell him what to do. Neither do you. Either come with me or I tell the feds out there that you are the right person after all. You'll be locked up for a long time, my friend. And Sarah will die."

# CHAPTER 64

He felt as if he'd been traveling for weeks, months. The boat from Saint Sebastian. The flight to Miami, then to Saint Louis, then to New York, Johannesburg, Kamalia, and back. He'd lost a full day between the attack in Villeneuve and landing at JFK. And now, arms handcuffed behind him, in the back seat of Billy Sandifer's car, heading upstate. His injured left hand throbbed and his head felt heavy, but he forced himself to stay awake, watching the passing signs, concentrating on remembering the route: George Washington Bridge, Palisades Parkway, Route 17. They were headed toward the Catskill Mountains. A few exits north of Monticello they turned off the highway. He'd already tried to engage Sandifer in conversation, to no avail.

Almost three hours after leaving JFK they turned into a dirt driveway that ran for nearly a half mile through very deep woods, ending at a small, ramshackle cottage.

"One of Mr. Mellow's estates?" Zach said, just to see if he

could get a reaction. Sandifer opened the back door and nodded to indicate that Zach should get out.

The air was cold and smelled of pine trees and rotting leaves. Zach was shivering by the time Sandifer unlocked the cabin door and shoved him inside. The cabin was low-ceilinged and dark. The walls were painted brown and covered with posters whose edges were curled and yellowed with age: they were broadsheets for demonstrations—in Geneva, Seattle, Buenos Aires. The scant furniture appeared to be relics of the seventies: a sagging sofa, beanbag chair, small plastic tables in gumdrop colors.

"Is this your place?" Zach asked.

"It's no one's place," Sandifer answered. He walked over to Zach, who stepped back. "I need to empty your pockets."

As Sandifer went through his pants and jacket pockets, removing cash, change, his cell phone and boarding pass, Zach quickly considered his options. With his hands locked behind his back he wasn't much of a threat. He could throw himself at him, perhaps knock him over. But unless he somehow managed to render him unconscious the move would do no good, and might even cause Sandifer to take revenge. He didn't think he could stand more punishment. His best bet seemed to be to get Sandifer talking, perhaps coax some information from him.

"Someone must own this place," he said while Sandifer rooted through his pockets. "I mean, even if this was some sort of commune, someone pays the taxes."

"No one knows it exists," he said. "Not a penny of taxes has been paid on this place." He sounded proud, boastful.

"The perfect anticorporate hideout." Zach looked around at the posters announcing marches and concerts. Neighboring cabins probably had antlered deer heads mounted over the fireplace; these posters were Billy Sandifer's trophies.

"Doesn't it kill you, working for Julian Mellow, after this?" He nodded at the various trophies.

"That was then," Sandifer said. He piled all of Zach's things on a table.

"Do you know what his companies do, Billy? I know, because I worked for him. I helped him buy those companies. One of them, the DeQuan Corporation, is the largest polluter of the Susquehanna River. They get more fines each year from the EPA than any other company in America, and they don't care, they don't even fight them, because it's worth it, Billy, it's worth choking off the river and paying the fines because the company is so fucking profitable. Pollution and fines are a cost of doing business, like rent and telephone. Another company, Alston Enterprises, ever heard of them? No one has, but they make the shoes that Walmart and Sears still sell under their own name. You know who sews those shoes and glues on the soles that fall off after a few weeks? Children, Billy, in Central America and Southeast Asia, children making twenty-five cents an hour so Julian Mellow, who owns 100 percent of Alston, can take out ninety-five million a year in profits from the company, and that was three years ago when I last saw the company's books. Who knows how much he's taking out now, and I'll bet those kids haven't had a raise in all that time. Doesn't that kill you a little bit, Billy, to be working for a man like that? You used to march against people like Mellow."

Sandifer turned on Zach's cell phone and clicked through his recent calls. Thank God he hadn't called Sarah from it.

"These children, Billy, they're ten, eleven, twelve years old. Younger than Rebecca, Billy, they're younger than your—"

Sandifer dropped the phone and charged at him, his right fist slamming into Zach's gut and sending him sprawling onto the floor. Arms cuffed behind his back, Zach couldn't break his fall and his head hit the floor with a force that temporarily blinded him. He wondered if he might be unconscious, but then heard Sandifer talking to someone. "I'll pick you up in a half hour," Sandifer said into the cell phone, then clicked off.

"What about Harry Lightstone, Billy?" Zach's voice sounded, even to his own ears, weak and unsteady. "How do your comrades feel about your working for a guy who wants to roll back pollution controls, eliminate import duties on goods from Central America and Southeast Asia?"

"I don't have comrades," Billy sneered, and left the cabin. He returned a minute with a length of coiled rope, which he proceeded to wrap around Zach's upper body and legs. Still on the floor, dazed, his vision blurred, Zach was in no shape to resist. His head throbbed, along with his left hand, and his shoulders screamed with pain from having his arms pinned behind him. Sandifer stood up, surveyed his handiwork, turned, and left the cabin.

A minute later Zach heard the car start.

He flexed his arms and legs to test the ropes; they were secure. He resigned himself to waiting for Sandifer to return with the person he was picking up. To keep his mind off what would happen when he returned he focused on one thought: Sarah was alive. If they had killed her they wouldn't be keeping him alive—he'd be of no use to them. So Sarah was alive and they didn't have her. He repeated this to himself, mostly silently but occasionally aloud, just to make sure he was still conscious, as he waited for Sandifer to return.

# CHAPTER 65

The helicopter first appeared as a speck on the horizon, a tiny blemish against the pale late autumn sky. As it approached it grew larger and noisier, and when it finally landed on the parking lot of the Jefferson Elementary School it seemed to suck the air from the entire area; Billy Sandifer actually grabbed the car door handle lest he be drawn into its vortex. The door opened the instant the chopper touched ground. From a distance, Julian Mellow looked almost ludicrously inconsequential next to the mass of gyrating steel. He walked quickly to the car, regaining his usual stature as he got closer.

"How far?" he shouted over the helicopter's din.

"Ten minutes."

"Good, let's go." He got into the passenger side of the car.

• • •

The cabin door opened slowly. There was a momentary pause before Julian Mellow entered. He had on a blue windbreaker, a checked shirt, and khaki pants—a country gentlemen inspecting the stables. After two years spent tracking him from a distance, following his every move, Zach was surprised by how *average* he looked. He'd once known that face very well, but in the intervening years it had morphed in Zach's mind into something grotesque—surely the evil inside him had to manifest itself on the outside. But Mellow looked handsome and composed and even benign. Only his eyes, avoiding Zach as they scanned the small room from one end to the other and back again, betrayed a hint of anxiety.

He stood at the center of the room, a few feet from where Zach was still trussed on the floor. Strangely, after all that had happened, Zach didn't know what to say and felt an odd reluctance to break the silence. Julian must have been feeling similarly, for he seemed paralyzed, his bottom lip turned inward. Only his hands moved, twitching inside his pants pockets like trapped mice. Finally, after what felt like an hour but was perhaps only a few minutes, Julian took his hands from his pockets and moved closer to Zach. *He's going to untie me*, Zach thought, and then Julian kicked him in the stomach with such force it sent Julian staggering back several feet.

Zach felt a surge of air rush upward through his chest and out his mouth. He couldn't even cry out or moan because there was no wind left inside him.

"How dare you?" Julian said, panting from the attack. He stepped forward, and Zach braced himself for a second assault. But Julian stopped, the effort at self-control visible in a stiffening of his arms and face.

"You thought you were indispensable. You were nothing." For

once, words were failing Julian as he tried to express not only the contempt but that most unfamiliar of emotions, frustration.

"There was at least one time I was indispensable," Zach managed to say, pressing his back against the cabin wall and shimmying up to a seated position. "Finnegan. With Finnegan I saved your ass."

"It had to be done."

"That's rich, Julian, it really is. *It had to be done.* You did it, Julian, not *it*. You set me up, you ruined my life."

"There was no choice."

"The way you talk about it, it's like you weren't even involved. *You* had a choice. *You* chose to destroy me. But it was all through lawyers then. You always have someone on hand to do your dirty work. You wanted Finnegan so badly that when you couldn't have it you did a stupid, reckless thing, buying those shares. You risked everything because you couldn't handle losing. And you know what? Your latest scheme won't work, either."

"It is working."

"I know all about all of it, beginning with the murder of Danielle Bruneau in San Francisco. And maybe Harry Lightstone will win on Tuesday. But you're still going to lose, Julian. Because nothing is going to bring Matthew back."

Julian charged at him, frantically kicking him in the leg and waist as if defending himself against an attack dog.

"Nothing will bring him back," Zach gasped as Julian continued to flail at him. "Nothing can change how you practically ignored him when he was alive."

The kicking stopped. Julian was breathing hard. "You're wrong," he said.

"You've been sending money to Sophie DuVal in Kamalia, because you want the government overthrown. But she's going to fail, the woman your son loved is going to die. It's all for nothing, Julian."

"Harry Lightstone will look like a genius when the fighting breaks out. He's been warning of it for weeks."

"And Sophie will die. Do you think that's what Matthew would have wanted?"

"You have no right even speaking his name."

"Did it gnaw at you, the fact that he kept five thousand miles between him and Mellow Partners? Your son was the one thing you couldn't take over. And now he's gone."

Julian kicked him, but the blow lacked conviction.

"Do you ever stop to ask yourself if it's worth it? Are you so full of hate that you really don't care who dies, that you're perverting an election?"

"Perverting an election? I gave you more credit, frankly. Every election is stolen, it's only a question of which thief gets away with the prize." His voice had firmed up now that he'd left the subject of Matthew. "Every politician is bought and paid for. Evangelicals, gay rights advocates, this minority group, that minority group, oil companies, Wall Street, steelmakers, importers, exporters, gun owners, SUV owners. They bid for the services of our politicians like dealers at an auction. I'm no different. I'm just smarter. And richer. And I want very little out of it, which is more than you can say for the others."

"What exactly do you want?"

"Revenge," he said so softly it was almost a whisper.

"The insurgency in Kamalia is going to fail. The man responsible for killing Matthew, Laurent Boymond, will survive."

"I will have my revenge."

"And what if it doesn't work?"

"It will."

"That's not what I meant. What if you get your revenge and that hole inside you is still there?"

He stared down at him for a few moments while Zach prepared for more abuse. "Where's Sarah?"

For a moment the pain in his head, his back, his legs, and abdomen vanished, replaced by one consoling thought: his assumption had been confirmed—they didn't have Sarah.

"I don't know."

"I will ask you once more, and if you still don't answer I will ask for Mr. Sandifer's help in getting the information."

"You're going to ask him to torture the information out of me? Why don't you do it yourself?"

"One last chance."

"Fuck you, you pathetic coward."

Julian took a deep breath, his hands balled into fists. He let it out slowly and headed for the door. Zach heard Julian and Billy talking outside. He tried hard not to think of what Billy was about to do. He feared the pain. He feared his own weakness. He tried to clear his mind but her location only burned brighter, like a flashing sign: *Nassau Hotel, Miami, Nassau Hotel, Miami.* What if the words leapt from his lips on their own, an instinctive attempt at self-preservation, dooming him and Sarah? How much more pain could he endure?

The cabin door opened and both men walked in. Julian stood as far from Zach as the small room permitted, but Billy walked right over to him, a pistol in his right hand.

"All I have is this gun," he said. "Six bullets. The first one goes into your right knee. Then the left knee. I haven't decided where the third one goes. You can save yourself a lot of trouble by telling us where she is."

"Are you going to watch?" Zach said to Julian, who glanced away but otherwise made no move. "Do you think you can handle it, Julian?"

"Where is she?" Julian hissed. "Just tell us." He seemed more scared for himself, what he was about to witness, than anxious about the fate of Zach's kneecaps.

"Fuck you, Julian. And you too, Billy. *Sellout.*"

Sandifer glanced at Julian, who nodded.

"Shoot him," Julian whispered, turning away from Zach.

Billy stepped closer to where Zach was sitting and extended his right arm so that the pistol was just a few feet from Zach's right knee. Zach pulled his legs into his body, an instinct rather than a conscious attempt at protecting his legs, closed his eyes and prayed that he'd lose consciousness when the bullet hit.

What he heard next was not gunfire but the chirping of a cell phone. The three of them looked around, as if a small animal had scampered into the cabin. By the second ring they had all discovered the source: Zach's phone, on the orange plastic table.

Only one person had his cell number.

"Okay, I'll tell you where she is," he said quickly, hoping to distract them from answering. "I'll tell you, right now."

The phone rang a third time.

"She's in New York, staying with a friend, I'll give you the—"

Julian flipped open the phone and answered. "Hello?"

"DON'T SAY ANYTHING!" Zach screamed at the phone. "GET OUT OF THERE!"

Julian flicked the phone shut, waited a few seconds, then reopened it. He pressed a few buttons and a moment later turned to Zach.

"Missed calls indicates a Miami area code. The number ends in zeros...a hotel? Let's try redial." Julian pressed a few buttons and a few seconds later Zach just barely heard a woman's voice from the phone's tiny speaker. Julian hung up. "She's at the Nassau Hotel. Miami."

"You want me to go?" Billy asked Julian.

Julian thought a moment. "No, I can handle it. I'll have the chopper take me right to the plane, I'll be there in four hours. You wait here, keep him alive until you hear from me. If Sarah heard him just now she might run, and he's our only connection to her." He turned to Zach. "Your girlfriend spared you a great deal of pain. If she's still at the hotel, you will die a quick death, which is more than you deserve." He considered Zach for a few moments, looking down at him like a new rug he wasn't quite sure he wanted to keep, then quickly left the cabin. "If he tries to escape, shoot him," he said on the way out.

• • •

# CHAPTER 66

Moving confidently toward the presidential palace, Sophie felt herself part of a great choreographed dance. She was with ten others, all men. On other streets that fanned out from the palace bands of rebels were closing in. At seven forty-five on a Saturday morning the streets were nearly deserted, the shop windows shuttered. An ominous silence cloaked downtown Villeneuve, as if the population were holding its collective breath.

She had reconfirmed her plans the night before, then given the signal to Rémy, who passed it along the chain of rebels. She'd visited Claude DuMarier personally, stealing into his house through the kitchen door like a servant or mistress. He had assured her that the guards at the south gate would be off duty Saturday morning, at his orders. Only a skeleton crew would be waiting for them inside—*my worst men,* DuMarier had called them. Le Père would be in residence, and the head of the military would be with him; the two would attend a special celebratory mass in the private chapel in the palace's east wing in commemoration of the successful coup two years earlier. "They kill and steal as much as they want, then beg for forgiveness the next morning so as to start the day with a clean slate," he said with a serious tone, as if describing a clever strategy. Many members of the government would be there, too, gathering early for a midday ceremony of some sort in the grand Chambre d'Etat. Where would DuMarier himself be during the uprising, Sophie wanted to know. *On the morning plane to Paris.* It chilled her, that the plan to liberate Kamalia depended on the avarice of a slimy traitor, but there it was.

One block from the palace, in front of a small tobacco store, she raised her hand to stop the men behind her. Like most other stores the tobacconist was still closed. She tried the front door and was gratified but not surprised when it opened; she had become very good at making plans—and spreading around Julian Mellow's money. Inside, behind the small wooden counter, were ten Kalashnikov rifles. She called for the men to come inside and handed them each a rifle, offering a firm *bon courage* to each. In their eyes she saw fear and determination and hunger for glory. She'd run small tutorials on how to use the Kalashnikov, but most had never actually fired one. Perhaps, if all went well, they wouldn't have to.

"We will wait in here until eight o'clock exactly," she said. Small groups of rebels surrounded the palace, each securing their weapons at the shop or home of a sympathizer (or, as in the case of the tobacconist, a paid supporter). Since Zach Springer's visit and the raid on her house she had stayed with one such sympathizer; perhaps that night she'd be able to return to her own place. In the past days, her thoughts often returned to the photograph of Matthew on the small table next to the front door; she couldn't shake the feeling that she had abandoned it.

The short wait felt interminable. The men smoked cigarettes and said little, shifting their weight from foot to foot as they tried to relax, running their fingers gingerly over their rifles, wondering, no doubt, if they would be firing them that morning. Sophie's mind had already entered the palace, whose floor plan DuMarier had supplied, though she'd been to any number of events there, back before Le Père, when she and Matthew had been courted by the democratic regime as models of the new Kamalia. She pictured herself entering the palace grounds through the east gate, crossing the small courtyard to the enormous east door, built to withstand siege, which would be left unlocked, DuMarier had assured her. Inside, an immediate left. The chapel was the second door on the right. Others would charge up the south staircase and secure the second floor, while another group would secure the north wing. It would be over in a few minutes. A bloodless coup. Much as she wanted Le Père dead, killed by her own hands, she knew that the future of Kamalia would be better served by keeping him alive. She imagined a public trial for crimes against humanity, following the release of political prisoners, one of whom, Roger Derain, would act as interim head of the government until elections could be held, most likely in January. Perhaps Le Père would receive a sentence of death—she would be there for his execution, holding Matthew's photograph.

She opened the small locket she wore around her neck and kissed the tiny photo of Matthew.

"It's time."

The air had warmed up during their brief hideout in the shop, or perhaps it was anticipation. The palace was girded by a circular road, four lanes across. The city's broadest avenues fanned out from it in a five-pronged star pattern. It had been designed by a Frenchman after the Place Charles de Gaulle in Paris, but the area had never quite lived up to the plan's grandeur; one block from the ornate palace and the grand, if decaying, limestone public buildings that surrounded it, the city relaxed into ramshackle one-story shops and homes that looked almost embarrassed by their place of honor along the broad boulevards.

They walked quickly to the Place du Palais, and when Sophie reached the corner her spirits soared: almost simultaneously, bands of armed rebels appeared around the circle and, presumably, on the other side. As planned, all of them quickly moved to the south gate, brazenly occupying the street and forcing the sparse Saturday morning traffic off the circle.

The palace was a two-story building, modeled, Sophie had heard, after a French château along the Loire. It had always struck her as an absurd symbol of Kamalia's vain aspirations; it didn't look out of place so much as out of proportion. It was too big for the small park in which it sat, too formal for the honky-tonk city over which it loomed, too grand for the third-world country that its occupants sought to rule. And the damp tropical climate had had its way with the palace's pretensions, riddling it with pockmarks and sending voracious, giant-leafed vegetation up its walls faster than the understaffed maintenance crew could cut it down. It was ringed by a fifteen-foot fence composed of steel spikes two inches apart, connected by steel bands at the bottom and top, each capped by an ornate finial, once gilded, now a rusty black. There were four gates, the grandest to the south, through which visiting dignitaries passed, the others used for deliveries and more prosaic arrivals and departures.

Despite DuMarier's assurance that the south gate would be

unguarded, she was hugely relieved to see it untended. Also buoying her was the sight of the entire rebel army, more than eighty strong, mostly men but with a few women, walking with long, confident strides toward the gate. Gone was the slump-shouldered Kamalian shamble. The collective determination and pride would carry them to victory, she felt sure.

"Comrades!" she shouted in front of the gate. "COMRADES!" The air went silent. "We have longed for this day for two years. Many of our friends have been imprisoned and some of them have been killed. We have lost our freedom and our livelihoods. Today we change all that. Today we take back our country for the people. Today we begin a new chapter. *Bon courage, mes amis.* We will meet next in the Chambre d'Etat! *Allons! Allons! Pour Kamalia!*"

She thrust open the gate—unlocked, as promised—as shouts of *Pour Kamalia!* rang out behind her. The south door was less than thirty yards away, across a dusty and, most importantly, deserted courtyard. The words *bloodless coup* floated into consciousness as she broke into a run, her right hand holding aloft the rifle.

Then a shot rang out, a series of shots.

Still running, she turned back and felt her insides drop.

The tight mob had dispersed to either side of the courtyard, revealing several fallen bodies. At the rear she saw some comrades attempting to retreat back through the gate, but it had been closed behind them. In front of the gate, and to either side of the mob, stood soldiers in full uniform, dozens of them, all carrying machine guns. She and her comrades were trapped in the small courtyard. Men were throwing themselves at the fence, as if hoping to topple it, only to be gunned down, shot in the back by round after round of machine gun fire. Comrades were falling like dominoes, unable even to fire back.

She had been betrayed.

*They* had been betrayed.

Rage propelled her forward. Screaming, firing the rifle to either side, she sprinted for the door, hoping that it would be unlocked as promised and that there would be someone alive to follow her. Behind her, earsplitting gunfire was punctuated by the shrieks and moans of her comrades.

She reached the door, dimly aware that this in itself was a miracle. She threw her body against it but it didn't move. Her nostrils burned from the smell of gunpowder, her ears rang with explosions. For a moment she stood there, her back to the ambush, immobilized by the weight of the betrayal—and of her responsibility for the carnage taking place behind her. She waited for a bullet in her back to release her from that weight.

The bullet never came.

Instead, she felt hands grip both of her arms and turned to find two soldiers, huge men in military fatigues and helmets, gripping her, lifting her, carrying her away. The courtyard was an agony of fallen bodies, most of them lifeless, some writhing and moaning until a spasm of bullets from the ring of soldiers surrounding the courtyard stilled them. To one side of the gate, Rémy Manselle had managed to climb the iron fence only to be shot down when he reached the top; his body landed on the hard ground with a sickening thud she heard even over the din. She saw that several men had managed to escape before the gates had been closed. They were running toward the promised sanctuary of the US embassy.

The rest, all of them, were going to die, trapped in the courtyard like cattle brought to the slaughterhouse.

Why was she being taken away? She needed to break free, to join her comrades not in their final struggle, for no struggle was possible, but in their final glory.

She tried to push her captors away but their grips were unyielding. They dragged her to the back of the palace as if she were a small child being led to punishment by angry parents. They turned the corner and walked quickly to the palace's north door; as they pulled her inside she was already aware of the sudden quiet from the west courtyard. The gunfire had ceased. The moaning had stopped. It was over.

• • •

# CHAPTER 67

Zach played out the scenario in his head, over and over. Julian on his helicopter, then his plane, then the short cab ride to South Beach, up the elevator to the fifth floor of the Nassau Hotel and into Sarah's room. It was hard to imagine Julian lowering himself to dealing with Sarah personally. Violence, like so much else, was beneath him. And then there was the risk of getting caught. But whom could he send? His companies employed hundreds of thousands of people, but he could hardly call up an employee and order him to Miami to execute an unarmed woman. He'd use his own gun; Julian, at the recommendation of Mellow Partners' security consultant, owned a small pistol, and he'd have no trouble transporting it from New York to Miami—one of the perks of *flying private*, as the Gulfstream crowd liked to say.

Each time, the scenario ended with Sarah innocently opening the door. His mind couldn't go further. He had to warn her.

In ten minutes Billy would be back from taking Julian to the helicopter. Zach rolled from one side to the other, surveying the cabin. If only he could get the ropes off his feet, he'd be able to stand. He noticed that the slate hearth extended a foot from the fireplace, and that its edge was relatively sharp. He rolled himself across the room and positioned himself so that his legs were facing the fireplace, then lifted them up onto the slate ledge. He shimmied to his right, then a bit to the left; finally, his feet were where he wanted them, the ropes around his ankles directly over the edge of the slate. He began moving his legs from side to side, forcing the rope into the sharp corner. After a long minute of effort he saw some fraying, but at that rate it would be an hour or more before he made any real progress. He shimmied to his right and tried another spot, then a third, where he felt some resistance as he worked his feet from side to side—some sort of nub on the slate, a flaw. He concentrated on pressing his feet into the ledge and a minute or two later the rope was cut nearly in half. Encouraged, he worked harder and faster. Finally, the rope split and his left foot dropped to the floor.

Slowly he got to his feet, feeling the effort in every bone and muscle. He flexed his legs until he could safely move about the cabin without fear of tumbling forward. He crouched before the fireplace and ran the handcuffs along the ledge, but quickly realized that the slate was no match for steel. He could run, but the road was at least a half mile down the long dirt driveway, and he didn't recall seeing any houses nearby. In any case, Billy would be back before he reached the road.

He'd have to get the key from Billy.

He searched the cabin for something that might help him. Candles and matches by the fireplace…he could burn down the place, but how would that help? Billy had locked the cabin door, so he crossed the room and powered his shoulder into a back window, shattering several panes of glass along with the rickety wooden framing. He repeated the action until he'd managed to push out most of the glass, then carefully hoisted one leg up over the sill, pressing his body against the side to stay balanced. Once he was straddling the sill he slowly brought his other leg across and jumped down.

Outside, he was tempted to run into the woods. Eventually he'd find a house with a telephone, even if he had to walk for hours or a day. But by then Julian would be in Miami. Running away wasn't an option.

Across a small patch of what had once been a grass lawn but was now a raggedy expanse of weeds and debris there was a small shed. He pulled open the door by pressing his right elbow against the wooden handle. Inside he made out an old, rusted rotary mower and, next to it, a red can of gasoline. There was also a rake, shovel and various other yard tools. He crouched to his knees, with his back to the gas can, and managed to lift it with one shackled hand, his left—his right was still tightly bandaged and in no condition to do any lifting. The can felt full. He went back to the cabin, hoisted the can over the window sill, his back to the cabin, and let it fall inside. Then he climbed in.

He squatted in front of the can, picked it up again, and carried it behind him to the table. Once it was on the table he unscrewed the cap, still with his back to it. The cap off, he picked up the can and poured a third of its contents in a six-foot-long puddle that began about two feet from the cabin door. He put down the can and, in the small kitchen area, found a large stock pot in a lower cabinet. He filled this with the remaining gas and placed it next to the puddle, at the point farthest from the door.

He heard an approaching car. Crouching in front of the fireplace ledge, he managed to pick up the large box of kitchen matches with his shackled hands and slide out the inner compartment. Most of the matches fell to the floor but he was able to secure one with his left hand while holding the box in his right. Pain shot through his wrists, particularly his injured left fingers, as he angled both hands to light the match on the side of the box. The first swipe was unsuccessful, and on the second he dropped the match.

The crunch of tires on the dirt driveway grew louder. He got a second match and, pressing it as firmly as he could against the side of the box, gave it a swipe. He smelled sulfur but didn't hear the sizzle of ignition. Backing up a few feet, he pressed the hand holding the box against the cabin wall for greater stability. The cuffs dug into this wrist he ran the match along the striking surface.

He heard it hiss.

Outside, the tire crunching stopped. He forced himself to walk very slowly toward the kitchen area, worried that the match behind his back would extinguish. When he reached the table he carefully angled the lit match to the candle. The flame was biting into his fingertips. He pressed his arms back from the shoulders and just managed to connect the match to the wick. Then he turned around; the candle was lit. He picked it up, still in its holder, and backed across the room to the puddle of gas.

A car door slammed.

Slowly he crouched down and placed the lit candle on the floor near where the puddle of gas began by the door. He stood up and pressed his back to the wall next to the door.

Seconds later he heard a key in the lock, and then the front door swung open.

# CHAPTER 68

Billy Sandifer first looked down at the candle, then across the cabin to the corner where Zach was supposed to be tied up. He took a step forward and Zach leapt at him, aiming low, for his knees. Billy lurched forward and fell face down into the puddle of gas. Zach kicked over the pot, covering Billy's chest and gut with gas.

He was tempted to go after the pistol in Billy's right hand but stayed on plan.

"Stop!" he yelled as Billy started to get up. "I'll kick over the candle!"

Billy rolled over and aimed the gun at Zach's head. But his eyes took in the fact that Zach's foot was touching the lit candle, which was an inch away from the puddle.

"Shoot me and we both die," Zach said. "Put down the gun."

When Billy didn't move Zach nudged the candle even closer to the puddle with his right foot; it almost tipped over.

"No!" Billy shouted.

"Then put down the gun, *now.*"

Billy appeared to weigh his options, his eyes darting between Zach and the candle on the floor. He looked less nervous than calculating. Finally, he dropped the gun.

"Push it over to me," Zach said.

Billy complied. Zach wanted to crouch down to pick it up, but he'd have to turn his back and he worried that such a move would give Billy the chance to roll away.

"Now the handcuff keys, the car keys, and my cell phone."

Again Billy hesitated, seemingly weighing the benefits of complying. Moving very slowly, as if fearful that he might knock over the candle himself, Billy emptied his pants pockets and slid the keys and the phone toward Zach.

"Now what?" he said with a leering grin. "How you gonna pick up that gun, Zach? Or are you gonna light me on fire?"

Billy was picking up on his indecision, and that could be fatal. Zach wanted more than anything to knock over the candle and get out of there but his foot felt paralyzed. He thought of Sarah, how she had urged him to shoot Billy from the boat off Saint Sebastian. He'd hesitated then, too. He could make up for that mistake with one small movement of his right foot.

But he didn't, and he hated the look of smug relief in Billy's eyes as he watched Zach slowly crouch, his right foot still touching the candle, his back to the keys on the floor. His knees throbbed as he slowly, very slowly, lowered himself. Finally, he reached a squatting position and began to bend backward from the waist. Was it even possible, what he was trying to do, some strange yoga move that involved muscles and tendons he hadn't known existed? He felt the key with his right middle finger. It *was* possible. Gently he teased it toward him until he could just feel it with his thumb. Another half inch and he'd be able to grasp it.

At last he pinched it between his thumb and index finger. His right foot still touching the candle, he started to rise, fingers gripping the key, but about halfway up he felt his right knee buckle and he began to fall to the side, away from Billy, who seized the opportunity to spring at him. If Billy reached him before he could knock over the candle it would all be over. His life. Sarah's life.

As his shoulder hit the floor Zach kicked at the candle with his right foot.

The candle holder seemed to teeter on one edge for a moment. In that long moment, Zach had one thought: he'd let her down again.

The candle fell over. The puddle of gas erupted in flames. Billy, midlunge, seemed to disappear in a blaze of light as his clothes caught fire. He shouted something and fell back into a smaller puddle that hadn't yet ignited.

Billy was rolling around the floor, screaming from behind the flames. Zach sat up. Working as quickly as he could, he gathered the cell phone and keys. A small wooden chair caught fire.

Billy managed to stand up and charged at Zach, who threw his entire weight into him, sending him back to the floor. The cabin's floorboards had ignited, and sparks had lit one of the posters. Now completely engulfed in flames, Billy tried to stand up a second time but fell back, a hideous noise emanating from his mouth, something between a yelp and a moan.

Clutching the keys and phone, Zach left the cabin and ran to the car. He turned his back to it and deposited the car keys and cell phone on the hood. Holding the handcuff key in the fingertips of his right hand, he carefully maneuvered it, and after several failed attempts he felt it slip into the keyhole on the left side. He twisted it, felt a dull click, and both arms fell to his side. Immediately he removed the other cuff, retrieved the phone and car keys, and got in the car.

He drove off quickly, looking back in the rearview mirror just once. Flames jutted from the cabin's windows and danced across its roof. The front door flew open and Billy Sandifer ran out, a shimmering meteor of fire. As Zach turned a corner, he saw a ball of flames rolling in the tall grass in front of the cabin.

When he reached the road Zach stopped the car and dialed Sarah at the Nassau Hotel. Her cell phone was back in Saint Sebastian. The receptionist connected him to her room but there was no answer. He was connected to hotel voicemail.

"Sarah, it's me. Leave the hotel. Get out of there. Julian knows you're there, he's coming to get you. Call me as soon as you're safe." He gave her the number of his burner phone. "I'm coming to you. I love you."

He hung up, redialed the hotel, and asked for the number for the local police department. Moments later he was spilling out his story to the operator at the South Beach police precinct who, sounding equal parts annoyed and skeptical, connected him with a detective.

"There's a woman at the Nassau Hotel, room 506. She's in serious danger. I tried to contact her. You have to get over there and protect her."

The police officer, a Detective Martindale, sounded as annoyed and skeptical as the operator, but Zach refused to hang up until he got his assurance that he'd go over to the Nassau and check out the story. Then Zach put the car in drive and sped off, heading south for LaGuardia Airport.

# CHAPTER 69

"Talk about an October Surprise," the CNN anchor was saying. "You won't find anything more surprising than this. I must warn you, these images are difficult to watch. We strongly suggest that young children not view the footage we are about to show."

Julian used the remote to turn up the volume on the small television in the Gulfstream. They were still ascending to cruising altitude, but he hadn't waited for the pilot's authorization to turn on the TV. It was the weekend before Election Day, the race a statistical dead heat, as the pundits never tired of calling it, and violence erupting in Kamalia—he wasn't about to let FAA regulations get in the way of monitoring a situation that he had largely created.

On the small screen was a grainy black-and-white image of a large, two-story building of white stucco. "What you're seeing is the American embassy in Villeneuve, about two hours ago," said the CNN anchor. "The embassy is just a few blocks, we're told, from the presidential palace, where earlier an attempted coup was brutally put down by the private security force that answers to President Laurent Boymond, or Le Père, as he's known to Kamalians. Virtually all of the insurgents were killed in a small south courtyard to the side of the palace. On the right of your screen, you can see two men in military uniform. These are members of Le Père's private security force. About two hours ago, some two dozen members of this force stormed the US embassy. We are told that the embassy is secured by two US marines, who were easily overwhelmed. No word yet on their fate. The intruders spent roughly fifteen minutes inside. Gunshots were heard, we have been told. As for the motivation for storming the embassy, there has been no official word from either Kamalia or the State Department. However, representatives of Agence France-Presse, the French news organization, have reported that several of the insurgents somehow got into the embassy as they fled the massacre at the presidential palace. The Kamalian government believes— and at this point we have no confirmation—that there was a preexisting plan for the insurgents to seek refuge in the embassy if the uprising failed. Whether the storming of the embassy was an act of retaliation or an attempt to secure these insurgents is not known. Now, watch this."

Julian leaned closer to the screen. The front door of the embassy opened. Two uniformed soldiers emerged. One held the hand of a white male adult, the other held a white woman. Between them were two young girls.

"You're watching the US ambassador, Ray Knapp, his wife, Paula, and their two daughters. As you can see, they are in great distress."

Somehow one of the girls, who looked to be about five or six, wriggled free of her mother's hand and ran straight toward the camera, which Julian guessed was positioned outside a gate of some sort, probably the entrance to the embassy compound. Her parents screamed at her to stop, calling her name, Julia, over and over. Suddenly her father broke away from the guard holding him and went after her. He got halfway to her when he was shot down. Now the mother and both girls were shrieking. Paula Knapp charged at the guard who'd shot her husband. Julia tried to run back to her as her mother began to pummel the guard, the younger daughter clinging to her.

Suddenly the picture went black.

"We don't know why we lost video. What we do know—it has been confirmed by Agence France-Presse—is that all four members of the Ambassador's family, including..." His voice broke. "...including his daughters, are dead." He touched the tiny audio feed in his right ear. "We are going to take you to Madison, Wisconsin, where Senator Harry Lightstone is about to make a statement. As you know, the senator has made the situation in Kamalia a centerpiece of his campaign, long before today's events. It will be interesting to hear—okay, we're taking you live to Madison."

Harry Lightstone stood in front of a low brick building—a union hall, perhaps, or school—a phalanx of reporters in front of him. His always somber face looked especially gloomy. "First of all, my condolences to the Knapp family on what appears to be an act of brutal savagery."

Julian listened with impatience, eager to get to the inevitable segue from outrage to politics, in which Lightstone would pin the tragedy on the Nessin administration and somehow, without directly saying so, imply that he had warned about such a situation. The segue occurred about five minutes into the speech.

"In our global political economy, events like this one do not occur in a vacuum. They result from a complex mix of policies and personalities that transcend borders. Our president had refused to deal with the mounting crisis in Kamalia even as I urged him, from the floor of the Senate and from the campaign trail..."

Julian flicked off the television. He liked the bit about "from the floor of the Senate." Lightstone had never once mentioned Kamalia from the Senate, and wouldn't have mentioned it as a candidate had it not been for Julian's *encouragement*. Hypocrisy in full bloom—it was almost enough to put a smile on his face. Killing those two girls had not been part of the plan—only the ambassador and his wife were supposed to die—but it made for very effective TV.

It distressed him, having to take care of the business in Miami on his own. He was accustomed to delegating. Ironic, in a way, that the most ambitious project of his career should involve just two people, one of whom was an ex-con. Perhaps he should have had Sandifer kill Zach, and then sent him to Miami to take care of the girl. But that would have been riskier than the current strategy, if not quite as unpleasant: Zach was the only link to Sarah, and if she should escape from the Miami hotel, she would, at some point, try to contact him. He absently ran his fingertips over the pistol in his jacket pocket. At least he wouldn't have to trudge through a metal detector.

He tried to focus on the job at hand, eliminating Sarah Pearlman, but his mind kept returning to that godawful cabin upstate. *Should* he have killed Zach? Why hadn't he? He felt the contours of the gun under his jacket. *Focus.* Could it be that he didn't want to be the one to kill Zach? That after all he'd done, that one act—firing a single bullet—made him uneasy? Was there, perhaps, some remorse left in him, some guilt? He shook his head, as if to expel it. Remorse, guilt—weaknesses that spawned muddled thinking and poor decisions. He'd built a fortune moving money from one investment to another. Actually running things was something he delegated to others. Now he was faced with doing something that couldn't be delegated. Sarah Pearlman had to die. And he had to do it himself. *Do it himself.* A concept he was uncomfortable with. But it had to be.

*Focus.* In three hours he'd end the life of Sarah Pearlman, by himself, and then make the call that would end Zach Springer's life, too. And then he would watch the election returns.

# CHAPTER 70

Zach sat in first class on an American Airlines flight to Miami from LaGuardia. He'd arrived minutes before the flight was scheduled to depart and there was only one seat left. As soon as the seatbelt sign was turned off he went to the bathroom and used his cell phone to dial the Nassau Hotel. Sarah was still not in her room. The pilot had announced that the weather in Miami was eighty-two degrees and sunny, which perhaps explained why Sarah wasn't inside. He dialed the Miami Police Department and, after a long wait, during which someone rapped on the bathroom door, he was connected to the detective he'd spoken to earlier. He and a partner had gone to the Nassau Hotel. Yes, there was a Sarah Pearlman registered there. No, she wasn't in her room.

"Go back, make sure she's okay," Zach said.

"We can't protect someone who isn't there."

"She's in danger. I'm begging you…"

"Listen, we're busy down here, this election coming up, there's talk of irregularities at the polls, a lot of us are having to watch polling places, not our usual beat."

"Please, just go to the hotel, tell her to get out of there."

"My partner and I, we'll stop by again in an hour, how's that? If she's there we'll tell her that…" He paused, as if reading a report. "That Zach Springer thinks she's in danger."

Zach ran through the timing in his head, over and over. Julian had an hour's head start and had taken a helicopter to his plane. Zach's drive to LaGuardia had taken two hours. A half-hour sprint from the car to the plane, with a stop at the ticket counter. A three-hour flight. He figured Julian had a two-hour lead, maybe three.

"Okay, thanks. But no later than an hour, it's important that you get to her within the hour."

He hung up and consulted the *New York Times* a flight attendant had handed him. During takeoff he'd circled the paper's general information number and the name of a reporter who was covering the election in Miami: Gordon Lewis. As the detective had pointed out, there were rumors of election fraud swirling around several swing states, including Florida. He got through to the reporter and quickly launched into his prepared pitch.

"I have information about polling irregularities," he said, back in the first class bathroom. "I'd like to meet you later to tell you what I know."

"You and half the people in Florida." Gordon Lewis sounded skeptical and tired.

"What if I had proof?"

"Everyone has proof."

"I work for Julian Mellow. I know you know who that is."

"I'm on loan from the business section. I interviewed him once."

"Do most of the people who call you with tips work for one of the richest men in America? I mean, I'm guessing most of them don't work at all, and don't have homes, and don't even speak coherently."

"You're not exactly the most articulate person I've talked to today."

"Just let me come by late this afternoon. Give me five minutes."

There was a long pause, and then: "I'm working out of our Miami bureau this week. Call me from the lobby. If I have time, I'll come down." He gave Zach the address. "But I'm warning you, I'm on deadline and the election this week means—"

"I understand," Zach said. He heard a flight attendant's voice on the other side of the bathroom door. He hung up, flushed the toilet for effect, and unlocked the door.

# CHAPTER 71

Sophie couldn't summon the resolve to raise her head when she heard her name. She'd lost track of time: had she been in the small, windowless room, somewhere in the palace, for an hour? Two hours? Days? She didn't know and didn't care.

"Come now, you must rejoice that you are alive, when so many of your comrades, nearly all of them, in fact, met a different fate." Claude DuMarier lifted Sophie's chin with his hand, which she swatted away. "Why so angry? I saved your life, you know."

She looked up at him for the first time. Instead of his customary military uniform he wore a white dress shirt and navy blazer. But the familiar leer was there.

"You betrayed me, betrayed all of us."

"You would have failed with or without my help. I merely expedited things."

She leaped from her chair and flung herself at him. Two guards, who had been standing quietly behind her, pulled her off and shoved her back in the chair. DuMarier motioned for them to leave the room.

"You will be punished," she said, hoping it was true. "My comrades and I, we have supporters all over the world who will see to it that you don't escape retribution, starting with Julian Mellow. Do you think you can betray a man like that and get away with it?"

DuMarier's laugh rocked his entire body. "Betray Julian Mellow? Oh, my dear, you are so naïve it is almost touching. Who do you think has arranged for the private plane that is waiting to take me away from this hellish country once and for all?"

"But…" She felt a spasm in her gut, then a wave of nausea. Julian had set her up to fail? Impossible. "Matthew, he would never have—"

"Betrayed the memory of his son? Yes, that is why you are alive. It will not hurt that you will be a recognizable face for the American media, worth more alive than dead. Since his son was killed Monsieur Mellow has had one thought: the destruction of Le Père. But he was never so foolish as to think that you and your friends could do that. Only the great United States of America can bring down a government. The slaughter of a hundred insurgents, the imprisonment of an internationally recognized fashion model, what happened earlier at the US embassy, those poor little girls… in these events, not your little insurrection, are the seeds of Le Père's destruction."

"The embassy, you…"

"Yes, I have been busy. Monsieur Mellow leaves nothing to chance, it is why he is who he is. We allowed a few of your comrades to escape to the embassy, as planned, *as Julian planned*, and then we had no choice but to go in and get them, *n'est-ce pas?* But I must leave for the airport now and begin my new life in France, a very good life. And this is why I have come here." He stepped toward her and lowered his voice to a whisper. "I will be a very rich man, Sophie. In a country not like this one, a country where all the comforts and pleasures that money can buy are at one's fingertips." He actually rubbed his right thumb across his fingers. "I would like to propose that you come with me. Monsieur Mellow will not be happy—you are more valuable to him as a prisoner in Kamalia, but I have confirmed that the money has been transferred, so this one thing will be beyond his control."

"He betrayed us..."

"Perhaps you are thinking of my wife, but in France this will not be a problem. You will have your own apartment in a good arrondissement, an allowance."

She flew from the chair and spat in his face.

He stared at her for a few long moments, perhaps considering whether to strike her, then calmly took a handkerchief from a pocket and wiped his face. "*Eh bien*, you have chosen your fate, to rot in prison until the Americans come, assuming they come. That will depend on whether Monsieur Lightstone wins tomorrow. Perhaps it will be better for you if he loses, because you can be sure that Le Père will not allow you to be rescued."

She raised a hand to strike him but he grabbed it and forced it down, then took her other hand and held it by her side.

"Beautiful women have choices, Sophie. It is a shame you don't know that." He pulled her to him and kissed her roughly on the mouth. She bit down hard on his lower lip. He howled as he shoved her across the room. As she hit the wall she felt the wind rush out of her.

"*Putain*," he snarled, dabbing his bleeding lip with the handkerchief. "Stupid whore." He crossed the room and opened the door. "Take her to the prison."

• • •

# CHAPTER 72

Julian walked confidently across the lobby of the Nassau Hotel, a small deco-style building that retained the faded, depressing air that had been renovated out of its more fashionable neighbors in South Beach. He'd called the hotel from the taxi on the way in from the airport and managed to secure Sarah's room number. And he'd had the taxi drop him off at a florist, where he bought a small bunch of roses; who would detain a well-dressed man, his face obscured by flowers? Just before entering the Nassau he'd tried Sarah's room again; she was still out.

On the fifth floor, where Sarah was staying, he saw a maid's cart outside a guest room. He softly knocked on the door and entered. She was a short, squat woman, visibly tired after a long day cleaning rooms. He closed the door behind him.

"I almost finish," she said as she continued making the king-size bed. Behind her was a vacuum cleaner, plugged into the wall. He crossed the small room and used his right foot to turn it on.

"*Que?*" she said, turning around. By then he had the pistol out of his pocket. "*Dios mío,*" she said.

"Give me the master key," he said.

"*No comprendo.*" Tears were already streaming down her plump cheeks.

"The key." He pointed with his free hand to the access card hanging from a cord attached to her belt.

With some difficultly she unclipped the cord and held out the card, which he took from her.

"Please, you want money, I give you, here, see?" She reached into her apron pocket and took out a fistful of bills, the tips from a day's hard labor, perhaps ten or fifteen dollars. "You have it, yes?"

For some reason that small wad of bills enraged him, maybe the notion that anyone, even a hotel maid, could equate his mission with so meager an offering. When he showed no interest in the money she began to moan. "Why, I no understand..."

"Because I can't leave you alive to identify me," he said.

"*Que?*"

"Go into the bathroom." When she hesitated he repeated the instruction and she obeyed. In the windowless bathroom he told her to turn on the shower. When she did, he closed the door.

The first shot hit her stomach, sending her back onto the sink. He fired again, this time just above her right eye. She fell onto floor.

Between the vacuum cleaner and the shower and the closed bathroom door, he felt confident that the two shots had not been heard outside the room. And the hotel felt empty, though he had no evidence other than a deserted lobby and the fact that November was far from peak season in South Beach. Quickly, he went to the hallway and pulled her cart back into the room. He picked up the vacuum, shut the door, headed down the hall to Sarah's room, and used the master key card to unlock the door.

Her room was identical to the one he'd just left, but it had a woman's presence, a vague scent of powder or body lotion in the air, various feminine garments hanging from doorknobs or folded and stacked on whatever surface was available. The room itself, like the one he'd just left, was what he'd expected, given the shabby condition of the lobby: a queen-size bed covered in a cheap-looking floral comforter, a desk and matching bureau pocked with dings and old cigarette burns, a TV bolted to the top of a minibar. The single window looked across a narrow alley to another stucco building. This room, too, had a small, windowless bathroom.

He moved the desk chair to a spot behind the door, so that Sarah wouldn't see him when she entered, sat down, placed his pistol on his lap, and waited. It seemed unfathomable that it had come to this: hiding in a third-rate hotel room, having shot an innocent woman, about to commit a second murder. It had been an unshakable tenet of his life that there was always someone else on hand to get things done. Other people, other people's money. Now he had no one.

He almost jumped from the chair when the phone rang. He noticed that the message indicator light on the phone was already on and waited until a few minutes after the phone stopped ringing to call in for messages. There were two, both from Zach, both frantically warning her to get out. The most recent was the most disturbing. "Get out of the room! I'm in Miami. I'm coming to the hotel. Leave the room. Go to the nearest police station."

How had he made those calls? Where was Sandifer? The fact that the message light has been on when he entered the room meant that Sarah hadn't picked up the first message, but what if there'd been an earlier one, and she had fled? He erased both messages, sat down behind the door, and used his phone to call Billy Sandifer's cell. No answer. How had Zach managed to get away?

He pressed 1 to erase the messages, as instructed, hung up, and waited. An hour. Two. And then heard the door unlock.

# CHAPTER 73

Sarah entered the room carrying a beach bag and towel and closed the door behind her. Halfway across the room she must have spotted him in the mirror over the desk, for she turned quickly and let out a short scream. He aimed the pistol at her as he stood up.

"Hello, Sarah."

She backed up until she hit the television, hands covering her mouth. "Please don't hurt me," she said. "I don't know what's going on. I don't know anything about what you're doing."

She dropped her things and sidled across the room, back against the wall, until she was in the corner. He stepped closer. He raised the gun and pillow.

There was a sudden knock at the door.

He shook his head, signaling for her to say nothing. A second knock, this one somewhat more insistent. "Miss Pearlman? It's the Miami Beach Police. Are you in there?"

Julian stepped closer to her, until the gun was just a foot or so away from her chest. He heard muffled voices from the hallway: "Go get a room key and we'll look inside."

"Ask what they want," Julian whispered to Sarah. When she hesitated, he added: "If they come in the room you'll die first."

"What do you want?" she said.

"Sarah Pearlman?" one of the policemen said.

Julian nodded at her and she said, "Yes."

"Can you let us in, Miss Pearlman?"

Julian shook his head and whispered, "You just got out of the shower."

"I just got out of the shower!"

"Are you all right, Miss Pearlman? We had a report that you might be in danger."

"From who?" Julian whispered.

"From who?" Sarah said.

"Name of Zach Springer."

"He's insane," Julian whispered. "He does this all the time."

"He's insane! He does this all the time."

"We really need to see you, Miss Pearlman."

She repeated exactly what Julian dictated: "No. This is what he wants, to humiliate me. I can't let you in."

"We can't leave without—"

"Get a warrant!" she said as directed.

There was some muffled talk between the cops, then: "Okay, Miss Pearlman. As long as you're okay."

"I'm okay," Julian whispered.

"I'm okay!" Sarah said.

"Enjoy your stay in South Beach," one of the cops said with undisguised sarcasm.

Julian felt his knees weaken, his hands trembling. That was as close as he'd ever come to defeat.

"Sit down," he said to Sarah, motioning to the desk chair. When she complied he sat on the edge of the bed, gun pointed at her chest, and waited.

• • •

# CHAPTER 74

Zach's taxi pulled up to the Nassau Hotel just as a Miami Beach Police car was pulling away from the curb. He took that as a hopeful sign that nothing had happened. Again, he ran through the timing and guessed he was about two or three hours behind Julian. He paid the driver and got out. Crossing the small lobby, he took added comfort in the calmness that pervaded the space—nothing suggested a crime scene. He took the elevator to the fifth floor, sprinted down the long, dimly lit hallway to Sarah's room, and knocked on the door.

"Sarah? Sarah!" He heard some sort of movement from inside the room. "Sarah! It's me, it's Zach!"

A moment later the door opened and she was standing there. He felt the weight of the past twenty-four hours fall away as he took her in his arms and moved into the room. She was okay.

"I tried calling…Sarah, Julian knows where you are, he—"

He was standing just to the side of the door, a gun in one hand. The pistol was aimed at Sarah's back.

"Shut the door, Zach." Julian's voice was flat, disapproving. When Zach hesitated he raised the pistol and said: "Shut it or she dies now."

Zach shut the door. "Let her go, Julian. She's not involved, she doesn't know anything."

"Too late for gallantry. Sarah, pick up the remote control from the desk behind you."

Her hand trembled as she obeyed. Her eyes were bloodshot and teary, her face ghostly pale.

"I'm sorry, Sarah," Zach whispered.

"Now, turn on the television."

"But I—"

"NOW."

She flicked on the TV to a news show. A political commentator was noting that Harry Lightstone had pulled ahead in most national polls, thanks largely to his prescient position on Kamalia. The bloodbath at the US embassy there had sparked outrage among American voters over the Nessin administration's failure to anticipate what the Lightstone campaign had been warning about for months. The scandal involving the vice president's blind trust had also hurt the incumbent.

"Fitting background, don't you think?" Julian said, his voice still flat but a bit less disapproving. "Turn up the volume." Sarah pressed the volume button. "*Louder!*" She cranked up the volume until the analyst's voice ricocheted off the room's walls.

"Now turn on the vacuum," he said. She looked momentarily confused, then even more terrified. "NOW." Her hands shook as she switched it on, filling the room with a roar as loud as the television.

"There'll be an investigation," Zach shouted. "They'll connect us; I've been talking to people."

Julian could barely hear him. "I have no choice. Goodbye, Zach."

Slowly, deliberately, he moved the pistol from Sarah to Zach.

"No, please, don't!" Sarah yelled.

Zach lunged at him, leaping across the six feet that separated them.

Julian fired. Zach's sudden movement had cost Julian his aim—the bullet missed him. Julian stumbled back, hitting the wall next to the bed. Zach fell forward and to the side, hitting the wall next to the door. He heard a loud noise, a thud, behind him and turned. Sarah was slumped on the floor, blood pooling around her head.

He knelt by her side. "Sarah. Sarah! Oh, God, Sarah."

A bullet—the bullet meant for him—had entered her forehead over her left eye. The blood, however, was leaking from the back of her head. He put his lips on hers, gently, and waited for the next shot. He didn't care what happened now.

"Get up," Julian said from somewhere very far away.

Zach took her hand and squeezed it. Someone on the television was talking about martial law in Kamalia, another place very far away.

"Get up!"

"I'm sorry, sweetheart," he whispered. "I'm sorry."

"One last time, Zach, get up. You can't help her."

He leapt to his feet and flew at him, prepared to dig his fingers into Julian's throat, rip his eyes out, bite out his heart.

Something stopped him.

First, a sound, another explosion. Then a burst of light, just in front of him, like camera flash. But this flash felt physical; it froze him for a long, empty moment.

Then he began to fall, as if in slow motion. His eyes were fixed on Julian. He didn't want that. He didn't want Julian's face imprinted on his eyelids as they closed.

Sarah.

He tried to turn to her, but his feet felt glued to the floor.

Sarah.

The floor rose up to meet him. If only he could turn just slightly he'd see her, and remember.

Sarah.

# CHAPTER 75

Julian stood for a few moments in the center of the room, as still as the two bodies at his feet. He felt a profound sense of awe at what he'd done. The only two people in the entire world who could harm him were gone. He'd done this. Alone.

He waited, listened. Had anyone heard the shots? The lack of commotion in the hallway was a good sign, but he would do well to get out of there quickly. He clicked off the TV.

He went to the bathroom, got a tissue, and carefully wiped down the pistol, which he then placed near Zach's right hand. Fortunately, Zach had managed to twist toward his girlfriend with his last bit of life, as if he'd wanted one final glimpse of her. It would look like he had shot her, then himself. The important thing was that his name never be involved. He quickly searched through Sarah's belongings for any reference to him. Finding none, he turned to Zach's body, searching his pockets and removing scraps of paper with phone numbers, Zach's cell phone, and, in his jacket pocket, a piece of yellow foolscap on which he had scribbled notes punctuated by underlined words connected by arrows. *Mellow, Lightstone, Sandifer, DuVal.* Names that should never have appeared on the same page, and now never would.

"Sorry, Zach," he said as he placed the paper in his pants pocket. "You lose."

He left the room, took the service stairs to the lobby, and exited the hotel through a back door that opened onto an alley. In less than a minute he was lost in the throng of South Beach tourists making slow progress along café-lined Lincoln Avenue.

An hour later he was on the Gulfstream, banking over Biscayne Bay as it turned north.

## TUESDAY, NOVEMBER 3

# CHAPTER 76

Julian was in the living room of a well-known hedge fund investor when Harry Lightstone's victory was called by NBC. Caroline had persuaded him to attend the party, and he'd agreed only because he'd been so anxious all day that he decided any distraction—even a roomful of Park Avenue grandees—would be better than waiting at home for a call or visit from the Miami police. Several television sets had been moved into the room, where they clashed absurdly with the gilt-and-brocade Louis the Something décor. Most of the attendees knew Marcella Lightstone from the charity circuit; Lightstone's victory would not only mean lower taxes, it would mean more or less unfettered access to White House dinners and perhaps even the coveted overnight. The mood was buoyant. One of their own had gotten in. Or the husband of one of their own.

"Lucky bastard," someone said to him as they watched a second network declare Lightstone the winner. "Those little girls getting gunned down in...what's that country called? That's what put him over the top."

"Kamalia," Julian said.

Things had gone as planned in Kamalia, at least. DuMarier had delivered exactly as ordered: the ambush at the Palace, the flight to the embassy, the massacre there. He'd paid an extra hundred thousand to have Sophie spared. Julian had convinced himself that keeping her alive would work to his benefit: she would be a rallying symbol, focusing the world's attention on Kamalia, which could only help his cause in the long run—his work was far from over as far as Kamalia was concerned. But perhaps it was sentiment at work, too. She'd been Matthew's great love.

"Kamalia," someone said. "Who would have guessed?"

"Voters were looking for a reason to go one way or another," someone else said. "No one really believes that the government can do anything."

"Anything right, you mean."

"Exactly. So when a candidate actually gets something right, like Lightstone with Kamalia, they all jump on board. Maybe, finally, someone who can do something."

"Scary thought, the government doing something."

Widespread laughter as a third network called the election for Lightstone.

"Looks like you pulled it off, Julian," someone whispered behind him.

"*What?*" He turned quickly and realized with huge relief it was Caroline, looking straight at him, wearing a beautifully tailored Chanel suit and diamond earrings, holding a glass of Chardonnay that would remain nearly full all night. He hadn't shared a single fact about his involvement in the election with her, and never would. It was almost gratifying to see the hurt in her face at being excluded: she always seemed to expect or need so little from him, but perhaps she wasn't as self-contained as she liked to appear.

"Lightstone will lower our taxes," he said, trying to sound cheerful and ironic. "Perhaps now we'll be able to afford that new car."

"I still don't understand what you're doing," she said. "Lightstone carrying on about Kamalia. I got the connection to Matthew. But I read this morning in the *Times* that Sophie is being held in jail. How has that helped, Julian? Would Matthew approve of what you've done?"

"What makes you think I had anything to do with—"

"Don't patronize me."

A few heads turned their way. Caroline managed a wan smile and touched his arm with her free hand.

"I'm not through yet," he said, once attention returned to the televisions.

"Oh, no."

He surveyed the room, anxious faces calculating the impact of the returns on their businesses, their influence, their incomes. It wasn't true that all politics is local. All politics is venal.

"Has it been worth it, Julian? Is it helping? I've never seen you anxious before, distracted. I've never known you to risk so much. Has it brought any peace? Is it helping?"

"Not yet."

"Will it?"

He continued to look around the room.

"Will it?"

"I've had enough," he said at last. "Let's go home."

"I want to stay."

• • •

He left the party without thanking the hosts. He'd be invited to their next soiree anyway. On the sidewalk he headed west, toward

Fifth Avenue, trying to concentrate. *Focus.* Left foot, right foot. Ignore the returns. Ignore Caroline. Ignore everything.

Left foot, right foot.

The moment would pass if only he could clear his mind.

Left foot, right foot.

Three blocks to go. Control, focus, discipline, rigor.

Left foot. Right foot. Faster, now.

Crossing Madison. Almost home. Fifth Avenue in sight. Almost running.

Leftfootrightfoot. Halfway to Fifth.

Leftfoot—

He ducked into an alcove between the front steps of two townhouses, leaned face forward into one of the stoops and began to sob, fists pounding the concrete. He felt his entire body vibrate and half expected the building to tremble.

It wasn't helping.

"Matthew," he whispered between sobs. "Matthew."

It wasn't helping.

Not yet.

# PART IV

# CHAPTER 77

The black Town Car pulled up to the northwest gate of the White House. Julian opened the back window. A Secret Service officer inside a small guardhouse spoke into a microphone. "May I help you?"

"I have an appointment with the president," Julian said, then added, "President Lightstone. My name is Julian Mellow."

"Just one minute, sir."

As the guard made a phone call from the booth, Julian considered with some satisfaction the ease with which his assistant had arranged the interview. The inauguration had taken place only two days earlier, and while Lightstone had spent the months since the election assembling a cabinet, it was a safe bet that he was still a very busy public servant. Not too busy, apparently, to make room in the third day of his presidency for Julian Mellow. Julian had considered calling for an appointment on the first day, just to demonstrate that he could, but he worried that doing so would draw too much attention to him. The new president was being closely watched by the press. So he'd waited.

"Everything is in order, sir."

A gate slowly swung open and the driver eased the car into a small fenced holding area, stopping just in front of a second, inner gate. Here, another guard approached the car and asked Julian for photo ID. He handed him his driver's license. The guard went into another, larger security booth, then returned to the car. He handed Julian his license and a plastic-encased badge, with Julian's photo imprinted, attached to a thin lanyard.

"Please wear this at all times, Mr. Mellow. Your driver will wait here for you."

Julian got out of the car. Inside the security house he emptied his pockets, walked through a scanner, collected his cell phone and keys, and walked through the now opened gate toward the West Wing.

It had been an anxious eight weeks, waiting for this day, unable to share his expectations and plans with anyone. At first his anxiety had focused on being connected to the deaths in the Catskills and Miami Beach. That hadn't happened. Then his focus shifted to executing the final phase of his plan. The election of Lightstone had brought no more satisfaction than the closing of a large deal. He was accustomed to the deflating emptiness that followed each success, the need to fill it with the next thing, and the next thing after that. It was time for the next thing.

A door was opened by another uniformed guard. "Welcome to the White House, Mr. Mellow. Please follow me."

He'd been there many times, for state dinners and with small groups to meet with whoever was occupying the Oval Office at the time to lobby for a bill or policy change. Access had long since ceased to be an issue, a source of satisfaction. But this was his first solo visit, and he wasn't immune to a sense of awe as he was led up a short flight of stairs and down a long, wide, red-carpeted hallway. He remembered the peculiar smell of the place from earlier visits, the reassuringly disinfected odor of a first-class hotel room. He remembered the buoyant spring in the thick carpet that seemed to impart a spirit of all-American optimism. He remembered the hushed aura, the sense that he was heading into the silent center of a vast storm.

They entered a large, windowed office. Behind an oversized wooden desk sat an attractive woman in her thirties or early forties.

"Good morning, Mr. Mellow, right on time! I'm Eleanor Forsythe. The president will see you."

*Of course he will*, Julian almost said. She circled the desk and opened a door.

"Mr. President, Julian Mellow to see you."

He entered the Oval Office.

"Julian," the president said with so little enthusiasm the last syllable faded to a sigh. He stood up from behind the famous desk and walked slowly toward the seating area.

"Mr. President," Julian said, not without a touch of irony. They shook hands. Lightstone had lost even more weight, adding new shadows to his already craggy face and causing his suit jacket to hang limply from his famously broad shoulders. The press was full of reports of the president putting in long hours, a fact that made the public nervous; voters never liked to see their leaders sweat. Still, there was no denying that Lightstone looked the part of commander-in-chief; he may have lost weight during the transition, but he'd acquired gravitas—though perhaps it was only the setting that made it seem so.

"Are we being recorded?" Julian asked. He sat opposite the president on one of two facing sofas.

"No, we are not being recorded."

"Good, then I'll get to the point. I'd like to discuss your policy toward Kamalia."

Lightstone crossed his legs and clasped his hands behind his head, as if relaxing into a discussion of baseball or movies—a power display. "You're not one for small talk, are you Julian?"

"You're a busy man. So am I."

Lightstone winced at the comparison. "Frankly, I was surprised you hadn't contacted me earlier. I expected your call every day since November third."

"I wasn't even invited to the inauguration, or any of the parties."

"Would you have come?"

"No. I think Caroline was disappointed, though. Now, about Kamalia. Your policy of negotiation with the Boymond regime is not going to work."

"It's only been three days. We are sending a special envoy to negotiate the release of American prisoners. The UN is considering sending a delegation to investigate human rights abuses. This ex-model, Sophie DuVal, there are rumors that her treatment has not exactly been ethical, and there are hundreds like her."

"That's not enough."

Lightstone unclasped his hands and let them fall to his side. His face turned rigid. "I find nothing in your background that qualifies you to lecture me on foreign policy. If you want to talk about interest rates, we can do that, but please leave the subject of—"

"Here is what must happen. You will issue a direct ultimatum to Le Père Boymond, demanding that he step down. The muder of the Knapps, his human rights violations, and his ongoing threat to the stability of the region make it unacceptable that he remain in power. When he refuses to obey, which he will, you will send in troops to remove him. Most likely he will capitulate without a struggle. Even so, he will be killed. He cannot survive the invasion, and neither can his generals or ministers. Not one of them. You will see to that."

"Good God," Lightstone said. "Is that what this has been about?"

From the moment he learned that Matthew had been killed, exacting revenge on Le Père and his henchmen had supplanted every dream and ambition he'd ever possessed. It had been what kept him alive, the one thing that enabled him to lift his head from his pillow each morning and the only thing that allowed him to close his eyes at night. He wanted them all dead, not merely deposed or exiled. Dead. They had to be wiped out, dozens of them. Swept clean. If he could have arranged for the annihilation of every citizen of that jerk-water country he would have done so, but an invasion would have to do. Unfortunately, even the richest, most influential man in the world couldn't invade a sovereign state. Not on his own, at any rate. And thus, in a hotel room in San Francisco, had his plan begun.

"I want this to unfold soon. Immediately. There is a great deal of animosity toward the Kamalian government right now. The memory of those two children gunned down is still fresh."

"Of course it is. Your television stations continue to run that awful footage, night after night. Interviews with every relative you can dig up, schoolchildren who knew them, former nannies. A two-hour special in prime time. It's shameless."

"The public wants revenge. A successful invasion, democratic elections…you will give them what they want. You'll demonstrate, after Iraq, that we can still have our way."

"It remains unclear to me what you did or didn't do to affect the outcome of the election, but there is absolutely no way that—"

"Shall I tell you what I did? About a plane crash in Maine? A bogus drug sale in Washington? A phony request for a stock trade inside a blind trust? A deliberately unsuccessful insurrection in West Africa? The gunning down of two children in Kamalia, American children? Would you like the details? Because I have them all written down, with evidence. And there are videos, too, one shot in a hotel room in San Francisco, the other at an elite boarding school in Connecticut."

Lightstone sat silently, eyes fixed on the famous rug, the edges of his mouth turned down. Could he really be contemplating the extraordinary nature of his ascension for the first time? Was his hubris really so great that he thought that the chain of unlikely events that had catapulted him to the White House was somehow the result of fate, *his* fate, his destiny?

When he finally spoke it was in a faint and trembling voice. "Releasing that information would destroy you."

"And you. If the invasion of Kamalia does not happen, it won't matter what happens to me. I won't care."

"This is about your son."

"About Matthew, yes." Now it was Julian's voice that trembled.

"I can't do it," Lightstone said. "I can't pervert our foreign policy to satisfy the revenge fantasies of a murderer."

"Then you will not survive your first year in office. You'll be forced to resign; there may be criminal charges."

Julian stood up. Lightstone remained seated, and didn't look up from his lap.

"Le Père deserves death. His country deserves freedom."

"And our soldiers, do they deserve to die in the streets of Villeneuve?"

Did Matthew deserve to die, after fighting to improve the lot of the people of Kamalia? The death of a thousand soldiers, ten thousand, would not come close to redressing what had happened to him.

"If you act quickly the government can be brought down with minimal casualties, a handful at most."

"Even one life…"

"I expect to see the ultimatum issued in your State of the Union address next week. Then you will move quickly. The longer you wait, the more prepared Le Père will be."

Lightstone said nothing.

"Goodbye, Mr. President. You will not hear from me again, *ever*, assuming this goes as planned. No one must survive, remember that. There is nothing more I want from you. Not a thing."

Julian crossed the room and opened the door through which he'd entered. A guard snapped to attention as he stepped into the antechamber.

"Your meeting ended earlier than expected," said Eleanor Forsythe, standing up from behind her desk.

"I didn't want to keep the president longer than necessary," Julian said. "He's a very busy man."

## MONDAY, FEBRUARY 15
### PRESIDENTS' DAY

# CHAPTER 78

On television, the streets of Villeneuve look almost familiar. Every network has had a makeshift bureau there since the failed insurgency in November, and though there hasn't been much to report, they've made a point of running at least a handful of stories each week in order to amortize their investments. Masters Broadcasting, the largest owner of network outlets, has taken the lead in running Kamalia stories. Most of them focus on the two Knapp children, the pieces growing increasingly pointless as hard news becomes increasingly rare. Anyone who ever worked in the US embassy, even to serve drinks at a party, is interviewed, and they all attest to the little girls' intelligence, generosity, affinity for the locals. So now, with actual news coming from Kamalia, the country feels oddly recognizable: the traffic circle ringing the president's palace, the broad, faux-Parisian boulevards fanning out from it, the dusty, half-paved street lined with dilapidated huts where the "real" Kamalians live—always, somehow, the same street, the same colorful laundry hanging out to dry, the same mangy dog sniffing the same overflowing can of trash.

But now, instead of tiny French cars hurtling along these boulevards and streets there are US Jeeps and tanks, and the sidewalks are strangely deserted. Occasional glimpses of local citizens show them to be less frightened or relieved or grateful than vaguely embarrassed, their country having fallen to the invaders in a single afternoon. The only bloodshed appears to have occurred in the palace itself, where Le Père and most of his closest aides, perhaps as many as two dozen, have been shot to death along with the two or three guards who didn't desert them the moment the first tank appeared at the south gate. Already there is talk of multiple assassinations. One Kamalian, his face blurred by the networks to maintain his anonymity, claims that the leader had already surrendered when he was shot. Other ministers were similarly executed. In Washington, President Harry Lightstone declares the near-bloodless (American blood) takeover a great victory for democracy, an event that will liberate all of western Africa from the threat of Kamalian tyranny and serve as a beacon of hope for other tyrannized people. The shadow of Iraq has been lifted. Images of the Knapp girls being gunned down are replaced by footage of Sophie DuVal, hardly able to stand on her own, emaciated even by supermodel standards, being escorted by Marines from prison. "*Le Père est mort*," she manages to say when a microphone is thrust in her face, her voice not only weak but flat. "*Vive Kamalia*." She almost lacks the energy to get out the last syllable of her country's name, and when asked if she will play a role in the new government she shakes her head with a faint grin that reveals two missing teeth, but no pleasure.

At the Dade County Correctional Center, a maximum security prison hospital, the television is always on in the physical therapy room. There are only two PTs for the thirty or so patient/inmates who need them, and they all have very different disabilities, so there is a lot more TV watching than therapy in the physical therapy room. Some patients are in wheelchairs, others use walkers. Some can't seem to stop speaking, though they never make much sense. Others never speak at all but stare up at the television screen, faces blank, waiting for their five minutes of therapy.

Zach Springer falls into this last category. He doesn't speak, though it is suspected by the doctors assigned to his case that he is able to. He walks with the use of a cane, because his right side is nearly paralyzed: he can move the fingers and wrist of his right hand but not the arm itself, and his leg hangs limp, useless. His right eyelid droops, as does the right corner of his mouth; in fact, the right side of his face, where the bullet entered, seems perpetually exhausted, while the left, if not exactly energetic, is at least firmer, taut. The doctors at Dade pretty much ignore him, as do the PTs, but every few weeks he is visited by a court-appointed physician who asks him a few questions, requests this or that movement in order to determine if he is fit to appear in court for indictment. So far, the answer has been no.

He spends his days watching television and trying to reclaim the past, which seems both nearby and inaccessible—a former address to which there is no longer reliable transportation. He remembers details, but they feel disconnected, so he passes the time attempting to string them together into a coherent narrative. Some days he manages to find himself in room 506 at the Nassau

Hotel in South Miami Beach. Then Sarah crumples to the floor and the connection to the present is broken. He doesn't remember the second gunshot, the one that sent a bullet into his frontal lobe and out the back of his head, somewhere just north of the cerebellum, paralyzing his right side, cutting off speech and apparently making coherent thought a Herculean undertaking, although perhaps the painkillers and the crushing monotony of life in the Dade County Correctional Center have something to do with this.

Other times his pierced brain takes him back to before everything went haywire. Only the smallest details come through. Sarah getting ready for school, standing before the sink in bra and panties, brushing her teeth. The hot summer day when they went to five different movies in the big multiplex across from Lincoln Center, paying once and gleefully sneaking into whatever was playing next. The field trip to Ellis Island when one of her students—he even remembered her name, Keisha—asked him if he was going to marry Sarah and he said definitely yes and Keisha asked if she could come to the wedding. Sometimes he feels a dampness on the left side of his face, where the tear ducts are still functional.

Kamalia. On the TV screen it's all jerky images and American correspondents in their absurd khakis describing an entire Boymond administration wiped out, no one left to stand trial, rumors of human rights abuses against men who had themselves been flagrant abusers of those rights. Already there are calls from senators for an investigation into why so few were allowed to live to stand trial. He has never felt more powerless—incapable of walking, of talking, of telling the world what he knows...or thinks he knows...or once knew. But watching the news in Kamalia, the body bags leaving the palace, the US tanks moving through Villeneuve, so much more substantial than the buildings lining the dusty streets, the interviews with bewildered citizens who seem at once frightened and resigned, as if the invasion was just another tropical storm recently endured—fearsome but, inevitably, temporary—he knows only one thing for sure.

All this is happening because of one man. An invasion had

been launched, a leader and his thugs executed, a country thrown into chaos, because of one man.

This strikes him as strangely fitting for a country that has always been at the mercy of strongmen—first tribal leaders, then communists, then reformers, then a dictator, one leapfrogging over another into power. At least with those men the country knew who was controlling its destiny. This time, when the dust, literally, settled, would anyone know that it had all happened not because of geopolitics, not because of the deaths at the embassy, and certainly not because of any grand scheme to democratize sub-Saharan Africa, but to avenge the death of a single person, a rich man's son? Would anyone ever know?

# CHAPTER 79

On another television screen, in an office on 57th Street in Manhattan, Julian Mellow watches American soldiers carry body bags out of the presidential palace, one after another.

He feels, for the first time in almost two years, a sense of… no, not peace, he will never feel that. Closure? No, he despises psychobabble. He feels…satisfied.

Yes, satisfied, the way he feels when a deal finally closes and he can hand Stacy the small clutch of papers for filing, knowing he will never have to see them again. Billions have been transferred from one entity to another, much of it into his own accounts, more often than not. Nothing, fundamentally, has changed, other than figures on various balance sheets. But there is a sense that order has been restored, equilibrium.

He feels that now. Nothing will bring Matthew back. There is no *closure*, no *healing*. There never will be. But the accounts have been balanced.

And perhaps there is the tiniest satisfaction that he has brought all this about?

He has never been a man who needed to share his triumphs, and there have been many. Not even with Caroline. And yet this one victory feels vaguely hollow. He has grasped, still holds, the ultimate power, and only two other people, the president of the United States and the first lady, know it.

Well, three actually. The survival of Zach Springer was a terrible surprise. The papers were all over the story for several days: the lovers returning to Miami after fleeing the country, some sort of argument, the beautiful former teacher shot, then her boyfriend's suicide. There are unexplained details, of course, particularly the frantic calls to the police before the shooting. The suspect is in a near-vegetative state, however, unable to answer questions, let alone be indicted. The story has faded from prominence.

He knows he will have to take care of Zach, but with Billy Sandifer gone that will be difficult. This thought reminds him that the institution housing Sandifer's daughter has been calling, looking for its annual check. He makes a mental note to ask Stacy to inform the Newman Center that he is no longer responsible for the girl's care. The fewer the connections to Billy Sandifer the better.

Zach will be taken care of, and if he can't use Billy Sandifer to do his bidding, well, he has other allies now. He smiles at the notion. Yes, he has other connections now. Powerful men. Leaving the Oval Office four weeks ago, he'd assumed that he'd pulled his first and last string; he'd wanted only one thing from Harry Lightstone.

But now he wants something else, another favor. And perhaps there'd be another favor after that, who knows? If even a fraction of the true story behind Lightstone's improbable rise to the White House were to be revealed, he'd be impeached, perhaps jailed, no matter how vigorously he denied knowing what had happened. It would be a shame to waste the leverage he'd worked so hard to create. Political capital, it was called. He'd earned more of it than anyone in history, and it would offend his sense of balance not to spend it in some way, starting with the elimination of Zach Springer.

• • •

# CHAPTER 80

The walk back to the room he shares with three other damaged souls is a major event in Zach's day. It is slow, painful work, his left hand gripping the walker, his right foot pulled along like a heavy, useless sack. Most days he puts off the return trek for as long as possible. His room, which had been built to hold just two beds, feels more depressing than the public room, and that's saying something. But the news reports from Kamalia, which dominate every station, are unbearable. As he shuffles to his room he hears a newscaster's voice growing fainter as he reports that few if any members of Le Père's government have survived the invasion. "There is an eerie silence surrounding the palace, which until yesterday was the center of…" The voice trails off.

*I was there. Four months ago. Or four years.* Which is it? He wonders if he can talk. The Dade County Homicide Bureau thinks he might be faking aphasia. He keeps expecting them to prick his foot with a pin to see if he howls. But they don't, and in fact he isn't sure what he's capable of. There is no one to talk to. Nothing to talk about.

He turns into his room and finds it empty, all four beds unmade, the familiar chemical stench of urine. Striped shadows line the floor and sheets, almost cheerful if you didn't know they came from the steel bars on the windows. The man in the bed next to his is paralyzed from the waist down, shot in the lower back during a robbery attempt. The guys in the beds opposite his had been injured while in prison and are in much better shape. Walkers, they are called (*You take the walkers,* one attendant will tell another when they come in to get them ready for their therapy. *I'll handle the chair.*)

He shuffles to his bed, slowly turns his back to it, and sits. The relief of finally arriving: a sigh travels through his body, even to places he can't feel anymore. But instead of lying down he reaches with his good, right arm to the bedside table and opens the drawer.

Inside is one object: his wallet, returned to him by the police sometime after he was brought here. It is practically empty. Cash, credit cards, receipts, his and Arthur Sandler's licenses—all of it has been removed. It looks rather pathetic in this state, flabby. Why they saw fit to bother returning it is beyond him, but he is grateful. It is all he owns, this limp piece of old leather.

Slowly he removes the remaining items. His blood donor card. New York City Public Library card. Expired health insurance card. Frequent flyer cards from every major airline—relics from another life. There are photos of his late parents, but they seem to belong to someone else's life, too. There used to be a small picture of Sarah, but the police must think it might be useful for the trial, when and if it happens. Finally, he removes the last item in the wallet, which he always puts back behind everything else, as if that would save it if they came looking.

And he knows they will come. In fact, he can't understand why they haven't come for him already. Every time the door to his room opens he assumes it will be men from the government, from the president, sent to finish what the bullet to his head hadn't quite done. What was arranging the death of a cripple in a county rehab center next to ordering an invasion in West Africa? Julian Mellow could probably have the entire center bombed to the ground if it suited his purposes. He has unprecedented influence and access. He has power.

But they haven't come for him yet. He looks at the photograph, as he does every day. He has thought of asking one of the attendants to take it home for safekeeping, but they would view his handwritten plea with disdain, one more sign that he lost his mind when he lost the use of his left side and voice.

He takes an envelope from the drawer, already stamped. He'd traded two desserts with a roommate for it. Slowly, he writes the address he's memorized from the single copy of the *New York Times* available to patients in the common room, then adds the name of the reporter he'd talked to, the one who had interviewed Julian Mellow: Gordon Lewis.

The photo is of decent quality, shot with a cameraphone, emailed to a computer, printed in black and white, folded and refolded many times. But the image is clear enough. Two men, one wearing a blazer and slacks, the other in sweatshirt and jeans, one a wealthy financier, the other an ex-con.

Yes, the image is clear enough. Reassured, he turns it over and writes in a slow, careful hand: *On left, Julian Mellow. On right, Billy Sandifer, who burned to death October 22. Find the connection.* He wishes he could sign it, but he can't risk calling attention to himself, not yet.

The news from Kamalia has sent him back to his room early, intensified his need to look at the picture one last time before sending it out into the world. Perhaps he dreamed the entire thing. What proof does he have, other than the increasingly cloudy workings of his damaged mind? But the image in the photograph is clear, it is real. He puts it into the envelope and seals it. Tomorrow he'll drop it in the mailbox in the hallway and then someone else will see it, use it. And one day, if he can get out of here before they come for him, he will launch his life's campaign, now that everything else has been taken from him: bringing down Julian Mellow and the president of the United States.

# ACKNOWLEDGMENTS

When I began this novel, the notion that a billionaire from New York could essentially acquire the White House seemed so outlandish I worried readers wouldn't buy the story. But sometimes truth really is stranger than fiction. This is, of course, a work of fiction, and any resemblance between my characters and actual persons, living or dead, is purely coincidental. But rather uncanny, don't you think?

Thanks, once again, to the great team at the Jean V. Naggar Literary Agency; no author has been better served than this one. My editor at Diversion Books, Randall Klein, worked his magic with a firm and wise hand. Jane Margolis, Maggie Margolis, and Carole Zelner, as always, added their indispensable perspectives.

CPSIA information can be obtained
at www.ICGtesting.com
Printed in the USA
BVOW08s0031100117
473066BV00001B/1/P